Ain't Noboc

WHEN WE

DANCE

Book 1

By

Tracey Gerrard

CONTENTS

ACKNOWLEDGMENTS

Big Charlie, Lisa, Millie, little Charlie, Sharon, Sarah, Margaret, Catherine, Serena, Vicky and Angela. You all played a part in getting me to this point, no matter how big or small or whether you knew it or not. So, I thank you with all my heart. I couldn't have done it without you all.

I would like to thank Gold Wind Limited for publishing my book and everyone who has clicked on the 'Buy Now' button. I hope you enjoy reading it as much as I did writing it.

Chapter 1

Holly

Standing in front of my floor-standing oak mirror, the mysterious woman observing me is unrecognisable. I've been pampered to within an inch of my life, courtesy of my two closest friends Olivia and Sarah. I was taken yesterday morning, snatched from my own apartment by them both, along with their husbands Jack and Nick.

Stopping first at our favourite café, Sandra's, for coffee and croissants. We've been meeting there at the family-run coffee shop for years. Its warm and friendly atmosphere is inviting, which is why it has so many regulars.

Afterwards, both Jack and Nick whisked all three of us off to Paint, Pout and Primp where we were treated to the full works. It's well known for having mind-blowing massages. So, after taking full advantage of the soothing essential hot oils, relaxing whale music and lavender-scented flickering candles, we elected for the manicure and pedicure.

Sitting there feeling relaxed and content, my ears become alert to what Sarah is saying. "Waxing next, girls," she declares.

"What?" I question.

"You know," she whispers as she points down to her nether regions, nodding her head to the same area while waving her hand around it. "A landing strip or the full works, Holly," she says, smiling.

"Not bloody likely. Why would I put myself through that torture when I've had such a relaxing morning? You're crazy if you think I'm letting anybody rip hot wax off my women's bits."

"Oh, it's not that bad," Olivia chimes in. "I've had it done many times. They rip the wax off that quick it's just like taking off a plaster," she states, her face looking as if it's no big deal. Well they might have had their hairy bits subjected to hot wax many times but me, never! I usually shave that area myself.

*

I'm lying on my back, legs up bent, ready to be subjected to my pussy becoming hot and bothered and not in a good way. *If you know what I mean.*

An overly tattooed, five foot, pink-haired masochist smirks at me. My scream pierces her ears as she rips off the hot wax.

"Bitch!" I want to shout out, but I don't. I also want to bring my foot up and kick that smirk off her overly pierced face, but I don't. No, I just lay there, inhale through my nose, and breathe out through the sting. After the initial shock, I calm myself down even though my pussy feels as if it has been stroked over by a red-hot poker.

Mary Masochist the beautician, hands me a tube of cooling cream. Thanking her, I adjust my clothes and make my way to the front counter, where I find Olivia and Sarah giggling like adolescent teenagers.

The glamorous woman behind the counter offers Sarah three bottles of lotion, telling her to use after showering. "It gives an all-over light, glowing tan," she states with a smile, baring her perfect pearly white teeth. Sarah passes one to me, pops a bottle in her bag and gives the last bottle to Olivia.

At one o'clock we meet the boys for lunch at The Golden Fleece, another regular place. Then after a mushroom omelette, salad and one glass of house wine, we make our way home.

Waking this morning, I feel the effects of yesterday's massage. I'm so relaxed I don't want to move from my king-size bed. Leisurely stretching my arms above my head, I turn to look at the alarm clock. It's nine thirty and I need to get a move on, if I want to get to the gym, then hit the shops to treat Olivia and Sarah for their kindness and friendship and get back in time for Sarah's cousin coming over to curl my hair. Nick is dropping Sarah and Olivia here at five o'clock so we can do our make-up and get dressed for tonight's ladies' night out. I make quick work in getting ready for my daily workout at the gym, taking a change of clothes so I can go shopping straight from there.

*

It's seven thirty. While Olivia and Sarah are in the kitchen eating nibbles and having a glass of wine, I am finishing getting dressed, just adding a few extra little touches.

Looking at the finished product, I'm speechless. Gold, glossy, curly locks fall softly onto my shoulders. My usual pale complexion has a natural glow while enhanced sapphire blue eyes sparkle seductively. Lush red lips ripe like fruit ready to be devoured, turn up a smile.

Black and gold silk covers my body, stopping mid-thigh; velvety sleek ribbon fastens loosely around my neck, leaving silky smooth shoulders bare. I turn to see golden curls cascade on to the sleek skin of my back; the feeling is sensual as the curve of my spine comes into view all the way down to the base. I stand four inches higher than normal due to black and gold strappy heels. My only thought is WOW! I haven't seen myself look this good in a long time, if ever.

Just over a year ago, I hid myself away after catching my husband Rob, well, ex-husband now, in the throes of passion at The Devonshire Hotel room 324 with his ex-girlfriend Rachel. Apparently, when she cheated on him after being together for six years, he hadn't gotten over her. In fact, and these were his words. *"I'm sorry, Holly, I never wanted to hurt you. It's just that I've always been in love with Rachel since I was eighteen. She's the love of my life,"* he declared.

"Well why the hell were you with me? Why did you ask me to marry you if you still loved her? We've been married for almost ten fucking years, you bastard," I ranted at him.

I was hurt, angry and ashamed that I'd played second fiddle all this fucking time. No wonder he always looked as if he wasn't with me half the time.

SLAP!

I couldn't help myself, plus he deserved it. I didn't wait for answers. Looking at the red handprint on his face, Rachel had scurried off into the bathroom now locking the door behind her. I rubbed my stinging hand down my thigh and headed for the door. Slowly I turned back, to look at the man I had trusted. The man I had loved and thought loved me. I opened the door holding back the stream of tears I knew would fall as soon as I left the room.

"You deserve each other," I spat out. Then I left.

Eagerly, I hurried along the narrow corridor and down the several flights of stairs, not wanting to take the lift and chance running into anyone. Once I was through the foyer past the reception desk, I broke out through the double doors, focusing on the carpark across the road, where both Olivia and Sarah were waiting to take me home.

Within two weeks I'd filed for divorce and put the house up for sale. I'm now renting a three-bedroom apartment in Cedar Court, of which Nick and Sarah are the landlords. Rob is shacked up with Rachel.

I handed my resignation in at the bank where I'd worked at for nearly eleven years. Rob had been one of the area managers and Rachel was working at one of the other branches. I couldn't see any other way of keeping them out of my life. Did I say that's how they had met back up again after all these years, at one of the bank conferences which my cheating ex-husband went to regularly?

Although Rob had said that he did love me, just not in the same way he loved her, this didn't soften the blow any, in fact it was like being hit by a freight train. So, I hid away in my new little home, not wanting to listen to friends and colleagues ramble on, *"Oh, I'm sorry to hear about you and Rob."* Or, *"What a bastard he is."* As well as, *"I thought you two were good together."*

No, I re-joined the gym, which I visited every day at its quietest time, and only associated with Olivia and Sarah who were my solace. They put up with my months of moping around. I didn't want to discuss what happened and I didn't want to go out.

However, the whole recluse thing has ended due to my so-called overprotective friends.

It's Sarah's younger sister Chloe's hen night next week at the prestigious club Aphrodite, and she was given complementary tickets to the VIP lounge at the nightclub Eruption, for tonight. Both clubs are housed in the same building within the heart of the city centre, where Eruption has been up and running for the last six years and was voted one of the top night spots in the north. Aphrodite has only been open for two years but gets outstanding reviews, catering to large parties as well as stag and hen parties.

Which is why Sarah, Olivia and myself are joining Chloe and three of the bridesmaids Helen, Suzy and Julie at The Night Owl Bar around eight o'clock. Then we will make our way over to the club for nine thirty. Olivia's eldest daughter Lucy, who's at university, was supposed to be joining us but had to back out because of an exam in the morning. She has sent her apologies and said she will be there for the hen night.

I'd declined the invitation numerous times, not ready to face the world yet, but after a night in with my interfering friends and their husbands, who have taken it upon themselves to become overprotective brothers, in a good way, though – oh, and several bottles of wine – a few home truths became known.

Chapter 2

Holly

One week earlier

"Holly!" my best friend squeals at me across her kitchen table.

"Olivia!" I squeal back.

Her husband sits there grinning at us both like a Cheshire cat.

"You have to go next week," she sighs. "The tickets came free for the club when Chloe booked her hen night." She continues with her ramble. "It's been organised for months."

"She's right," her husband Jack says. "Since splitting with Rob, you haven't been on a girls' night out."

"I know, I know," I respond to the truth he throws out.

My cheeks heat up as I exhale, a little ashamed of myself for not taking up the invitations I have had to go out with them. Apart from going to the gym, I haven't been interested in going anywhere or doing anything in the last year.

Olivia crosses her arms over her double-D chest and puts out her bottom lip while Jack gazes at her lovingly, knowing his wife is only nagging at me because she wants me to have a bit of fun.

We've all been friends since we were teenagers, even though

Olivia and Jack are older than me by four years, meeting through Jack's younger brother Nick. They married at nineteen when Olivia fell pregnant with twins, Lucy and Jackson. Happy with their lives, they went on to have another two children and have a four-year-old granddaughter.

"Listen Holly, I think a good night out with the girls as well as a no-strings fuck is just what you need." This just falls casually from her mouth as if it's the most normal thing for me to do. With her eyebrows raised and a smirk on her cunning face she turns to Jack. "Don't you agree?"

"I do," he replies as he snakes his arm round Olivia's waist.

Looking at me, Jack's mouth opens and closes just as quickly. I throw a questioning look at him.

"What were you going to say?" I quiz.

"Just that if you don't get laid soon, you will end up a born-again virgin." Jack lifts his drink and takes a large gulp while shrugging his shoulders at me.

To both Olivia and Jack, sex is no big deal. They don't hide the fact that they're still strongly attracted to each other. When they were younger they would not think twice about bunking up somewhere when we were all out. Even now given the chance they would sly off for a quick fumble.

My expression must be a picture because Olivia cracks up laughing, and I follow. The difference between us is like chalk and cheese yet we are the best of friends; they're like the family I never had.

As we all cackle like hyenas, the door opens and Nick and Sarah stroll in. "What are we laughing at?" she asks.

Jack is sitting back on his stool now and Nick takes a seat at the side of him. While Sarah gives Olivia and me a kiss on the cheek she grabs herself a wine glass, and fills it before taking a large mouthful. "Woah, I needed that. I'm getting some practice in for next week, ladies." She smiles around her glass.

"So," Nick says, "what's put a feather up your arse then?"

"What do you mean?" I query, knowing full well he's after what had tickled the three of us as they entered. That's all I need, all four of them on my bloody case. Between them they would have me registered on every dating site going, speed dating and set up on endless blind dates. Anything to get me out of my rut.

"WELL," Jack pronounces, a little over the top. "We were just saying if Holly," he nods his head towards me while pointing his bottle of beer in my direction, "doesn't get laid soon, she'll end up a born-again virgin." Sarah starts to choke on her wine, spitting it all down her sleeveless floral dress. Nick is trying hard not to follow her with the spraying of his drink but is failing miserably, as he turns purple in the face. Eventually they both contain themselves and return to the table, after cleaning Sarah's wine-covered dress.

As I take in the friends before me, I'm so glad to have them in my life. These are the people that have been constant throughout my teenage and adult years.

At five years old, I was put up for adoption when the child services concluded that my mother (who was a heroin addict) was putting my life in danger. I was constantly left alone without food, while she went shoplifting, so she could feed her habit. The last time she left me alone she had gotten herself arrested and didn't inform the police for two days. Apparently, it slipped her mind that she had left me home alone.

I was adopted into a loving, calm environment, with good Christian parents. My new mum and dad slipped into their role easily and catered to my every need. Although I missed my mum at times, I wanted to please Mr and Mrs Spencer, so I became the ever-loving Christian daughter.

Always doing my homework on time and getting top grades in school. Never complaining when I couldn't play in the street with the other children or attend school friends' birthday parties. I ate all my meals and did my chores around the house. We attended church every Sunday and always went out for dinner afterwards. During the week, my parents would take me to the park after school as well as bowling. I also attended dance and swimming lessons. The children I could play with were all from our church. This was their life and the life that had taken me out of the squalid home I had lived in with my birth mother.

I'm not sure when it was that I started to refer to Mr & Mrs Spencer as Mum and Dad. I just remember the beaming smile it had put on their faces, which made me feel all warm and gooey inside. I had been able to do something so small, but to them it was the biggest thing in the world.

When I was thirteen, my parents re-mortgaged our house and moved to an area with a better high school. The one I had attended, had been put into special measures due to the Ofsted report, so without a second thought we moved to a new house. My parents' life revolved around me and what was best for my well-being. They had moved from their marital home for me and for my education.

Over the months, my father had started to work longer hours at the office and my mum had taken on a part-time job at a florist in the city centre. They didn't tell me, but I knew it was due to the extra money they had to pay out each month on the mortgage.

My grades at school were still on a high and I was moved to the top set in maths. That is where I met Sarah and Nick. We were grouped together along with a girl called Sammy. Even though I wasn't allowed to socialise out of school with any friends I had made there, it was agreed that I could meet with Sarah and Nick at their homes or they could come to mine if we were revising or had homework to finish. This is how I met Olivia and Jack and Mr and Mrs Anderson, Nick, and Jack's parents.

My parents mellowed over the next few years, allowing shopping trips into the city centre with Sarah and Olivia and any family get-togethers at the Andersons'. They were always wary of people I encountered, knowing what kind of start I'd had in life; they didn't want me to end up down the same path as my birth mother. That was never going to happen.

Mum and Dad liked the Andersons and knew they were good people. As they got to know Olivia and Sarah, they allowed me to spend more girl time with them, experimenting with hair and make-up.

Life was good – I had a loving family, fantastic friends and knew what I wanted to do when I left school.

Then just after my sixteenth birthday, my world was turned on its axis.

It was a late February evening; my parents were attending a works party for my father's boss, who was retiring, and I was at the Andersons' along with Sarah, just chatting. I'd told my parents I would be in by ten and not to worry. So, like the good girl I was, at ten o'clock I got up to leave. As always Nick and Sarah walked me the few hundred yards to my home. Chatting in the doorway as usual, we noticed a police car pull into our small cul-de-sac.

Within minutes everything had become a blur. The police had asked me to step into the house and sit down, Nick had run home to fetch his mum and dad and then I'd been informed that my parents had both died in a car crash. From what the police could tell, they had hit a patch of black ice and my dad had lost control of the steering wheel, hitting a tree, both dying on impact.

Mr and Mrs Anderson took me into their home straight away, enveloping me into the bosom of their family.

A loud bellow brings me back to the here and now. "Where the hell have you been hiding!"

"Oh, fuck, you're in bother now," Jack sniggers.

I feel him before I see him, as I'm cocooned by two mighty arms. Mr Anderson has become my surrogate dad; he even gave me away on my wedding day. Oh, and he's a force to be reckoned with.

"Put her down, Jay," I hear Mrs Anderson tell him. After a grunt and a groan and a kiss on the top of my head, I'm released from the bear hug then placed into the warm embrace of his wife. "Ignore him, sweetheart, I know it's been hard for you," she says soothingly. One thing about Mrs Anderson, she knows how to show her affection. As her hand strokes my straightened hair the other one lifts my chin, so I'm looking directly at her. "It's time to let it go and move on, Holly," she utters lovingly.

As my chin quivers, pools of wetness flood my eyes. These people have been nothing but loving, caring and understanding towards me since I was sixteen. They encouraged me to continue with my education and went along with my plans to marry Rob, even though they didn't care for him. The guilt washes over me for not visiting them this last year, cutting their telephone calls short and when they called on me at my home, hurrying them out with any excuse I could think of. Just because I was embarrassed about Rob being unfaithful and once again feeling dejected that someone I cared about had been taken from me.

"I'm sorry," is all I can mumble out.

"No need for apologies," she expresses as she continues to hold me tight. "Just remember you're like a daughter to us and we've missed you so much, sweetheart."

"M-me t-too," I stutter out.

Jack's voice cuts in to our little mother and daughter hug.

"Come on, Mum, leave Holly alone now, you've had your moment," he laughs.

Drying my eyes on the tissue Mrs Anderson has given me, we move and sit with everyone else around the table.

Jay is in full voice, giving his sons shit about the investment they want to get into. He stops immediately, when Sarah speaks. "Ivy, are you coming on the night out with us next week?"

"What night out?" Jay quizzes, his eyebrows lifting as he glares at Sarah then shifts his glare to his loving wife. Nick gives out a chuckle and mumbles something about his dad being a caveman. It's quite funny really because as old as they are, they are still very flirty and affectionate towards each other.

Olivia looks at me surreptitiously, then jumps right in. "The one Holly is refusing to go out on because she's still upset over that bastard ex of hers."

"Is this true, Holly?" Jay asks.

I swallow hard and try to answer his question without sounding ridiculous. "It's not because of him, I just…" And I can't finish what I was about to say because I don't have a good enough reason not go with them. So, I just shrug my shoulders and bite my lip, a habit I have when I can't think of anything to say.

"Love, you should go. Enjoy yourself," Ivy suggests.

"Yes, you bloody well should, and forget about that poor excuse for a man you called your husband. He was never worthy of you and I should have said as much before you married him," he voices.

I'm a bit annoyed at Sarah and Olivia because they've only

mentioned it to get Jay on my case. So, I just dive straight in with the attitude. "I'm not a child. You all don't need to tell me what I should and shouldn't be doing, I'm thirty-seven and capable of making my own decisions." My hand is waving around, making sure they're all aware I'm speaking to each one of them.

"We know that, Holly," Jay expresses with concern. Getting up from his seat and stalking round the table until he's stood at the side of me, he puts my hand in his and continues. "Holly, you didn't have a good start in life because of your birth mother. When you were adopted by William and Anna, no child could have wished for a more loving couple to raise them. They smothered you with love and affection, you were their world." My eyes start to tear up again with the mention of my parents. I know that I meant the world to them, they showed me every day just what family love was. Jay squeezes my hand when he sees I'm a little choked up, but he carries on with what he wanted to get off his chest. "However, and this is no disrespect to William and Anna, but you had a strict Christian upbringing and missed out some experiences. Which is not a bad thing, but if you remember you were nineteen before you went to a party."

Cutting him off, I say, "I went to all the parties that you had at your house," my head nodding towards my four friends that I want to laugh at because they remind me of when we were teenagers and Jay would lecture us. Well not me as much as Jack, Nick, Olivia, and Sarah: make sure you're home on time, keep together, stay away from drugs, and always use protection. Good advice, really. Although I don't think Jack and Olivia listened well enough.

Jay continues with his lecture.

"I know you did, love, but that was different," he says as he squeezes my shoulders. He carries on about how I spent a lot of time with adults and not mixing with children of my own age, until I met Sarah and Nick. Also, when my parents died, I spent more time in church trying to find answers to questions: why was my real mum a drug addict and needed that more than she needed me? Why were my adopted parents taken from me so cruelly? Listening to Jay ramble on about my upbringing, I'm awakened.

Awakened to the fact that I was sheltered and protected so much from the outside world, that I never got to experience a normal childhood or adolescent years. Focusing on my school work and pleasing my parents was paramount. Nothing else would come first. I owed them that for taking me out of the squalor I'd encountered in my younger years and giving me a loving home and family. Sadly, this did not put me in good stead for my adult years.

After my parents died prematurely, Ivy and Jay took me in and kept up with the whole protection of Holly. Jack and Nick became the overprotective brothers I never had. Olivia the big sister I needed. Sarah I'd got to know well through our school years.

Sarah and Nick were very good friends; it was a big shock when she went off to university and both embarked on relationships with other people. They'd been friends since they were young children and only started a physical relationship when they were seventeen. It was obvious to a blind man they were meant to be together, but both wanted to make sure it was the real thing. That's why they wanted to experience seeing other people. If Nick and Sarah still felt the same about each other afterwards or couldn't go through with seeing other people, then they knew it was meant to be.

Before Sarah had finished university, they were back together, claiming that they had both been idiots for trying the separation. Happily, they have been together ever since, with two children, Jaden aged twelve and Emilia who is ten.

My friends have been fortunate to experience a wonderful life and I'm overjoyed for them.

Me, not so much.

Not wanting to get into a relationship with anyone until I thought I'd found the one, I waited until I met Rob, thinking I had found my happy ever after.

How wrong was I?

Taking in everything I know, I need to move on and start living for me and not let the hurt and upsets I've endured over the years stand in my way any longer. Jay is right. "Start living a little, Holly," I hear him say, which brings me back to the group.

"You're right," I murmur.

"What?" Olivia groans while taking a bite of her pizza.

"I'll come out next week," I reply.

"What about the hen night?" Sarah adds, rubbing Nick's arm excitedly.

"And the hen night," I tell them.

"Good, its sorted then. You're going out." Jay points at me. "And you're not," he whispers into Ivy's ear, but its loud enough for us all to hear. She bats him away, letting him know that if she wanted to go out she would, but she'll give it a miss this time. Nick jumps in, letting his mum know that we will be going to a night club which she is a little old for. Ivy is more than aware of this but doesn't want anyone telling her what she can and can't do. Placing her dark-rimmed glasses on the bridge of her nose, she advises her son not to knock the old bird in the room as she could give us all a run for our money. Jack and Nick laugh at their mother while Jay takes her by the hand, twirling her around. With one hand on the small of her back, he dips her gracefully. When he brings her back to her feet, he plants a kiss smack on her lips. We all give them a round of applause for their little show.

When they finish chuckling, Ivy says, "I never liked clubbing anyway. Even when I was a spring chicken. And you three," she points her finger at the three women in the room, "are no spring chickens."

"Thanks Mum. I love you too," Olivia says sarcastically as she blows a kiss at Ivy.

Olivia has called Jack's parents Mum and Dad since she was a teenager. Not having a father in her life and her own mum always out with different men, she was left to fend for herself. She never went without material things and she knew her mother loved her. She just liked to go out and enjoy herself. Olivia's father had been around when she was younger but moved to Scotland when she was six. She had gone to visit a few times but didn't get along with his new wife. So, over the years, Olivia and her father would meet up when he was travelling through Yorkshire on business, which had gotten less and less over the years.

*

Ivy and Jay say their goodbyes, announcing that they had only stopped by for ten minutes after eating out at the new Italian restaurant Marco's, which had only opened recently. As Jay pats his two sons on the back he chuckles, then states, "Got to go, boys, I'm on a promise," wiggling his eyebrows at Ivy.

"Get out! You dirty old bastard," Jack chokes out as he throws a piece of pepperoni pizza back on his plate. Olivia lets out a little squeak when Jay pulls her plaited hair.

"How do you put up with that miserable bugger?" he laughs. Jack's face scrunches and he mocks a shiver, as if he's disgusted with his dad. He's not, they pull one another's leg all the time.

As they head out of the door Jay calls out, "There's life in the old dog yet." Then the door closes behind them.

Jack shakes his head at his dad's antics and I can't help but ask, "Do your parents still have sex? I mean, they're what, sixty-five?"

"Noooo!" Jack grimaces.

"They stopped having sex after they had Nick. Couldn't run the risk of having another like him," Sarah answers as she is just about to take the last bite of her cream cheese bagel. She doesn't get the chance because Nick swallows it before it reaches her lips.

Jack and Nick's parents have been gone about half an hour when Sarah asks, "Holly, are you definitely coming out next week?"

"Yes. I said I would, I'm not going to change my mind. Don't worry," I tell her.

"Good," she says as she claps her hands together. Then she turns to Nick and says, "Tell her."

"Tell her what?" he questions. I can see Sarah's eyes go wide. Then she nudges him.

"You know, who you saw yesterday."

"Oh," Nick says, shaking his head. "I'm not sure if that's a good idea," he mumbles to Sarah.

"Well if you got something I should know then please inform me now." I've had three glasses of wine and I'm feeling a little jolly. But his face tells me it's something I'm not going to like. So, I park myself firmly on the chair, and grip my glass tighter while I take a sip.

"I saw Rob yesterday," he says hurriedly. I wait and nothing else comes out of his mouth. He just sits there taking another swig of his bottle.

"And?" I drawl out, trying to coax something else out of him. My calm manner hopefully lets him know that I'm not that bothered about his name being mentioned.

"And Rachel," he murmurs.

"Oh," I hear Olivia gasp.

I nod my head in acknowledgment, hating the mention of her name. Why the hell didn't she come back and claim him before I got involved with him?

"Hmmm," Nick continues. "They got married two months after your divorce." His voice is edgy. "And they're having a baby. She's three months." My hand tightens on the glass I'm holding. Hearing they're going to be parents, enrages me. I'd asked and pleaded with Rob for us to start a family. Only to be told, "*Not yet, honey. We're not ready. My career takes too much of my time. If we have children,*" not *when,* he said *if,* "*I want to be at home, not at work all the time. I would prefer to be at home with you and our children.*" Then he would kiss me as if I was his world and I believed him.

It was all a lie.

He might have wanted children one day, just not with me because he'd not got over his first love.

"Fucking hell," I hear Jack rant. "What a fucking dick," he rambles on. "Listen Holly, don't give it a second thought. He was never good enough for you, with is finicky fucking ways," he spits out. "Don't wear this, wear that. The selfish bastard never supported you in getting into a career you wanted. He held you back, keeping you in that mind-numbing bank job. That wasn't you. It was all about him and you couldn't see that. You wanted to please him because that's what you do."

Everyone is gripped by Jack's outburst. I've never heard him go off on one over someone's relationship. He normally doesn't give a shit. I take another sip of wine; I'm on my fourth glass now. Olivia topped it up when she thought I wasn't looking. Three glasses of the Californian rosé are enough for me. Feeling the effects of the fruity pink stuff, I don't really give a shit about what my ex is doing and who he is doing it with. Although, I do care about Jack and how critical he has become because of Rob. I need to calm him down. "Jack," I say quietly.

"What!" his tone is clipped. Everyone's heads snap towards him and all eyes drill into him.

"Sorry Holly. I didn't mean to snap at you," he says calmly while peeling the label off his bottle of lager.

"It's OK, I know you didn't," I say soothingly.

"No, it's not all right, Holly. You see that's what I mean about you, always ready to forgive, wanting to please everyone. It's time you got what you wanted. Do what you want, please Holly. Not for us, not for William and Anna or Jay and Ivy, YOU, HOLLY," he states, pointing at me. "And fuck everybody else. Release what's in here." He pats his chest, letting me know he means my heart.

Olivia rubs his shoulder and down his arm. "You need to chill, Jack," she states.

"I'm trying to put some sense into her head," he proceeds with his lecture. "We met you when you were that skinny little thirteen-year-old. With your head constantly stuck in a book. Shy and timid, you always looked as if you would break like a little china doll when anyone spoke to you. Trying to be the goody two shoes to please your parents." His mention of my dead parents, the ones who took me in at five years of age and doted on me, giving me love I'd never known and shelter I needed, brings tears to my eyes. "Holly, they were lovely people and you did please them. God, if you had rebelled a little, you know, got into a bit of mischief now and again," he chuckles. We all do because that wasn't me. "They would have still loved you." And he says what we all thought. "But that wasn't you." He sighs. "You feared being rejected. The same happened at my mum and dad's house. Always the one to help. How many times did they say, 'You're only young once. Go out enjoy yourself? How many times did we say the same thing?" He points around the table. "You worked like Trojan to get your degree. Taking on a part-time job at Micky's place. Bringing in customers he could have never done without your expertise. You were in your element. My dad offered to help you set up your own business when Michael had to sell the place. But that boring prick had to turn on his charm and take over, helping you get the job at the bank so he could weasel his way into your good books.

"He didn't know you, Holly.

"That wasn't you sitting behind a desk day-in, day-out. Playing the dutiful wife when he wanted to host a party to benefit himself. To push his career, not yours. He never once thought about what you wanted." He sounds exasperated.

I know Jack's right, everyone does. But I never stood up to Rob and told him what I wanted. I gave into him all the time. Me in the bank away from the bars, where I had loved working. Researching what the clientele wanted, then scouting for bands, organising music nights from battle of the bands, to resident band and karaoke nights. Themed nights were a great success. Building up the restaurant, again giving the customers what they wanted and catering for the elderly, young and families. Jack brings me back to the here and now.

"You know, Holly, he persuaded you to apply for that job, knowing he could influence the interviewers into giving you the job. Then he'd have you close by away from the bars where you might meet someone, who let's say," he makes air quotes, "might be a little less boring than him." Nick lets out a chuckle and nods his head in agreement with his brother.

Olivia takes her turn and buts in. "So, let's sum this up," she says. "Rob loved Holly but not like he did Rachel. He didn't want anyone else getting close to her, so he helps her out getting the job at the bank where he knew she couldn't meet anyone else because she was stuck in the office all the time. Then he dated her for twelve months before proposing. He then went on to marry Holly knowing he had feelings for someone else. That's just fucking crazy," she states, placing her glass onto the table. "In fact, it sounds ridiculous."

Nick jumps in before Olivia has a chance to say anything else. "I'm with Jack," he tells us. "I know it sounds a little strange but it's credible. Rob was still hung up on Rachel when he met Holly, but he started to have feelings for her, that's for certain. When Holly was told Micky's was closing he was already wanting to ask Holly out. So, helping her get the job at the bank would give him brownie points plus stop all the men flirting with Holly if she landed another job in a bar. He'd been cheated on already and didn't want that happening again."

"He didn't know me very well, if he thought I would betray him in that way," I butt in.

"No, he didn't," Jack says dramatically. We're all absorbed with Nick's intense speech and let him carry on with his ramble.

"After you had been together for a while he probably thought, 'Yeah, let's get married and do the whole family thing.' Although, he couldn't go through with having children, that was probably too much to get into. He loved you and he needed you as much as he needed his job, but he loved Rachel even more. Which is why when they met at a conference it was easy for him to rekindle their relationship. But too hard to tell you he wanted to end your marriage."

"Well it's his fucking loss," Sarah says. "Let Jay help you put that business idea together. You've got the money now to get it up and running; these two will help." She points at Jack and Nick. They nod in agreement, lifting their bottles, and clinking them together. Olivia puts her arm around me, squeezing my waist.

"Me and Sarah will help you with anything you need, Holly, you know that, right?"

"Yes, I know," I say. I know they will always be there for me just as I am for them.

"You also need to stop moping around. It's time to step out of that rut and start meeting other men. We know you don't have much experience with men but it's not like you didn't have the offers, before and after Rob came along," Sarah expresses. Her face lights up and a smile appears on her face. "Have a little fun, Holly," she continues. "Let's face it…" She giggles as she takes a sip of wine. We've all drunk quite a bit and I'm sure we will be feeling the effects in the morning. Once Sarah's finished her wine she then goes on with her little rant. "Let's face it, honey, any woman who hasn't had an orgasm through penetration, especially by her husband, needs to get out and start living a little." She grimaces as soon as the statement leaves her mouth. She's well aware this is a step too far. We all are. Olivia's hand goes straight to cover her mouth with an OMG while two wide open mouths as well as two pair of emerald green eyes stare, gobsmacked. "I'm so sorry, Holly, I never should have said that," she says, all apologetic. Regretful of her comment, she hurries to my side and throws her arms around me. "Please Holly, forgive me?" she asks, her hazel eyes pleading for absolution.

I already have.

We've had a lot to drink tonight and I know she didn't mean to blare out my sex life in front of her husband and his brother. I cradle her in my arms, kiss the top of her head and give her a reassuring smile, letting her know all is well.

"WOW!" comes from Jack as he rubs his hand and strokes his greying goatee beard. Nick's hand goes the other way as he rubs his shaven head.

"Not sure we needed to hear that little bit of information," he declares while chewing the inside of his cheek.

"No, neither am I." Jack gives a little chuckle when he finishes with, "Well, it is what it is. Like I said, go live for you, Holly, and please have a little fun while doing it." That's his way of giving me brotherly advice without embarrassing me any further.

Time's getting on when I glance around the table, noticing the laughter and topic of conversation has now moved from my personal life to Nick. I'm grateful for that. We can all move on without falling out over Sarah's slip of the tongue, however, I am exhausted with it all. Yawning, "I think I'm ready for bed," I tell them.

"You want a lift? We're calling a taxi," Sarah asks.

"No. I think I'll take Olivia up on her offer and sleep in the guest room," I say while nodding my head towards a sleepy Olivia. Her head is resting on Jack's shoulder, all snuggled in while her eyes flicker shut. Jack gazes down at her with doting eyes. Without a word, he scoops her up in his muscular arms, cradling her in his embrace. Passing his door keys to Nick, he mouths, "Lock up," then stalks out of the kitchen and up the bedroom stairs. After giving Sarah and Nick a goodnight kiss, I pick up my phone and bag, leaving them to lock the doors while I make my way to bed.

Chapter 3

Holly

Present day

"Come on, Holly, the taxi will be here in ten minutes!" Sarah shouts through the crack in my bedroom door.

"On my way," I answer. I apply one last coat of lip gloss, slip it in my bag and make my way to the kitchen where I know Olivia and Sarah anxiously wait. They haven't been clubbing in a very long time, none of us have, and we can't wait to hit the dance floor. Entering the kitchen area, two pairs of loving eyes rake over me as if they're seeing something for the first time.

"WOW! You look good," Sarah states while taking a sip of wine.

"Good as in I'll do, or I look fine?" I ask with a nervous giggle.

"Nooo," Olivia says. "Good as in hot, hot, hot, my good woman. You're going to be beating them off with a stick tonight," she laughs as Sarah thrusts a glass of wine into my hand.

"Get that down your neck before the taxi arrives," she laughs while placing her empty one on the black marble-effect kitchen worktop.

"Thanks," I tell her, taking hold of the glass of rosé and downing it one. This isn't my normal way to drink the fruity stuff, I'm normally quite sensible, but I need a little Dutch courage tonight.

I've no sooner got my breath back from finishing my drink when Sarah's phone comes alive letting us know the taxi has arrived.

*

Making our way through the sea of heads towards the bar of the Night Owl, we can see it's standing room only. This place stays busy until just after twelve, that's when most of the younger end, mainly students, move on to the clubs, and the older end make their way home. Only tonight this group of over thirty-fives will be sharing the dance floor with the barely dressed younger generation.

Just as we pick our drinks up from the bar, Sarah pats my arm to get my attention. Pointing across the crowded room, I can see her sister Chloe and three of her close friends, Helen, Julie and Susan stood near one of the alcoves, frantically waving at us. Taking in the crowds of people in this place, it's going to be a bit of a squeeze to get to them. We make our way across to where they are standing, fighting our way through various groups of young students here for discount drinks. There's been a football match on earlier and a crowd of rowdy supporters are making a spectacle of themselves. Eventually, we reach them where Chloe is being entertained by five young men; they must have found out she's getting married soon and decided to treat her to an early hen night.

Olivia holds up her glass of wine. "Look at that, I paid four pounds fifty for that and I've only got three pounds left," she complains.

"When did you have the chance to drink that? I had to guard mine with my life, so it wouldn't get knocked out of my hands!" I shout over the loud music and the chanting from the five men who are encouraging each other to take off an item of clothing.

"I haven't had a bloody drink yet," she declares. "I spilt one-pound fifty's worth down some dickhead's back when he stepped on my foot," she grimaces. I giggle because I'm sure she will have spilt it on him on purpose. In fact, I'm surprised she didn't kick him in the balls.

Chloe gets my attention. "You look stunning," she states, stepping away from one of the men who's been trying to twirl her around.

"So, do you," I greet with a hug. And she does. Her silky black hair has been pinned up with a few loose curls hanging down, while her hazel eyes have been given the smoky affect, her cheekbones have been worked on so they look more prominent and her fitted red dress enhances her breasts, giving one hell of a cleavage. It stops at her ankles with a split up the middle, stopping mid-thigh. She really does look beautiful.

Grabbing my hand, she pulls me into her. "Thank you for coming, Holly. You're going to have a fantastic night," she chuckles. She knows my story but it's not about me tonight, it's her night.

"It's not about me, Chloe," I reply to her. "This night out is for you so let your hair down and don't worry about me," I say while giving her a warm hug.

"Oh, that's next week, honey. Tonight, is just a bonus but I want you," she points her finger at me, "and everyone else to enjoy themselves. We haven't been out together in ages," she states. "Plus, we must have fun tonight, so everyone will turn up next week," she laughs while taking a drink of her wine.

"Don't be silly; we'll make our own entertainment if the atmosphere is shit in the club."

"Thank you," she says as she hugs me tight. Chloe's grip tightens on me. I know she can get overemotional when she's had a few drinks. "I'm so, so glad you decided to come out tonight," she repeats again. As if on cue I'm saved from her over-the-top show of love when 'Play That Song' by Train blasts through the speakers and the rowdy bunch of lads decide to give Chloe their rendition of the song.

Leading her by the arm, one of them looping hers through his, they perch her on the high- backed stool she'd been sitting on when we first arrived. Then all five of them break into song. She's subjected to a little hip thrust and arse wiggles. She can't contain herself and gives one of the tight-fitting arses a little slap. This gets a cheer from the men and whistles and screeches from the ladies. As soon as the song ends 'Dancing on the Ceiling' by Lionel Richie replaces it. This is a big favourite of Olivia's and gets her up on the seat singing, grabbing my arm to join her.

What the hell? I think to myself. *Have a little fun.*

We're both up on the seats when one of the men breaks loose from his mates and joins us. Only he is stood in front of us giving his version of the Chippendales.

The man's about twenty-five, standing around six feet tall with mousy blond hair. He's clean-shaven and slim built. When the instrumental part of the song plays he wriggles out of his Ralph Lauren polo shirt then kicks off his shoes. So-called mates of his start chanting, encouraging him to keep going while they dance behind him in sequence. It's a fantastic routine and I'm sure this isn't the first time they've put on a show for the ladies.

Women and some men have surrounded the man who is now unfastening the button of his jeans very slowly and seductively. Once the button is undone, he gets a round of applause, squeals, whistles and a chorus of, "Off, off, off!" from the female supporters. He quickly shimmies out of dark blue denim jeans that cover his long, slim, but ever so muscular legs. You can tell he works out. A lot! Mr Chippendale then starts limbering down until he squats on his haunches.

That's when a woman lunges forward with what looks like a tube of hand lotion, but I could be mistaken, which she tries to thrust into Chloe's hand. Gesturing to her to rub it on the man's chest. Chloe screams, "Noooo!" loudly, shaking her head to indicate she doesn't want to. She looks to us her friends for moral support. She's head over heels with her man and wouldn't dream of touching another man in fun or not. She looks like a scared kitten, her face blushing crimson with embarrassment. That's when I take pity on her and do something that is so out of character for me.

Grabbing the small bottle of lotion from her trembling hands, I use Olivia's shoulder to balance as I try to get down. Before I have chance the other men that are with him give an almighty cheer and come to my rescue, taking me by my hips and lifting me off the stool. Once I'm placed on the floor, I stalk over to the nearly naked man and straddle his tanned thighs. He sniggers at me as I hitch up my dress, gathering the bit of material in front of me and tucking it under my crotch so he can't see my lacey black knickers. I shake the lotion a little then proceed to squirt it on his broad chest and onto his muscled abs. Within seconds he's taken my shaky hands in his. Because I am a little nervous, I've never done anything like this before. We both rub the white cream into his firm chest, his hands placed on top of mine. "Oh my god," I hear Olivia screech while she continues to jig up and down on her seat.

"You little hussy," Sarah laughs out as she claps along with the music and the show we're putting on.

I haven't got a clue what's got into me and where the courage came from to put on such a show. I know if I don't stop laughing soon I may wet myself. Everyone who can see is enjoying the display. You can tell by the number of screams, squeals and whistling. Oh, and lots of chanting. I move my weight slightly off the man's thighs, so he doesn't start to struggle, although the gleam in his eyes and grin on his handsome face tells me he's enjoying himself immensely. I hope his dick behaves itself and doesn't start enjoying it too much. I laugh to myself.

We're suddenly halted with our little show when a couple of burly bouncers arrive in front of the crowd. "Come on now, ladies and gents, the show's over," one of them grunts out.

"Get your clothes back on, sir, we don't have an entertainments license," the other big guy says, smirking as he does.

"You've had your bit of fun," the grumpy one says, although his eyes hold some amusement. One of them throws the guy's clothes at him while the other helps Olivia down off the seat. There's boos coming from the crowd. However, the bouncers just take it all in their stride, with a, "Yeah, yeah, boring bastards, that's us," one of them claims with a chuckle and a shake of his head.

Chloe's friends' faces are awash with colour. I don't think they've laughed as much in a long while, I know I haven't. This is nothing new for Olivia and Sarah. Their husbands, Jack and Nick, would strip many times in their younger years, just to give their ladies a show.

The stripper has re-clothed now and he's subjected to pats on the back from his mates. Chloe gives him a hug and a kiss on the cheek, thanking him for the entertainment. When she's finished he stalks over to me and grips me in a bear hug, where I squeal loudly. He then dips me to one side, lowering over me and plants a kiss smack bang on my lips (no tongues). When he releases me I feel my face burning up; it must be the colour of Chloe's dress. "Thanks love," he says. "I love a lass whose game for a laugh," he comments, raking his mischievous eyes over my heated skin.

"Wow, you're welcome," I reply, chuckling and a little shocked at myself for my open display.

The crowd has dispersed now, gone back to what they were doing before our little floor show. The Night Owl's answer to the Full Monty have said their goodbyes and are heading out the door, with another round of applause from the crowd.

Sarah turns to me still giggling like a little school kid. "That was so entertaining, Holly. I think I wet myself a little at you being so brazen. I can't believe you did that. Who knew?" she says, shaking her head.

"Yeah, who knew?" I agree with her because I wouldn't have believed I had it in me to put myself on the spot like that.

Helen, Suzy and Julie are still wiping the tears of laughter from their eyes when Chloe gathers everyone together. "I think we should finish this drink and visit the ladies' to dry her knickers." She throws her chin up at Sarah. She nods in agreement. We all burst out in fits of laughter again, while Chloe chunters on about fixing our make-up.

Half an hour later, after consuming another glass of wine that had been paid for by the wannabe Chippendales, taking a trip to the ladies to replenish our mascara and lipstick, oh, and let's not forget drying Sarah's wet knickers as well as Suzy's, who said that she'd not wet herself, she had just got overexcited with the whole show and the young man I was straddling, we descend on Eruption; giggling, sniggering and making a damn fine show of ourselves. We are in fine party spirit as we're led into the VIP lounge.

Chapter 4

Vlad

Why the hell have I agreed to this? I ask myself as I make my way past the masses half my age and dressed in next to nothing, queuing to get into Eruption.

My sons have twisted my arm to join them at the club along with some golfing friends of mine, to celebrate my forty-fifth birthday. It's just after ten when I arrive and I'm running late. They asked me to be here for nine thirty, but I wanted to spend some time with my youngest, Lucas, when he got home from school. He's not thirteen yet so a little young to join his three brothers and me.

Do I feel forty-five? No, not really, my boys keep me feeling young. Do I look forty-five? Maybe. I certainly don't look like the father of a twenty-seven-year-old, plus one at twenty-five and another at twenty-one. Yeah, I know I started young, but I wouldn't trade them for the world. I am the proudest father ever to walk this Earth. Everything I've done in my years of existence I have done to keep them safe. Bringing them here to England twelve years ago was the best decision I ever made. Keeping them away from the dark world I had grown up in and worked in was always my end goal.

As I approach the entrance to the VIP lounge in the club, I'm stopped in my tracks when a large hand slaps me on the shoulder. "Are you a member?" the rough voice of the hand asks. I smile straight away, knowing I'll see Frank when I turn around. Frank is the head of the security team here and a very good friend. I would not have opened this place if it wasn't for him.

"Happy birthday, you old bastard," he greets me with.

"Fuck off. I'm only three years older than you," I laugh at him, shaking his overly large hand. Mine are big but look half the size of his. This man might work for me, but he's been a good friend I couldn't have done without.

When Sebastian was twenty-one and had almost finished his business degree. He asked me about buying this space to open a night club. The building it's housed in, is joined on to the restaurant I own. His ideas were: I would hold the license till he and his brother Nicholas were old enough to take over. We could put in for building permission to allocate offices, extra kitchen, storage space, exit door into a private staff carpark between the club and restaurant. He had a designer draw up the plans to show me. He had done his homework. I knew his plans were good, he'd even got Nicholas on task coming up with ideas. I still wasn't persuaded. I had one problem. A big problem really – drugs.

Nightclubs are notorious for drug dealers and I would not sit back and watch my sons get involved in anything that would put them in any danger, but I promised them I would think about it and look in to it. And I did.

During one of my nights out with a couple of friends I'd known for a good few years, I had a lengthy conversation with the head of security for the nightclub we had been visiting. Frank had worked in clubs since his discharge from the army and understood my concern. He did inform me that with the right type of security; CCTV, bouncers, drug checks and regular police checks they shouldn't be a problem. So, I asked him to join my sons and I for dinner at Dimitri's, the restaurant I owned. I hadn't bothered to change its name when I bought it from the parents of an old school friend, who had moved here from Russia when he was fourteen. The place was a going concern and a little gold mine. I hadn't changed much, except for expanding the kitchen, décor in the restaurant, casual waiting staff and a new chef when one retired. All the staff were happy and so were the clientele. The restaurant was full most weekday evenings and booked solid every weekend. This made me a very happy man.

After meetings with the council, building contractors, the police, persuading Frank to come and work at the club, alongside countless part-time staff, Eruption opened its doors a year after we bought the seven thousand, five hundred square foot area. My boys were overjoyed and so was I. With not having to put a great deal of my time into the restaurant I was able to support Sebastian and Nicholas with the club and when I wasn't around I knew they were in good hands with Frank.

*

Dean, one of the regular waiters, opens the door for me to the lounge and straight away I spot my boys stood at the far end of the room. They're propping up one of the high tables along with Dave and Mark, two friends I play golf with. With a proud smile on my face I stride across the room to meet them. Passing one of the bars I'm subjected to wolf whistles, 'woo woos' and laughter. The exquisite sound halts me in my tracks. Turning quickly, the sight I see before me takes the breath from my lungs. Her head is thrown back as she laughs, showing the delectable column of her neck which I would love to run my mouth over, sucking and nibbling as I make my way down her stunning body. She sees me staring. The innocent smile that radiates her beautiful face, floors me. It's almost angelic, but with a touch of mischief. The angel laughs again, and her eyes sparkle like a thousand stars in the dark night sky. She would bring the strongest of men to their knees and she's just floored me, knocking me completely on my arse.

Her friends are chuckling at our flirty interaction and I suddenly remember where I am. Stealing my eyes back reluctantly, I turn to face the giggling idiots I call my sons. Yes, there've caught sight of the whole seductive situation and I'm sure they will give me shit as soon as I reach the table. Before I make my way over to them I turn to the vision at the bar and send her a beaming smile and a cheeky wink then stroll casually to where my sons wait.

A shot glass is thrust into my hand which doesn't even touch the sides. Another is replaced straight away and this time I feel the burn kick in, bringing me back from the reverie I was in.

"Fucking hell! Paps, you've only just walked through the door and the ladies are eyeing you up," he chuckles out while slapping me on the back. Sebastian, my eldest, smiles around the bottle he's drinking from then drags me into a bear hug. "Happy birthday, big guy," he greets. "Why don't you have a little fun tonight? It is your birthday," he suggests, motioning with his bottle to the bar, where I stare spellbound. Shaking my head at him, I want to say no but it gets stuck in my throat.

"Maybe I will," comes flowing out instead. His eyes light up with my response because in the twelve years we have lived in England, they have never seen me with a woman.

Oh, they know I've had plenty. More than my fair share over the years. But my family life is kept very separate to my sex life. My boys come first, they are all I have, and no women will come between them and me. I have never taken a woman home since we came here, if needs must I always go back to their home or to a hotel room. They get what they want, and I get what I need, a quick release. I'm only too pleased to inform any woman that it's just sex and nothing more. Just one night of pure pleasure. Controlled by me.

Although, I think my control has just been tested by the little gem at the bar. Grinning like an idiot to myself because I'm tempted by the challenge set before me.

Daniel steps in and nudges his elder brother out of the way, who's still struck dumb from my answer to his question. "Come here, you, big brute," his deep voice booms around the room and once again I'm enveloped in a man hug. "Happy birthday, old man," he sings to me then smacks a kiss on top of my forehead.

My sons are well built but Daniel is the one who twins me. We are both six foot three, broad shouldered and weigh around the same. Our features: high cheek bones, strong nose and chiselled chin are almost identical. They all have my dark blue eyes, almost black sometimes, and my mouth shape. But with him it's like looking in a mirror except for our hair. Mine is dirty blond or was, it now has speckles of grey which show even though I have it cropped short. Daniel's is almost black like his mothers, and very long. Tied in a fucking ponytail which I would love to take a sharp pair of scissors to and cut the fucking thing off. "She's very pretty," the voice of the ponytail tells me while wiggling his eyebrows at me.

"Who?" I question. I know who he means. Every time I glance over, and our eyes meet, my heart beats like drum, the pulse in my neck is like a ticking time bomb and my chest feels as if it's been sat on by ten fucking sumo wrestlers. I've never felt this way before, not with their mother or any woman. It scares the shit out of me because if she asked me to jump I would probably ask how high. I'm fucked, and I haven't even spoke to her yet.

"The sweet little thing at the bar, that took your breath away as you stalked across the room with that broody look you've got going on. You turned a lot of heads, for a man your age, you should be grateful you can still pull the ladies," he states all matter-of-fact.

"She did not take my breath away," I lie.

"You keep telling yourself that but we," he points to his two brothers, "saw the whole eyes meeting across a crowded bar thing."

"The bar is not crowded," I cut in with as that's all I can give him. She did literally take my breath away.

I'm suddenly rescued by Dave and Mark, from three pairs of dark questioning eyes, when they call me to join them at the table. They both wish me a happy birthday and some dark liquid in a shot glass is placed in front of me. It tastes like cough mixture and I screw my face up as it lingers on the back of my tongue. Dave laughs at my disgust and passes me a vodka shot which I drink off to chase down the aftertaste of the cough mixture. Dave and I met twelve years ago; he's the head of the children's department at the hospital that Lucas attended regularly when we first came to England. Mark, I met there too. Dave, was his three-year-old daughter's doctor. They both played golf together and over a short period of time I got to know Mark. Through visits to the outpatients' department they invited me to join them in a game of golf. Over the years knowing them we would meet up once a month for a game of golf, a few drinks in the club house then on to a club. Dave was newly married at the time, so he went home early. Mark had never married his daughter's mother and had sole custody of her so if his parents could take care of her, he was game for a night out. Although Sebastian was nearly seventeen when I started going out, I liked to make sure there was an adult there. So, Mrs White, my housekeeper, would stay over and look after them.

"You know, Vlad, it couldn't be more obvious you're interested in the little lady at the bar," Mark comments.

31

"Yeah, it's sickening the way their eyes keep meeting across the room," Dave expresses while throwing his head back, laughing.

"Go talk to her," Sebastian suggests, nudging me with his elbow. The boys have joined us, sitting around the table now. Listening to them chat and laugh at my expense, I decide to put them and myself out of our misery.

Standing confidently, my focus is set on the beautiful woman at the bar. "Would you like another drink, lads?" I ask five open-mouthed men. Nicholas is the first to speak.

"We have a waiter to fetch our drinks, Father," he voices with a smirk on his face.

Placing my hands on his shoulders and bending down so I'm level with his ear I whisper, "I'm aware of that, Nicholas, but I think I'll go have a little fun." Then I stalk off towards my conquest.

Leaning against the bar, Dean nods his head, letting me know he'll be with me in a minute. He can take all night because I'm happy enough stood behind this woman listening to her sing along with her friends. I watch, hypnotised by the sway of her hips that move in time to the music. Her voice is like velvet and the sweet smell of summer mixed with strawberries dominates the air around her.

Curly blonde hair shines like rich gold and falls gracefully down her smooth naked back. Just as I'm taking all of her in – long, slender, toned legs; firm, peachy arse; two dimples at the base of her spine that I would love to dip my tongue in while my hands stroke the firm cheeks of her fine arse – she turns gracefully. Spins on her heels till she faces me, and I feel like a kid in a sweet shop who has been caught with his fingers in the candy jar. Only I haven't touched. Only looked.

Our eyes connect, and we're lost in our own little world. Her eyes are sapphire blue, pure, sparkling like the jewel itself. I can see the world through them; her world. Scared. Lost. Wanting to explore this, whatever this is between us, but needing reassurance. I smile, encouraging her. One side of a lip rises, creating a masterpiece. Her confidence has returned, and she places delicate fingers on the knot of my tie. Deftly, she runs them down my chest till she reaches the buttons of my Armani jacket. Once there she makes short work on unfastening them. My heart is hammering wildly in my chest and my hands itch to touch her. But they don't. I won't let them. No, I will let her set the pace for now. She continues exploring, her fingers lightly dancing across my shoulders while she sways that delectable arse to the back of me. I'm frozen. Can't move and I don't want to. Her French polished nails rake over the back of my neck, stroking over a tattoo of a black-handled dagger surrounded by thorns I have there. This sends an electric shock straight to my groin. My heart rate is soaring and the heat between us is combustible. She trails her hands back round to the front of my chest and once again she's stood close to me but not close enough. My hands take on a life of their own and suddenly take hold of her slim hips, bringing her even closer. Her breath hitches in her throat, as does mine when we connect.

Wild blue eyes pierce through me and the confidence she had starts to deplete as if she's just realised we're on show to everyone. Not that anybody gives a shit.

Just when I think she's about to break our contact, another song kicks out from the speakers. She smiles sweetly at me while she slips my jacket off my shoulders and places it on top of the bar. There's a squeal of delight from one of her friends and I can hear whistles coming from the table where my boys sit. I don't give a shit who's watching; if she wants to have a little fun, I'm game.

Suddenly, her tiny hand grips hold of my tie and I'm being led to one of the empty tables ahead of us. Not knowing what she is going to do next excites me even further so I follow like a little lost puppy. It doesn't take long, though, for me to find out, when she quickly pulls out one of the chairs and proceeds to step onto it. My arm shoots out to support her and I'm greeted with a sexy smile.

"OMG!" is shouted from one of her friends.

Followed by, "Oh, no she isn't."

Then a clarification from another friend of, "Oh, yes she is."

She still holding my tie and beckoning me with a curl of her finger to join her, everything about her screams at me to follow up on this little show but I shake my head, laughing at the thought I have. I'm the fucking owner of this establishment along with my sons. I own the fucking restaurant next door and the club adjacent to that. If my customers saw me God knows what they would think.

I briefly pull my eyes from her to see Frank stood there, arms folded across his huge chest, eyes glaring at me and face saying, "What the hell, Vlad?" I can practically hear him shouting it.

Loud bellows hurl at me, "Go for it, birthday boy." I know that's Daniel challenging me to join her up on the table.

"Up, up, up!" is chanted from Sebastian and Nicholas, while Mark and Dave shout at me to get up there and not leave the little lady waiting. Once again, I shake my head. What am I doing? This isn't me. I don't follow. I lead. However, this woman has me in a tailspin, wanting to follow wherever she wants to lead me.

Screams of laughter surround me followed by hoots and whistles. I know why. Without realising it my body has betrayed me and I'm up on the table, stood in front of the flirtatious, arousing angel. *What the hell?* I ask myself but before I have time to rationalise my hands take over. Gripping her hips tightly, I bring them flush with mine so there's no room between us.

I've taken over the control.

Hands travelling, feeling their way until they reach the sides of her ribcage. While her arms fly up reaching for the stars, skilful fingers stroke up her side up past her waist towards the bare skin under her outstretched arm. She gives out a little giggle as if she's ticklish, good to know for future reference. We are still joined together, her heat pushing into mine as my hands hold tight on to her waist, hers placed on my shoulders. Gyrating our hips, I then dip her, so she's bent over my arm. Masterfully bringing my other hand to her neck, my outspread fingers play, stroking slowly down past her breastbone till they reach her stomach. Once there I bring her back up. Her face is flushed, her breathing is heavy. People around us cease to exist. The table we are stood on is circular and large, big enough to seat a party of ten around, but I still should be careful with the delicate angel in my arms.

Bringing her close to me again, I raise our arms high then spin her fully around. She spins easily on her toes, flowing like a ballerina during a pirouette. This gets a cheer from our audience and I brush my lips lightly against her cheek. She smiles shyly at me then places her hands on my chest.

My heart is still pounding. It has been since I first caught sight of her.

I may have a heart attack very soon.

Just as I'm trying to get my heart rate in order she kicks it up again, by shimmying down my body, stroking my heated form all the way down. Knelt before me, her luscious lips at my growing manhood, I smile.

Fuck, now I need to calm that down because as much as I like seeing her knelt there, I really do not need to be getting hard like a randy teenager. Placing my hand in hers I bring her back up so we're facing each other. I shake my head at her because she knows she's playing with me, mouthing the word *naughty* at her. She bites her lip to try and stop her laughter, but I can see it in her eyes that she's happy I was affected by her little performance.

Turning her around so her back fits snuggly with my front, I control the rest of our dance. Spinning her around, rotating our hips and letting my hands freely feel their way around her body until the song ends.

We're both stood there, our foreheads resting together, panting, blood heated to a temperature where we should be in flames.

Her eyes are hooded, and her face is flushed. Dancing with her is like nothing I've ever experienced before. I feel like we've just become one, like making love for the first time. As framed eyes flicker fully open, lust oozes from them and her luscious lips call to me. Brushing a chaste kiss across them, I can't help but take a little nibble. She gives my hand a little squeeze that's when I hear the cheers, whistles and clapping of hands. Stepping back from me, her face suddenly full of shock, our tangled fingers unwrap.

Sudden awareness comes to us that we are not alone and are visibly on show to an audience.

Frank stands in front of us, hand held out to help my sexy little angel down from the table. Not a cat in hell's chance am I letting another man touch her.

Before she has time to reach out for his hand, I'm off the table, taking her by her hips and delicately placing her on the floor. My hands are still placed on slender hips as we stare, lost in each other's eyes, neither one wanting to break the spell we're locked under.

"A word, please," Frank's stern voice cuts in, ending our brief encounter.

She steps back from me and a blush rises from her neck and onto her lustful face. That's when I see the lost, scared look on the face of the woman who not minutes ago had desire radiating from her. Quickly, she turns to her friends and hurries to where they wait for her, losing herself in the middle of the crowd.

I stalk back to the table, annoyed at Frank for interrupting us and angry with myself for feeling the way I do about some woman I have just met, whose name I don't even know. Snatching the bottle of beer out of Nicholas's hand and placing it to my lips, the little shit sniggers at me. "Don't," I warn him. I'm not impressed and need a minute to cool down before I can deal with his smart comments. Frank appears at my side holding a glass of what looks like Brandy.

"Sorry mate, didn't mean to spoil your fun but you know the rules even for you."

"Yes, I know, no dancing on the tables…"

"We need a couple of new erotic dancers at Aphrodite if you and the sexy little thing want a job," Nicholas laughs at me.

I slap him round the back of the head for his cheek and he chuckles at me again.

Looking across the room, a shy smile greets me from the little angel at the bar. I send her one back, knowing by the end of the night, I will have danced with her again, know her name and made her my angel.

Chapter 5

Holly

We've been on the dance floor for over half an hour and I'm dying for the toilet and a glass of water. Grabbing Olivia's hand, I tell her I'm going to the ladies'. "Hold on!" she shouts. "We'll come with you." She drags Sarah with us, leaning into her to let her know where we are going.

Water is what I've been drinking since I decided to make a show of myself, dragging the most intimidating man I have ever come across up onto a table and dirty dancing with him. It was one thing in The Night Owl with Mr Chippendale, that was just a bit of fun. This was something else.

We noticed each other as soon as he entered the club and what an entrance he made.

Confidence surrounded him.

He walked with purpose and seemed to control everything within radius. As soon as our eyes connected, I gave out a giggle. My girly parts heated up and I had no control of how I was feeling. My skin became flushed and my breath quickened. This had never happened to me, never, and suddenly I became a different person, wanting him all over me like a rash. But he scares me like nothing before. It's not the fact that he's well over six feet tall, tattoos that start on the nape of his neck and run God knows where down his oh, so, sexy body. Or the fact that he has a scar running from above his right eye and slightly down the side towards his cheekbones that most women would kill for. Oh, and the husky, slight Russian accent. No. It's the fact that he can turn me into this different person who becomes wild with need. Just one naughty smile or cheeky wink and I'm a goner. All my Christian upbringing thrown to the wind; that I've only been with one man and don't have much sexual experience, doesn't even get a mention. Because just one touch from him, one brisk brush of his lips on me, one look from those demanding, dark, intense eyes and one pull into his firm, masculine body and I am his. And this is what I'm afraid of.

A man like him would break my heart, chew it up, and spit it out.

I'm not the one-night-stand woman, that's why I've only ever slept with my ex, but that would be all forgotten with a man like him and I would hate myself the following morning.

*

There's a queue for the ladies' when we arrive so we're stood outside the door waiting to get in. Chatting away about the events of the evening, Sarah nudges me with her elbow and nods her head to the side. Looking up, I follow her line of sight and that's when my eyes land on the most breathtaking man I've ever seen. He's exiting the gents' and walking in our direction. No, he's not just walking. His gait oozes confidence, his strides are long and precise, his posture upright and determined as he dominates the area around him.

The wicked grin appears on his face as our eyes reach out to connect. "Ladies," he greets us with a nod of his head. Then the sexy wink makes a devilish appearance before he turns into the VIP lounge. And I'm a mess on the floor.

"WOW," I say dreamily as I imagine all things dirty, he could do to me. What the hell? I never have thoughts like that, I leave it to my two close friends.

I must be staring at the door he just sauntered through longer than necessary because I hear Olivia's voice. "Earth to Holly," and then a clicking of fingers in front of my face breaks the spell I've been put under.

"Fucking hell!" Sarah screeches out. "He's got your attention."

"He certainly has," Olivia comments with a wide smile on her face.

"I don't know what's wrong with me," I say, shaking my head at them both. "No man ever, ever grabs my attention like that. He makes me want things… Feel things that…" Wow, I' m still shaking my head at them.

"We know. So, let's get in the ladies' then back in there, quick-smart," Sarah squeals while dragging me through the cloakroom door.

We're back in the VIP lounge where Chloe and her friends have joined us, needing a well- earned drink. They have been on the main dance floor of the club for well over an hour. The lounge has filled up some since we arrived earlier, I'm assuming with other hen and stag parties who also received complementary tickets. The dance floor is heaving and the music filters through the speakers louder than ever. Bodies are pressed together, bumping and grinding while roaming hands run suggestively over bare skin.

After watching them for a short time, I think back to my hen night. It was nothing like this and this is just the start; they have the main event next week at Aphrodite. Mine consisted of Olivia, Sarah and two friends from the bar I had worked in when Rob and I first met. We had a pampering party at Olivia's then went out for a meal; we were home for eleven thirty.

"Looks like your man has bought our drinks again," I hear Sarah shout over the music. Looking at the table I can see two bottles of champagne placed there by the waiter.

"How do you know they're from him?" I ask pointing at the very expensive bottles that the waiter is now pouring into eight champagne flutes.

"Because my dear," she says, giving me an over-the-top smile while snaking her arm around my shoulder, "when I went to order them from the bar, this hunk of a man here…" Sarah starts to fan herself dramatically. The waiter is cute and fits his white T-shirt snugly. She continues, "He told me Mr Petrov was paying for our drinks."

"So, you ordered the most expensive drink, Don Perignon rosé."

"No. I asked what champagne they had, and he recommended this. I don't know what it costs," she says, shrugging her shoulders.

"It's around two hundred and fifty pounds a bottle," I tell her, laughing at the way her eyebrows shoot up and nearly reach her hairline as she takes in the price of the two bottles on the table.

"Fucking hell," she chokes out while informing the girls about the champagne the waiter is handing out.

I pull him to one side, to ask him about Mr Petrov. "Will he not mind you recommending this?" I ask, pointing to the drinks and angling my head towards Mr Petrov's table. At least I know his surname now.

"Not at all. He said, whatever you wanted, and he does not do cheap. If I had suggested anything else he would not have been happy." He gives me a tight smile.

"Well thank you, that's very kind of you," I tell him.

"Not a problem, Miss, whatever you want, you only need to ask." His smile is wider now, showing his pearly white teeth which makes him look cuter and more approachable.

"There is one thing," I say before he has time to walk away.

"Yes?" he enquires.

"What is Mr Petrov drinking, and the others around his table? I'd like to buy them a round of drinks back just to say thank you from our party."

"Mmmm." He studies me for just a moment before he answers. "Well, it is his birthday so they're celebrating. The last lot of drinks was Courvoisier."

"Then get them another round and I will pay for it," I state.

"OK, no problem," he says, nodding his head.

"Oh, and tell him I said thank you for the champagne and the drinks from earlier. And wish him a happy birthday from me." The waiter nods his head again and returns to the bar.

'Cheap Thrills' by Sia filters through the speakers and Chloe, joined by her friends, makes her way to the small dance floor. I want to join them, so I finish my glass of champagne and follow them.

Once there the music takes over my body and soul, the way it used to over ten years ago before I married Rob. He wasn't a dancer, he didn't even like to slow dance. It was a challenge getting him on the dance floor for our first dance as man and wife.

I'm lost in my own little world, letting the beat of the music take me high and forgetting everyone around me. With my eyes closed, my hips swaying, and my hands raised above my head, I sing along to the words. Thoughts of Mr Petrov stroking over my overheated body, I have my hand running through my hair and down my body, feeling every curve. For the first time in my life a man has made me feel sexy. Suddenly, the music changes to 'Ain't Nobody', by Rufus and Chaka Chan, a fantastic eighties number.

I open my eyes to see the dance floor is packed full when two strong hands grip my hips. The powerful woody scent of his aftershave encompasses me, and I know it's him back to claim me. A firm chest is pressed into my back while the smoothness of his chiselled jaw skims across the bare skin of my shoulder. Light kisses run up my neck until his mouth is level with my ear. "Miss me?" he whispers confidently. The huskiness and the slight accent ignite a fire within, causing a shudder to run down my spine. His hips lock with mine and his strong hands are still firmly in place. Curving my arms above my head I continue to move in unison with him. My head turns slightly to the left, so I can see his handsome face. A boyish grin appears on his face and I send him a shy smile. I'm anything but shy at this moment in time as I let our hips sway together while the tips of his fingers play seductively up and down my body. He throws the cheeky wink at me then spins me round so my face is level with his chest. I place one of my hands round the back of his neck and stroke the nape where his tattoo starts with the tip of my thumb. His eyes close slowly. I know this affects him, it did at the bar earlier in the evening. Running my other hand up using my nails to rake over his firm abdomen till I reach his chest, I then tweak his left nipple.

Dark eyes fly open. It's then the song ends, and I'm dragged off the dance floor at rapid speed. My hand is held firmly as we pass the smoke glass windows that look out to the main area of the club. We pass his group of friends, who are now lounging on the black leather sofas, laughing when they see the urgency in the man who has a firm grip on me. We exit the lounge, past the ladies, and down a dimly lit corridor where we land outside a door. He quickly punches a code into it, and wastes no time pulling me through and pinning me up against the wall.

His mouth crashes into mine....

Chapter 6

Vlad

I'm on her like my life depended on it, taking what she's offering. Our tongues dance together, searching for control. She tastes sweet and smells of strawberries. My hand grips her peachy arse, lifting her so she can feel my erection on her heated area. She complies with a little squeal and soft warm legs wrap round me when I thrust my hardness against her. I fit between them perfectly and take this opportunity to roll my hips against her. She strokes the sensitive part at the back of my neck. The little minx has learned quickly this is a turn on for me. Her other hand strokes my chest and up on to my shoulder. Mine skims across her flat stomach and travels until it reaches her heavy breast. Her nipple is erect and my thumb caresses slowly. There's a gasp from her throat which I swallow up in our kiss. My want for her is intense and I growl when she circles her hips against my hardness.

I want her like nothing I've ever wanted before, and I know the feeling is mutual, I can see the hunger in her eyes, the heat between us is off the scale. But I want more. I can't take her here the way I would any other women just to get my fix. No, she's more than just a quick fuck.

Reluctantly, I pull away my lips from hers. She's breathless and so am I.

The corridor is dimly lit but I see her.

Lustful eyes draw me in. The pull so strong, it will take all my strength to let her go. Not that I want to. Her swollen lips are parted, and her cheeks are flushed. She looks at me, searching my face for something, then she speaks.

"I… I don't know your name," she stutters out. Oh, she'll get to know my name because she will be screaming it many times. My lips turn up a smile when I think of all the ways we could get to know each other and how she would sound calling my name while she comes so hard.

Taking my time, stroking her collarbone with my lips, nibbling up her delectable neck until my mouth meets her ear, I whisper, "Vlad. My name is Vlad, just so you know what to scream out when I give you the biggest orgasm of your life, angel," before I latch on to her neck, sucking and marking. Her whole body shudders in my arms.

Resting my forehead on hers, I suck in her bottom lip and give it a little nip. Her eyes are closed but soon fly open when I run my finger down her cheek and take another bite on her bottom lip. I can't help but go back to her slender neck and run tender kisses down it.

"Holly," she murmurs, halting me. Such a beautiful name.

I place her on the floor and take her face in my hands, stroking her cheeks and down on to her lips. "Holly," she whispers again. "Just so you know what to yell out when…" She doesn't finish but the shyness in her voice does.

Her name is as beautiful as her and I find myself saying it out loud.

I need to know for sure if this is what she wants because I want her, but not here.

"Holly, do you want this?" Our foreheads are still resting together. She swallows, and her tongue comes out to lick those perfectly swollen lips. "Do you want me, Holly?" I ask while stroking one hand up her thigh till I reach the edge of the lace on her knickers.

"Y-Yes," she quickly replies while she nods her head.

"No, not like this," I whisper.

"What?" she suddenly blurts out, her face asking why and body screaming for me to take her. I will give her something but not me. Not yet. I'm straining painfully in my pants, fucking rock hard but I won't take her here. I chuckle to myself. I'll need a very cold shower or will have to take myself in hand when I get home.

My fingers still stroking her bare thighs, I breathe her in. "Holly," I say firmly. Her eyes look up to meet mine. "I want you so fucking much but not like this, not up against a club wall." She looks at me as if she can't believe what I'm saying. Her eyes leave mine and drop down towards the floor. "Holly, look at me," I say while lifting her chin with my fingers. She gazes directly into my eyes and that lost look appears on her angelic face again and melts my hardened heart a little bit more. I need to make it clear I want her but not here and not for just a one-night stand. *What the fuck am I thinking? This isn't normal for me.*

My lips claim hers again while my fingers feel their way to the dampness between her legs. I kiss her passionately as I massage her swollen lips through the soft material of her knickers. Her chest rises and falls rapidly, and I can feel her beginning to shake. I know it won't be long before an almighty climax rips through her, but I need to get her number first. So, I'll keep her on the edge just a bit longer.

I stop my hand and move it back to her thigh. "Holly, where's your phone?" I ask.

"Huh?" comes her reply.

"Where's your phone?" I ask again. Her pupils are almost dilated, and face flushed. This mixed with her swollen kissed lips takes my breath away.

She inhales sharply as if she's annoyed at me. "My phone is in my bag with Olivia," she spits out at me. She is annoyed I've left her hanging but I'll take care of her once I get her number.

Taking my phone from the back pocket of my trousers, I ask her for her number while I let my thumb trace over heat again. Only this time I move the material out of the way and seek out her clit. Breathless, she relays her number to me, which I type into my phone as her body melts into me. Slipping it back into my pocket. I continue with giving Holly what she wants.

But she surprises me when her head that has been resting on my shoulders, lifts. Looking confident she floors me with her question.

"You don't want this?" she asks while her hand motions between us. I answer her straight away.

"Yes, Holly, I want you. But I want you in my bed when I fuck you hard." I stroke my fingers over her heat again, making her breath catch and her head fall on to my shoulders again. "I want you gripping my sheets when I place my head between your legs, dragging your orgasm out while you scream my name," I whisper seductively. Her body shudders again and I know she's not going to last much longer. Rubbing my fingers a little faster, I then slip one inside her and she's so fucking wet for me. I could come right now, like a randy fucking teenager.

I continue with my seduction as I insert another finger. "I want to feel your nails rake down my back, your teeth biting into me while you come so hard around my cock," I say slowly. And there she goes. Her body shakes as she grips my fingers like a vice then her teeth bite into me, drowning out the scream that's coming from her.

Her arm holds tightly onto my neck as mine hold her firmly while she comes down from her high. It takes a while. She's limp when she nuzzles into my neck, placing sweet kisses there and onto my jawline. "Hi," I greet when her face lifts to mine.

"Hi," she says back, smiling.

"You OK?" I ask, chuckling at the sweet smile of content on her face. My thumb runs over the soft skin of her cheekbone.

"Yes," she smiles shyly. "Although I could do with a glass of water," she says, looking down at the visible erection in my pants. A giggle erupts from her and I'm curious to what has her in such a pickle, lifting one of my eyebrows to question her. She places her hand on the thick bulge in my trousers. "What are we going to do about him?" she asks while giving him a little rub. Taking a deep breath, I remove her hand and bring it to my lips.

"He will be just fine and will wait till we meet again." She nods her head and leans in to kiss me.

"Let's get you that glass of water and back to your friends. I want you to text me tomorrow then we can arrange when I can take you to dinner." This is all new to me but there's nothing more I want.

"OK," she agrees, as we walk back to the lounge hand in hand, stopping on the way for her to freshen up in the ladies' and me in the gents'.

All eyes are on us from her friends and my boys as we make our way to the bar. I motion for Dean to get two glasses of water; once we drink them I tell Holly I need to go home as I have an early start tomorrow. I don't but I know if I stay any longer, I will do something I will regret. She gives me a gentle kiss on my cheek before she sashays off to her table. I can still feel her on me but it's not enough. Striding over to Mark, Dave and my boys to collect my jacket. They don't ask me questions because they know I won't answer them. I tell them I'm leaving, and my boys hug me. Mark and Dave shake my hand and we arrange to meet up in a few weeks. Before I leave the club, I march over to where Holly is stood, take her hand and stake my claim. Our lips lock passionately and I'm finding it hard to let her go. Eventually, we pull apart both breathless. "I look forward to hearing from you tomorrow," I whisper in her ear. She nods her head and I leave the club a happy man.

Chapter 7

Holly

It's official, I'm a hussy. A brazen hussy. My friends laugh at me; I know they're laughing at me. I've been sitting here for the last half hour, in my kitchen with my head in my hands, not because I have a hangover. Well I do, but that's not the only reason. "Holly, it's not that bad," I hear Olivia say.

"Oh, it is. Believe me, it is," I tell her, lifting my head to look at her.

"No, it's not, we've all done it," Sarah relays.

"Well you're a pair of shameless tarts," I snigger at them then drop my head back in my hands.

They both chuckle at my comment.

"Oh, I'll let you know, that this pair of shameless tarts," Olivia says, pointing between Sarah and herself, "married the men we had sex with in a club."

"I didn't have sex with him. I-I just let him…."

"You let him give you the biggest orgasm you've ever had and you're complaining. Did you enjoy yourself with him last night, Holly?" Olivia asks.

"Yes," I murmur.

"So, what's the problem?" she questions while looking at me as if I'm an idiot.

"That is the problem, I enjoyed myself a little too much. He makes me…" I stop myself to think what to say for a minute.

"He makes you what, Holly? Want something different than your usual boring life? A little excitement maybe? Well there's nothing wrong with that," Sarah adds.

"You're thirty-seven, Holly, it's about time you let your hair down. So, text him. Phone him. Arrange a night out. If he's as keen as he seemed last night, he'll take it at your pace or just have a little fun with him. No big deal," Olivia stresses then throws my phone at me.

"I can't text or phone him," I argue.

"Why?" she asks, frowning at me.

"My phone's flat," I answer.

"Well bloody charge it," she says, getting off her seat. She snatches the phone out of my hand and starts rummaging around in my kitchen drawer, I'm presuming for the charger which isn't there, it's plugged in the socket by the kettle. "Where is it?" she shouts, getting all flustered with herself. She is funny when things start winding her up. I don't want to aggravate her any more. I can see Sarah smirking; she knows Olivia doesn't have much patience, so I point towards the kettle. Olivia storms over to where the charger is and plugs in my phone.

Stomping back to her seat, she huffs and puffs. "Holly, you're not a prude. You've put up with us and the dirtiest two bastards you could ever meet. I don't understand what the problem is. He's a ruggedly handsome man, who takes care of himself. Did you see the suit he was wearing? And that watch, so he's not short of a few quid. The man has sex appeal in buckets, he walked around like he owned the place. He obviously has a thing for you because he could have had any woman he wanted in there last night."

"Apart from us," Sarah states, smiling. "We're happily married. Oh, and Chloe because she's all loved up with Michael. But Olivia is right, you two looked fucking hot together on that table then on the dance floor. You really did put a lot of women's noses out of joint…"

"He scares me," I blurt out, cutting off Sarah.

"In what way?" Sarah asks. Olivia just sits there calmly watching me.

"To be truthful I really did enjoy being with him. The look in his eyes, as if I was the only woman in the room. How he held me in his arms when we danced, electricity surged through me to every nerve ending when his fingertips stroked over my bare skin. I had no control, he took it from me and made me his. He could have stripped me naked and used me any way he wanted, and I probably would have said thank you." I laugh out loudly, covering my mouth. Then I remember his smell and OMG how big he was.

"That's great how he made you feel," Olivia says. Her eyes light up when she picks up that I've got a little grin on my face. "Why have you got that look on your face, Holly?" She questions raising one eyebrow.

"What look?" I try to cover it up, but she can see it in my eyes, she can read me like a book.

"The one that says, you've got something else to say. Come on, woman, spit it out," she sings.

I can't hold it in. These two are my closest friends and I really need their advice because I do want to contact him, it's just I'm scared of a man like him.

"He smells fantastic. All woody and manly, you know the one that as soon as you breathe it in, you're addicted. The one that hits the parts that have never been hit before. And he's so big and wide. It wouldn't fit, I know it wouldn't," the panic in my voice causes me to screech.

"Calm down, Holly, I'm sure a man like him would make sure he didn't hurt you," Sarah says, trying to calm me down. I take a deep breath to get myself together. I know she's right but when you've only been with one man who was of average size, coming across a man like him is bloody scary.

"So, you little floozy, how do you know how big and wide he was?" Olivia asks, rubbing her hands together as she shifts forward in her seat, leaning her elbows on the breakfast bar. I decide I might as well get it all out and over and done with, they know most of what happened anyway.

"I felt it. Pressed up against my back. Rubbed up against my crotch. In my hand. Believe me after all the things he said he wanted to do to me, with me, I nearly knelt before him and begged him. I felt wild." They both sit there in shock, mouths wide open before they screech like banshees at what I just revealed to them. I shake my head at them trying to suppress the nervous laughter that wants to erupt.

"Oh, Holly, ring him. He's just as affected as you are if he was as pent up as that. I am one hundred percent sure you could have him on his knees begging," she laughs out.

"What would I do with him?" I ask them both. "You know I'm not that experienced with men and you saw him, he will be a god between the sheets." Sarah composes herself before she speaks.

"Let him lead you, Holly, if you're not confident."

"Yeah, he looks all domineering. He'll take care of you," Olivia adds.

"Domineering," I squeal.

"You know," she laughs.

"You mean handcuffs and whips? I don't think so," I say firmly.

"I think what she means," Sarah says while elbowing Olivia, "is a man like him will help take care of your needs before his own then talk you through what he wants, so to speak. Eventually, it will become second nature to take care of each other. Instead of being with someone who only thinks of themselves," she explains.

I know she's talking about Rob. He was never adventurous in the bedroom department, but I can't just blame him, neither was I.

"OK, I'll text him once I've showered," I tell them. What's the worst that could happen? I get my heart broke. Or it could be the bit of fun that's been missing in my life.

"Promise?" Olivia asks.

"Yes, I promise. My phone will be charged once I've showered so I'll do it then," I reassure them.

"Do you have his right number?" Sarah queries.

"Yes, he texted me last night on the way home in the taxi," I tell them, smiling, remembering the butterflies in the pit of my stomach when the text arrived. Wow, I feel like a giddy teenager instead of a divorced thirty-seven-year-old woman.

"What did he say?" they both ask in unison, shocked that I hadn't mentioned this already.

"He just texted me goodnight, nothing else, and I texted him back the same."

"Well at least he gave you his correct number," Sarah says.

"He asked for mine and put it in his phone when we were having our little bit of fun," I let them know. "Anyway, isn't it time you two got home to your families so I can shower?"

"Yeah, we're going, but don't forget your promise. Then ring us both with all the juicy gossip," Olivia says, getting off her seat and picking up her bag.

"I know," I state while walking them both to the door. After saying goodbye and giving each other a hug, they both leave. I walk back into my kitchen area and pick up my phone to check the charge, that's when I notice a text from Vlad. The time is one fifteen and he sent this at ten this morning. I open it and read.

Chapter 8

Vlad

Tapping my fingers on my dark oak desk, twirling a pencil between my long fingers and staring at my computer screen without seeing what's there is on repeat, I anxiously wait for a reply from Holly. My phone sits across the room. I placed it on the window ledge over an hour ago. Why? To stop myself from looking at it every two minutes. Although I had asked her to contact me today, I couldn't wait so I sent her a message.

I'd been awake since seven this morning; to be truthful I hadn't slept much at all. Too much pent-up sexual energy curtesy of said woman.

After an hour on the treadmill followed by a shower, I ate breakfast alone. Lucas isn't at home to distract me, he stayed at Sebastian's last night. Izzy had offered to have him stay over so I could go with my sons to the club. Nicholas and Daniel have their own little apartment and must have chosen to stay there last night because their bedrooms here are empty. So, I came into my home office to catch up on some paperwork. Only I haven't got a single thing done. My mind kept wandering to the angel I met last night. The connection we had. How our eyes drew each other in and led us to follow what we couldn't deny. Her smell, her laugh, her touch igniting a fire so deep, I'm like a volcano ready to erupt.

This isn't normal for me. I never give any interaction with women a second thought, sexual or not. But, with Holly I want more. Not wanting to wait any longer, at ten o'clock I texted her. But she hasn't got back to me yet. It's now after one and my patience is wearing thin, my mind wandering to alternative reasons why she hasn't got back to me. Maybe she doesn't want to pursue what transpired between us last night. What if she met somebody else? Fuck, I hope not.

Or, it could be she is still in bed recovering from last night and has not seen my text yet. I need to calm myself down.

Getting up to give my legs a stretch, I hear my phone ping alerting me to a text message. Almost tripping over the bin at the side of my desk, I make the quick dash to retrieve my phone like a Tasmanian devil. My mouth twitches upwards and my heart pounds when my little angel's name appears on the screen. Yes, I've gone there (MY ANGEL). Swiftly, I swipe the screen.

HOLLY: Hi Vlad. Sorry I didn't reply earlier but I've only just got home from Olivia's.

My phone had died through the night so only saw your message when I put it on charge. In answer to your question. I have the worst hangover not use to drinking that much champagne which leads me to your next question. I'm sorry I will have to decline your invitation to dinner due to so-called hangover.

Good explanation but I'm sure we can arrange for tomorrow evening instead.

VLAD: Sorry you're still recovering Angel, maybe drink more water next time.

Hope you're feeling better soon. How about dinner tomorrow?

I've kept it short, no point in beating around the bush. Her text message comes back quickly.

Holly: Sorry Vlad, I'm away tomorrow until Monday, maybe some other time.

Reading her last message has me cursing. I was hoping to get to know her a little better over the weekend. I hope she's not trying to brush me off; she did seem keen last night but that could have been the alcohol. I wonder where she's going. Maybe I should start up a conversation about what it is she's doing, keep it light and friendly. Quickly I type up a message.

VLAD: Yes, we can arrange to meet some other time.

Are you going anywhere exciting?

Walking over to my chair, I patiently wait for her to get back to me. I sit comfortably in my leather recliner; I have nowhere to be. A message comes back five minutes later, and I eagerly read it.

HOLLY: I'm having a relaxing weekend, staying in a cottage on the Northumberland Coast.

VLAD: Are you going alone?

If she's going alone I don't mind joining her, although she wouldn't be doing much relaxing. She texts me straight back this time.

HOLLY: Nosey.

VLAD: Just making conversation. If you want company, I'm all in.

HOLLY: I'm not going alone.

My chest tightens with the thought that she could be going on a short break away with a man. And I now need to know who she is going with, but I don't want to scare her off.

VLAD: May I ask who you are going with?

Keep it polite.

HOLLY: Yes, you may.

VLAD: Well…

HOLLY: Well… What?

Is she really trying to get me worked up? My angel has suddenly become a little devil. A smile creeps on my face.

VLAD: WHO ARE YOU GOING WITH? Do I need to remind you who you were with last night and how he can make you feel?

I press send and then regret it. Maybe shouty capitals are too much, as well as a reminder of last night. It's too late now. Plus, I want her to remember our encounter. I'm not kept in suspense long as my phone lights up.

HOLLY: NO REMINDER NEEDED! I'm not likely to forget in a hurry. I don't make a habit of going to night clubs and I certainly don't let men I don't know seduce me.

I curse myself. So much for keeping it light and friendly. If I was her I would block my number. I need to make this right.

VLAD: I'm sorry Holly. I didn't mean for things to be awkward between us, I should not have sent that last message. It was insensitive of me to bring up last night and the shouty capitals were sent with a touch of humour following your messages. Please accept my apologies.

I place my phone on the desk and my head in my hands. I'm not used to this texting back and forth with a woman I want to impress. As a rule, I never ask for their phone number and I would not give mine out either. She has not got back to me yet and my palms are sweating. God, I'm a lost cause. How can I go from someone who could not care less about meeting a woman one minute, to needy bastard overnight?

Standing from my chair, I pace over to the far side of my office to make a coffee. A very strong coffee. Suddenly, the vibration of my phone coming to life on my desk has me nearly scalding myself. Within in seconds I'm sitting back in my chair with my phone in my hand. Nervously, I swipe the screen.

HOLLY: Apology accepted.

I thank all that is holy, and a smirk crosses my face, at the fact that she must be as desperate as I am. Well, desperate might not be the right word to use but I have certainly made an impression on her. Never in my life have I been so eager to get to know some woman, not even my late wife.

Immediately, my fingers set about typing a message back.

VLAD: Can we start again?

HOLLY: Yes.

This is good news but where do I start? At the beginning.

VLAD: Hi

HOLLY: Hi yourself.

VLAD: How about we take turns in asking a question about each other?

HOLLY: Okay. You want to go first?

VLAD: Err, ladies first.

HOLLY: Well. I know your name, Mr Petrov, and that it was your birthday yesterday. How old are you?

Well, she knows more about me than I know about her. She must have got the extra bit of information from the club last night. Let's even it up.

VLAD: I'm forty-five. And you are? Surname and age please.

HOLLY: Spencer. Holly Spencer, and I'm thirty-seven.

VLAD: Beautiful name for a beautiful woman.

HOLLY: Thank you. Occupation?

VLAD: I run a restaurant. You?

I haven't lied, I just haven't added on that I own the nightclub she was in last night and the one next door to it.

HOLLY: Unemployed. Have been for over a year now. What's your favourite colour?

Her last answer has me wondering what happened just over a year ago? Was she finished from where she worked? Made redundant, fired or resigned? Has she fallen on hard times: struggling to find a job, not able to pay her bills? These things concern me, and yes, this is insane, I've only just met the woman. But I want to know more, I want to know her. I need to find out more.

VLAD: My new favourite colour is the one that set its sight on me last night. The one that made my heart race faster than a champion Grand Prix car and had me wanting things that I've never wanted before. (Sapphire blue). That sparkle like the gem itself. What happened with your job?

I wait, hoping bringing last night up won't embarrass her again.

HOLLY: Oh, smooth lol. You don't want to know my favourite colour?

VLAD: Yes, I do, and a whole lot more.

HOLLY: I don't really have a favourite colour. I resigned from the bank I had worked at for over ten years.

And I'm asking the question.

VLAD: Why?

She doesn't get back to me straight away and I'm hoping she has not decided that it's too personal, maybe it isn't. She could have just wanted a change, or something could have made her want to give a steady job up. It might have been stressful, she might have been some high flyer in the banking world. My phone lights up, bringing me out of my musing.

HOLLY: My husband, well, ex now, decided I wasn't good enough for him and he reacquainted himself with an old girlfriend of his. They both worked for the same bank, so the best thing for me to do at the time was to resign.

Wow, I was not expecting that. I know what it is like to be deceived, betrayed, have it flaunted in front of you by someone you love. It hurts like a bitch, but you either live with it or move on. My mind goes back to Russia, the country I once loved until... I shake myself out of that thought, and quickly start typing a message back to Holly.

VLAD: I'm sorry to hear that someone you cared about deceived you in the most unforgiveable way Holly, but I must ask you, was he BLIND?

HOLLY: Thank you but I'm over the deceit. What do you mean was he blind?

VLAD: I'll get straight to the point Holly. If you were in my bed every night. If I woke up to you each morning. If you were mine. I WOULD NOT BE LOOKING ELSEWHERE. But I'm glad he did what he did. I know it sounds cruel, but I wouldn't have met you. I would not have held the most beautiful, sensual woman who drives me crazy with her laugh, her shy but devilish smile, her eyes that sparkle, yet hold so much sadness and the sounds she makes when she lets go in my arms.

Selfish, I know, to cash in on something that brought a whole lot of heartache, but that's life. On the other hand, making her aware of just how beautiful others think she is, especially me, might just show her that her husband was a fool.

HOLLY: I appreciate your kind words, but they're not needed. I'm over the past and moving on with my life, slowly. And really, you brought up last night again.

Yes, I did, and I'm not sorry at all.

VLAD: I'm not going to apologies this time Holly, not for telling you the truth and believe me I don't make a habit of texting back and forth with women. This is all new to me. But what happened between us needs to be acted upon. Now we can take it as slowly as you want or as fast, I'm all in. Need I remind you that you still haven't answered my question from earlier. Who are you going with on your relaxing weekend?

HOLLY: We can take it slow; well not a snail's pace, but I would like that. And the people I'm going away with are an older couple that have been like parents to me since I was sixteen. I've haven't seen much of them in the last year, so we are going to spend some quality time together.

I now want to know what's happened to her parents. Are they still around or not? There is so much I want to find out about the angel who had me captured quicker than the SAS sweeping in on their targets. The one who leaves me breathless and has haunted me all night long. But I won't ask them now. Some things should not be asked in text messages. Plus, I'm happy with what she's given me already. We can take it slow, I'm sure I can persuade her to speed things up a little. If last night is anything to go by we were both out of control, doing things we wouldn't normally do. Furthermore, I now know with whom and why she's having a weekend away.

VLAD: Thank you for giving us a try, I'm sure we will have lots of fun together and thanks for answering my question. At least I can sleep peacefully until Monday knowing why you're there and not have nightmares about some man taking you from me. Please promise me you won't dance with anyone but the elderly gentleman if you go out.

I sound desperate, but I don't give a damn.

HOLLY: I'm laughing at you. Last night was something I won't forget. I don't normally entice men on to tables and put on an exhibition for all, but I will confess that you make me want to do things I wouldn't normally do. With you dancing came naturally, as if we had held each other all our lives. So, on that I will promise not to dance as we did last night with any other man while I'm away.

Fucking hell, this woman surprises me at every turn. One minute she's shy and embarrasses easily the next she's laying it out there, telling me how it is.

VLAD: You laugh at me all you want, sweetheart. I'm just delighted we're on the same page about last night. I will happily wait until Monday to hear from you now, although I don't think you're as shy as you would have me believe. My angel has a little devil in her that likes to play out now and again.

HOLLY: Well I didn't until last night. I think it's you who brings out a little mischief in me. So, be careful Mr Petrov, you may get a little more than you can handle.

I can't help but laugh at the little minx. Maybe I have brought out a devilish side to her, but she's brought out a whole new man in me.

VLAD: Bring it on, woman. Can't wait to handle you again. LOL

HOLLY: I am going now, I have things to get ready for tomorrow.

VLAD: Okay. Have a very relaxing weekend, don't forget your promise and phone or text me when you get back.

HOLLY: I will, to all three. Enjoy your weekend too X

Resting my head back on my chair, I'm a very happy man. Though I'm not sure what to do about the little X she sent on the end of her last text. I know when Izzy my daughter-in-law and Rebecca my granddaughter put it at the end of their text it's meant as a kiss. Do I send her one back like I do with them? They're my family who I love and will do anything for – even my boys put them on the end of their text to me, although I think they do it just to get a reaction from me. They say it's because they don't have a mother to text, so they treat me as both. They are good lads but fucking idiots at times. Fuck it.

VLAD: X

I'm still resting my head on the back of my chair and the smile on my face is still fixed in place as I press send. Am I happy? I'm fucking ecstatic, can't wait for Monday.

Chapter 9

Vlad

Since my last message to Holly I haven't stopped smiling, thinking about our meeting last night, the messages to each other today and where I could take her when we eventually meet up. Questions pop in and out of my head constantly. What does she like to do in her spare time? I know she isn't working, so she has plenty of that. Where does she prefer to eat? If she's divorced, does she have children?

With my feet perched up on my desk and my head still resting on the back of my chair, I'm content. That's until I hear a commotion at my office door. I know who's there. I don't need to lift my head because I'd bet my fucking life that when I look up, there will be three grinning idiots I call my sons staring at me.

Last night's attraction was not just a surprise to myself but will have shocked the hell out of them. I didn't stick around long enough after my little tryst with Holly for them to tease or try and extract any information from me.

Nicholas is the first to interrupt my thoughts.

"Hi, Paps. You look like the cat who got the cream, with that smirk plastered on your face," he laughs out at me.

He's my second eldest and is the clown of the family. He likes to joke around a lot and has a very fun-loving personality. Unfortunately for me, I get to bear the brunt of his sarcastic humour. I love him just as much as his brothers, but he drives me to despair most days.

"I feel like the cat who got the cream," I tell him. Sebastian and Daniel look at me with amusement in their eyes.

"Wooh, did you get laid, old man?" he questions while getting comfy in the chair opposite me and planting his size ten feet up on my desk.

"I don't kiss and tell, Nicholas," I answer, throwing a pen at his head and motioning for him to take his feet down. He sits there observing me with inquisitive eyes.

They all know it was very out of character for me to behave the way I did last night, especially in front of them and in one of my own establishments.

Daniel strolls round to my side of the desk and places his hand on my forehead. "Are you not feeling well, Paps? Do you have a temperature?" he asks then tries to swipe my mobile phone in the process. However, I'm a little bit faster than he is; safely the phone is tucked away in my pocket.

"You two are such nosey bastards," I point out.

Nicholas regards his brother and I know I'm going to be bombarded with their piss-taking antics. So, I brace myself for whatever they're going to throw at me.

Only, what I hear is nothing but a shock. In all the twelve years we have lived in England, they have never once questioned or commented on me never bringing a woman home. Neither do they ask what I do or where I go for entertainment.

"Ah, kiss and tell. Who are you kidding? We hear you don't even kiss the women you screw around with, Paps." This statement just leisurely falls out of Nicholas's mouth.

"Yeah, you're a hit with the ladies," Daniel intercepts. "With the whole brooding bad boy image you have going on," he chuckles.

My mouth falls open and I rub my hands over my shocked face. I can't speak. I have nothing to say to their comments, so I just go with... "What?"

"Paps, you don't think we hear what some of the women you've played around with say about you? We've had their younger sisters trying to get off with us, hoping we are a chip off the old block." Nicholas points between himself and Daniel. "You know we have met up with women in the club that have made your acquaintance. They're more than happy to let people know that they have been with one of the owners."

Sebastian does not say a word. He doesn't have to; the surprise on his face tells me he didn't know they were going to bring up my private life.

It's not like I've ever lied to them about it, I just never mentioned it and they don't ask. My sons have always been brought up to respect women, never wanting to put my distrust of the opposite sex on them. I have my reasons for this. They know what their mother put me through and I know not all women are the same. My daughter-in-law is a beautiful, caring woman, a devoted wife to my son Sebastian and loving mother to their children. With all that said, women know what they're getting with me, I put them under no illusion that there will be nothing more than a good hard fuck.

Sebastian shifts on his feet and places his hands in his pockets, waiting with bated breath for what these two are going to say next, or for what my reaction is going to be. So, I'll play their game and ask, "What do these women say about me?" I relax further into my chair, placing my hands at the back of my head and watch them with a smug smirk on my face. Daniel's the first to inform me that I'm well known for fucking hard and fast, giving women just what they need.

Then Nicholas follows with, "It's a one-time thing, no seconds, no dates and no exchanging of phone numbers. No exceptions." They both shrug their shoulders at their comments and I just nod my head at them. It's nothing I don't already know.

My body stiffens, and I grip the arms of my chair as I hear the words, "Mother dear really did a number on you, didn't she?" Nicholas emphasises. My eyes lock onto Sebastian who's glaring wildly at his brother's remark.

"Nicholas, enough," he spits out with the sternness of an older brother.

What started as a bit of fun has now taken on a more serious tone and I'm wondering where this is going to lead. I don't wonder for long because Nicholas has not finished with his little son-to-father talk.

"I know I've crossed the line," concern on his face as he shifts forward in his seat, "but, I saw you last night, letting your hair down, enjoying yourself, and it was not the alcohol. Or, the fact that it was your birthday. It was all to do with the woman you spent all night eyeing, flirting and dancing with. And I'm almost certain, in fact, I'd bet my share of the club that's who you were texting and who put that smile on your face." He sounds exasperated.

Looking at Nicholas, I see concern etched in his eyes, and the concern is for me. It's easy to forget that he's not a child or teenager anymore. He's twenty-five and I still worry about him, about all of them. All his life he's kept us entertained with his pranks. Always the one to take a serious situation and turn it into a joke, amusing his brothers endlessly with his sarcastic wit and quick one-liners. When Daniel woke with nightmares, he'd be the one to get a smile out of him.

Daniel was only nine when we moved here, and it hit him the hardest. Losing his mother, the move and starting a new school, all played a part in him having frequent nightmares. He didn't understand what she was like, what she put us through. I suppose he missed her and his home, unlike his brothers and myself who were glad to get away. Although, as he got older, he must have remembered certain things because he would question Sebastian and Nicholas about her and Russia. "Dad," Daniel utters. I smirk at him because they very rarely call me that. Papa, Paps or Father along with old man, big guy, depending on how they're feeling, are normally what they bellow around the house.

Searching my sons' faces, it's then I see that the roles have reversed, and it's not me who is concerned for them but the other way around. "Paps," he says this time. "You don't have to be alone anymore, we're adults. Do you not think it is time you found someone who makes you happy?" Daniel suggests.

"Not all women are the like our mother," Nicholas states, raking his hand through his mousy blond hair while he studies my reaction to their mother being mentioned again.

I sit there watching the anxiety etched on my three sons' faces. Poor Sebastian looks pale with worry. Does he think I'm going to flip because his brothers mentioned their mother? Well I'm past letting her name infuriate me. There was a time when any reference to her would antagonise me. It was like showing a red rag to a bull.

Slowly rising from my seat, my boys stare with wide eyes. I stroll over to Sebastian's desk and pick up one of the black leather chairs. Striding back, I place it next to where Nicholas is seated. "Sit," I order my eldest. Daniel has already got himself settled on the other side of his sidekick Nicholas. All three are glancing at each other, bewilderment covering their faces. I chuckle to myself because the expressions that they are wearing, say, 'Are you seriously going to scold us as if we're teenagers?'

Keeping them guessing, I perch my rear on the edge of my desk and cross my arms over my chest, then sigh lightly as I prepare to let them know what's going on in my head.

"Sebastian, Nicholas, Daniel," I start. "I brought you here to England," my hand waves through the air, "over twelve year ago, to give you a better life and put behind us all the danger, unhappiness and hurt we had endured. I hope you will agree with me that I have done just that." All three, nod in agreement but say nothing.

"Seb," I greet with admiration and as much love for him as I had when he was born. "You have grown into an exceptional young man with a family of your own to care for, but never once do you neglect that you have younger brothers or a father who loves you dearly. I am so proud of how hard you work and the man you have become. It has been a delight and an honour to be your father which I intend to enjoy a lot longer." His blue eyes glisten; he swallows, trying to fight back his emotions. I rise from my desk; he stands from the chair he has been sitting in. Hugging him tightly, showing him the love of a mother and a father, that's what I have tried to be to all my sons over the years. After patting him on the back, we both return to where we were sat.

Nicholas and Daniel watch me with the same look on their face as Sebastian.

"You two," I point at them, "like your brother are remarkable young men. Again, no matter where you are or what you are doing, you are always there for each other and your brothers. I am proud of how well you did at school and how hard you both work to achieve whatever goal you set yourselves. And I'm sure when the time is right, when you marry for love and have children you will be as devoted as Sebastian." Tears spill from their eyes and Nicholas holds up his hand.

"Stop. Why are you telling us this? This was about you, not us, Dad. We just want you to have something, someone in your life that makes you happy," he expresses.

"Your concern for me being on my own all these years is not needed. I've been happy to watch my sons become the strong men you are. Furthermore, I will continue to watch Lucas grow into a strong man like you three," I beam proudly at them. "I've been happy to keep my…" I cough into my hand, not sure how to word my next statement. But we never hold back with what we want to say, so I carry on. "I've always been happy to keep my sex life separate to my family life and never wanted to bring a woman into our lives or home. Plus, I've never met a woman that's got me wanting any more than a few hours of her time," I explain.

Nicholas stops me when he adds, "Until last night." His brothers smirk at his comment and wait for my reaction. I'm not going to lie to them, I do want to pursue a relationship with Holly. Wow, just thinking of her, saying her name in my head gives me goosebumps and puts a smile on my brooding face. I nod my head at them and repeat Nicholas's words.

"Until last night."

"Fucking hell, I know that look," Sebastian snorts out.

"Yeah," Daniel jumps in. "It's the same fucking lovestruck one you had when you were chasing Izzy," he teases. Sebastian chuckles at him while slapping him round the head.

Nicholas then opens his mouth. "Papa is in love," he jokes.

"No, I'm not, you set of idiots." I laugh at them, shaking my head. "I'm just…" I don't finish because I don't know what I'm feeling. I know it's something I haven't felt before not even with their mother.

"Yes?" they all say together, wanting me to finish what I was going to say.

"Just what?" Nicholas enquires.

"I don't know." And I don't know what I'm feeling. I know she excites me in ways I've never felt before. Her not responding straight away to my text had me pacing the floor like a caged tiger. As soon as she contacted me my heart raced.

"I'm fucked," I mumble.

"Yes, you are," Sebastian agrees. "I knew Izzy was the one when she came flying through the office door at the club. She looked like a drowned rat and as fragile as a newborn puppy. No sooner did her big chocolate eyes lock with mine, I was hooked. She had sadness and mischief rolled into one which made me want to wrap her up in my arms, take her home and keep her there, safe. But as you know, she didn't make it easy for me. I had to prove myself to her and I think that's what you might have to do with the woman you met last night."

"I'm up for the challenge. Anyway, what makes you sure she will play hard to get?" I ask him.

He nods at Nicholas to answer my question. "I was dancing with one of the women she came into the club with and she gave me a little bit of information about your lovely Holly," he informs me.

"Well whatever it is, I'm sure I will find out from her."

"You don't want to know?" he questions.

"No, I'm a patient man." Although, maybe not so much where she is concerned.

"Yeah, you keep telling yourself that, old man," Daniel says, grinning at me.

"Hey, this is where you're all hiding," says the voice of my youngest as he hurries through the door. He has an inset day, so no school today, and probably wants to spend the day with his brothers.

Both sides of his mouth turn up, beaming at them. "Are you not working today?" he probes.

"No, we are discussing our father's love life," Nicholas tells him.

"Uh, he doesn't have one," Lucas says, shrugging his shoulders while sitting his bottom on the edge of my desk.

"He does now," they all say in unison.

Chapter 10

Vlad

What a fucking weekend it's been. I contemplate it all, removing my coat and shoes and depositing them in the oversized walk-in wardrobe. I didn't even attempt to enter the kitchen tonight, just slowly took my aching and overly tired body up my stairs, heading straight for a hot shower. It's Monday evening and since Friday I've had one hectic weekend.

The early hours of Saturday morning had Daniel phoning me letting me know we'd had a couple of drug dealers trying to sell their shit in Eruption. Things got a little out of hand when the bouncers tried to secure them while they waited for the police. Frank, with his level headedness was able to contain the situation until the police arrived. Although I didn't have to go to the club, the fact that someone had been able to smuggle them in, enraged me. So, no sleep for me for the rest of the night.

Late Saturday afternoon Izzy was taken to hospital with stomach pains. Straight away I was by her bedside along with Sebastian. She's a little over four months pregnant and every twinge and ache has them both in a panic. I don't blame them. I'm right behind them in getting Izzy and the baby checked out, especially after the miscarriage they had early last year. Even though the pains were nothing to do with the baby they kept her in overnight, some infection in her water

I think they said, and her blood pressure was slightly raised. Sebastian wanted to stay at the hospital which meant I was having my grandchildren Joseph and Rebecca overnight. I normally work early Sunday morning until lunchtime on paperwork for the restaurant, that didn't happen. Making pancakes for breakfast with syrup and fruit for our Princess Rebecca because she wanted an American breakfast took priority. She has her father, uncles and me eating out of the palm of her hand.

Mrs White, our housekeeper, had been the only woman around the house for many years before Izzy came along. Not having any daughters, she quickly became part of the family, claiming her place in our hearts. My other sons looked upon her as an older sister. When Sebastian and Izzy found out they were having a girl I knew none of us would be the same again. No sooner did she scream into this world she had every one of us wrapped around her little finger.

After cleaning up the flour and batter off the floor and the kitchen work surface, as well as the mess Lucas and Joseph had made grilling bacon for sandwiches, we took a trip to the park.

By the time Sebastian arrived to pick up his little darlings, we had had pancakes and bacon for breakfast, a trip to the park and a game of football. Then I'd cooked fishfingers and chips for my nearly five-year-old (going on eighteen) granddaughter, burgers for the boys and myself. For desert we baked one of the apple pies from the freezer that Mrs White had made. She keeps everything well stocked for my sons who will turn up day or night to get their fill.

I had played with My Little Ponies, brushing and plaiting their hair so Lucas and Joseph could pick whose were the prettiest, mine or Rebecca's. They were happy playing on their video games. Like I said, she has us eating out of her hand. This all took precedence over any work I had to do.

Monday morning came around fast; I was in the office for six, so I could get yesterday's work out of the way before the meeting I had at one o'clock. The meeting I had booked with a very well-respected business man. Alex is an elderly gentleman who owns a significant amount of property, some of which he is selling. I'd approached him weeks ago about one of the run-down buildings he has. My sons and I had discussed buying property to turn into affordable apartments. I had mentioned this to Alex who agreed that he would give me first option to buy and we had negotiated some figures over a few drinks. Today's meeting was to get the ball rolling with his final asking price and get our solicitors on with drawing up the paperwork. Only, Alex couldn't make the meeting because his wife had surprised him with an early sixty-fifth birthday present, a Caribbean cruise for three weeks. Which left me with his wet-behind-the-ears grandson. Twenty-two years of age and couldn't tie his own shoe laces without his mother's help. Honestly, my twelve-year-old could organise himself better. And the jumped-up little shit had the audacity to try and up the price well above its value. It's alright if it works, he would have made his grandfather a lot of money. But, I'm not some wet-behind-the-ears kid, so his overconfidence got him nowhere.

Like a lot of men and women in business, we don't take kindly to some kid thinking we don't do our homework on any ventures we want to get into. That's why eventually I told him to go home and I would deal with his grandfather when he came home from his cruise. He wasn't happy that I didn't want to do the deal with him and suggested that his grandfather might pull out of the agreement we had. I chuckled at that. I knew his grandfather and if someone had tried to put one over on him he would have told them to fuck off. So, that's what I did, then left him open-mouthed as I stalked out of his grandfather's office.

*

The end to my day just got a lot better. I've showered and poured myself a double brandy. Lucas is staying with Nicholas and Daniel; he likes to stay with them one night a week, either at their apartment or here. They opted for theirs to give me a bit of peace and quiet.

Sitting my back against the soft leather headboard, I have my drink in one hand and my phone in the other with a huge grin on my face. My little angel has just texted me. It's only one word but it's all I needed to brighten up the end of the day.

HOLLY: Hi

VLAD: Hi yourself

I know it's a short text back, but I want her to lead today's conversation.

HOLLY: Hmm, you asked me to text you when I got back so here I am. Texting you, that is.

From her message I deem she's a little nervous. Looks like I'm going to be the one to open a conversation.

VLAD: I'm glad you remembered. How was your weekend?

HOLLY: Good thank you. Very relaxing. How about yours?

No need to go into detail about my hectic weekend. I would rather find out about her and make plans to take her out.

VLAD: Busy as usual, lots of boring paper work…

HOLLY: Sorry, I won't keep you. You must be tired.

Quickly, I message back because I'm not letting her go yet.

VLAD: It's fine, I'm not too tired to talk to you.

HOLLY: OK, if you are sure. What would you like to talk about?

VLAD: Us.

My answer is one word because I know once we meet again we will be an us.

HOLLY: There is no us, Vlad.

I ignore the word no, I won't accept no where she is concerned.

VLAD: There will be when you agree to let me take you to dinner.

HOLLY: You are very self-assured that if we meet up, there will be more than dinner happening

I chuckle to myself because I am confident that it won't be just dinner. Our encounter last week proved that there's a strong attraction there, we couldn't keep our hands off each other. But, it's more than that. I want more.

VLAD: I did not mention anything but dinner. You know I'm a gentleman, Holly.

I leave it at that. I could have it taken further last Thursday, but I knew as soon as I held her in my arms I wanted more. In fact, to be truthful I probably should have realised it as soon as our eyes met across the room. I was captivated.

My phone starts ringing, and Holly's name lights up the screen. I answer it straight away, not wanting to waste another second.

How desperate am I?

"Holly," is all I say.

"Vlad," comes her sweet voice. My name is like smooth velvet rolling off her tongue. My heart skips a beat and flutters with excitement.

We're both silent for a brief while, so I decide to break the quietness. "This is a surprise. It's good to hear your voice again, I was forgetting what your sweet voice sounded like."

"I thought I would give you a chance," Holly says.

"Well that's very kind of you, Holly," I laugh. "But what are you giving me chance to do?" I ask, still laughing.

"You said that you're a gentleman so I'm giving you a chance to prove it," she answers nervously.

"Well then Holly, how about you let me take you to dinner, tomorrow, and then you will see just how courteous I can be?" I invite.

"Sorry, Vlad. I'm busy over the next three or four days. I'm meeting with friends tomorrow evening, child minding on Wednesday and on a hen night on Thursday," she reveals.

It will be hard to wait until the weekend. Sounding desperate never looks good on anyone, so I don't mention we could meet tomorrow for lunch.

"What about Friday?"

"Not sure Friday's a good idea, I might be tired and a little hung over. What about Saturday?" she suggests. And I'm fine with that. Well, not fine but like I said, I don't want to be too eager.

"I'll book a table for six o'clock and pick you up."

Who am I kidding?

"Saturday at six sounds good," Holly relays back.

"Fantastic. Although I'm not sure I can wait until then to speak to you. I might have to call or text you before then," I tell her with a chuckle because I couldn't sound more like a love-struck teenager.

"I will look forward to that, Vlad.," she says while softly laughing.

Her laugh is beautiful. I find myself laughing with her even though I know she's sniggering at how needy I sound. Not wanting to let her go just yet, I continue with our conversation.

"So, Holly, what are your plans for the rest of the evening?"

"Hmmm, not much. I'm already in bed, so I'll probably read until I fall asleep. What about you?"

There we go. My mind and body take over the life of a twenty-year-old and as soon as it enters my juvenile mind, does it come tumbling out of my mouth. "Have you ever had phone sex, Holly?" *Fuck*, I chastise myself. "I'm really sorry. I can't believe that came out of my mouth," I choke out. Hearing her laugh on the other end of the phone, gives me hope that I haven't fucked up and maybe she might be game for a little fun over the phone.

"No, Vlad, it's something I've never done. I'm thirty-seven years old and maybe my sex life has not been as interesting as yours or my friends' for that matter," she tells me still with a hint of humour in her voice.

"Again, I'm sorry Holly. But, I can't help myself with you, I end up acting like a randy fucking teenager. I'm not normally like this," I explain.

"What are you normally like then, Vlad?" she purrs out.

The sexy sound of her tone has me conjuring images of her in sexy underwear, no underwear at all. What she would feel like under me, my hands wandering, stroking her soft, silky skin.

I'm aware I haven't answered her question yet. Making dates over the phone isn't something I do. I enjoy sex as much as the next person. but I don't flirt to get it. I don't have to. For some reason women find me irresistible and can't wait to have me in their bed or up against a wall anywhere really. And I don't even have to try. Holly is something different; I find I want to talk, flirt and get to know her.

"Sweetheart, I'm forty-five and phone sex is something I haven't tried yet either," my voice taking on an even lower tone than normal.

"Why mention it then?" she quickly asks.

"I'm not entirely sure. It could be that I've had a hell of a few days. I find you incredibly beautiful and sexy. Your call brightened up my evening and knowing you're laid in bed probably in lacy underwear or naked…" I don't finish because she jumps in.

"Wow, what happened to you being a gentleman?" she chuckles.

"Fuck if I know," is what falls out of my mouth and I'm apologising again. "Sorry Holly."

She giggles at my pathetic attempt to rescue myself for my bad language.

"No need for apologies, I'm not a prude," she assures me. "My friends curse like sailors, I'm known to say the odd profanity myself. Come to think of it, so-called friends are well known for being intimate anywhere they damn well please, therefore I'm sure they will have had phone sex many times. Olivia and Jack have been together since they were teenagers and they're forty-two and still very touchy-feely," she divulges.

I'm glad to hear her friends are devoted to each other; let's hope it's the kind of thing Holly wants because with me it will be all or nothing.

I don't mention phone sex this time, although she didn't say she wasn't up for it, just that she had never done it. "Your friends must be very much in love," I say, wanting her to know that I'm not just interested in sex.

"Yes, they are. The desire you see in their eyes for each other is something to behold. They've always shown how much they love each other and don't care who witnesses their passionate embraces," she sighs.

There's happiness in her voice for her friends but sensing it is something she has never experienced, tightens my chest. "Holly?"

"Hmmm."

Why would any man in his right mind cheat on this woman? She deserves to be worshipped, to have someone who will show the world what she means to him. I'm not the touchy-feely type as she says her friends are. I never got the chance with my wife. Saying that, I did a lot of that with Holly last week. I held her hand, kissed her, ran my fingers over her silky skin in front of the whole club and did a few other things behind closed doors. I did not care who was watching when I kissed her up on that table, whispering in her ear while my hands skimmed over her tight curves. Holding hands on the way back to the lounge felt right; everything felt normal with her.

She brings me out of my thoughts. "You still there, Vlad?"

"Yes, sorry I was just thinking."

"What about?" her soft voice asks.

"You."

"What about me?"

"I was just thinking that when we do meet up, you will see how much you are desired because I will be doing a lot of flirting, touching and let's not forget whispering all my dirty thoughts while my lips caress your delectable neck. You will realise how crazy a real man is for you." My gravelly voice is getting lower.

"Well, I will look forward to that," she tells me on a raspy whisper, her breath catching.

My cock springs to life; the tone she uses tells me she will be looking forward to our meeting. I know she's affected as much as I am.

"So, will I, Holly. So will I."

"Maybe I should go now. You've had a long day and I'm meeting Olivia early in the morning," she murmurs.

"OK, sweetheart. We will talk soon." I'll let her go but she can expect me to be expressing my desires throughout the week.

"Goodnight Vlad," she says quietly.

"Goodnight Holly."

Looking at my phone after I ended our call, my cock is still twitching with the thought of her naked in bed and my hands take over my phone. Before I know it, I've sent her a text message.

VLAD: Just because we're not having phone sex, doesn't mean I can't get off thinking about you naked in bed, with me kissing, stroking your silky, smooth skin, pleasuring you while whispering all those things we could be doing together.

A few moments my phone pings.

HOLLY: Hmmm, sounds very erotic. Maybe I will do the same. Thinking about all those things has certainly got me all hot. Goodnight Vlad.

The little tease. I think I may have met my match.

After taking care of the hardness my angel has caused, I fall into the deepest sleep dreaming of her.

Chapter 11

Holly

"Aunt Holly, we're here," Megan sings at me through the intercom.

Megan is Olivia and Jack's four-year-old granddaughter. She's been living with them since her mum, their eldest daughter Lucy, went off to university to finish her degree in psychology.

Lucy was only eighteen when she ended up pregnant after a drunken fumble at a party. She had just finished her A-levels and was due to go to university. Finding out two weeks before her start date, her education was then put on hold until after Megan was born.

Although Olivia and Jack were only a year older than Lucy when they had her and her twin brother Jackson, it was not what they wanted for their only daughter. A little shocked to say the least about her revelation, they sat down and discussed what Lucy should do after the baby was born.

Between the three of them, they decided that once Megan was a year old, Lucy would go off to do her degree. Her parents would look after Megan Monday to Friday with the support from Jackson the doting uncle. Jay and Ivy the proud great grandparents and the two younger uncles would help too. Since I was Lucy's godmother and had taken care of all my friends' children when they were small or any time they needed an extra shoulder to cry on, I would gladly help with the little pumpkin.

I had been the one Lucy had confided in when she thought she was pregnant. She came flying through my door like a force ten gale waving a pregnancy kit around. "*I need to pee on this quickly. I can't take the suspense anymore,*" she shouted then disappeared into the bathroom. Once I heard the sobbing that's when I entered the room Lucy had run off into and held her like her mother would have done if she had been there. Unfortunately, we had to wait a week to let the new grandparents know as they were sunning themselves in the South of France and we did not want to ruin their holiday. They had both worked so hard to keep Jay's business going when he handed it over to them and Nick. They had also expanded it. With four children to raise they never got a break, they didn't even have a honeymoon. So, this week away meant a lot to them.

Lucy drives back from Liverpool every Friday evening and returns Monday morning, except if she needs to study for an exam. Megan gets a phone call from her mum as soon as she wakes in the mornings and before she goes to bed in the evening. The little girl loves asking her mum what she has been doing at school in her posh little voice.

She now gets quality time every Wednesday with Aunt Holly. Today, there's an inset day at her school, so instead of me picking her up from her reception class at three, she is here at nine thirty.

I press the button on the intercom to let them in and open the front door, waiting.

Her giggles echo across the landing as she steps out of the lift. As soon as she comes into view she thrusts out her little chubby hand, which is holding a bunch of pink carnations. "For you," she squeals. "I picked them by myself," she sniggers, "out of Grandpa Jay's garden." She continues sniggering. Bending down to her level, I take the bunch of flowers from her.

"Thank you, sweet pea. Does Grandpa know you stole these from his garden?" I whisper, my eyes widening and a little grin on my face.

"Nooo," she whispers back. Holding her tiny hands in front of her, she shakes her head. "Don't tell him, will you Aunt Holly?" her little face scrunching up.

"No, I will not. Let's go and put them in a vase, my little sweet pea, and we will say nothing to Grandpa Jay," I tell her while taking her cute little hand in mine and skipping off into the kitchen.

She continues with her giggling. "I'm not a sweet pea. You're silly."

"Yes, you are. You're my little sweet pea as well as my little pumpkin," I say as I scoop her up in to my arms. She plants a sloppy wet kiss on my cheek and I return the kiss with one just as sloppy on hers. Then we head for the cupboard to rummage for a vase.

Olivia laughs at the interaction between her granddaughter and best friend and steals a piece of my toast. "Help yourself, Olivia," I say with a smirk on my face.

"I have," she mumbles around the toast and shrugs her shoulders.

"Have you had breakfast, Megan?" I ask the little pint pot that's trying to scramble up on to one of the breakfast stools. Once she gets herself comfy, she informs me.

"I had porridge with Granddad Jack and a slice of toast. He lets me help now, you know," the little madam adds on with a smile that's only for her hero – Grandad Jack. It's their thing, no matter what's happening or how busy he is Jack shows his love for his granddaughter. He always makes her breakfast and they eat together. He spoils her rotten with outings to zoos, parks and children's productions at the theatres. He reads to her every evening too, but he did the same with his children. Like I said, lots of love.

"Well would you like another piece of toast with jam on top of it?" I ask her.

"Yes please, Aunt Holly," folding her sparkly pink covered arms as she answers. She's wearing one of her favourite long-sleeved princess T-shirts with black leggings and sparkly pink pumps.

Her nanna puts her arms around her granddaughter and squeezes. "You are such a polite young lady," she tells her.

The little pumpkin nods her head slowly. "I know," she giggles out. I laugh with her.

"She gets it from me," I inform Olivia then pop a piece of toast into my mouth. Olivia throws her eyes up at me and Megan just giggles.

"Have you time for a coffee?" I ask her.

"Yes, I've got half an hour," comes her reply with a wink. I know she wants all the juicy gossip as to what Vlad and I have been talking and texting about.

"Holly," Megan sings out, "Can I watch CBeebies while you and Nanna have your coffee?" she asks oh so sweetly while her big brown eyes look up at me.

"Of course, sweet pea, go turn it on," I say while helping her down from the stool. No sooner has she got settled on the sofa with the volume up then Olivia's on my case. The woman's relentless. She's like a dog with a bone.

"Sooo, what time did you get off the phone last night with the Russian god? Are you still seeing him on Saturday? Is he still flirty? Oh my god, I can't believe you two get on so well. I predict a hot, loving relationship blooming," She blows out then takes a deep breath, coming up for air.

"Woah, I thought you were going to burst a blood vessel then," I snort out.

"Well I only have half an hour and you know I need details," she exhales.

"I'm not telling you what we talked about until the early hours," I say with a smirk on my face.

Although he was flirty on the phone, he was also genuinely polite. Asking questions about my childhood. Did I have brothers and sisters? Were my parents still around? What job did I hold at the bank and how long had I been friends with Olivia, Sarah and their husbands? I didn't really find much out about him other than he came to England twelve years ago, he runs a restaurant and he enjoys a game of golf in his spare time. I'm not even sure if he's the manager or the owner because he'd change the subject back to me. He seemed content to let me ramble on about my adoptive parents and my friends.

"Holly, I have half an hour," Olivia says, tapping her phone and bringing me back from my thoughts.

"Sorry. We got off the phone about one thirty. Yes, we're still going out on Saturday, he's picking me up at six and as for hot loving relationship, who knows?" I say, shrugging my shoulders.

"Oh, come on, Holly. You two looked pretty hot together last week."

"Maybe," is all I say then I show her my phone with the text he sent me this morning at eight o'clock.

VLAD: Morning Angel. Hope you slept as well as I did. I dreamt of you all night. Best sleep ever… Anyway, have a fantastic day with the little one and I will look forward to hearing your sweet voice tonight.

HOLLY: Good morning to you too. I'm glad you slept well courtesy of myself and I hope your dream was satisfying… Have a great day and I will look forward to speaking with you tonight when you can tell me all about your dream.

VLAD: Where do you live? I can be around in no time at all and show you if you prefer.

HOLLY: No can do, big guy. I'm childminding soon.

VLAD: OK, I suppose I will just have to go to work thinking of you. You do realise I'm not going to get any work done.

HOLLY: Well get your head out of the gutter and focus on your job?

VLAD: OK, sweetheart. I need to go, running late now speak to you soon.

HOLLY: Bye Vlad

VLAD: Bye Holly

"Wow, you little flirt," she states, fanning herself.

"I know," I say, laughing. "I can't help myself with him. He brings out a side of me I didn't know existed."

"See, I'm right, hot relationship," she claims as she licks her finger and pokes my face, mimicking something sizzling.

"You're crazy," I say, amused at her actions.

"Yes, that is true, but it does not make my assumptions wrong, Holly."

Megan shouts from the sofa, "Are we going to the park today, Holly?" This stops our conversation and I answer the little cherub with a simple yes.

Olivia kisses Megan and me goodbye and leaves us both to get on with our day.

I pack our bag ready to start our day out when Megan skips into the kitchen area. My apartment isn't very spacious; the kitchen and living room are open-plan so I can watch her from one while she is in the other. "Aunt Holly, can I watch a little bit of Snow White before we go out?" the sweet little thing asks while scrunching her cute button nose up and holding up her thumb and finger to show me a little bit.

"Of course, it's still early, we don't need to go out just yet," I reassure her. "You can watch half while I tidy up the kitchen and put the washer on then we will walk to the park. We can feed the ducks while we are there. Then have dinner. After that we will get the bus to town and do a bit of shopping and when we get home you can watch the other half. Deal?" I hold my hand up and meet her high five as she tells me deal with a happy smile on her face. She then skips back to the living room to put on Snow White.

I've cleaned up in the kitchen and put one lot of washing in, when I decide to check my phone. Grabbing my cup of coffee and phone, I perch my bottom on the stool. With no new messages, I scroll through the conversations between Vlad and me. I have quite a few from Monday evening and a few from Tuesday morning but it's the ones from Tuesday night that I fix on. Scrolling back and forth, I can't pick out what it was that had him calling me. We had just been leisurely texting when my phone rang, and Vlad's name appeared on the screen. "*Holly,*" was his first word. His husky voice alone sent my body into shock, making my legs turn to jelly and I had to sit down quickly. But what came out of his mouth after had me nearly on my knees begging for him to come around and take me anyway he wanted.

"Holly, I'm not going to lie to you. I want you." His tone was confident. *"Everything about last Thursday night is still with me, crystal clearly. The way our mouths crashed together, how our tongues consumed each other. Our bodies moulded perfectly together, the heat almost combustible. Sounds we both made while pressed against the wall but most of all how you looked as you came apart in my arms.*

"If it was just sex, Holly..." he continued while I just listened, muted, my pulse racing, palms sweating as I tried hard not to scream at him to come to mine and make me his. *"Holly if it was just sex I would have gave you what you wanted that night and fucked you hard and fast against the wall. Yes, I am sexually attracted to you and can't wait for the day*

when I have you under me in my bed, up against the wall in the entrance to my home because we can't get there fast enough. In the shower while we wash off the smell of sex from the hours of fucking the night before and on the worktop in my kitchen after we have eaten breakfast together.

"That's not all though, I want to get to know you, who Holly is."

Well, I couldn't breathe after his rant. My brain couldn't get passed his bed and walls so when I tried to speak I stuttered, *"How many walls do you have in your home?"*

A loud chortle erupted down the line. *"My home has many walls that we could explore. Oh, and lots of surfaces,"* came his answer in a suggestive tone.

The shock of his boldness should have had me slamming the phone down. But with him, it makes me want him even more. I think it's the fact that he says what's on his mind and boy does he. I might not have had much experience with men and normally I wouldn't react to a man like him; to be truthful someone of his stature would scare the hell out of me. Even though he does scare me, it's not because he intimidates me. No, it is because I want what he's offering, he brings out another side of me, a cheeky, sexy side which I like, and he wants. So, I answer him with a bit of tease in my tone. *"Well, Mr Petrov, you must have a lot of stamina for a man of your age."*

He quickly comes back at me, chuckling. *"Oh, Holly. This forty-five-year-old will not be needing Viagra while you are getting accustomed to the walls and surfaces in my home."*

We both crack up laughing, then bring our conversation back from the gutter.

*

Once, Megan has watched her fill of Snow White, we collect our things; bread for the ducks, rain coats just in case, bottles of water and Megan's princess purse – she likes to take her own money to pay for ice creams at the park. Then we take a leisurely walk down to the park.

We play on the swings, roundabout and some new chairs that you sit in then spin. Megan shows me how she can scamper up the climbing frame and spin down the fireman's pole which has me anxiously waiting with my arms out ready to catch her if she falls.

Following a short walk around the lake we stop for an ice cream and feed the ducks. There's a small café at the end of the park so we opt to eat there before taking the bus ride into the town centre, where Megan can buy something out of her spending money.

It's ten past five when we arrive back home, and I am shattered to say the least. We decide on something quick to eat so while I place the fishfingers and chips in the oven, Megan puts away her leggings and another Disney T-shirt. As I'm setting out the plates and drinks Megan comes hopping into the kitchen. "Can I colour for a while, Aunt Holly?" she asks, still trying to hop on one leg without falling over. While we were travelling on the bus, Megan informed me about a new friend she has at school. Her name is Rebecca and they both like skipping, playing with the hula hoops and hopping around the playground. She too loves anything Disney.

"Of course, Megan, I'll let you know when the fishfingers are ready," I tell her, giving her the bag with her new colouring book and crayons in. She hops into the living room then sets out her things on the low coffee table, letting out a little yawn. I think once we've eaten, it will be bath and pyjamas time.

I wasn't supposed to be having her overnight, but I thought Olivia and Jack could do with a night on their own therefore Nathan and James are staying at their grandparents' and Megan is staying with me. She has her nightclothes and uniform here so we're all set for her sleepover.

Once we've eaten and washed the dishes, I let Megan go back to watching her film. When it is finished she can have a bath, hot chocolate then bed.

Looking, through my bag, I can't seem to find my mobile. Quickly, I check my jacket pocket and search through the bag of shopping I've yet to put away. Megan's bag has been checked too but no phone. Realising I must have dropped it in one of the shops or on the bus, I decide to contact my service provider from my landline.

They cancel my SIM card and tell me I need to inform the police. Once I have a log number from the police my replacement phone will be sent out. Unfortunately, this leaves me no way of contacting Vlad, nor him me. He was supposed to be ringing me tonight. Will he think I'm ignoring him? I have no other ways of contacting him, I don't even know where he works. My spirits have been lifted over the last couple of weeks, looking forward to the night out we had last week then the hen night tomorrow. Meeting Vlad and the way he makes me feel has had me floating on a cloud all week, but my mood has just been deflated.

I don't have time to dwell on it too long because I have a little girl to take care of. So, I decide to file it for now until I have Megan ready for bed.

By the time she's snuggled in to bed it's seven thirty. I make myself a coffee and phone Olivia on my landline.

"Hi," she greets.

"Hi, sorry for phoning. I know you and Jack wanted some alone time."

"You're fucking joking. It's been like a frigging knocking shop in here. What with Jackson calling around to talk to his dad. Then Sarah and Chloe panicking about tomorrow night," she exclaims.

"Why are they panicking?" I question.

"Who knows? Everything is in order. Lucy's train gets her here for three and her dad is picking her up. All the girls are meeting here at seven for a couple of drinks before we head off to Aphrodite. Oh, and Lucy is home until Monday."

"That's fantastic, Megan will be thrilled to see her mum."

"Anyway, what were you calling about?" she asks.

"Well, I'm in a bit of a panic," I utter. A little bit embarrassed that I've only known him less than a week and that apart from our initial meeting last Thursday night, we've only spoke over the phone.

"What's got you in a pickle, sister?" she sniggers.

I explain the situation of the lost phone and it's too late to get a replacement out for tomorrow. She is aware that I have a couple of old mobiles in the kitchen drawer, with pay-as-you-go sim cards, so I can use one of them when I set off out in the morning to take Megan to school.

"It's just Vlad was supposed to be phoning me tonight and he won't be able to. Since, I've lost my phone he has no way of contacting me, or me him." I must sound pathetic and whiney.

"Wow, you really like this man, Holly." It's not a question.

"Yeah, I do," I admit, just realising that I can't wait to hear his husky, sexy voice. My stomach flutters with butterflies whenever his name appears on my phone. Never have I been this excited over a man, before not even with Rob, my ex-husband.

"Listen, Holly. He was in the VIP Lounge last Thursday with a group of fellows."

"Yes, it was his birthday," I tell her.

"Most people who were there last Thursday were given complementary passes because they had booked their hen or stag party at Aphrodite for tomorrow night. I bet he will be there tomorrow and you can explain how you lost your phone and was unable to contact him," she states. "So, don't panic, you will see him tomorrow. If he isn't there then we could call into Eruption; the waiter and that big house bouncer seem to know Mr Petrov well. I'm sure they will be able to help us get in contact with him," she explains.

"I suppose you're right," I agree and leave it at that. We chat about the day Megan and I have had then we say our goodbyes.

Chapter 12

Holly

Arriving inside the main entrance of Aphrodite, we are welcomed by a bronze god. His smile alone would have many women swooning at his feet.

He's kitted out in a pair of black dress trousers which fit tight around his thighs, outlining the muscle beneath, and I'm almost sure there's going to be a nice firm arse on the other side. The white T-shirt he is wearing clings to his broad chest and his arms are lightly tanned, pure muscle.

"Good evening, ladies. You're the last of the hen parties to arrive tonight, my name is Chris and I'm all yours for the evening," he greets, with a smirk. The smile meets his sparkly, emerald green eyes. There's a day's worth of stubble on his chiselled face and his dark hair is cut close to the scalp.

We all give our hellos with a few giggles and fucking hells from the younger end of the group. Sarah jabs me in the ribs; when I peel my eyes away from the Adonis, she's laughing at her sister Chloe. Chloe's eyes are glued to Chris and her mouth is wide open. Placing my hand under her chin, I tap it. "Close your mouth, dear, you're drooling," I say, grinning at her. She swallows hard, adjusting her stance.

"Why the fuck am I getting married, when there's men like him around?" We all laugh at her comment because we know she's madly in love with Michael, her soon-to-be husband.

Following Chris through into the club, just one look and you can see why it's named Aphrodite.

Dim, soft lighting and the humming of 'Fever' by some female artist streams through the speakers. There's large screens with silhouettes of men and women dancing provocatively, giving the ambience a sensuous feel.

We're led past a crescent-shaped bar and I can see that there's one of the same across the other side of the room. The top half of the club is a sea of heads mingling, laughing and drinking. Polished dark oak wood covers the floors with rich black leather sofas situated around along with high tables and chrome, black-seated stools. There's a small cocktail bar in the far corner which is lit up with florescent lighting.

We're led further into the club and our seating area comes into view. A set of stairs are cornered off with thick black rope and a nickel-coloured clasp. A six-foot-six bouncer stands at the side of it, wearing a well-fitted suit that displays his fine physique. He has a menacing look about him, which fades when a smile appears on his rugged face and he greets us with, "Good evening, ladies, enjoy yourselves," as he lifts the rope for Chris to lead us to our table.

Across the other side of the room there's another bouncer guarding a twin set of stairs.

Circular tables house the area covered with expensive-looking tablecloths and sparkling wine glasses. At separate tables groups of men and women watch the show that's taking place.

Situated within the spacious area are chrome poles and at least five of them have dancers hung around them. The men are stripped down to well-fitted black shorts outlining their firm buttocks with a good size package at the front, and the women are attired in pearly white bikinis with one of them just in her bikini bottoms.

There's wolf whistles from the men when the other woman discards her bikini top. The dance is tasteful and erotic at the same time.

We take our seats at the table and champagne is passed around. Staff pass by with trays of canapes, offering them with genuine smiles.

Taking in the show that's happening, the beauty of these people is in abundance. The two male dancers mount the pole with ease. One is halfway up, his legs apart in a V shape; his strong arms pull him further up the pole, multiplying the definition of his muscles. The other one has one leg hooked around, while he hangs upside down. He then proceeds to lift his body up, unhooking his leg, and pulls himself further up the pole.

Both men show strength, stamina and overall prowess as they continue to deliver a well-rehearsed performance. Once they are finished with their routine the lights dim a bit more and the music kicks up a gear. The dance floor fills quickly.

*

I'm on my way back from the ladies' when I decide to call to the bar for a glass of water. The cocktail bar is the nearest and is very quiet, to say this place is filled to the rafters. I've enjoyed the evening immensely so far, laughing so hard I nearly wet myself at some of the antics and positions the dancers and strippers put Chloe and the other soon-to-be-married men and women in, on the stage.

My head is feeling a little woozy with the champagne. I need to slow my pace otherwise I won't last the whole night.

My mood took a downward turn earlier when I realised Vlad was not here. Sarah, Olivia and I looked for him amongst the crowd as well as the men he was with last Thursday. Unfortunately, none of them were here. After, a long chat with my close friends, I decided to put him out of my mind until tomorrow. Hopefully, he will phone when I have my new one up and running, if not we will call into Eruption tomorrow evening. Fingers crossed the waiter or bouncer will be able to help me out with his number. Sarah told me if I open an online account with my service provider I should be able to look at any calls I have made and get his number from there. So, there's hope yet.

When I reach the bar there's only one member of staff working. "Hi there, honey, what can I get you?" she asks this with a cheery tone in her voice.

Straight away I answer, "Just a glass of water please, I need to sober up a bit," pointing to my head as I ask.

"Coming up. Would you like ice and lemon?" she calls back while going to retrieve a glass from the back of the bar.

"Yes, thanks," I reply.

She's a bubbly little thing. Around her mid-twenties, curly auburn hair, high cheekbones, she stands about five foot six but she's in three-inch heels. As she bounces back with my glass of water, I notice her pregnant belly. She has this cute little bump at the front and nothing at the back. When she places my drink on the bar I notice her face contort as she gently rubs her stomach. Concerned for her, I ask, "Are you OK?"

"Yeah, thanks, just a slight twinge," she breathes out then smiles at me. Her face is pale, and I can see there's worry etched on it.

"Are you sure? I can get someone if you like." I look around and see a couple of bouncers chatting.

"No." She shakes her head. "No, honestly I'm fine. My husband is in the club somewhere, I'll give him a call if it gets any worse," she says, waving her mobile phone at me.

"OK, if you're sure." She nods her head to let me know she's fine.

I stay and chat with her for a while, not wanting to leave in case she gets any more twinges. Not sure why I feel I need to stay but I just have this feeling that I need to be here.

She pulls up a stool behind the bar and gets herself comfy. After she drinks a glass of water, her colour returns a little and we settle into light conversation. Over the next half hour, I learn her name is Isabel, but she gets called Izzy. She's married with two children. Joseph or Joe as he likes to be called is nine and Rebecca is nearly five. They don't know the sex of the baby yet. Although Izzy enjoys the odd shift behind the bar on party nights, she is one of the managers who organises the entertainment.

When I had finished my water, she offered to make me a cocktail, a Long Island iced tea. I accepted but now I'm feeling the effects. A giggle escapes, when I wobble on my bar stool, trying hard to move across the bar away from the overly loud group of women who have joined us.

Deciding it's time to join my friends, I slip off the stool and leave Izzy to tackle the cackle of women who have had one too many. Who am I to talk? Gingerly, I make my way across the room, letting the bouncer guide me down the steps to our table.

Olivia, Sarah and the rest of the girls are shaking their bottoms on the dance floor, my head is a little fuzzy courtesy of the cocktail, but I opt to join them.

"Where have you been?" Olivia mouths over the loud music.

"Chatting at the bar," I mouth back.

She dances along side of me and links her arm through mine. "Oooh, do tell." She's a little tipsy.

"There's nothing to tell," I laugh. "I was chatting with one of the bar staff who wasn't feeling well."

"Oh, boring. No sign of the Russian mafia boss," she asks, screwing her face up.

I chuckle at the nickname she's bestowed on him then show a disappointed face and shake my head. She hugs me gently, reassuring me that we will sort it out tomorrow.

An hour later my feet hurt, I'm in desperate need of the ladies' and gasping for a glass of water. We've danced for a solid hour and the buzz I'd had from the Long Island iced tea has worn off.

Olivia and Sarah follow me to the toilet which is overly quiet. This is due to the gorgeous dancers and entertainment about to make another appearance.

Grabbing Olivia's arm as we make our way towards the crowd of guests in the top half of the club, "Hold on while I get a glass of water from the bar," I shout to her.

"Get the waiter to bring you one to our table," she says, nodding her head towards one of them as he passes by, balancing a tray of drinks in one hand.

"No, it's fine. The bar area is empty, and I could do with a breather from the crowds." She knows I'm out of practice, so she gives me a light kiss on my cheek.

"OK, honey, we'll see you back at the table." She raises her voice over the screams and whistles that have just erupted. The next show has just begun, and the crowds are loving it. Sarah kisses my other cheek then they both hurry past the bouncer and towards our table, leaving me to wander over to the cocktail bar.

Izzy has just finished serving a couple of men when I take a seat on the bar stool. She looks up and greets me with a smile. "Back again! Would you like another cocktail?" she asks, grinning.

"Bloody hell, I don't think so. Just a glass of water please, I'm not sure I could manage any more alcohol right now." I've had more than I would normally; a couple of glasses of wine and few shots at Olivia's. Champagne and cocktails in here are more than enough for me and the night's not over yet.

Perched on the stool, I wait for Izzy to bring my water. She's rubbing her swollen stomach again as she adds ice to the glass. Just as she approaches me, the glass slips from her hands, her face pales and within seconds she's on her knees gripping the stool she was sitting on earlier while her other holds her stomach.

A small moan escapes from her and before I know what I'm doing, I'm clambering over the bar, discarding my shoes as I do. I guide her to the floor away from the broken glass. "Izzy are you OK?" I hear my concerned voice ask. Of course, she's not OK or she wouldn't look as if all the blood had drained from her.

She lightly holds on to my hand while she rubs her belly. "I feel sick," she mumbles out.

Nervously, I look around for something, someone to help. I shout frantically to the beefy bouncer that I can see about twenty feet away from the bar. He must be blind because he didn't see me vault over to the woman who's squeezing my hand a little tighter now. I wave one of my arms to get his attention. The other one is in a vice-like grip.

She's moaning about a dull ache she has at the bottom of her stomach, followed by a stabbing pain, and I don't think that's a good sign for a pregnant woman.

The sharp-suited security man comes barrelling over. Quickly he vaults the bar. "Izzy, love," he soothes.

I recognize his face from last week; he was working at Eruption where I met Vlad.

"Phone an ambulance!" I yell at him. He glares at me then nods his head and produces his phone. I'm knelt at the side of a scared woman, rubbing her back while she sobs through her pain.

"R-Ring Seb, Frank," she stutters out through her sobs. The man has an earpiece in and I can hear him talking to someone through it.

He kneels with us. "Izzy, sweetheart, the ambulance is two minutes away and Sebastian's on his way up from the office. I've given instructions to the door staff to bring the paramedics straight through to the bar. Don't worry, love, you'll be OK," he consoles her.

"Thank you," she utters, tears still falling from her scared-looking eyes.

I stroke her arm. "You're going to be fine, Izzy," I reassure her as I pass her a tissue from my bag. She wipes her nose and face.

"Hmmm, I'm scared."

Looking at her pale face and quivering chin, she looks like a scared little shaking kitten. Placing my arms around her shoulders I pull her in, trying to sooth her. "Shush," I tell her. "The ambulance will be here soon." I know she's scared, being pregnant and having stomach pains would frighten any woman.

I'm knocked slightly off balance when two strong-looking arms with shirt sleeves rolled up take her from me. "Izzy, baby, I'm here. Don't cry, sweetheart," the smooth, calming voice says. I can't see his face because he has it nuzzled into Izzy's neck. This must be her husband Sebastian. It's soon confirmed when Izzy speaks.

"I'm sorry, Seb."

"What are you sorry for, sweetheart? You and the baby are going to be just fine."

"But…" She doesn't get to finish what she was going to say because he envelopes her into his big, strong, comforting arms again. She sobs into his shoulder while he strokes her hair, kissing her head.

Frank, the bouncer, announces the paramedics are here. They quickly hurry towards us and crouch down at the side of Izzy. Sebastian moves back to give them space. I'm still sat on the floor. Just as I'm about to move back, her hand grabs me. "Stay, please don't leave," she pleads.

"I'm not going anywhere," I assure her, rubbing her hand.

Sebastian looks at me quizzingly, then mouths 'thank you'.

After, what seems like forever but has probably only been a couple of minutes the paramedics have made their assessment. They tell the young couple that she needs to go to hospital, just to be checked out.

I'm stood back now watching them fasten Izzy into a chair while Sebastian holds her hand. You can see the love he has for his wife and how scared this young couple are. "Come with us, please?" Izzy asks me.

"What?" I question.

"Will you come with us to the hospital?" she asks again, a pleading look in her eyes. I don't know why she wants me there, she doesn't even know me. But I'm a caring person so I'll go. Before I have time to reply her husband speaks.

"Izzy love, we'll be fine. This lady is here enjoying herself. She doesn't want to spend the rest of the evening at the A & E."

"No, it's fine, I'll come," I say, not wanting to leave this scared woman.

"We can only take one of them in the ambulance with us, love," the older paramedic states.

"It's OK. I'll jump in a taxi," I say.

"Dad," Sebastian calls while staring over my shoulder, "will you follow us and bring, urr, sorry love, I don't know your name." He looks at me and shrugs his shoulders.

I'm just about to tell him my name when a voice I know all too well speaks from behind me.

"Holly."

My skin heats up as the sexy, husky sound strokes over me and seeps into my pores. Sebastian studies the man over my shoulder then his eyes land back on me. "Holly," he greets. "My dad will accompany you to the hospital." The left side of his mouth turns up into a grin as he's just realised who I am.

Standing on shaky legs with bare feet, I turn to see one handsome face. His dark gaze roams over me until our eyes meet and we're both stuck there, lost in us. The club has just become a very small place, where there's only him and me. Eyes saying everything our mouths cannot.

Just one word slips out. "Vlad."

Chapter 13

Vlad

Her smile lights up the room when she turns to see me standing behind her. Realising how much she is pleased to see me, my darkened mood lifts and I return the smile.

I've been stood behind her a few minutes, arriving just after the paramedics. I knew it was Holly straight away. The fall of her glossy hair, the curve of her hips along with her firm arse and muscular, slender, tanned legs. Her sweet voice reassuring Izzy, caring for my daughter-in-law, melted my heart a little more.

Our eyes stay locked. Both enthralled with the electricity that radiates between us. We remain like this for a few minutes and I want to ask her why she snubbed my calls and texts. I don't get the chance because once she utters my name, "Vlad," I want to hear her say it over again. I want to hold her tight in my arms all night long.

Our spell is broken when one of the paramedics says, "Excuse me, love." Her eyes drop from mine as she turns to the paramedic at the side of her.

"Sorry I'll get out of your way," she tells him. Holly steps away then she turns back to me, the sweet smile still glowing.

"Come," I say, holding my hand out for her to take. I need to return to the office to shut down my laptop and collect my car keys and I'm not letting my little angel out of my sight. She slips her delicate hand into mine easily.

Shouting over my shoulder to Sebastian, telling him we will meet them at the hospital, I lead us both through the back of the bar, down the corridor towards the office.

"Vlad, my shoes." Holly's voice holts my hurried stride.

"What?" I look down to see a pair of bare feet with French polished toenails. She's looking down too, wiggling them. "Where are they?" I question.

"They're at the other side of the bar. I took them off when I climbed over to get to Izzy."

Sapphire-blue eyes flicker between me and her cute feet as her smile radiates her face. My mind races to getting lost in those deep blues while having her feet stroking up my calves, putting a different kind of smile on her face.

Quickly, I pull my phone from my pocket and call Frank, asking him to collect Holly's shoes from the bar. I try to keep my mind off pinning her up against my office wall but her body language screams for me to hold her and make her mine.

We enter my office and I close the door behind us. No sooner does she go to speak, all bets are off because the first thing I do is pin her up against the door, placing my hands at either side of her head as my mouth goes in to devour those luscious lips.

I stroke and taste her bottom lip with the tip of my tongue, waiting for her to open so I can explore. I don't wait long. She opens and we both take what we want. Our tongues tango, teasing, as we compete for control. She wraps her arms around my shoulders and her nails stroke over the sensitive part of my neck, sending a rush of heat straight to my groin. Pulling her tightly in to my body so she can feel what she is doing to me, we both moan loudly. Holly's leg comes up to my hips and wraps around me. Taking a firm hold on her arse I hitch her up, so she can wrap the other one round; she's in the perfect position for me to give her what she wants. But we don't have time for that. We are here to collect my keys, so we can get to the hospital.

Reluctantly, I pull away from her lips and place my forehead on hers, we're both breathless and wanting to take this further.

I'm still wanting to know why she didn't answer my calls so as I kiss along her jawline to her ear, I ask. "Why did you not return my calls or texts, Holly?" My voice is calm but firm. "You could have just told me if you didn't want to see me, although your body is telling me otherwise. It would have been the polite thing to do."

"I couldn't," she murmurs.

"Why not?"

She moves away from me and picks up her bag from the floor. I didn't even hear her drop it. Once she has it, her hand starts rummaging around in it. She brings out her mobile phone, wiggling the damn thing in my face. "Look," she says. I take it from her, not sure why though. "Look," she says again, so I look, frowning because I haven't got a clue why I'm looking at her phone, until she speaks again. "This is one of my old phones with a pay-as-you-go SIM. Yesterday, when I was out with Megan I lost my phone. I don't get a replacement until tomorrow. I don't know your number by heart, or where you live or work, so I had no way of contacting you. All the texts and calls you sent me yesterday or today I didn't get," she breathes. She sounds exasperated and upset. I do the only thing I can and take her in my arms, holding her tight.

"It's OK, no harm done. You're here now," I whisper in her ear.

I'm a happy man again. In fact, I'm ecstatic. I knew there had to be a reasonable explanation for her not returning my calls, and now I know.

There's a knock at the door and Frank walks in, dangling Holly's shoes on his fingers. I take them and we both thank him, Holly giving him a shy smile. He nods his head at her then gives me look as if to say, 'I'm not your lackey.' Tipping my head back, I laugh at him then thank him again. He leaves, and I stride over to my desk, shutting down my laptop and picking up my car keys. Once I've done what needs doing, I take Holly's hand and lead her to our private carpark, stealing a quick kiss on the way because I'm a happy man. A very happy man.

My sleek, black Jaguar XJ Sedan sits pride of place amongst my sons' cars which causes a low whistle from Holly when I press the button to unlock the beauty. I chuckle at her and pull her into me. "You approve of your ride, my lady," I jest.

"I do. It's, hmmm, sexy. Just like you," she punctuates as she strokes her hand over the bonnet and, rises on her tiptoes to kiss me. I help her out by dipping my head, so she can reach me. I savour her taste of champagne and sweetness; her braveness to initiate a kiss makes me smile.

We don't stay locked together long, as I'm aware I need to get to my son and daughter-in-law.

*

We've arrived at the hospital and been shown to a cubicle where a doctor is looking over Izzy. It didn't take us long to get here and we didn't talk much in the car. Holly sang along to a CD of Rag'n'Bone Man that my youngest Lucas had been listening to when I picked him up from school. I just held her hand in mine, stroking my thumb over her knuckles while she put her head back on the head rest and closed her eyes. I expected her to ask questions about my family and the club, but they never came.

We are sat outside the little room waiting for an update when Holly's phone comes to life. "Shit," she curses, and stands quickly.

"What's wrong?" I query.

"I forgot to let my friends know I was leaving," she sighs. She quickly types a message back then holds her phone firmly in her hand. A message comes back, and she lets out a laugh throwing her head back with, "The hussies," coming out of her mouth. I don't want to know what comment her friends have sent back knowing she's ended up with me, especially if she had told them all about our little hook-up last week.

"Everything alright?" I ask her, taking her hand back in mine and raising my eyebrows at her.

"Yeah, they're fine. Now they know where I am."

The curtain opens and Sebastian steps out, eyeing our hands joined together. His lips turn up into a smile. I know he's laughing at me, remembering my little tantrums and outbursts over the last twenty-four hours, all because I hadn't heard from the little angel who's currently dragging me into the cubicle. Apparently, the doctor stepped out as well and I didn't see him. That's what happens when you're focused on one thing; Holly, my angel. The little minx that has my mind in a whirl, my heart beating faster than a speeding train and my groin constantly twitching.

Izzy is sat up on the trolley with a bit more colour and a relaxed smile on her face.

"How are you feeling? What did the doctor say?" Holly asks before I've even time to open my mouth.

"I have a bladder infection," Izzy tells her. "I was in last week with a urine infection; they kept me in overnight then sent me home with some medication. But I felt sick after I had taken it so now I've ended up with it getting worse. They are giving me some other medication to take, but they won't let me home tonight."

"Why not?" I ask concerned.

"They're waiting for blood to come back which could take a while because they are busy. Plus, they want to make sure the tablets agree with Izzy," Sebastian answers, rubbing his hand over the stubble on his chin with one hand while the other gently rubs Izzy's back.

"It could be tomorrow morning when they send me home," Izzy says.

"It is tomorrow morning," Holly yawns out. "It's almost one thirty," she yawns again looking at her watch.

"Could you pick the kids up from Mrs White in the morning?" Sebastian asks me.

"Yes. What time?"

"I've texted Tom, he said you can collect them about ten."

"Are they not at school?"

"No, they have another inset day. He will drop Lucas at school though. That way we can get a bit of sleep and pick them up from you later in the afternoon or you could bring them home when you pick up Lucas from school," he states, smirking and winking at me. He's a little shit. He knows fine well I will have my grandkids anytime and do what I can to help them out. But it does mean I will have to drop Holly home straight from the hospital and not take her home with me as I had planned. Probably a good thing as she keeps yawning. I'm sure all the champagne and dancing has tired her out.

"OK," I answer my son.

"I'll phone a taxi," Holly says, fidgeting with her bag and her phone.

We all stare at her, then ask, "Why?" simultaneously.

Holly's blue eyes roam between us. "Hmmm, well, Izzy needs to rest," she points to Izzy who has a grin on her face, "and you need to get home. If you're looking after your grandchildren tomorrow you need to get some sleep," she states as she tucks a loose piece of hair behind her ear. I smile at my little angel, pleased that she cares enough for Izzy that she needs her rest. I look at Sebastian who has himself seated at the side of his wife, smirking at me.

I know why.

I turn to Holly and take her hands in mine, pulling her into me. She falters a little, a blush runs up her neck and onto her beautiful face, but she lets it happen. She's a little embarrassed that I'm taking her in my arms in front of my son and his wife. Well, she needs to get over it because if I have my way, we will be spending a lot of time together. Which means my sons will see us holding hands, cuddling and stealing kisses. It won't bother them or me and she needs to get used to it. I also need to let her know, I'm not old and need plenty of sleep to take care of them. And she certainly will not be getting a taxi anywhere. I will be driving her home.

I consider her tired eyes then place my lips on hers gently then remove them. I don't want to scare her too much; we have an audience. "Holly," I speak softly.

"Yes?" she whispers.

"Firstly, I'm forty-five, not sixty-five. I don't need to go to bed at a reasonable time, so I can take care of my grandchildren in the morning."

"I… I didn't mean that," she stutters out.

Seb and Izzy chuckle like school kids. I throw them a look and shake my head at them, meaning, 'Grow up.' Then I turn back to the woman who thinks she's getting a taxi home.

"Secondly, there will be no ringing of a taxi. I will be driving you home, OK?" I say that a little firmer.

She nods her head at me.

"Good, and when I kiss you in front of my family don't be embarrassed. It doesn't bother them." She looks over at them both; they smile nicely at her. "It certainly doesn't bother me, and it shouldn't you." I stroke her chin with my thumb.

"OK," she chokes out.

"Right, now we have that cleared up, we will leave these two in the capable hands of the doctors and nurses and I will run you home." I take Holly's hand and walk over to the bed, giving Izzy a kiss on the cheek and Sebastian a hug goodnight. Sebastian embraces Holly, thanking her for being there for his wife then Holly leans in and gives Izzy a cuddle. We all say goodnight then I lead us off to the carpark.

Once we're outside, I'm jabbed in the side of my ribs by Holly's elbow. Looking down at her she doesn't look happy. "What the hell was that for?" I ask, dropping her hand and rubbing my side. She looks a little flustered, but she soon gets to the point. Her finger comes up and prods me in the chest. I let out a chuckle; this gets me a frown from my little minx.

"You," she prods again. I take it, not sure what I've done to deserve it but I'm sure I'm about to find out when my little woman stands in front of me with her hands on her hips.

"Did you have to embarrass me like that in front of your son and daughter-in-law?" She's not happy with me. There's a glare at me and her hand comes up to prod me again. I can't help it this time. I let out a belly laugh and quickly take the prodding finger in my hand. She glares at me again. She looks all red-faced and I get a pout as well and a stamp of a foot. "Don't laugh, it's not funny," she warns.

"Sweetheart, I'm not laughing at you and I didn't mean to make you uncomfortable in front of them." I take her in my arms and pull her in to my chest. She doesn't stop me so that's a good thing. "Listen, I've told my sons about you. Christ, they even saw me dancing on the table with you last week…" She cuts me off.

"Wait." She holds up her hand, pulling away from me.

"What?" I question.

"You said sons."

"Yes. Four of them." I hold up four fingers, wiggling them at her.

Her mouth falls open and her eyes widen. She holds four fingers and wiggles them back at me mouthing, 'Four,' I nod my head at her, she just shakes hers and tries to pull away. I don't think so. I keep hold of her hands in mine.

"Why haven't you told me? It's not like you never got the chance. How old are they? These are things you could have mentioned while we were chatting over the phone," she says.

"I know. It's not like I wasn't going to tell you. I love my boys. They come first, them and my grandchildren." I place my hands on either side of her face and gaze into those shocked eyes. "Holly, you have to understand, I don't date. My sons have never seen me with a woman, you are the first." I try to make her understand.

"But I only met Sebastian and Izzy by accident," she states. "Would you have told me if I hadn't met them at the club?" she asks, stepping back from me so my hands slip from her face.

"Yes, once we had had a proper date," I express.

She shakes her head at me and mutters, "I don't believe you." Then she turns on her heels and stalks off in the opposite direction of my car. Where the fuck does she think she's going? It's the middle of the night. I call after her, but she ignores me. This is why I don't get attached, too many fucking complications, but this woman has gotten under my skin. I need her to believe me when I say I would have told her.

"Holly," I bellow. "Get your arse back here. Don't make me chase after you because I will throw you over my shoulder and spank that sexy rear of yours." Fuck, what am I saying? That's not going to bring her back but, yeah, I would love to spank that peachy arse of hers while taking her on all fours. To my surprise she halts and turns around. She's a good hundred yards away in a not so lit up car park but I can see the glare she's giving me all too clearly. She starts walking towards me with a sway in her step; looks like I'm going to get another prodding of the finger. I'll take it. It's better than her ignoring me.

I stride towards her, meeting her in the middle. "I can't believe you shouted that out in a hospital car park—" I cut her off.

"Sweetheart, believe me, you try to walk away from me in the middle of the night, putting yourself in danger, and I will spank you,"

I say firmly, taking her hands in mine. She goes to speak again, and I cut her off. Yes, I know I'm being rude, but she needs to give me a chance to explain and now is not the time. "Please, let me explain. I would never lie to you, angel, I will answer any questions you want, tell you whatever you want to know and yes, I would have told you about my sons," I say, stroking her cheekbone with my thumb. "But not tonight. You're tired, I'm tired, and I need to get you home."

"You will tell me anything?" Holly asks, looking up at me.

I get lost in her sparkling eyes. I close the distance between us. Our lips are but a few centimetres apart. Her eyes glisten like the ocean itself on a clear, starry night. I know she has every reason not to trust me, I have told her next to nothing about myself. Plus, after what her husband did to her, she probably won't trust me for a while. I must make her see I would never hurt her or lie to her; not sure how I'm going to do that when there's so much about my past I can't tell anyone.

"Anything," I whisper into her lips as I close the gap further until our lips touch gently. We stay like this for a short while when Holly pulls away.

"Take me home, Vlad, I'm dead on my feet," she sighs. Grabbing her hand, I lead her to my car, open the door and wait until she's secure in her seat. I close the door then round the car to my side where I take a deep breath before I climb in and hit the road.

We arrive outside Holly's apartment block, nice area and only a ten-minute drive from mine, how convenient. "Holly, we're here," I utter. She's had her eyes closed all the way to her home. Not sure whether she was asleep or just didn't want to talk to me. She opens her sleepy eyes and turns to face me. Her head is still resting on the seat.

"You could have told me about your sons. It doesn't make any difference to me. I mean, it wouldn't have stopped me from wanting to see you again." Her voice is throaty. I know she's sleepy. She looks so damn cute. I lower myself in the seat and place my head near hers, running my thumb over her ripe lips.

"I could have told you, should have told you, but I was too busy being interested in you. We didn't discuss much about me. Did we." It's not a question.

"No, but you will tell me?"

"Yes, tomorrow."

"Saturday, we're not meeting tomorrow," she informs me.

"Right, our date. Yes." She nods at me. "OK, give me your phone," I ask politely.

"Why?"

"So, I have your number and I can contact you tomorrow."

"Oh, right."

She hands her phone over and I quickly type in my number then ring my own phone, so I have hers. I give her it back. "There, now I can get you on either one."

We exit the car and I walk her into her block. There's a security man sat at a small desk when we pass through the foyer. He looks up waves at us then averts his eyes back to the screen he'd been looking at.

Holly, tells me that there's eighteen apartments in this block, spread over four floors. The first two floors have six one-bedroom apartments each. The third has four two-bedrooms and the fourth has two three-bedrooms. Holly's is on the fourth in one of the three-bedroomed which she rents from her friends. I'm glad to see that there's a security man on site – at least she will be safe if she comes home late. She tells me he starts his shift at nine in the evening and finishes at seven in the morning. There are two of them that alternate their shifts; there's also a maintenance man through the day. The building is all marble and chrome, with just a small entrance.

The lift dings when it arrives, and I follow in after Holly. She looks up at me when I press the fourth floor with a questioning look. "You don't need to come up, I'm fine now," she says.

"I know. Humour me. I'm a worrier, I want to make sure you get through your door safe."

She giggles at me. "OK, no problem."

Once the door closes, I manoeuvre myself so I'm behind her then I pull her into me. She doesn't stop me, just snuggles her back into my chest. I dip my head into her hair and inhale the sweet smell of strawberries, summer and sweetness. My nose trails down, just below her ear and I place my lips gently on the soft skin of her neck. Her body moulds into mine further and she moves her head back a little to give me better access. I nibble, suck and have the urge to mark her as mine. Fuck, I'm acting like one of my sons, not a forty-five-year-old man. But that thought doesn't deter me as I continue leaving my mark. It doesn't seem to bother Holly either because she gives out a little moan as I suck a little harder and hold her a little firmer, my arms around her waist.

The sound of the lift landing on her floor halts our little moment. "Vlad," I hear her softly whisper.

"Hmmm." I'm very content here just holding her against me.

"You're not coming in," she says.

"I'm not," I reply dazed. She has me under her spell and I would do anything she asked.

"No," she tells me as she stands up straight, holding the door open button on the lift panel. "Thank you, for bringing me home. I live there." She points to the door nearest the lift and I make a note of the number sixteen, for when I need to buzz to get in. I move a step closer and lower my lips to her, giving her a gentle kiss goodnight. She lets me. Then I thank her for looking after Izzy. I tell her I will phone her tomorrow, wish her goodnight and watch as she enters her apartment. Once I hear the door lock, I return the lift to the ground floor and make my way to my car.

Chapter 14

Holly

Knock. Knock. Knock.

Oh, God. I've got Woody Woodpecker pecking at my head. "Be quiet," I whisper to nobody. The builders have been in the apartment next to me all week, fitting a new kitchen, and they've picked this morning of all mornings to start hammering again. I didn't get to bed until after two and all though I'd slowed down my drinking through the night, I still have the worst hangover ever.

When Vlad drove me home in the early hours, I had taken two headache tablets, downing them with a pint of water, hoping I would not wake up with a raging hangover. Unfortunately, it didn't work.

Knock. Knock. Knock.

The noise continues as the alarm on my phone decides to cause me more distress. Half asleep, I drag myself out of bed in search of the sound that's making my ears ring. Fumbling, I trip over my clothes that I discarded on to the floor, too tired to put them in the washing basket, and end up stubbing my big toe on the bedside table. My eyes become unstuck from last night's minimal sleep and a loud curse erupts from my throat. That's when I spot my phone on my dressing table. The ringing has stopped now and I'm thankful; so has the knocking from next door.

I stagger in to my bathroom, hitting the walls too many times. I really need to go back to sleep. Some people can cope and function easily with a few hours' sleep. Not me, no, I need eight of them.

Just as I'm finishing up in the bathroom the loud knocking starts again, only it's not next door's, it's my door. My phone starts again only it's not the alarm as I thought. No, someone is calling me.

Vlad's name flashes like a beacon warning me. I'll say warning because this man could be dangerous to my health. As soon as I hear his husky voice or feel his masculine touch, he dominates me, taking any control I have and ripping it to shreds. I know what my ex-husband did to me would be like a walk in the park if I was to let Vlad fully in and he hurt me; my heart would never recover.

I open my door at the same time as I answer my phone. "Morning, beautiful," I hear in stereo. Stood before me is one fine specimen of a man. Dark, piercing blue eyes, roam over me. I'm standing there in a pair of pyjama shorts with a thin vest covering my boobs. The desire and heat from his stare warms my blood to the point, I feel hotter than the Sahara. The morning stubble heightens his sex appeal and causes a flutter in the bottom of my stomach. He's wearing a dark blue T-shirt which fits his muscular body perfectly, short sleeves showing off the various black and blue swirls tattooed onto his skin. The faded jeans he's sporting fit his powerful thighs like a glove. Hell, even his feet look sexy in a pair of black Adidas trainers.

I glance back to his handsome face and he's smirking at me. "Like what you see, angel?" he laughs. Shit, I must have lingered a bit too long in the ogling area. I must blush at this point because he continues with his cockiness. "I like this colour on you, sweetheart," he says and runs his long fingers down my overheated cheeks. "Are you cold? Or are the girls just pleased to see me?" he emphasises on the girls, averting his eyes to my boobs.

Cheeky bastard. Sure enough, when I look down, my nipples are stuck out like sore thumbs. I roll my eyes at him and quickly fold my arms over my chest. "Do you not have a filter on that mouth of yours?" I ask as I stand to one side to let him in. "And why are you here?" I question, closing the door behind us. He turns and places his arms on either side of me, trapping me between him and the door.

"Apparently, I have no filter around you, things just fall from my mouth. I can't help it, you seem to bring out another side to me that I didn't know I had."

"You and me both," I mumble, but he hears me.

"I've come to take you out for breakfast," he says, stepping back so I'm no longer trapped between him and the door. "So, go get some clothes on, angel, because as much as I like seeing your very beautiful sexy body, I don't want anyone else to see it," he says, placing his hands on my shoulders. He winks at me, steers me so I'm facing in the direction of my open-plan kitchen and living room, then he slaps my arse. I give out a little yelp and he laughs.

"Stop," I say. "What do you mean, breakfast? What time is it?

"It's seven fifteen and it's breakfast time. Now go get dressed, woman," he commands.

I raise my eyebrows, place my hands on my hips and stand there firmly. I'm not jumping to his orders. My body might betray me when he has his hands on me that's different. For some reason I don't mind him being a little dominant or his dirty talk. It's not something I ever imagined I might like but then I've never met anyone like Vlad.

He realises that I'm not going to move. Running his fingers through his short hair he asks, "Please will you get dressed? I only have two hours then I have to pick up my grandchildren and you wanted me to tell you a little about myself."

Well I would have waited until tomorrow for any information he wants to give me but I'm all for getting to know a bit more today.

"OK," I say. "How is Izzy this morning?" I ask, genuinely concerned. I'd already assumed she was a nice person before I found out she was related to Vlad. I make my way in to the living room and gaze up at this very large man who is staring back at me with a softened look on his face.

"She's well this morning and hopefully will be home by dinner time. Everything is good with the baby too." He smiles and it's one of a proud father and grandfather. It amuses me that this man who looks so intimidating can be so affectionate, caring and charming. He certainly doesn't look like a father of four and a grandad.

"What have I done to deserve that little grin on your face, angel?" he asks, smiling back at me. I love the terms of endearment he has for me. Rob never really called me anything but 'love'.

"Nothing," I tell him. "I'm just pleased everything is good with Izzy and the baby, that's all." He nods at me and takes a seat on my sofa, his muscular body getting comfy while I step into my bedroom to get dressed.

Within half an hour, I've had a quick wash and brushed my teeth. Dressed in a pair of skinny blue jeans, black button-down, sleeveless blouse and a pair of canvas pumps, now I'm humming to the radio, sat in Vlad's Jaguar on our way to some restaurant to eat breakfast and hopefully I will get some information about him.

"Would you like to start now?" Vlad's voice asks over the song playing.

"Start what?" I question, turning in my seat to face him. He glances at me then quickly averts his eyes back to the road.

"With what you want to know about me," he says, keeping his eyes on the road ahead. It's still rush-hour traffic, but he seems to navigate the vehicle easily in and out of the lanes.

I'm keen to learn more about his sons.

"You have four sons and two grandchildren."

"Yes," he confirms.

"What are their names and how old are they?" I probe. He doesn't falter with his answer.

"Sebastian, who you met last night, is my eldest and he will be twenty-eight in three months."

I'm good with numbers but this doesn't take a mathematician to work out that Vlad became a father at a very young age.

"Bloody hell," slips out. "Wow, you were seventeen when he was born." It's not a question.

"Yes. Seventeen years and three months," he chuckles.

"What about the other three? How old are they?"

"Nicholas will be twenty-six in five months. Daniel has just turned twenty-one two months ago and my youngest is Lucas," he says with the biggest smile on his face. "He is twelve years and six months." Bloody, bloody hell. Some fathers couldn't tell you how old their children are without thinking about it. I know if I asked Jack he wouldn't be able to tell me without thinking about it, in fact he would probably consult with Olivia to find out. The engine cuts and I realise we are in the same carpark as last night. I can see the three exit doors with signs above them and Vlad has parked his car in the same place.

My door opens, and Vlad's hand reaches for mine. I let him help me out, then he keeps a tight hold on it as we stroll towards one of the doors. Once he's tapped a code into the control panel, the door opens, and he leads me into what looks and feels like a cold store. There is shelving with boxes, tins and plastic tubs. We then enter a passageway and follow it to another door; when we step through we end up in a kitchen where there is a man and a woman chatting. The man who is dressed in chef's whites turns and greets Vlad with a genuine smile. "Morning, Vlad." He crosses the kitchen and slaps him on the back with his greeting. The woman rushes over.

"Look who's here," she gushes as she pinches Vlad's cheek. He blushes a little and I can't help but let out a little chuckle at their interaction. Then all eyes fall on me. "Who is this stunning little thing?" the woman asks, who I would think was in her late fifties.

"I was just about to ask the same question," the man says, lifting an eyebrow at Vlad.

"This is Holly," Vlad tells them while he snakes an arm around my shoulder and pulls me into his broad chest. "She's a friend who has agreed to join me for breakfast," he continues as they both smile enthusiastically at him. "This is Steven who is the chef here and this is his lovely wife Maureen who manages the restaurant." They both put their hand out to greet me.

"It's lovely to meet you, Holly, let's go through to the restaurant and I'll take your order," Maureen says. We both follow her into the main restaurant. "Do you want your usual table?" she asks Vlad. He shakes his head and tells her anywhere is fine. We're led to a table situated in an alcove by the window.

She takes both our orders for scrambled eggs with wholemeal toast and tea for two. Once she's gone, I take in my surroundings.

Rich mahogany wooden floors coordinate the bar with its highly polished glass mirrors, sparkling crystal flutes and tumbler glasses which gleam amongst the various bottles of beers, spirits and wines. The rich mahogany extends to the table and chairs with their midnight blue seats and cut-glass candle holders that sit in place on the white tablecloth. Matching holders stand in the corner areas of the backrests and a wide set of stairs leads to a balcony. Light beams through the long windows with flowing drapes giving off a warm feeling. I'm sure in the evenings with the glow of the lights it would have a romantic mood.

I look up to see Maureen has returned with our tea and Vlad observes me meticulously. He takes the tray from her and starts to pour. We both thank her, and she disappears again.

"This place," I wave my hand around, "is yours?" I ask. Vlad nods his head at me while taking a drink of his tea.

"Yes," he says once he's placed his cup on the table. "It belonged to a friend's parents."

"A friend?" I question, tilting my head to the side, letting him know I need more information.

He smiles, causing the laughter lines that edge his dark eyes to deepen, making him look even sexier. I stare in awe.

"Dimitri and I went to school together in Russia," he continues. "When he was fourteen, his parents came to live here in England and bought this restaurant, hence the name. I had always wanted to come to England so when they decided to retire twelve years ago, it was the right time for me to make the move. I bought this place from them and my home." His face lights up as he tells me. His English is excellent for someone who only came here twelve years ago as an adult. It is obvious he is Russian, but I would have thought he had been here a lot longer.

"Your English is very good," I say.

He nods his head at me before he speaks. "Yes. My mother was English." A beam of warmth washes over his face at the mention of her. I assume he was close to her. Although, I did not expect to hear his mum came from England, I play with the menu on the table, hoping he will pick up on my hunger for more.

He does. "She was born in a little mining village here in Yorkshire. Her mother died when she was a little girl then when she was eleven her dad and two older brothers were killed in an explosion at the pit where they all worked," he explains.

"I'm sorry to hear that, it must have been horrific for her." I know only too well what it is like to grow up without your real mother then to have the other people who have cared for and loved you taken away from you as quick as putting a light out. Tears threaten my eyes and I hold back on the urge to hug him for his mother's loss.

"Holly, are you OK, sweetheart?" I hear Vlad's concern.

Looking at him, I shake my head and swallow down the sadness I feel. "Sorry, I just find it all very upsetting, for someone so young to lose their entire family," I choke out at the same time as Maureen appears with our breakfast. She considers both of us cautiously while placing the scrambled eggs on the table.

"Enjoy," she says. "If you want more tea just shout me." Then she disappears behind the bar.

The eggs look hot and fluffy; my stomach lets out a growl reminding me that I am hungry. I unravel my cutlery from the serviette and tuck in. Vlad follows me in devouring his breakfast. After consuming a few forkfuls of my scrambled egg, I swill it down with a drink of tea then I continue with my questioning.

"How did your mum end up in Russia?" I ask, placing my fork on the table and picking up a piece of hot buttery toast. Vlad swallows the forkful of his food. I watch his Adam's apple bob up and down.

"She only had one relative, an aunt who lived in Russia. A neighbour took her in and contacted Maria, her auntie. Once the funeral was over she took her back to Russia with her. Maria's husband had an older daughter who looked after my mother; they became good friends, like sisters. She had a new family and friends, she was happy... My mother died just over a year ago."

I sit there, listening to Vlad speak about his mother with love in his voice but sadness in his eyes. His hand rests upon the table so I place mine on his. "I'm really sorry to hear about the hurt your mother went through at such a young age and that she is no longer with you," I empathise. Vlad caresses my knuckles with his thumb.

"It's fine, Holly. I don't dwell on the past."

I nod, "OK," not knowing what else to say.

We sit there silent in our thoughts for a short time, Vlad still holding my hand while we drink our tea. It's not uncomfortable but reassuring.

Despite Vlad's admission that he doesn't do relationships, I assume he must have been in one or been married at some point. With no ring on his wedding finger, it leaves me wondering about his son's mother. "What are you thinking about?" Vlad asks, his head tilted to one side and a smirk on his handsome face. That naughty smile of his puts my heart rate up and has my face blushing. God, he's too sexy. He has stopped rubbing his thumb over my knuckles now. He holds my hand in his and strokes my wrist lightly.

"Nothing," I whisper, caught by his dark intense stare.

I'm drawn into them like a moth to a flame, unable to break the powerful spell he has on me. "I can tell you have more questions, Holly, so let's just get them out of the way." He lets go of my hand and pours out some more tea, taking back my hand in his once he has finished. I decide to ask about his father before I ask anything about his wife. He hadn't mentioned him when we were talking about his mum. "Is your dad still alive?" I ask quietly.

His body stiffens, and he sits up straight. Dark blue eyes turn almost black as he blows out a long breath and his jaw tightens. Bloody hell, I've hit on a sore subject. Maybe I should just quit with the questioning for now. "No," he snaps when he answers my question.

"Sorry, I—"

"He died not long before we moved to England," he cuts in.

"I'm sorry to hear that, Vlad."

"Don't be. It was a long time ago. Like I said, I do not dwell on the past."

His whole blasé approach, the way his body reacted, rigid and tense when I mentioned his father, has me wondering what kind of relationship they had. I decide not to pursue it any further. Maybe when we have known each other a bit longer he might enlighten me.

Changing the subject, I ask about Joseph and Rebecca; this has the desired effect because you can see the darkness lift from his eyes and his mouth turns up into a wide grin.

"Sorry," he says as he relaxes back into his chair. I know what he is sorry about, but I still ask.

"What are you sorry about?"

"I should not have used that tone when you asked about my father."

"It's fine. I'm sure you have your reasons for getting riled up about him," I say. "Although, your face lit up like a lightbulb when I mentioned your grandchildren," I smile.

"Yes, they do bring out the softer side of me." He flashes a warm smile.

For the next half hour, we chat and laugh about his sons and grandchildren. He tells me that Lucas his youngest and Joe his grandson are both quiet boys when they are on their own but together they're like a tornado and hurricane rolled into one. Rebecca, his granddaughter, has him wrapped around her little finger. She has him playing with My Little Ponies, her Disney princess dolls and drawing in girly colouring books. I can't help but laugh at this man because seeing him with his youngest son and grandchildren would be the cutest thing in the world. Vlad looks intimidating with his size, tattoos, scar and the whole broody look. But, when he talks about his family, you know straight away that they are his world. How much I would love to be one of the people who brought that look upon his handsome face.

I watch mesmerised as he continues to chat about his family. The laughter lines around his eyes and mouth deepen, giving away his age which make me chuckle. This gets me a raised eyebrow from him; I'm sure he knows I'm studying him attentively. There's a twinkle in his dark blue eyes which reminds me of a clear, dark night when stars dance around the open sky. The overnight stubble on his face is calling out to me, taunting me to stroke my nimble fingers over it. I resist the urge. The tense and rigid man has gone now completely, leaving a relaxed and loving man in its place.

Vlad looks at his oversized watch. "We need to get going shortly, so I can drop you off home before I pick up the kids from Mrs White," he says.

"OK, let me go to the ladies' then I'm ready when you are." Vlad points me in the direction of the toilets then gets up to talk to Maureen who's pottering about around the bar.

I find Vlad sitting back in his seat waiting for me when I return. Although I had decided not to ask him about his son's mother, I can't help but want to know. He stands when I reach him. "Can I ask you something before we leave?" He nods his head and motions for me to sit down. He takes his own seat and waits for me to speak. It takes a while because I don't want to upset him if the woman had died or bring on the anger he had when I mentioned his father. You never know, she might have cheated on him. God knows why, he's every woman's dream.

"Your son's mother, is she still around?" I utter. And straight away I wish I had kept my mouth shut. I kick my questioning mind up the arse. Why do I always have to know all the bloody details to everybody's life?

I hear his breath sucking in between his teeth and watch as he holds on to the table with a deathly grip. The scowl on his handsome face and his tense body tells me everything I need to know, that she probably did the dirty on him. "You don't have to answer that, Vlad. Sorry, sometimes I never know when to keep my nose out." I point to my nose. "One day someone will hit me in it for being so nosey." I laugh a little, hoping to bring back the man who was sat here a few minutes ago. Note to self, do not mention Dad or wife ever again.

"Over my dead body," comes the rumble of his husky voice.

"Pardon?" is all I manage to say.

He takes my hand in his. "Nobody will ever raise a hand to you without having to deal with me first." His voice is menacing. His eyes close and he blows out a breath. "Sorry, Holly, it enrages me to think about anyone hurting you."

I can't believe this man, he's only known me a little over a week and yet the thought of anyone hurting me has him all riled up. I don't say anything, just nod my head. We both sit there for a moment, silent, and when I go to get up, resigned to the fact I'm not going to get an answer to the question about his wife, he speaks. "My wife died over twelve years ago," he mutters. I sit there, wide-eyed, unable to comment because the reaction I got when I first asked about her was not of upset but of anger. Plus, his dad died twelve years ago, maybe that is why he's bitter. Losing them both might have been too much to deal with. I can relate to that. There's also the fact that Lucas is only twelve. My mind is in a whirl, that two people who are supposed to mean the world to you have him looking like he could kill with the mention of their name, but people deal with grief differently. There's also the fact that he brought his sons here after the death of his father, so maybe it was too much for him, losing his wife and father as well as having to bring four boys up, and just as the thought enters my head, it's like he just read my mind. "She died a few hours after giving birth to Lucas," he reveals. This time there is no emotion in his voice. He sits there with my hand in his and an expression on his face that I cannot read.

Just when I thought I was getting to know him he dances around, reacting to his feelings like a jack-in-the-box, making my head spin. In the last hour he's gone from warm, caring and loving to angry, irritated and cold. I would have at least expected to see some sadness on his face and in his voice. But I don't. All I see now is a cold, icy stare. I don't pull him up on it, no, I just say, "I'm sorry for your loss, it must have been hard for you bringing up a baby and three young boys," hoping my mention of his sons will end this troubled state I've put him in, with prying into his life. I should have just waited for him to tell me.

He nods his head then stands. "I'll be back in a minute," he says, his accent thick and harsh.

Sitting there twiddling my thumbs, looking around the empty restaurant that I'm sure will be open for lunch in the next few hours, I'm not sure if I should walk out the door or give him the benefit of the doubt. With me he is kind and considerate, a gentleman. I've seen him with his son Sebastian and his daughter-in-law Izzy and he is nothing but a loving, caring father. When he speaks about his other sons and grandchildren, you know they're his world. But, bringing up his past, the death of his wife and father, you see a different side to him. One I don't like and don't care to be around.

He's been gone around ten minutes when I stand ready to leave.

I've played the rejection of my mother, the loss of my adopted parents and the deceit of my ex-husband in my head. My reaction when people mention them is of sadness and loss as well as anger for a short time. I'm trying to wrap my head around why he could look so cold when he told me about his wife but I'm at a loss, only that people deal with things differently.

"Are you ready to go?" comes the husky voice of the man I met over a week ago. When I look up, I don't see the coldness of the man's stare or the tensed body of the man who sat here gripping the table as if he could snap it in two with his bare hands. No. Vlad rounds the bar, stalking towards me owning the area. Owning me. His eyes are smouldering, ablaze with lust. As he reaches me his hands come up to cup my face and his lips cover mine, fiercely taking what he wants from me. One hand moves to the small of my back and he pulls us together so there is no room for air between us. His heartbeat is rapid and so is mine. We devour each other there in the middle of the restaurant, starving for the taste of each other. All of what was in my head a minute ago, is gone, sucked out of me by a man that's so far out of my league, I'm at a loss what to say next to him.

A small cough stops us and we both pull apart, panting. He takes my hand in his. "Let's get you home." He gives me his signature wink and I feel a hot flush rush over me. I'm so confused with him. One minute I want to leave, run out of the door, and the next I want him to rip my clothes off and claim me.

We make our way back to mine in a flash. I've just sat there humming to the music on the radio while Vlad was content listening while he drove. We've pulled up outside my block and Vlad has his head resting on mine, one hand round the back of my neck and the other holding my hand.

He takes a deep breath before he speaks. "When we go out tomorrow, can we focus... talk about now and the future and not the past? Well, not my past anyway," he asks, his eyes pleading for me to not let his earlier emotions get in the way of the here and now.

I've decided I will speak to Olivia and Sarah and see what they think of Vlad's reactions. I want to give him a chance. I can see his past is hard for him but I'm out of my depth. I don't have much experience with men, only my ex-husband, and look how that turned out. So, for now I will give him the answer he wants and have a girly chat. I nod my head and whisper, "OK." As I'm getting out of the car Vlad gets out too. He rounds to my side and steals my mouth again; I don't stop him. I can't. His mouth, his touch, his eyes, once they're on me I'm gone. He breaks our kiss and we're both breathless again.

"Go, before I'm late for my grandchildren," he grins while turning me towards my apartment block and slapping my arse. I let out a yelp and giggle like a bloody love-struck teenager. I look over my shoulder at him as I walk towards the entrance, shaking my head at him. He throws a sexier-than-hell wink at me and blows a kiss before he jumps back in his sleek black car and drives out of the car park. I walk through the foyer to the lift on jelly legs, knowing that Vlad, intimidating, dirty talking, sexier than hell, confusing man, could have me bending to his will. But I don't care.

Chapter 15

Holly

Vlad is on his way to pick me up and I'm a nervous wreck.

When I got back home yesterday morning, after having breakfast with him, I went back to bed for a few hours. I put Vlad's reactions out of my head and slept until two in the afternoon. Once I had showered and made a sandwich for my late lunch, I called Olivia and Sarah. They both laughed so hard when I explained what had happened the night before. How Vlad had turned up out of the blue behind the bar when I was trying to comfort Izzy the bartender, who turned out to be his daughter-in-law. I relayed the rest of the evening to them, then how he knocked me up out of bed and dragged me off for breakfast.

After explaining my reservations over his reactions about his wife and dad, they both understood but urged me on to give him a chance, explaining that everyone's experience of grief is different. This I know already. Olivia gave me her view on his past life in Russia, suggesting that his life might not have been all that rosy there and that's why he came to England. Making a home for them and building up his business. Sarah agreed. Which led me to the decision I already knew I would take, which is to give him a chance and live in the here and now.

Around six o'clock, Vlad had phoned me. Hearing his husky voice sent my blood soring into outer space and had me wanting to hear his dirty talk over the phone. I knew it wasn't going to happen though because I could hear children in the background, laughing and screaming. Vlad told me he was keeping them overnight even though their mum was home from hospital. Both Izzy and Sebastian were shattered so Vlad had suggested letting Joe and Rebecca stay with him and Lucas. Sebastian had jumped at the offer to snuggle with his wife in bed for the rest of the day and have a lay in the following morning.

Vlad explained that last year Izzy miscarried at three months so when she fell pregnant this time she worried a lot. Now they have her on the right medication for her infection she feels better and she had spoken to someone this morning about panicking every time she gets a twinge. Even though she has had two other children and knows what to expect she just can't help fearing the worst. Whatever was said to her, it had lifted her spirits a bit because Sebastian had said she seemed relieved and wanted to go home.

The giggles and screams got louder while we were chatting. I heard a loud high-pitched scream that had me chuckling when I realised it was Vlad. When I asked him if he just screamed like a girl, his voice cracked with a loud, raucous laughter. Apparently, he was being attacked by Lucas, Joe and Rebecca, they were bombarding him with scatter cushions and shooting bullets from their Nerf guns at him. This had him running through the house and locking himself in his office.

I could picture the scene even though I didn't have a clue what the children or the house looked like. My whole body tingled with anticipation that maybe one day I would be with him, squealing and giggling as we skipped and danced around the house trying to escape from the bombardment of scatter cushions and foam bullets.

A sigh spilt from my lips when I heard Vlad's words through my cloud of dreams. I listened to him speak, how he is looking forward to our evening out and how he can't wait to taste my luscious lips again. My heart rate kicked up listening to his seductive tone and my legs quivered with anticipation when he told me how good it will be between us. I'm not sure whether he meant the evening out or sex.

What I do know is I'm not very experienced when it comes to men, only having my ex-husband as a sexual partner. We were not very adventurous in the bedroom department or affectionate towards each other. Maybe before we got married we were but it's hard to remember. Over this year I've often wondered why I married him. Olivia and Sarah's words have rung through my head on many occasions. *"Are you sure this is what you want? Do you love him enough to marry him? Does he make you feel like your life would end if he wasn't in it?"* And in all honesty, I had to answer no but at the time I didn't care, I just wanted someone to make me feel something, to have someone there in the evenings. To have someone to hold. I know he never looked at me like my friends' husbands look at them. Jack and Nick have always been the devoted husbands, worshipping their wives like they're goddess and in turn Olivia and Sarah idolise them, putting them right up there on a pedestal.

After my chat with Vlad, I came off the phone light headed and wondering what this man sees in me. On the three occasions we have met he looks at me like he's the predator and I'm his next meal. I'm sure he's going to be so disappointed when we eventually have sex. I say have sex because I know I will not be able to refuse this virile man when he decides the time is right to take it further than the night we met in the club.

This morning after I'd been grocery shopping, I decided to phone Vlad to find out where he would be taking me, so I could pick out my outfit for the evening. Truth be told I really wanted to hear his sexy, husky voice again and couldn't wait until six.

"Hi, honey," I greet him with when he answered his phone.

"Hi, sweetheart. This is a surprise." The warmth in his voice wraps around me like a winter duvet. I want to climb through the phone, sit in his lap and let him envelope me in his manly arms. "I hope you are not ringing to cancel our date, my little minx," he jokes. I want to know what his reaction would be if I had, so I decide to make him sweat.

"Vlad, I'm sorry. I haven't been feeling well since I came home from shopping. I think I am going to have to cancel on you. I—"

"Are you kidding me?" he snaps before I have time to tell him what's wrong with me. I cover the phone with my hand to hide the chuckle that slips out. I knew it would wind him up, he's been looking forward to this night out as much as I have.

"I have a terrible migraine and feel a little sick and lightheaded." I finish what I was going to say.

"Oh," he says quietly this time. "Holly, do you need me to get you anything from the chemist?" he asks, concern etched in his voice.

"Hmmm, no. It's fine. I think I will just go to bed." I extend the lie, hoping he doesn't say 'OK'. I don't need to worry because he persists with his worry.

"I don't think you should be on your own, sweetheart. I'll call to the chemist then to the supermarket. Once you have had a sleep I'll make you something light to eat." His tone is not up for discussion. I need to stop this. This is ridiculous, I should never have tried to have him on. I've seen his reactions when I tried to walk off on Thursday night when we were in the carpark. He thought I was putting myself in danger. Then when he told me about his mother, putting tears in my eyes; he didn't like me being upset. I also heard his comment to my joke about me being nosy and someone hitting me in it one day.

"Vlad—"

"Holly don't try and stop me, I will be round at yours within the hour." His voice is firm.

"Vlad, I was joking!" I shout to stop him from dropping what he's doing and barrelling over to my apartment.

"What?" he questions, not sounding thrilled about my little wind-up.

"Sorry," I giggle. "I couldn't help it. I didn't think you would get all nursey on me."

"Well, what did you think I'd do? Leave you on your own while you're poorly That will not be happening," he grunts.

"Sorry," I say again, sounding like I've just been told off.

"You will be. That warrants a spanking, my little minx." His gravelly voice now takes on a seductive tone.

"You're joking? Right?" I say, laughing at him.

"Oh, I don't joke when it comes to warming your perfectly shaped cheeks with the palm of my hand, Holly." His accent is a little stronger and heats up the parts that only he can ignite. God help me. I can't believe I'm turned on by his domineering comments.

We're both quiet for a few seconds.

"Why did you phone me, angel?" he asks, breaking our silence.

"Oh, I wanted to know where you are taking me."

"Why?" he asks.

"So, I can dress accordingly."

"Well, I'm not telling you where we are going, and it doesn't matter what you wear, you will stand out amongst the crowd, beautiful," he states.

"Oh, smooth."

"Not really. I could have suggested something you could wear but it would be inappropriate for where we are going." His playful, seductive tone makes another appearance, giving me the courage to tease him a little.

"Are you having inappropriate thoughts about me, Mr Petrov?" I purr.

"Am I allowed, angel?"

"No." What I really want to say is yes and please enlighten me to them in that husky tone that has me crazy with lust.

"OK, then I am not." His voice is soft and smooth this time.

"Liar."

"As I'm sure you are aware by now, whatever I am thinking when I speak to you or around you, I don't lie. The truth just comes pouring out, whether it is inappropriate or not." Yeah, I know this, it doesn't matter how dirty his thoughts are. "Wear what you want, Holly. Every time I see you, you look more stunning than the last," he says, bringing me back from my thoughts.

"Sweet talker," I tell him.

"Sweet. Me?" I hear him laugh. "I do dirty talk really well, if you're interested," he sniggers.

"Oh, I know. But that's not what I phoned for," I say. I need to get off this phone before I tell him to cancel the restaurant and get his sexy self to mine sharpish. "Well, I'm going to go now so I can find something that will keep me in the beautiful and stunning zone."

"You do that, and I will brush up on my sweet and dirty vocabulary since I sense you enjoy them both a lot."

"Bye, Vlad," I say, needing time to get my head straight before he picks me up at six. He has me wanting things I wouldn't dare to dream about when he speaks those suggestive words.

"Bye, angel," he chuckles, ending the call with, "see you at six, my little minx."

*

My doorbell rings announcing Vlad's arrival. I breathe in a few times, trying to shake off the nerves but the butterflies in my stomach are still in fine flutter mode. This is our first proper date and I want to make a good impression. Taking another check in the mirror to make sure my make-up isn't too heavy or smudged, I then pick up my black stilettoes and matching bag, chucking my lipstick into it. My door raps again, letting me know I've taken too long getting my act together and Vlad is getting impatient. Quickly I hurry to the door, dropping my shoes so I can slip my feet into them, then pull the door open.

My eyes pop out of my head when they catch on to the sight before them. Vlad must have really picked up on me observing his unshaven face yesterday because he has left it on, modelling two days' worth of stubble. His dark blue eyes bore into me as I shift my gaze, wandering up and down the very expensive-looking charcoal grey suit contrasting with a lighter grey shirt under it. The fit exaggerates his muscles further, making him look even more powerful. If that's even possible. There's no tie this time; he's left a couple of the top buttons open and you can just make out the blacks and blues of a tattoo.

I wobble a little on one of my very high shoes and grab the door handle for support, so I don't make a fool of myself and topple over. Blowing out the breath I'd been holding in while ogling this fine specimen of a man, I bend down to slip on my other shoe and go to say hi. Only, it's swallowed up when I find myself pinned against the wall in my hallway and the strapping body of the fine specimen of man is pressed against me while his lips claim mine.

Chapter 16

Vlad

I couldn't help myself. Seeing her standing there. Eyes wild as they roamed over me. Full of lust dragging me in. Her soft golden hair draped down one shoulder, exposing her slender neck on the other side. An all-in-one sleeveless crimson red trouser suit, cut low into a V showing off her cleavage, had me trembling. I'm sure she had worn it just to get a reaction out of me. Well it worked. She's fucking lucky I didn't throw her over my shoulder, spank her arse for being such a tease then have my way with her hard and fast up against her fucking door. But I didn't. Being a gentleman is very trying.

I stride into the doorway, lifting her chin, and seize her succulent sweet lips. They're warm and inviting, sending an electric shock through me with such force I become light headed. This is what she does to me. My heart races and hot blood travels straight to my dick, making it harder than an iron bar. I know I need to pull away before this leads to something we both know will be explosive, but it's a struggle.

I want to wine her and dine her, be the gentleman I said I would be, the man she wants and needs, the one who will always put her needs first and protect her fiercely.

We continue with our greed for each other, our tongues tangled together. Her hands entwined in one of mine, pinned above our heads while my other explores the soft curves of her body.

Reluctantly, I pull away and release her hands, laying one of mine on her throat while our foreheads rest together. I can feel the pulse in her neck trying to thrash its way out. One of her delicate hands lies trembling on my chest as the other goes up to her lips. She carefully strokes her index finger over them and a, "Wow," falls softly from them.

It takes a minute for us both to get our breath back. We just stare into each other's eyes, knowing whatever happens between us, it will be something neither of us have experienced before.

Once we have both gained back some equilibrium, I bend down to help with the high-heeled shoe she was trying to put on when I arrived. Then I put my arm out and ask, "Ready to get out of here, angel?" She holds her finger up indicating to give her a minute, turning towards the mirror in her hallway where she runs her fingers through her soft hair, laying it back over her shoulder, then adds a coat of lip gloss to her swollen, freshly kissed lips.

We arrive at the Italian restaurant, Marco's, with half hour to spare. I'd booked the table yesterday morning after dropping Holly off home. Knowing the owner here has its advantages. Saturday nights are normally fully booked, weeks in advance. We're led to the lounge area next to the bar and a waiter tells us our table won't be long. He takes our drinks order; a glass of house rosé for Holly and a glass of Pinot Noir for me.

"When did you book the table?" Holly asks, her eyes wide and full of excitement. "Olivia and Jack tried to book in here for tonight but were told it was fully booked; they've been trying to get a table since Jack's parents told them about it a couple of weeks ago. They have had to book in for next Saturday night," she tells me, waving her hands around while she scans the restaurant, eager to give the details to her friends. I smile while lifting my glass of pinot that the waiter has just dropped off. Holly sips at hers and a, "Hmmm," of appreciation follows as she replaces her glass on the table. "Wow, that's good stuff," she shivers. "It's strong, taste it," she says, picking it up and passing it to me. I take it from her, give the glass a swirl and drink. To my surprise it's fruity, crisp and is very strong.

"It's very refreshing, with a bit of a kick," I chuckle. I may change and join Holly with the house wine; one sip has her giggling away as if she's drunk half a bottle. Maybe it's nerves, I know I was a little nervous about our date tonight but now I know she's happy, I've calmed down a bit.

We sit there chatting and laughing about my sons for the next half hour. Once we're shown to our table Holly's eager to look at the menu. "Hmmm, I can't wait to try the king prawn linguine with garlic and lemon. Apparently, it's better than sex… And, I can't believe I just said that," she blushes, covering her face with the menu. I snort the wine out of my nose when I erupt with laughter. I can't believe she has said it either. I don't know her very well but the colour of her face when she said it, tells me she doesn't normally blurt out comments that have the word 'sex' in them. I can't help but make her blush a little more. Pulling the menu from her face and lowering it to the table, I lean forward so only she can hear me.

"Don't worry, sweetheart, we will both try the linguine then go home and test the theory." I wink at her and get the effect I was hoping for and a little bit more. Her face turns almost scarlet, but she can't hide the fact that she enjoys a little flirting. Her lips turn up into a beautiful megawatt smile then she throws her napkin at me.

"You really need to watch that naughty mouth of yours, Mr Petrov, you're lowering the tone of this fine establishment," she says, waving her hand around.

"Ah-ah, look at you who is comparing their fine cuisine to sex. I think your mouth could be as naughty as mine given the chance, my little minx." I sit back in my chair, smirking at Holly's face that's trying to look all coy but failing miserably.

The waiter comes over to take our order which stops our little playful banter. We both order tender squid in a light batter with lemon and garlic for starters. Followed by the king prawn linguine for Holly and I decide on the lobster risotto.

Throughout the starter we laugh and flirt, receiving a few raised eyebrows from some of the other patrons. Once our main meal arrives, we tone it down a little and Holly enlightens me to when she worked behind a bar and waitressed at a bar named Micky's. The establishment sounds small and it would have probably closed, if the owner hadn't given her free reins to build the place up. What surprises me more is that she was so young when she accomplished this as well as undertaking her degree.

I watch as she tucks into king prawns, appreciating the noises and faces she makes. She could possibly be right that they are better than sex. The sound of ecstasy. The look of pleasure on her face as she closes her eyes and savours the taste, captivates me. Watching her swallow slowly, her sparkling eyes opening seductively. She's unaware how sexy she is but I'm more than aware as she causes a tingling in my boxers.

She chuckles at me as she places a prawn on her fork, leans over and offers it to me. "Here, try one. They're so—" Before she finishes my lips are round her fork and I devour her offering, wishing it was her I was tasting. "Good?" she asks, giving me that hypnotic stare and sweet smile. I nod my head in approval then offer her a taste of my lobster. I'm put through my torment again as she repeats the same sensual enjoyment.

By the time the waiter brings the bill, we have laughed all the way through our starter. I've gained knowledge of her past employment and had to tame down my sexual appetite over our main course. We intimately shared a piece of chocolate cake with a rich cocoa topping and Morello cherry sauce. I declined having a dessert but Holly couldn't resist giving the chocolate cake a try. I couldn't resist sharing it with her when she decided to feed me. Every time she had a piece she fed me a piece. I enjoyed it more than I thought I would. I am also aware that we have drunk a carafe of the house rosé. I had ordered it once we had finished the glass when we first came in and the light flush on Holly's face is telling me maybe she has had a little too much.

We step outside into the cool night air; it's ten forty-five and the streets are full of life. Holly wobbles a little on her heels, so I put my arm out for support. She links me and snuggles into me. I love the feeling of her body so close to mine and can't wait to feel her body naked under me.

Snuggled together, we wait for a taxi. "Dance with me," I hear Holly whisper into my shoulder. She's had her head tucked into it, guarding her face from the wind that has just kicked up.

"Pardon?" I ask, confused a little by her request.

"How far is your club from here?" she asks, looking up at me, her eyes full of mischief.

"It's just around the corner. Why?" I ask, knowing full well the woman in my arms loves to dance. She manoeuvres herself, wobbling on those damn heels again, until she is stood in front of me. Both her arms snake under my jacket, wrapping them around my waist, then she stands on her tiptoes, gently placing her lips on mine. It's not all-consuming or tongues. It's a soft touch that lightly brushes over mine, but it still captures me all the same.

Holly, pulls away, looking up at me with those deep blue eyes that have me hypnotised. "I want to dance with you," she whispers.

"You've had a lot to drink, sweetheart. I'm not sure if it's such a good idea to go clubbing."

She screws her nose up at me, causing me to chuckle at her cute look. "Yes, I have had more than usual but dancing will help sober me up," she says, patting my chest, then sticks the end of her tongue out at me and crosses her eyes.

She looks so fucking cute, I can't help myself. Bending down I take her tongue between my lips then lead us into a kiss that's so intense we get a few whistles and shouts of, "Get a room!"

Breaking away, we're both laughing at the fact we managed to acquire an audience. "Come." I put my hand out. "Let's go dance the night away."

*

We've been in the lounges at Eruption for about an hour and half. When we first arrived, we ordered a glass of iced water and found one of the plush leather sofas to sit on. Once Holly had drunk her water she had me up on my feet dragging me off to the dance floor and that's where we stayed until about twenty minutes ago. We may be forty-five and thirty-seven, but we sure put some of those twenty-somethings to shame. We're sat back on one of the leather sofas and Holly has just called one of the bar staff over and whispered something in his ear. "What has she ordered?" I question, raising an eyebrow at him.

"Shush, don't tell him!" Holly shouts over the music, shaking her head and putting her finger on her lips. She looks fucking adorable and a little tipsy. The poor lad looks like a deer caught in the headlights of a fucking truck. I may be his boss, but this woman has a way about her that has you jumping to her every whim. He stands there wide eyed and shrugs his shoulders as if to say, 'What do I do?' I wave him off.

"Go. Go get whatever she has asked for," I say, shaking my head at Holly. She grins at me and rubs her hands together then places herself in my lap, thanking me with one of her soft kisses. I can't help myself but lock our lips together; when we break apart her eyes are full of lust.

Five minutes later, our drinks are brought. Two fucking Long Island iced teas. This woman is going to be death of me; she may have sobered up a bit after dancing for nearly an hour but if she drinks this she's going to be worse than she was when we first arrived. She's fucking fast too. By the time I've thought about her getting drunk, she has two hands round the glass and the straw in her mouth sucking on it like a fucking baby suckling on a bottle of milk. Her eyes are wide, and I can see the smile hidden behind the glass. She's laughing at me. "Fuck it," I growl. I don't want her getting pissed. I thought by now we would be back at my house, in my bed with us both naked and Holly under me. Well, that's not going to happen tonight, I tell myself. As much as I would like nothing more than to take her back to mine and show her what a real man is capable of. How spectacular we would be together. It's not going to happen. I want Holly to remember every touch from my hands. Every kiss I place on her silky skin. Every time my tongue strokes over her erogenous zones. If it's anything like when we dance together then I can only imagine it will have a lasting effect that neither of us can explain or comprehend.

I watch as she downs it in one; her face contorts and pales as she looks up at me from her glass. I need to get her home before she's sick. I'm just about to suggest that we leave when she places her head on my shoulder. "Vlad," she slurs.

"Hmmm?" I reply as I run my hand through her silky hair.

I know she's regretting her last drink and I chuckle when she says, "Please take my drunken arse home."

Ten minutes later we're in the back of a taxi, heading for Holly's home. I have my arm around her and her head is placed on my chest. I can hear her lightly breathing out of her nose, giving out a little snore. Yeah, she's asleep.

Once the taxi arrives at her apartment block, I pay the man, get out of my side gently laying Holly's head on the headrest then I round the car ready to carry her. To my surprise her eyes flicker open. She looks tired and adorable. "Come on, sweetheart, let's get you in and to bed," I tell her.

"Are we home?" she croaks out. And I'm shocked when I answer her.

"Yes, we're home." It doesn't sound alien when she says 'we', nor does it sound wrong to answer with 'yes, we're home'. Suddenly, I'm more aware that it doesn't scare me to want this. I don't feel any selfishness in her like I have with many women that have entered my life. Then I think I already knew that from day one.

She doesn't allow me to carry her, slapping my hand away when I try. Her arm links through mine, staggering a little as she does. When she gains her balance, we set off at a slow pace through the entrance of her block and into the lift that is waiting on the ground floor. Once we are at her door she fumbles in her bag for the door key. I take the bag from her, retrieving the key and open the door. Holly kicks off her shoes and drops her bag on the small occasional table. I'm just about to ask her if she would like me to make her a black coffee, when she covers her mouth, and mumbles what sounds like 'I feel sick'. She takes off towards what I assume is the bathroom like a champion race horse and I follow in pursuit.

Kneeling on the black tiled floor, Holly retches the contents of her stomach down the toilet. I hold her hair away from her face and rub her back, trying to comfort her as tears saturate her bloodshot eyes. When she finishes she stands shakily, looking exhausted, and moves towards the sink where she swills her face. She turns to look at me, her face awash with embarrassment. I don't make judgement, I only hope I have not judged this woman wrongly and this is normal for her. Not wanting to linger on that thought for too long, I locate her pink and purple toothbrush and pop some toothpaste onto it then hand it to her for her to freshen up.

She finishes and turns to face me. "Let's get you ready for bed," I say, staring into her blue eyes that have a bit more focus in them now. She nods at me but doesn't speak. Without taking my eyes away from hers, I place my hand round her back and feel for the zip. Pulling the fastener down slowly, when I do the garment slides down her body and pools at her feet. Then she holds onto my shoulders for support, so she can step out of it. I can't move my gaze from hers. I wouldn't dare. I don't think I'm strong enough to look at her beautiful semi-naked body and not want to pin her up against the wall. I walk backwards, holding her hands and keeping her close, till I find her bedroom. Entering the dimly lit room, the curtains are slightly parted, and the moon is casting its light. "Where are your pyjamas, Holly?" my low voice asks. She goes to let go of me, wanting to walk over to drawers that she has pointed to, but I keep a hold on her hand, taking the lead towards the drawers. Fishing through the drawer with one hand, my eyes stay fixed on her mesmerising face. Locating a small T-shirt and a pair of shorts, I let go of her hands. My eyes flick towards the ceiling as my hands travel round her back to unclasp her bra. It falls down her arms and onto the floor. Making quick work, I slip the T-shirt over her head and onto her warm silky skin. Then I let my thumbs stroke down her body until they reach the top of her knickers. Hooking my thumbs under the elastic, I close my eyes and kneel before her. My restraint is verging on non-existent with this woman. I want her so much it's fucking painful. All I really want to do is rip off this tiny piece of material, hook her leg over my shoulder and taste her on my tongue. But I won't. She's had a little too much to drink, which I blame myself for, and she is tired. I inhale deeply and quickly strip them from her body then help her into her shorts.

"Thank you," she utters, letting out a yawn when her sleepy eyes close then blink open. I move us both to her bed where I remove the sheet and lay her down. Covering her over until she is nicely tucked in, I brush my lips over hers. I don't linger. Moving my mouth from hers slightly I look at her.

"Sleep, my angel," I whisper then move and kiss her forehead.

She turns her body, so she is laid on her side, and tucks the sheet under her chin. "Night, Vlad," she mumbles then I hear a soft snore coming from her.

Perched on the end of the bed, I decide to stay the night.

Stripping down to my boxers, I watch my angel sleep. There's a hint of a smile on her face and I wonder if she's dreaming about me. She inhales through her nose then lets out a shuddering breath her body moves slightly then she settles again. Chuckling to myself, I head to the bathroom. Once I'm back I gently lay at the side of Holly, I don't bother with the sheet, I think laying on top would be the best thing for the both of us. I watch the moonlight's shadows dance around the walls; hand in hand the light of the moon and the dark of the night hold each other, moving in sequence.

The breath on my face flutters and tickles while delicate fingers twirl with the short dark hair around my belly button. There's a long slender leg sprawled out over the top of my thighs and the sheet that covered Holly is twisted between us. My manhood has made an appearance due to the soft and gentle touches from her breath and skin. If I'd have been any other man I would have probably woke her, wanting her to take care of the throbbing she is causing in my boxers. But I don't.

Before sleep claimed me last night my mind ran to the problem from earlier. What if this is normal for Holly, getting drunk easily and needing assistance to make it home. I can't and won't tolerate a woman who doesn't care about the people around and how she is hurting them. In the dark hours of last night my mind wandered back to the anxiety and trouble my wife brought with her. After watching Holly sleep peacefully for a while, I knew I had to give her a chance. She's bewitched me, and I couldn't pull away even if I wanted to.

I turn to look at the time on my phone which I had placed on the bedside table last night after texting Sebastian. I'd asked him to pick me up from Holly's at eight o'clock then sent him the address. It's six fifty-five and I need to make a move. Gingerly, I remove Holly's hand from my stomach, then her leg, rolling out of the bed quietly so I don't disturb her. Grabbing my clothes from the chair where I had left them last night I make my way into the bathroom to dress.

Ten minutes later I walk out to find Holly sat up in bed her hair like a bird's nest and a look of bewilderment on her face. "Morning, honey," I greet her with, stalking over to her side of the bed and stealing a kiss. "You hogged all the covers last night, beautiful," I say, then brush my thumb down her heated face. I know she's wondering what the hell happened last night between us. Believe me, if something had she would have remembered because she would still feel me there. But I'm not going to tell her I was the perfect gentleman. I let her sweat for a bit first. "Would you like me to make you a coffee, angel?" I ask, trying hard not to laugh at her. She has questions on her face which I won't answer, not yet anyway. She nods her head at me. "Get dressed and meet me in the kitchen, my little sex kitten." I turn quickly, unable to hide the grin on my face when her blush deepens on her perfect skin.

Striding out of the bedroom door I hear her call, "Vlad." I don't reply, I close the door behind me and chuckle into the kitchen.

Our coffees are made, and I've had a message from Sebastian letting me know he's up and about and will text me when he is outside. I've just slipped my phone into my pocket when Holly strolls into the kitchen. She is freshly showered; her hair is tied back, and she is dressed in a pair of exercise pants and a hoody. The smell of strawberries invades my senses and without warning, I have her enveloped in my arms, my nose in her soft damp hair inhaling the refreshing smell, getting my fix of her. Then my mouth can't help butting in. Wanting to taste her skin. I trail my lips down her neck, along her jawline then to her lips, taking a little bite as my tongue sneaks into her mouth to get its fill. Our kiss is powerful, like two mighty countries joining as one. Holly's hand grips the back of my hair and I find myself lifting her up, so she can wrap her legs around me. I place her on the tiled island and shift my hips, so they fit snugly into her. Just as I get settled my phone vibrates in my pocket. I know it will be Sebastian without even looking but my option to ignore it doesn't stop Holly from pulling out of our embrace. "Vlad," she breathes, resting her head on mine.

"Hmmm," is all I manage.

"We didn't... you know?" she asks, moving her head away from mine while one hand rests on my chest and the other points between us.

"No, Holly, we didn't... you know," I mimic with a smirk on my face.

"Oh, thank God. I don't mean... Urrrrrr, that came out all wrong." Her flustered state has me laughing out loud. "Don't laugh. It's not funny, some things are a blur," she grimaces, as she puts her head in her hands.

I take pity on my little woman and decide to help her out. Taking her hands away from her face I ask, "What can you remember, Holly?"

She looks at me as if she trying to relay the night in her head. "I remember the very posh Italian restaurant, the beautiful food and extra strong wine, laughing and making a spectacle of ourselves in front of the other customers." I nod my head at her. She has that bit right.

"What else do you remember?"

"When we came out of the restaurant I was a little tipsy. I wanted to dance so we went to your club." She smiles. "Oh." She covers her mouth. "I drank that lethal cocktail in one, didn't I?"

I nod my head at her again. "Everything is a bit of a blur after that," she says, scrunching her nose up at me.

"Do you remember getting in the taxi?" She shakes her head. "The taxi ride home?" Again she shakes her head. "You fell asleep." I take her hands in mine just to let her know she doesn't need to be ashamed.

"I fell asleep. What an idiot I am. Why did I think I could drink that cocktail after all that wine?"

"Don't worry, I'm sure you won't be doing it again anytime soon," I reassure her.

"Oh my god," she says, her eyes wide. "You practically had to carry me to my apartment." Then realisation hits her, about her getting rid of the entire contents of her stomach. "I'm so bloody sorry." She covers her mouth again. "I threw up, didn't I?"

"Yes," I say.

"And you helped clean me up as well as getting me ready for bed." I don't need to verify this; she knows I did. "You were a perfect gentleman." She looks at me like I'm her hero. I place my hands on her thighs and rub them lightly. All the while she looks affectionately into my eyes.

"It was hard," I smirk at her.

"I bet it was," she says with a cheeky grin dawning on her angel face. She places her forehead on mine. "I'm sorry, Vlad, for spoiling our night. I don't normally get drunk like that or get sick," she declares.

"You didn't spoil the night. In fact, I think we had a fantastic night," I tell her.

"Well, I think you're just trying to be nice to me because I can't handle my drink."

"Oh, I think you did a pretty good job on the wine." I look down at what she is wearing. "Are you going for a run?" I query.

"I'm going to the gym, when you go. I need to work this hangover off. In less than two weeks I've been drunk three times. Last night was the first time I have ever been sick with alcohol. I don't usually drink that much. When it comes to alcohol I'm a bit of a lightweight," she tells me.

My phone rings and this time I answer my son. "I'll be down in five," I tell him. Looking at Holly and listening to her, I know I was stupid to even let it cross my mind that she could be anything like my wife. I take her in my arms and nuzzle my face into the crook of her neck. "Spend the day with me tomorrow, Holly," I whisper. "All day. I'll pick you up at ten and we'll take a trip to the coast." She nods her head at me. "Bring an overnight bag and stay with me." She nods again. Her eyes telling me it's something she wants too.

"I'd like that." The truth in her voice stands out.

"Good. I can't wait," I articulate then kiss her hard, letting her know just how good it will be. "I have to go, sweetheart, Sebastian is waiting for me. I need to go home and get changed before I go and tackle all that paperwork I have to do." Half-heartedly I pull away.

"OK, go," she says, not wanting to let go of my hand. I can't help but go in for another taste of her before I tell her I will phone her later and to enjoy her trip to the gym.

I leave her sitting on the kitchen worksurface after kissing the hell out of her. We are both giddy with the anticipation about tomorrow, knowing it will cement our relationship.

Chapter 17

Holly

Walking hand in hand across the warm, soft sand with Vlad, I have a smile as wide as the sea before me plastered across my face. He has been the perfect gentleman.

After he left my home yesterday morning, I didn't hear anything from him until late last night when he telephoned to let me know he would pick me up at ten this morning for our trip to the coast. He had asked me to bring an overnight bag and stay at his home, I had agreed.

To say I'm a little nervous is an understatement because we both know I won't be staying in the spare room.

It's been a long time since I was intimate with a man and shared the same bed. Although, I know Vlad had slept in my bed with me on Saturday night, I only knew this because I could smell his masculine scent on my sheets and the pillow he had used. He had woken and got dressed before I stirred on Sunday morning and it wasn't until he walked out from the bathroom that I realised he had stayed over and that he had taken care of my drunken state. Like I said, a gentleman.

Packing my bag and deciding what to wear for today had been a nightmare, underwear playing a huge part in my dilemma. I had chosen a pair of ankle-grazer red skinny jeans and a blue and red floral top, for today's outing, along with a pair of Converse pumps and a dark blue chunky jumper. It might be late April, but the summer sun hasn't kicked in yet. Eventually, I picked out matching lacy bra and knicker set, deep red with tiny dark blue flowers sewn on them. I also packed an outfit for tomorrow morning along with underwear and threw in a sexy nighty and dressing gown that was bought for me by Olivia and Sarah over two years ago, that I've yet to take the tags off.

Vlad can and does make me feel and want things that I have never experienced before or ever needed. Knowing the impact he had on me the first night we met, I'm sure tonight will be something I've never felt before.

He arrived at mine this morning at nine forty-five, taking me straight into his arms as soon as I opened the door. His lips full and soft attacked mine with such passion, he left me light headed and speechless when he let me go, sauntering off into the kitchen.

Half an hour later we were on the road, stopping once so I could use the ladies'.

The picturesque coastal town was busy, full of visitors taking advantage of one of the first beautiful sunny days we have had.

When we first arrived, we strolled around the shops eating freshly made doughnuts then stopped at one of the amusement arcades to play on the machines. We fooled around like two adolescents let loose without an adult, his hip lightly tapping against mine to get to a winning machine before me. Me pushing back at him so I could insert a coin first. His enthusiasm to win me a stuffed penguin on the shooting range was exuberant. His firing skills were remarkable, and I couldn't help jumping into his strong arms when he won. The delight that covered his handsome face made me fall a little more.

We chose to have fish and chips for lunch and sat in one of the many restaurants, then went for a walk along the beach, taking off our footwear and rolling up our jeans so we could paddle in the sea. We stood together, with my back to Vlad's front, gazing over the vast water rippling under the blue skies. While the seagulls cried overhead, sailing boats floated dreamily across the soft waves. All the time his masculine arms stayed wrapped around my waist while his chin rested on my shoulder and he stole little kisses here and there.

Vlad told me about when his sons were younger, not long after they first came to England, he would bring them here for the day. Building sandcastles with the younger ones, spending time on the arcade games, eating fish and chips then Sebastian and Nicholas would spend an hour or two on the fun fare, riding on as many fast rides as they could.

I was shocked when he brought up a memory of his mother telling him when he was a young boy how her dad and brothers would bring her here and stay in a caravan for a few days in the school holidays. Vlad went on to tell me that growing up he had always wanted to visit England and when his friend moved here with his parents, they had planned for Vlad to come and stay with them when he finished school. Only he never got the chance because he became a father at such a young age. He had to marry young and prove to himself as well as others that he was man enough to be a father and a husband.

I couldn't see the look on his face when he told me, but his husky voice was filled with emotion. The heartfelt shudder and sigh he let out told me everything. He had missed out on things that he wanted for himself at a young age and worked to provide for his family. Not sure what he worked as, and it didn't go unnoticed that while he spoke about his mother, he never mentioned his father. He also left out anything about his wife.

I didn't comment on what he told me. I was glad he had brought up a little bit about himself instead of me asking. So, I just held onto the arms that were wrapped around me, stroking the hairs and following the lines and twirls of the tattoos, while we looked out to sea.

We stood there just taking in the sea air, letting the water coil around our naked feet for a few silent moments, until Vlad spun me around to face him and took my hands in his. "Would you like to ride the ghost train with me, sweetheart?" he asks, wiggling his eyebrows at me with that knicker-dropping grin on his face.

"Will you hold me tight and keep all the monsters away?" I fool around, picking my pumps up off the sand.

"Always," he says, pulling me into him and taking my pumps from me.

"Well what are you waiting for?" I say, pulling him towards the benches off the sand, so we can dry our feet with the towel he has in the bag slung over his back.

We dry our feet and slip on our shoes. I decide to give Vlad a challenge. "You know, I've never been kissed on the ghost train. Maybe you could change that for me," I flirt.

His eyes light up and his lip turns up, giving me a dirty smirk. "Consider it done." He pulls my hand, leading us towards the fun fare. "Come on, woman, the quicker we get there the quicker I can be your first," he says, pushing me in front and slapping me on my rear. This gets us a look from a young couple passing by, hand in hand, walking a dog. They both giggle as they pass by. Vlad winks at them then hurries along, taking my hand.

Vlad takes me on the ghost train, the big wheel, rollercoaster and some other ride that flips us upside down and swings us around so fast it has me shrieking like a little girl and gripping Vlad's thigh so hard I'm sure I've left nail marks. On every ride he kissed me like his life depended on it. Placing his hands on the sides of my face, his dark eyes gazing into mine then claiming my lips. Once we had finished on the rides we decided to head off home, well, back to Vlad's. In all honesty today has been one of those days I will never forget and it's not over yet. I'm not sure what to expect when we get to Vlad's place, only that I don't want this day to end without Vlad showing me the animal side of him.

I must have dozed off on our way back home because I can hear the low rumble of Vlad trying to wake me. "Holly." He nudges me out of my sea air induced sleep. "Sweetheart, we're here," he soothes, as he strokes my cheekbone. I sit up quickly, stretching my legs out, and run my fingers under my eyes to remove any mascara that may have smudged while shutting my eyes. Don't want to look like an old lush, I'm still getting over the mortification of being sick on Saturday night.

Once I can focus, my eyes take in the immense grounds surrounded by woodland with a three-garage building to our right. Vlad is out of the car and opening my door when my mouth falls open. His home is huge.

Chapter 18

Vlad

Placing my fingers under Holly's chin, I close her mouth and put my lips to hers. "It's just a house, Holly," I whisper. She nods her head and steps back before she spins around to take in the scenery surrounding her. Yes, my home stands out in the area it is situated in and the grounds could house a football pitch, with its tall leafy trees and blooming shrubs kept to a high standard, edging the winding pathed road from the electric gates up to the house. Tom, my housekeeper's husband, who has become a good friend and someone I know I can trust, designed this garden long before I came to live here and has been tending to it ever since, priding himself on how fertile and green the grass is.

"Come," I say, taking her hand. "I'll put the car away later. Let's get in and I will show you around before we eat," I tell her. Holly takes my hand while I lead her towards the front door of my home.

"It's huge," she says seriously. I look at her and take her comment out of the context she meant.

"Yes, it is." I wiggle my eyebrows at her. "But you'll get used to it," I chuckle. She picks up on the innuendo and slaps me on the arm.

"You know what I mean," she laughs, screwing her eyes up at me. One thing I've come to notice about Holly, she likes to prod and

141

poke me, jab and slap me whether she is being playful or angry. I love it all.

"Ouch," I yelp, rubbing my arm and putting out my lip playfully.

"Sorry," she says, rubbing my arm. "But you always lower the tone," she giggles as I open the door. We enter, and straight away Holly's eyes widen again. "Wow! You could fit my whole apartment in your entrance hall," she exaggerates.

"I don't think so. I've seen your place and I'm sure we would have to extend to the kitchen to fit your apartment in," I chuckle, placing her bag on the floor and kicking my shoes off. Holly removes hers too and then rushes off to the open-plan kitchen, stopping on her way to take in the vast entrance with its highly polished oak wooden floors and winding staircase with thick, plush, dark blue carpet. She slides across the floor; on entering the kitchen she screeches, "I don't believe it. This is the exact same kitchen I wanted when I was still married to my ex," she gushes, waving her arms around excitedly, a huge grin on her face. "And this island... the colours I love." The exuberance in her voice calls me to her and I find I'm stood in front of her with my hands on her hips.

"Wanted," I say. She looks up at me and the smile leaves her eyes.

"Sorry, it's just... When I was still married, we had a lot of social parties, work related. Rob's work. Our home was... not as big as yours but it was adequate size for him to invite colleagues for dinner and get togethers to further his career. I loved to cook but wasn't happy with the kitchen and appliances we had so I found the one on the internet and showed it to Rob. Only he didn't like the colours or the design and that was the end of my new kitchen," she sighs.

I take her in my arms, shaking my head. What a fool he was. This woman should be worshipped. Given whatever her heart desires. If I'd have been in his position she would have had the world. "Anytime you want to cook feel free to use my kitchen as yours. Even if you just want to hang out in here, not a problem. But if you cook there are a lot of hungry males in this house, so you need to cook enough to go around my greedy brood." I lift her face to investigate her eyes and the happiness begins to return.

"Deal," she grins, putting her hand out to shake mine. "When did you get this?" her hand waves around the kitchen she loves so much.

"Hmmm, I can't take all the credit for this. My housekeeper Mrs White, Izzy and Sebastian chose it. I just paid for it. Well, they showed me three and this one was the one I preferred," I explain. "It was installed about two years ago."

"You have very good taste, Mr Petrov," she says, patting my chest.

"Yes, I do, and that is why I have you in my arms, sweetheart." I tap her nose with my finger and get the squint-eye face she pulled on me a few nights ago. She's so fucking adorable I can't help but lower my head and steal her lips. Holly breaks our kiss and moves around, wanting to explore my home further. Her gaze lands on the lived-in living room opposite the kitchen. I say lived-in because there's always children's toys, video games or schoolbooks hanging around but not tonight; someone has had a tidy round. Probably Mrs White.

We move over to the area and Holly sinks her toes into the luxury pile carpet, wiggling them as she does. Her fingers stroke along the soft mocha-coloured Italian leather sofa. My home is mostly decorated in shades of blues and browns which my boys and I have always liked. She walks over to the floor-to-ceiling windows, looking out through the patio doors.

Her eyes then focus on the television mounted on the other side of the room. She just raises her eyebrows at me and smirks. I shake my head and chuckle because it's big. But in my defense, anything smaller would look ridiculous in this house.

My stomach lets out a rumble and I realise we haven't eaten since well before we left the coast to come home. "Come on, let's order a takeout. You must be hungry…"

"Vlad, that's swearing. You don't order takeout when you have a kitchen like that to cook in. It's just not right," she says with her hands on her hips and determination in her voice.

"Sweetheart, it's quicker to order something and as much as I would like to cook for you it would take over an hour for me to make something half decent." I'm talking to her back now because my little minx has sashayed those hips of hers over to the kitchen and has her head in the fridge. "What are you doing?" I ask, standing behind her and because I can't help myself, I'm just a man, I place my hands on those hips that had attitude as they swayed across the room. I also run my thumbs over the firm cheeks of her bottom. This gets me a slap on my roaming hands as my angel turns around, arms full of chicken breasts, vegetables and a few other things she picked out.

"Stir fry," her flushed face says. I just stand there, dumb; my woman wants to cook for me. "Vlad, do you like stir fry?" I hear her say. And yes, I love stir fry and yes, if she wants to cook in this kitchen she loves so much, who am I to stop her? Especially if she is going to let me watch her parade around rustling up something for us both. I'm not a caveman – well, maybe a little in the bedroom – but no woman I've ever wanted so much has ever wanted to do anything for me. Then again, I've never wanted a woman as much as I want her. And there's nothing sexier than having that woman prepare a meal for her man.

Nodding my head to her question, she leans into me. "Vlad, go put your car away and I will whip us up something to eat. You can show me the rest of the house later."

An hour later, I've put away the car. We've eaten a delicious meal, loaded the dishwasher and wiped down the worktops. My dick overreacted to watching Holly move around the kitchen; every time she bent over I almost whimpered. I'm not sure how much longer I can remain this gentleman.

Holly's been to freshen up while I poured us both a glass of wine and now she lounges on the sofa, looking as edible as the meal she just cooked for us. It's time to snuggle with my woman.

Handing Holly her glass of Australian rosé, she takes a small sip and shudders. "Is it not to your liking, madam?" I jest, sitting down at the side of her, brushing my thigh against hers.

"It's fine," she says. "I just remembered the state I was in on Saturday night…"

"Don't worry," I cut in, taking the glass from her and placing it on the table. "I will keep my eye on you and not let you drink too much," I tell her as I lay my hand on her cheek, stroking my thumb over her blushing cheekbone. Moving my lips within millimetres from hers, she softly swallows, and her eyes fill with need. Her tongue dips out to taste her bottom lip and I can't stop myself from following suit.

Our lips lock. Our tongues taste. Arousing a need so strong, I'm helpless to stop what we have both been wanting, needing for what seems like a lifetime. So, I don't. Holly manoeuvres herself and straddles my hips, bringing us further together and causing a sensation so strong, I can't help but let out a moan as I edge us both to the end of the couch.

Without realising straight away I'm on the move, carrying us both across the living room, past the kitchen and to the foot of the staircase. All the while our mouths stay fused together. Stopping at the stairs I reluctantly remove my lips from Holly's. We're both breathless and needy. Placing my forehead on hers and looking into her seductive blue eyes, I don't have to ask if she's ready. We need no words. There's just one look from me and a slight nod from her and I'm moving up towards my bedroom, clutching Holly, never wanting to let her go.

As we enter, I switch the lights to dim. I want to see this woman naked before me, but I know she's a little shy. I lead us to the bed, my eyes never leaving hers, then lean in, kissing her as if my life depended on it. And I'm sure it does because if I don't get her naked soon, I may die.

Holly's hands tangle in my short hair while mine run up and down the soft curves of her body. She strokes her nails down the back of my neck causing a growl to erupt from my throat.

Breaking our kiss, I turn us around, so my legs hit the mattress of the bed. Then I sit down holding on to Holly's hips. She looks down at me, her wavy hair tugged out of the band she had it in earlier. Her eyes are heavy, and her chest is heaving. I need her naked. "Take off your clothes, Holly." My voice is low and commanding. She stares at me and just when I think she's going to deny me this one chance of her submitting to me, she steps back, lowers her head, shakes her hair, bringing it back up then runs her fingers through the silky strands. She gives me one look, one lick of her bottom lip then that devilish smirk appears, and her fingers start to slowly and seductively remove her shirt.

I sit there gripping my sheets as she places her fingers on the buttons of her shirt, unfastens one then places her hands on each side of the material, pausing, then rips the shirt clean open, buttons flying in every direction. She doesn't falter and neither do I. Her firm breasts are a beautiful sight and I must stop myself from going to her. Holly continues, her hands stroking down her smooth skin until she reaches the button to her jeans.

I don't normally want a woman to submit but I need this from Holly. I need to know she trusts me. Trusts me that I will take her through the night with her pleasure in mind.

She lowers the zip then places her thumbs inside the waistband and sways towards me, pushing the denim off her slender thighs as she does. Once they're laid at her feet she places her hand on my shoulder for balance and steps out of them. I can't help but lower my lips to her shaky hand and leave a little kiss. She may look confident and in control, but I see the tremble in her. Holly is nervous and so am I.

She is stood before me in lacy underwear looking like a fucking goddess and me her slave. Holly's hands move to the front fastener of her bra and I'm on my knees. Knelt there with my lips moving over her stomach, kissing and nibbling her strawberry-tasting flesh. One of my hands goes to hers to stop her from removing the material that covers her hard nipples and firm breasts. That is one job that I will take great pleasure in doing.

I keep my mouth on her skin, sucking and kissing as I move up towards her breasts; once there, I stand, catching her mouth with mine, and unwrap her breasts. Freeing them into my hands. Taking her hard bud between my fingers I roll it gently and then give a little squeeze. She moans into my mouth and wraps one of her legs around me, wanting, needing friction to quench the throb building within her. My cock is hard and aching to be inside her heat. I need to get us there.

Sitting my hand under her bottom, I'm aware her knickers are still in place and I am fully clothed. I turn and lower us on to the bed. My mouth runs wild over her luscious skin, biting, kissing and licking every inch of her. Her legs fall wide when I kneel between them and roll the lace down past her thighs. Once off, I take her in. Wet pink flesh ready and ripe and I can't hold back any longer when I look at Holly's face pleading for me to take her.

My tongue laps at the wetness, drinking it all in. Holly's hands are pulling at my hair and scratching, trying to tear off my T-shirt while her back arches. She moans loudly with pleasure as she is taken to the edge ready to fly off into the night.

Her hands pull once again at my T-shirt which I'm reluctant to remove. It hides my past.

Ink. Skulls of men that the dagger above them drove into. Greedy, vicious, cruel men that were eradicated, taken from this world all in the name of greed. My heart open, ripped apart by the people who were supposed to care, love me. Daggers piercing through the pieces every time I was betrayed. Jokers, dancing around my chest. Representing the fool. Me. How many times I played that man, forgiving the ones who hurt me. And then the devil, looking over at my heart ripped to shreds and the little fool that forgave. Laughing in his triumph. I can't let my past keep me from happiness any longer. I need this woman in my life. But, I know she will ask questions about the ink that covers me; the scars on me. I won't lie to her. I've already promised her that, but I will falsify the truth a little until the day she's strong enough to hear the truth. With that in mind I rip the shirt off and toss it on the floor.

Holly takes me in. Roaming her innocent blue eyes over the story on my body. I don't give her time to ask questions; my mouth is on her again, licking at the heated flesh. Devouring, drawing out her long-awaited orgasm. Her nails rake over my skin and moans echo around me as I take her to the edge and she tips over, squeezing my head between her thighs. Her body trembles while her orgasm claims her, and I don't move my lips until I know she's back with me.

Urgently, I join her at the top of the bed and take her mouth with mine, while my hands make quick work of removing the condom from my pocket and removing my jeans. Holly helps, pushing them down my legs with her feet, till I can kick them off. My boxers follow and my fingers fumble trying to rip open the packet. Once done I roll it on then lay down over my angel, taking her face in my hands. I kiss her fiercely, wild with the longing to be inside her. Moving my hand between us I feel her heat. She is wet and slick and so ready for me. Slowly I insert the tip and suck in a harsh breath. Inch by inch I move into her, coating myself in all that is her. She grips me tightly, her arms around me stroking my skin. Her lips biting onto my neck, marking me. She's marking me as hers and I follow. Nuzzling into the cruck of her neck, sucking while I move slowly in and out of her, whispering in her ear what she's doing to me.

Our need becomes more, and Holly moves her hips to meet mine. We meet each other as I pull out then thrust inside her. My heart is racing, and beads of sweat coat my back. Holly's moans drag me further in, causing me to speed up. I can feel the sensation at the bottom of my spine, letting me know I can't hold on much longer.

Hooking Holly's leg over my shoulder I drive in deeper, over and over, kissing her calf as I do. We're both shaking when it hits us. Crashing, lashing, ripping through with a force so strong, I can't help but roar while Holly lets out a scream. Even when I collapse on top of her she is still shuddering. Still gripping my hard cock with her tightness. Laying my head on hers we are both breathless and an aftershock shakes through me, causing my body to tremble again and I can't help but bellow out, "Fucking hell!"

I'm not sure how long it takes to get our breath back and our rapid heartbeat to slow down. I pull out of Holly, knowing we will be doing that again soon. Well, as soon as I get some energy back.

Laying on my back, I have Holly sprawled across my chest, twirling a lock of hair in my fingers. I know I need to move and get rid of the condom, but I can't. Her fingers are playing with the short hairs on my chest then she trails over the tattoos that mask my skin. We don't speak, we just lay there wrapped together, listening to our breathing become normal.

"I need the bathroom, sweetheart," I whisper, kissing the top of her head as I do.

"OK," she murmurs, then rolls off me on to her back. I can't help but lean over her and steal a kiss. "We'll be doing that again, angel." I wink at her and add, "As soon as I get my breath back," I chuckle then roll out of bed.

"Go. Do, what you need to do and get back here, I need to snuggle," she says, yawning, looking thoroughly fucked. And I love that look on her.

I stride through my walk-in wardrobe and into the bathroom at the other side to take care of business and return within minutes, to find Holly snuggled under the sheet cuddling my pillow. I climb in beside her, gently removing the pillow from her arms, and she cuddles into me.

We lay there for at least an hour just snuggled together, caressing each other. Face to face, arms and legs entwined, we whisper in the darkness of the night. Sometime after, we peacefully drift off to sleep. Waking a few hours later, we make love again.

Chapter 19

Holly

Peeling my face from Vlad's overheated chest, I glance at the clock on the bedside table. It's six thirty-five and my legs ache like I've run a bloody marathon. The morning sun is peeking through the open blinds, flooding the bedroom with light, as I take in the size of the bed I am laid in. Mine is a king-size and this is a hell of a lot bigger. I giggle to myself at the reaction I had to Vlad's wardrobe. I thought I'd stumbled into some movie star's dressing room, letting out a squeal as I paused to take it in.

We had drifted off to sleep an hour or so after our first round of mind-blowing sex. He had taken me high amongst the stars, dangled me there then let me go, floating amid the beauty of the sky until I drifted peacefully back to Earth. Only a couple of hours later he woke me with his tender touch and soft lips caressing my body then proceeded to take me to the outer limits again. After, I was in desperate need for the loo. Vlad pointed me in the direction. On entering, I staggered into the wall in shock. His walk-in wardrobe is like something Hollywood stars would have.

Rows of high-priced suits and shirts line the cobalt-blue walls and walnut shelving and drawers store the rest of his array of clothing. The walls above the drawers and shelving are lined with mirrors where spotlights sit discreetly, setting off a warm glow. Thick plush

149

carpet snuggles my feet like slippers and there's an overall smell of him. The masculine scent of his aftershave and other lotions filled the air and I needed to sit down on the comfy chair that sat in the corner of this fine room, to give my mind time to catch up. Everything about him is huge. From his six-foot-three height to the size of his home and size of his love for those he calls family.

Stepping through his wardrobe, I'm met with his oversized bathroom. The colours of the tiles and marble floor contrast with his bedroom and wardrobe. The bath is sunken into the floor and the shower stands in the far corner. Men's shower gels are scattered around as well as candles. The blue towels are folded neatly and of course they are Egyptian cotton.

After taking care of business in his bathroom, I got back into bed to snuggle up with Vlad and let him know how impressive his walk-in wardrobe and bathroom are. He just chuckled and pulled me into his hard body where we both drifted off to sleep.

Only now I am just realising why he is sat halfway up the bed, resting on his headboard and I am straddling his meaty thighs with my head on his chest. "Oh God," I say, louder than expected, looking up at Vlad's sleepy face while tracing my fingers over the disturbing tattoos on his chest.

"Why are you cursing?" His morning husky voice startles me. His eyes are still closed but he's more than awake. I can feel the rough pad of his thumb stroking up and down the small of my back and he's heard my torment. I sigh and bury my head further into him.

"What is it, Holly?" he queries, lifting us both so we're both sat up straight now with me still straddling him. Placing my head back where it was comfortable, I mumble into his chest, "I cannot believe I jumped you in the middle of the night." I lay there for a few minutes, replaying in my head how it happened.

I woke up feeling horny, so I took Vlad's hard length into my hands and whispered into his ear, "I want you." Well, there were no arguments from him. Swiftly he moved me so I was straddling him, where I proceeded to mount him like one of the dancers at his club ascending one of the poles. I can feel his shoulders shaking. The bastard's laughing at me. "We didn't use a condom." I'm still speaking into his chest but that should stop the laughter. He lifts my chin and his deep blues gaze into mine and there's still humour etched on his face.

"Is that what has my beautiful woman cursing, early in the morning?" he asks.

"Yes, it was very stupid of me…"

"Are you on the contraceptive pill?" he cuts in.

"Yes," I answer.

"And, I assume you were tested after your ex cheated on you?"

My face scowls at him. Yes, I got tested and yes everything was clear. I haven't slept with anyone since Rob and Vlad knows this. But, it's not me I have the issue with. Vlad is a handsome man, single and assuming he's not short of a bob or two, I know he would have warmed many women's bed.

He moves me this time, so I'm sat across his thighs cradled in his arms; he then lifts my hand and plants a soft kiss on the palm. "Holly," he says, "I always use a condom. I haven't been with a woman without one since…" He stops inhales then finishes. "Since my wife."

"Oh," is all I say. I don't want to spoil our time together, so I leave it at that. I know he wouldn't lie to me. Silently, we lay there, in our own little world, Vlad is first to break the calmness that surrounds us.

"What are you thinking about, sweetheart?" he asks, while he nuzzles into my hair.

"I'm thinking I need a shower," I answer him as I stretch leisurely across him and his enormous bed. "Do you really need a bed this big? You could hold one very large pyjama party in here," I joke, wiggling my toes under the cotton sheet.

"I do often," he muses. "But, I prefer naked parties with you, angel," he says, planting soft kisses down my neck. Turning quickly, I knock him away from me and scramble up onto my knees. I'm aware I'm still naked and Vlad is taking in my exposed state. But I'm anxious to hear his explanation to the first part of that statement he just divulged.

"What do you mean, you do often? In fact, don't answer that, I don't want to hear it," I tell him firmly as I slide to the end of the bed looking for something to cover myself up with. Embarrassed with myself for feeling jealous that I'm not the only woman that's been in his bed, I pull the sheet up, trying hide my discomfort. Vlad rises from the bed like King Neptune rising from the sea.

"Hey, what are you doing?" His voice is tense. He wraps his arms around me, shifting his body so he's sat at the side of me. "Holly, I didn't mean what I know you are thinking." He moves off the bed and crouches in front of me. "Look at me, angel." I can hear the anguish in his voice. So, I lift my head and study his face. He rubs his hands up and down his face. "Holly, I have four sons and two grandchildren. There is only one place in this very large house that I can escape to and it is only out there on the roof top," he points over towards the windows where I can see a door – I didn't notice it last night, other things on my mind, "that I get any peace and quiet. My sons think nothing about invading my privacy. It doesn't matter whether I'm asleep when they come home pissed, they will barge through the door, flop on the bed wanting to fill me in on what they have been up to. Some of it I don't really need to know." He shakes his head. "Then most of the time they end up falling asleep leaving me to get them out of their clothes and cover them up." I smile a little, relieved that I'd got his statement so wrong. "It's not bloody funny, lady," he chastises, pulling me onto the floor with him and sitting me on his lap.

"I could be working up here or in the shower, they don't give a shit. They sprawl out on here waiting for me to finish up whatever it is I'm doing. It was their idea to buy a super king size. When I told them I didn't need one, they just laughed and bought in anyway while I was at work." I know his boys love him dearly from what he's told me about them and what they do for each other I can tell they are very close.

"I'm sorry, Vlad, for coming across as a jealous bi—"

"Don't," he says, grabbing my hand and threading our fingers together. "You don't need to apologise, that should be me. I didn't think before I spoke," he chuckles. "But I never do when I'm around you." His lips gently touch mine and I fall into him.

We pull apart breathless. "Are you hungry?" My stomach rumbles on cue.

"Yes, I could eat something," I say innocently but Vlad raises one eyebrow and that dirty smirk appears on his face.

"You are so filthy," I laugh, slapping him on his arm.

"I never said a thing. It's your dirty mind, woman," he chuckles, raising me to my feet. "Go, get your shower and I will bring breakfast." He smacks a kiss on my lips then turns me towards the bathroom and slaps my arse. I let out a screech and he chuckles again while slipping on a pair of boxers. "I will meet you there," he points to the middle of the bed, "in fifteen minutes. Don't be late," he states then stalks out of the bedroom, leaving me watching his fine arse and a back heavily coloured in ink showing a mass of skulls. Like his chest these tattoos are worrying to me and I know I will have to ask him why he has them. Sometime soon.

Twenty minutes later, I have had a shower and I'm wearing one of Vlad's T-shirts. We are both sat cross-legged, eating poached egg on toast and drinking a cup of tea in the middle of Vlad's bed. He has been telling me more about his sons. How and when they first moved here; Lucas was only six months old and Daniel was nine years. Lucas' cot was in here and Daniel had nightmares, so he would end up in here as well. Sebastian was fifteen and Nicholas was thirteen. Nicholas, was the one who could comfort Daniel and get him to smile which led him to be in here too. Sebastian would just stay because everyone else were in here. Once, they had all fallen asleep again Vlad would collect the baby monitor and go to sleep in the next bedroom. I had to laugh at his screwed-up face when he commented on the smell in his room after three boys and one baby had slept in it all night.

I understand a bit more now about his comment from earlier because it's not just his sons that like to have him around, his grandchildren too like to snuggle with him when they stay over. Knowing what it's like in Olivia and Jack's house – they have the same relationship with their children and Megan their granddaughter – I know I've missed out on the love of having my own children and the happiness they can bring. But, I'm happy for my friends and Vlad that they have experienced it.

We finish our breakfast and our tea. We must have worked up an appetite because there's not a crumb left between us. Vlad takes the tray and places it on the floor along with our cups then settles himself in front of me. He takes my hands in his and his dark blue eyes glaze over as they climb up my body. "My shirt looks good on you, sweetheart," he flirts. "You know what else looks good on you?" And before I have time to reply, my back hits the mattress while my head lands on the pillow. Vlad hovers over me looking like he's just caught his prey. His prey being me.

"Me." He answers his own question.

His lips catch mine and drag me into his lair while one of his strong hands trails up the back of my thigh until he reaches my bottom where he squeezes firmly. His other lifts the shirt, trying to take it off. My hands are in his hair and my legs wrap around him voluntarily. He releases my lips and continues his search down my neck. I cry out his name when he latches on to one of my erect nipples. He climbs back up to my mouth, kissing and sucking as he does. His glazed eyes meet mine and then there's an almighty ruckus at the door.

Vlad's body stiffens. "Fucking hell, I thought I'd locked the door," he moans.

Suddenly, the sheet comes flying over my naked body and Vlad tucks it around me, cursing what sounds like the, "Fucking nosy bastards." The door comes flying open and I hide under not just the sheet, but the quilt Vlad had picked up from the bottom of the bed.

"Hi, Paps," I hear one male's amused voice. The bed dips and I know that the body of the voice has just sat on it. Right next to my feet.

"What the fuck are you doing here?" Vlad's voice is raised but not in anger.

"We missed you," says another male voice. This one seems to come from the doorway.

"Like fuck you did, you set of nosy bastards," he chuckles. He's laughing at them while I'm stuck under the quilt, sweating and almost suffocating.

"Why are you still in bed?" asks the voice that is sat on the bed that seems to be now sprawled out with us. Oh, how humiliating. I'm laid under here naked and nearly got caught in the act by Vlad's sons; he wasn't joking when he said he has no privacy.

"Nicholas, get off the bed," Vlad says firmly. I can't see his face, but I can hear the sniggers coming from the door way.

"Why? It doesn't normally bother you," he pats the bed only it's not the bed, it's my legs. "Oh," says the voice that I know to be Nicholas now. "Are you hiding someone under there, old man?" he chortles.

"Sebastian, stop laughing at him and get him off my bed and downstairs before I beat the fucking lot of you." Vlad sounds a little stressed now and I'm sure they are trying to wind him up on purpose. I can hear the cackling of all three of them and I know if I removed the quilt from my face I would see them all bent over laughing at their father's expense.

I can't stand it anymore. It's too warm under here so I remove the quilt from my head just showing my eyes and nose.

"Hello," Nicholas says, giving me a little wave.

I pull the quilt a little further down. "Morning," I squeak out, looking at who I now know to be Nicholas. The smirk on his face matches his two brothers who are stood filling up the doorway while their curious dark blue eyes roam between their father and me. How I didn't realise that Sebastian was related to Vlad when Izzy was ill at the club I will never know.

Observing these three young men, you can see that they have their father's genes. The dark, intense blue eyes, face shape and jawline and height, all resemble Vlad. Nicholas and Sebastian are a slimmer build and slightly shorter than their father, but Daniel equals him in size and build. His hair is the only difference – thick, long and chocolate brown, tied loosely down his back. I'm sure if you stripped him down and put him in a loincloth he could double up as Tarzan.

"You must be the lovely Holly," Nicholas interrupts my study of them and thrusts his hand out for me to shake. His smile is cheeky and contagious which causes my right hand to venture from its hiding place under the sheet. Tucking the sheet safely around the top half of my naked frame, I place my hand in his.

"I am," I greet. "And you must be Nicholas?" I say.

"That I am. I'm sure the old man has mentioned me." He juts his chin towards Vlad and I can't make out what Vlad mouths to him, but a burst of laughter erupts from the doorway.

Nicholas springs from the bed like his arse has just caught fire, dropping my hand. "Urrr, please tell me you two were not…" He doesn't finish, just shakes his hand and wipes it on his suit trousers, his body letting out a little shudder.

"That will teach you not to fucking barge in, nosy little shit," Vlad chuckles, getting out of bed in just his boxers. I can only imagine what it was Vlad mouthed to him and my face heats up with embarrassment. I pick up the pillow and burrow my scarlet face into it.

"I'll go put the kettle on," Sebastian sniggers. Which I'm grateful for; at least one of them is leaving. Nicholas shakes his head at his father and stalks off towards the bathroom. Only to return a moment later with a towel in his hand, mumbling something about being hungry and going blind. He too leaves, and Daniel follows chuckling at his brother.

"Sorry, about them," Vlad says, sitting down on the bed at the side of me.

"What did you whisper to Nicholas?" I ask, I needn't bother because I know the answer.

"I said that this hand," he takes said hand in his, linking our fingers together, "had just been wrapped around my cock." He smirks. Taking my hand back from him I slap him hard on his arm.

"I cannot believe you said that, Vlad. I won't be able to look at any of them again without feeling embarrassed," I tell him as I try to climb out of bed.

"Aw, Holly, it was only a joke," he says, not even flinching at the slap I had just given him. I don't make it off the bed because he wraps his strong arms around me and pulls me into him where I find myself sat on his knee.

Nuzzling his nose into my neck, "He's a drama queen, Holly. I knew what his reaction would be, and he knew I was only messing," he says, kissing my neck. I can feel his smile.

"How am I going to face them…?"

"Don't worry. Get dressed while I have a quick shower. Then we will join them in the kitchen and I will introduce you properly." He places me on my feet, steals a kiss then saunters off towards the bathroom, leaving me trying to pluck up enough courage to face the chuckle brothers.

Thirty minutes later, I am being led into the kitchen. Vlad is looking very handsome in a dark blue pin-striped suit, light blue shirt and clean shaven. He smells exquisite; fresh and clean blended with the spice and woody amber fragrance of his aftershave. I could eat him.

He holds my hand in his and we join his sons along with Izzy, his daughter-in-law. She either was down here when we were invaded by the chuckle brothers or she has just arrived. Their heads are huddled together; you can hear the cutlery hitting the plates and low voices chatting. Izzy looks up as if she heard our footsteps approaching.

"Morning." Her smile meets her eyes. "Holly, it's great to see you again," she beams.

"What about me?" Vlad questions, leaning down, tapping his cheek with his finger. Izzy gently kisses his cheek.

"Morning, Paps." He gets an adorable smile. One that a daughter would save for a father she looked up to. It's obvious that he cares for her like a daughter.

"How were the younger brood this morning?" he asks, while pulling out a stool and motioning for me to sit down. He takes a seat at the side of me, placing his arm around me; he then starts stroking my waist. I fixate on Izzy as she speaks to her father-in-law, too scared to look at the three men who have stopped eating now.

"Oh, you know. Getting Rebecca to wear her uniform and not something that is princess related is a nightmare." She waves her hand around. "Then Joseph and Lucas decide that they wanted to play on the PS4 instead of getting ready for school. I had to threaten them," she sniggers. "I told them that I would wash and dress them if they didn't get a move on. That had the desired effect because once I strolled into their room with a wet sponge and towel, they soon got their little selves in the bathroom. And your son was no help." She elbows Sebastian in the side who was happily rubbing his wife's back. "As soon as these two," she points between Nicholas and Daniel, "text him, he was up and out of the door," she relays.

"I'm sorry," Sebastian says while rubbing his side. "But, I wasn't letting these two have all the fun winding the big guy up." He motions with his head towards his dad.

So, that was what their intentions were. They just wanted to get a reaction from him. Vlad chuckles and I can feel the stare of his sons burning into me.

Vlad passes me a cup of coffee then starts to speak. "I think it's time for introductions," he voices. "Holly, you have met my eldest Sebastian and his beautiful wife, Isabel." His hand motions towards them. They both greet me with wide smiles and Sebastian takes my hand in his.

"It's lovely to see you again, Holly," he welcomes. "I hope our little intrusion this morning," he points between his two brothers and himself, "doesn't put you off us. We're not a bad bunch." Watching his mouth curve into a smile that just pulls you in, I find myself loosening up a little. The way he snuggles into Izzy and has what I can only describe as love for his family in his eyes, makes me like him a little more.

"It's fine," I speak. "I think I've got over the embarrassment of being descended on by the chuckle brothers." I'm hoping they don't take offence to the nickname I've bestowed on them.

"Oh, I like her," Nicholas laughs. This gets a chuckle from Vlad and the rest of them.

"And, this is Nicholas, my second eldest…" Before he has chance to say anything else, Nicholas is off his stool and rounding the breakfast bar. He takes my hand.

"It is a pleasure to meet you, Holly. Anyone who can put that look on this grumpy bastard here," he slaps his father on the shoulder, "must have something special going on," he finishes.

"Cheeky bastard," I hear Vlad mumble. I turn towards Vlad and he just shrugs his shoulders at me with that naughty look on his handsome face.

I sit up straight on the stool that I'm perched on. "Thank you," I say. "But, you should see the look he holds when he mentions all of you," I tell them.

"Aww, we can only imagine," Daniel comments mockingly, winking at his father as he does.

"Moving on from Nicholas, we have Daniel." Vlad moves his hand and points at him.

Daniel's arms are meaty and very strong looking. I soon find myself enveloped in them being pulled into his hard chest. "Hi," he says and gives me a squeeze then lets go of me.

"Hi," I chuckle as I get myself settled back on the stool.

"Keep your dirty hands off my woman," Vlad's deep voice demands, as he wraps his arms around me, so my back is against his chest. Then he lowers his mouth to my ear. "You might want to disinfect yourself, sweetheart, you can't be sure where they have been. Or who they have been with," he whispers then places his chin on my shoulder. This gets raised eyebrows from his sons and Izzy looks at both of us with an amused expression.

"I will have you know, we were tucked up in bed by eleven o'clock last night," Daniel counters Vlad's comment, pointing between him and his brother.

"It's who was in your bed, that concerns me." Vlad's eyebrows raise in question.

"Nobody. You don't get to stay this handsome by burning the candle at both ends," Nicholas jests, pointing to his face.

I smile at the banter between this family. It's direct and to the point. Intrusive but with humour. It's also very loving and caring.

Once they stop laughing at each other we slip in to light conversation. They all chat about Lucas, Joe and Rebecca. Then get excited about Izzy and Sebastian's upcoming scan next week. Vlad discuses some project they have going on with some property they want to invest in. And, Izzy informs Vlad that she and Sebastian want to move forward with some changes to the club Aphrodite.

I'm shocked at this because the club seems to be a little gold mine and doesn't look as if it needs a makeover. My shock increases when Vlad suggests bringing someone in to help Izzy with fresh ideas. That someone being me. He tells them all about my experience working and turning a run-down bar into somewhere people wanted to be. I tell them that I don't think what I did at Micky's was on the same scale as Aphrodite, but they just wave it off.

All the while Vlad's arms stay holding me while his chin rests on my shoulder. Every now and then he lightly kisses my cheek. I see the look on his family's face, one of shock and amusement. But nothing is said.

That is until there's a prediction and a bet.

Nicholas sits up straight, stretches his back out then whispers into Daniel's ear. Daniel gives a nod. "I have a prediction," Nicholas announces.

"What is it?" his sidekick Daniel asks.

"I predict wedding bells." His hand points at his dad and me while there's a satisfied look on his cheeky face. The coffee I had in my mouth spits out all over my hand and covers the breakfast bar in front of me. I can't believe what I have just heard.

"Pardon me?" I choke out, my body sitting back, waiting for him to say it again just to make sure I didn't hear wrong.

"Ignore him, Holly," Vlad says calmly. "I think I dropped him on his head when he was a baby," he suggests. I think he might be right. We've been together less than two weeks. Izzy and his two brothers sit there, not fazed by Nicholas's foreseen prediction into the future.

Nicholas sits up straight and folds his arms over his chest and lifts his eyebrows at his dad. "If you remember, old man, I predicted," he punctuates, "these two to be married within a year. And I was right," he smugly says.

"I'll have in on that bet," Daniel says, putting his hand out for Nicholas to shake.

"Six months," Nicholas says.

"Eight months," Daniel haggles.

My eyes go back and forth between them both. "Are you serious?" I screech, laughing at the faces of two men that look nothing but serious when they shake hands on the bet.

"Ten months," voices Sebastian. Izzy sits there rubbing her hands together, her lips bunched up and a questioning look on her face. Her mouth smiles excitedly, and she rubs her hands a little faster together. "Oow, I'm in," she squeals. "But I say eleven months."

My mouth is wide open, and my mind is whirling when I turn to Vlad who is shaking his head, saying something in Russian that ends in 'fucking crazy'.

"I think I must have dropped all of them on their heads and she's just hung around with them too long," he says, his expression apologetic. "Don't pay any attention to their silly games, I don't." I nod my head at him because I'm sure it's their way of seeing if I can take a joke. Well, let's play them at their own game.

Watching the four of them place their hands out, piling them on top of each other, I reach forward and put mine on top. "Twelve months," I articulate, then remove my hand with a smile and a wink.

Vlad chuckles at my little banter and grabs his jacket off the stool he had set it on earlier.

"I think on that note it is time to get to work," he says, still chuckling. He collects my bag and coat, helping me on with it. "I'm dropping Holly off home and I will see you four in work," he declares. They all get up from where they were sat, Nicholas moving so he is stood at the side of me.

"We'll walk out with you," he says, smiling, then links my arm through his.

"What are you doing, Nicholas?" his father questions from behind us.

"Just walking my stepmother to the car," he answers, patting my hand. I don't look at his face because I know I will see a playful grin there if I do. And I can't help letting out a little snort of my own. Well, he is funny.

Nicholas turns his head to look at me, eyeing me with an inquisitive look on his face. "You're not wicked, are you Holly?" he asks, his lip turning up slightly.

"Only in the bedroom," answers Vlad, sniggering from behind us. I don't know whether to laugh at Nicholas or turn around and slap Vlad for his statement.

"He didn't just say that?" Nicholas laughs. "You know, it took Sebastian six months to catch Izzy." He shakes his head. "You really need to play a little hard to get," he chastises.

I'm taken from Nicholas's arm and Vlad takes my hand in his. "Piss off, Nicholas," he tells him as we get outside, and his son just pats his back. He tells me to have a nice day and hopes to see me again soon. Daniel follows suit. Then Izzy and Sebastian come to say their goodbyes. Izzy asks me if I want to have lunch with her one day this week. I tell her I'm meeting with my two friends tomorrow; Olivia and Sarah and ask her to join us. She agrees, we exchange numbers and I inform her I will text her later with the details.

I'm sat in the passenger seat of Vlad's car with my eyes closed and head resting on the seat when he climbs in. "Are you OK, sweetheart?" his concerned voice asks.

Am I OK? I don't know. His sons are just crazy but funny and lovable.

A giggle erupts in my throat and before I have time to answer Vlad's question, my shoulders start shaking violently. I can't hold it in. Big fat tears of laughter fill my eyes as I reflect on the last hour and a half. From the invasion in the bedroom. The banter between the chuckle brothers and their father. Nicholas' prediction and the bet which I'm in on. Turning to look at the man beside me who just took their antics as if it is all in a normal day's work, "Wow. Did that just really happen?" I snort out, covering my mouth while I take in the look of perplexity on Vlad's face.

"Yes, I'm sorry," he says, moving my hand so he is holding it. "They can be a little… much to take on." He tilts his head to one side then opens his mouth. "But, they are…" I stop him.

Wiping my eyes, I breathe in deeply, containing the amusement that had come over me.

"Wonderful… and charming," I say, thinking about our introduction in the kitchen.

"They are," he beams proudly.

"Caring and considerate," I add, remembering how Sebastian helped Izzy off her seat, not allowing her to bend down to pick up her bag from the floor, and Daniel clearing away the pots we had all been using.

Vlad nods his head in agreement then leans in and steals a kiss.

"They are funny and crazy," I add, letting out another snort.

"Aren't they fucking just?" He rolls his eyes which makes me giggle again. "Please don't let them know that you find them funny," he says, shaking his head. "It will only add to my despair." Taking hold of his chin, I run my thumb over his bottom lip then move in and take his mouth with mine. Our kiss is warm and inviting; Vlad's hands come up to cup my face. Once we have had our fill, we break away, our heads resting together.

"I'll try," I whisper, knowing fine well I will not be able to resist being in on their craziness and after this morning I don't think they will let me.

Chapter 20

Holly

Walking into the coffee shop where I had arranged to meet up with Olivia, Sarah and Izzy, I see my two friends stood ordering at the counter while Izzy is seated on one of the ox-blood red, two-seater leather sofas. She has a bottle of water in front of her and is typing something out on her phone. As I approach her, she looks up, smiling as she does. "Hi Holly," she says, trying to get up from the edge of her seat. I motion for her to stay seated and lean down to give her a hug.

Olivia turns and sees me as I stand back up straight, so I wave her and Sarah over. "Wow, look at you," Olivia gushes, her eyes drifting up and down my body. I look down at myself then back to her cunning face.

"What's wrong with me?" I query. And I fall for it every bloody time.

"Oh, nothing. But I love this new look on you," she purrs while running a hand around my face.

"What new look?" I know I haven't changed my make-up.

"Oh, you know. That look that's says, 'I've been thoroughly fucked,'" she chuckles. Izzy starts to choke on her water at my friend's crude comment. I pat her back.

"I can't believe you just said that, Olivia Anderson."

"Why? It looks bloody fantastic on you. Whatever the big guy and you got up to, keep on with it. You have a beautiful glow." She waves her hand around dramatically.

I look at Izzy when she covers her mouth. "OMG!" she squeals, shaking her head. Sarah just throws her eyes up at Olivia and shakes her head too.

"Ignore her," Sarah says. "You know she can't help it, she's not right," she continues as she pulls me into a hug. "But you do look different," she whispers in to my ear as she lets go of me.

And I probably do. I feel different.

Why?

Because of The Big Guy. He makes me feel cherished and desired. His constant touch, caress, the way he sees me as if I'm the only person in the room when it could be filled with hundreds. How his words can turn me wild with lust, wanting what he's offering.

"Hi, I'm Sarah," I hear my friend saying. I remember that I haven't introduced my friends to Izzy.

"And this is Olivia," I smirk. "And Olivia this is Izzy, Vlad's daughter-in-law." I raise my eyebrows at her, grinning like an idiot because I know my friend, who is loud and in your face a lot of the time, can also be mindful about stepping over the mark, especially when she doesn't know the person. The colour of her face tells me she is a little embarrassed.

"Oh, I'm sorry," she says, bringing her hand to her chest, giving me her death glare.

"It's fine," Izzy chuckles out. "I'm not used to hearing Vlad been spoken about in that... context," she finishes with another chuckle.

"Good," Sarah says. "Because with this one," she throws her thumb over her shoulder motioning to Olivia, "you never know what filth will fall from her mouth," she tells her while taking a seat. "It's nice to meet you, Izzy."

"It's good to meet you too, both of you," Izzy greets.

Olivia joins them, sitting down, placing her latte on the table.

"Would you like a coffee or tea, Izzy?" I ask her, realising I haven't got one yet.

"No thanks. I'm fine with water," she tells me, lifting the bottle from the table.

"OK," I say then turn towards the counter to order my latte.

When I sit back down, Olivia and Izzy are in full animated flow, discussing Rebecca, Izzy's daughter and Megan, Olivia's granddaughter. "Can you believe this, Holly?"

I shake my head at Olivia. "Believe what?" I query.

"Izzy's Rebecca and my little Megan are only in the same class at school. Isn't it a small world?" Her face beams as she pats me on the arm. "Aw, it's so sweet, they play together at school. Your little goddaughter and Vlad's granddaughter are best mates." She grins.

"How have you found this out? I've only been gone five minutes," I ask. It's then I recollect the last time I looked after Megan and how she was all excited about her friend Rebecca from school.

"Your man's just texted, Izzy. He's having the kids overnight, so they can have a night off," Sarah relays.

"Wow. Yeah, Megan mentioned her friend Rebecca last Wednesday when she stayed over, only I didn't know you then," I nod my head towards Izzy. "And I never thought when Vlad spoke about her that she was the Rebecca that Megan was telling me about."

"Well, as much as I love my children, I am so grateful to my father-in-law. If it wasn't for him, we would never get a break."

"Yes, it's very thoughtful of him," I muse, remembering our conversation when he phoned me this morning.

He had asked if we could meet up tonight for a few drinks and something to eat at his restaurant, I had to decline. I always pick Rebecca up from school on a Wednesdays and as much as I wanted to go meet Vlad, I was not going to let my little pumpkin down. I love devoting my time with her at my place or at Olivia's. However, with spending so much time with Vlad over the weekend plus Monday, I haven't seen any of them.

My phone alerts me to a text message just as Olivia speaks. "Are you still picking Megan up from school today, Holly?"

"Yes. Why wouldn't I be?" I question while taking my phone from my bag.

"I thought maybe you might have made arrangements with your new man," she says with an amused expression on her face.

"No. I'm still having her, she can stay overnight and I will drop her at school tomorrow."

"Thank you," she says, squeezing my arm with a warm smile on her face.

"Are we not eating?" Sarah asks. "I'm bloody starving," she says, rubbing her stomach.

"Yeah, I fancy one of their jacket potatoes with tuna-sweetcorn and salad."

"I think I'll just have a Danish pastry. I'm not that hungry," Olivia says, shaking her head.

"I could eat something spicy," Izzy says. "I know I'll suffer tonight with heartburn but it's a price I'll have to pay. This little one," she points to her stomach, "has had me craving all sorts of crap that I would never eat."

"Oh, I was like that with Jayden, my eldest," Sarah tells her. "The spicier the better. I went through so many bottles of Gaviscon that the chemist couldn't stock the shelf quick enough. Nick, my husband, swore blind his son would come out with pink hair," she grins.

Izzy decides on the spicy cheesy panini, with chips and salad; Olivia chooses the cinnamon swirl. Sarah opts to have the same as Izzy and I know what I'm having. I make my way to the counter to order our lunch while reading the text message I had got. Sarah is stood at the side of me and chuckles when I show her the message.

Vlad: Fancy a play date after you pick the little one up from school?

"He's keen," Sarah laughs.

"Isn't he just?" I smile.

I don't answer him right away. If I was going to take Megan on a play date with Vlad and Rebecca, I would have to ask Olivia first to make sure it was fine with her. We place our order then return to our table. As we sit down, I get another text message.

Vlad: We are making home-made pizza; the boys are helping; the kitchen will never be the same again.

"I hope he's not sending you dirty text messages," I hear Olivia comment.

Looking up from my phone, I see two pairs of inquisitive eyes. Izzy is covering her mouth. I know she is dying to let out another squeal at Olivia's remark who is already smirking at me. Sarah sits there with an impassive look on her face. She knows it's Vlad and what the messages are about. I decide to put Olivia out of her misery and pass her my phone.

"You better not be showing me obscene photos, Holly Spencer." She shows me her pointy disapproving face as if she's Little Miss Prim and Proper while taking the phone from my hand. Izzy shrieks.

"Please don't show that to me!" I can't help letting out a wail of laughter when she covers her eyes with one hand while holding the other one up to stop Olivia from showing her.

"Oh, how sweet," Olivia expresses, putting one hand on her chest. "Look, Vlad wants them to have a play date."

Izzy takes my phone from Olivia, peeking at it through her open fingers that are still covering her eyes. After removing her hand from her eyes and reading the short texts, she places her hand on her chest. "Oh, that is sweet. The girls would love that," she says, passing my phone to Sarah. "I know Rebecca would. Poor kid, she's always stuck with the boys. She'd love to have her school friend over for tea," she beams.

"Aw, poor kid. C'mon Holly, text him back. Tell him you would love to join him, making pizza with the kids," Sarah states.

I wouldn't mind taking up his invitation, but I have someone else's child with me which means it's not my decision. "You don't mind if I take Megan, Olivia?" I ask her.

"Not at all. She never gets to spend time with her friends either, she'll be made up."

"What about Jack?"

"He'll be fine, Holly. She normally spends Wednesdays with you anyway. If she's with you he'll be OK," she tells me, shaking her head.

"OK," I say, grinning a little. His kitchen is out of this world and I can't wait to be able to use his multi-function double oven.

Our food arrives, and we slip into light conversation. I enlighten them to Vlad's kitchen, how it was the same as the one I had wanted. Izzy backs me up on all the appliances being state of the art. They continue conversing, both Olivia and Sarah, asking Izzy questions about her husband, children and the job she does at the club. I'm happy to see my two close friends making her feel comfortable within our little circle.

Once we've finished eating, Izzy sits back in her seat and rubs her swollen stomach.

"Hmmm, I enjoyed that," she says.

"So, did I," Sarah agrees.

"So, Holly," Izzy says, "are you interested in helping me with some ideas on how I can change Aphrodite?"

"What's this?" I hear in unison. Olivia and Sarah sit there waiting for me to inform them on Izzy's question. They both sit up a little straighter and give me a questioning look. One that says, 'What have you not been telling us? And you better tell us quick because we're a pair of nosy buggers.' I shake my head at them, grinning as I do.

"When I was out with Vlad last Saturday, I told him about when I had worked at Micky's…"

"Oh, fun times," Olivia breaks me off, her face lighting up with a wide grin. "And what do you mean 'worked'?" She slaps my arm. "You didn't just work there, you ran your little arse off to bring that run-down bar into a place that people wanted to spend their evenings enjoying the music and entertainment," she exclaims.

"Yeah, if I remember rightly, you thrived on the challenge to make it a place where all ages could enjoy their evening or weekend out," Sarah adds.

"I know. But Micky's was run-down, old and ready for closure. It wasn't that hard to do it up and bring in different bands for entertainment or organise the food, it just needed money spent on it. Aphrodite, is… well it's…" I stumble for words because I can't think for the life of me why they would want to alter anything. "I can't see why you would even consider changing the place, it's high-class with a lively, playful and erotic theme." I shake my head at Izzy.

"We are not wanting to change the décor or furnishings. We just want other ideas to bring in the customers and while I don't mind doing research and marketing," she points to her small bump, "this is going to get bigger, and I'm going to get tired, so I could use the help with moving forward with this before all the students we hired part-time finish," she tells us.

"What do you mean 'finish'?" I ask. Olivia and Sarah sit listening carefully.

Izzy sits forward, leaning on the table and opens her phone. She types something into it then leans over to show me. There's lots of data names, dates… "Eighty percent of the staff that work between Aphrodite and Eruption are students and seventy percent of them finish their degrees in the next few months which leaves us very short on dancers and bar staff," she tells me, putting her phone back on the table. "When we appointed the dancers just over two years ago, they were all given lessons on the poles and stage. We brought in a professional who choreographed a lot of routines then they practised in their spare time and added to them. It's hard work."

"I can imagine," Olivia says. Sarah agrees.

"What's the problem? Can't you just higher new staff?" Sarah takes the words out of my mouth.

"We could," Izzy replies. "We should have started advertising already so we can get them interviewed and trained up… But to be truthful we want a change."

"And, that's where you need the help?" Olivia asks.

"Yes. Like I said, new ideas, new themes. If we need to change some of the layout of the club, we can bring in the builders. So, I need someone who can be an all-rounder. Come up with ideas, do the marketing, if the room needs redesigning, so be it. We don't mind closing for a short time if we need to refurbish." Her phone chimes with a message which halts our conversation when she picks it up to read it.

"Sorry about that, Sebastian is outside waiting for me. We have a dentist appointment." She scrunches her face. "We need to pick the kids up early from school."

"OK," I say. The mention of her children reminds me that I haven't texted Vlad back yet.

"Maybe we could meet at the club tomorrow and talk some more?" she asks, tucking her phone in her overly large bag and slinging it over her shoulder.

"She'll be there," Sarah answers for me. I throw my eyes up at her and shake my head. My friends can't help but meddle in my life. "What?" she asks. "Come on, Holly, you know you will enjoy the challenge."

Olivia puts her hand on mine. "Why not meet with Izzy, have a look around? Get a feel for the place without your beer goggles on and take it from there." She smiles at me.

"I have to shoot," Izzy says. "We'll be dropping Joe and Rebecca off at their grandad's about three thirty then we will probably go home get changed and go out for something to eat. You can text me or phone anytime if you want to meet up," she states.

We say our goodbyes to Izzy then she hurries out of the door, leaving my two friends looking at me with amused expressions on their faces.

"What?" I ask, knowing they both have something to say.

"Nothing." Olivia is first to speak. But her eyes twinkle with amusement. "New man. New job. New life." Then putting her elbow on the table, she rests her chin in her hand and raises her eyebrows at me. "Just saying," as she shrugs her shoulders.

"I know what you are thinking Holly," Sarah comments, sitting up straight on her seat.

"You do? Well please enlighten me because if you're thinking what I am then you know it's a bad idea." All I can think, is that it's a little like déjà vu meeting my ex Rob then landing a new job, didn't turn out very well.

It's as if they have read my mind. "Vlad is not Rob, and this is a job you know you will enjoy, Holly." Olivia interrupts my doubts.

"There's no comparison. That man has it bad for you and you him. Take him up on his offer for a play date, speak to him about the job and then decide," Olivia finishes.

I look at my two friends; they always have my best interest at heart. I should have listened to them years ago and not married Rob. And I know Vlad is nothing like him. My ex never made my heart race with just the thought of him or turn me into a puddle on the floor with just one look. One smouldering look. "OK," I decide. "You're right. I won't get anywhere without taking a chance," I tell them, taking my phone from my bag and texting my man.

Holly: See you at four, I'll bring ice-cream x

Chapter 21

Vlad

My home is like a mad house. Holly and Megan arrived two hours ago and as soon as they entered through the front door the noise became a health and safety issue. I'm sure the noise pollution people would pull the plug on my sons and grandchildren.

"Megaaaan!" was the start of the noise. My granddaughter got overly excited when her best friend from school came walking through the door. The screech was so loud it set the dogs barking next door; when I say next door, our nearest neighbours are five hundred yards down the road. Once she calmed down a little, she asked Holly if she was Megan's mum. Holly informed my little soprano that she was Megan's godmother which sent her into a whirlwind, dragging Megan to her room to find a wand, a crown and wings to dress Holly up. Holly, being the fun-loving, caring person she is, took it all in her stride and squeezed into the child-size wings, placed the tiny gold crown on her head and stuck the sparkly wand in her back pocket. After I chuckled at her, my little minx whispered to the two plotting princesses who had changed into Cinderella and Ariel; they both scooted off again, giggling. Ten minutes later I'm wearing a pair of Minnie Mouse ears, the tip of my nose painted black and black whiskers are streaked across my cheeks. Apparently, Holly had said we need a mouse because there's a mouse in Cinderella.

Lucas and Joseph were respectful and polite when I called them into the kitchen to meet Holly and Megan. Joseph dropped his control pad for the games console onto the settee, and vaulted over the back of it. Once he spotted our visitors, he said hello, gave a little wave and raced back to his game. Lucas said hi to Megan and put his hand out for Holly to shake with an, "It's nice to meet you," then joined Joseph back on the settee. I had told them they had thirty minutes before we put the topping on the pizzas, so the girls had gone off to play in Rebecca's room and the boys were enthralled in some racing game. This gave me half an hour to get my fix of Holly. I really needed to taste those luscious lips.

We were stood in the kitchen when I placed my hands on her hips and pulled her into me. Her body warm and inviting, she's everything I didn't know I needed. The smell of strawberries invade my senses and I can't help but burry my nose into her hair, inhaling her sweetness. Moving from her hair, my mouth goes straight to its addiction – her lips. I steal a quick kiss then go back for seconds. Once we're locked together our tongues say hello and my hands roam from her hips around to those firm cheeks of hers. Holly's hands are on my chest then stroke up to my shoulders, one of them snaking around my neck where she ever so lightly runs her fingertips up and down the nape of my neck. A growl escapes from my throat which all too soon ends our moment. Holly pulls away from me and shakes her head. She looks up at me then her eyes dart across the room towards the boys who are too engaged in their game to notice us. But I understand. I don't want her getting embarrassed if they were to turn around, and spot us kissing like two teenagers.

I take her hand in mine and we sit at the dining table where Holly proceeds to enlighten me about Izzy's job offer. I can see she has reservations. I'm not stupid. I know she's worried about helping Izzy and Sebastian out and our relationship. It was my idea that they asked her. But, I get the feeling she doesn't want history repeating itself. Not going to happen. I might own Aphrodite along with my son and his wife, but I leave the entertainment to them. I don't get involved, unless they ask. We don't have time to discuss it though because we're disturbed by Nicholas and Daniel. They got wind from Sebastian, the traitor, that Holly was coming over and we were making homemade pizza.

The laughter from my two idiot sons when they see what Rebecca and Megan have got us wearing, fills the house. Lucas calls to them to play on the game with him and Joe. He enjoys challenging them; he beats them every time. Both Holly and I sit at the table watching my sons and grandson interact.

Within minutes of them setting up to play a new game, there's cheating going on. Nicholas picks up one of Megan's paintbrushes and snakes his arm behind Lucas, brushing the soft bristles over his ear. He then sits back as if he hasn't done anything. This distracts Lucas as he scratches at his ear like a dog with fleas. Holly turns to me and chuckles out, "That's mean." I tell her to watch because I know it doesn't matter what they do to distract him, he will still win. He continues to take his turn, getting to the end of his seat to focus better. He loves kicking his brothers' arses.

He stands, shouting, "Take that!" and continues battling against a three-headed monster. Lucas sits back down on the edge of the settee and Nicholas leans around him again to tickle his ear. He brings his arm swiftly back and runs down his leg as if he is dashing something off it. Daniel chuckles when Lucas rubs at his ear again; this gets him suspicious of his brothers and he turns to eye them both. He curses when he flicks his head back to the screen and his man is on the floor. He hasn't been defeated but he needs to use one of the artefacts he has collected to get him out of shit.

Holly taps her fingers on the table and I can see mischief written all over her when she reaches out and grabs a handful of grapes from the fruit bowl. She turns to me, popping one in her mouth then offers me one. I place my lips on it and suck it in. She has two more and before I've even swallowed the grape she gave me, she has launched one across the room and hit Nicholas on the back of the head. The purple grape bounces off his head and onto the floor. He turns to look behind him while Holly and I sit at the dining table, holding hands and trying to suppress our laughter. He squints at Holly when a chuckle escapes her but turns back to the game.

They play the game for a further fifteen minutes trying to distract the poor kid. Joseph is oblivious to them trying to sabotage Lucas. Between coughing and burping noises, he just giggles at them. Lucas leaps up from his seat again. "You can't beat the master, take that!" he shouts. "And that's why I'm the champion," he sings, dropping his controller on the floor and jumping in the air. He then proceeds to grab one of the scatter cushions and beats Nicholas with it. "Even with your feeble attempts to distract me, I still beat your score," he says then snatches another cushion and hits him with that one. Nicholas can't do anything for laughing. He's curled up in a ball while Lucas continues to smack him with the cushion.

Joseph jumps up to help Lucas and before you know it there's an all-out war going on in my living room. Two grown men are getting the shit kicked out of them by a nine-year-old and a twelve-year-old. To be fair Nicholas and Daniel can't do anything for laughing at the two boys who are putting their heart and soul into trying to knock Daniel on his arse. He dropped to his knees to help them out which was stupid of him because Joseph slung himself around his back and tried to choke hold him. It wasn't long before the two big kids of the family had had enough and dangled both Lucas and Joseph by their ankles to try and get them to give in. Calling, "Enough, it's time to make pizza," was all that was needed to stop them and get their attention.

*

Time has whizzed past since Holly arrived. When I look at my watch it's quarter past six and I know my woman will be going in half an hour. She said she wanted to be home by seven, so she could give Megan a quick bath before her bed time.

We've all eaten, and everyone helped to clean up. The noise calmed for a short time while we were eating. Well, apart from the noise coming from my sons who you would think had never been fed. I swear they were doing it on purpose. I'm sure animals on a farm eat with less noise. Every time I glared at them they just sniggered at me. I apologised to Holly for their rudeness, only she found them very amusing and chuckled every time she saw me give them a look. Then we had them winding up not one little princess but two. And oh, can they act like little divas. They had them both crossing their chubby little arms across their chests and stamping their feet. Screeching and screaming at the top of their voices when Daniel pulled their pigtails and Nicholas stool their crowns. Putting one on his head and giving the other to his side-kick. The fucking idiots don't know when to stop.

After getting the girls all riled up they left. Lucas and Joseph went to the living room to watch a film and we were left to calm down two four-year olds who still had more energy to get rid of. Holly took them both upstairs to Rebecca's room and came back down ten minutes later smiling. She assured me they were calm and had got them drawing pictures for Megan's mum and grandparents and for Sebastian and Izzy.

Pulling her into me, I nuzzle into her neck, just staying like that for a few minutes. "Thank you," I whisper.

"What are you thanking me for?" she asks as she wraps her arms around me.

"Oh, I don't know," I answer, shrugging my shoulders and looking into her warm sparkling eyes. "You probably had a nice quiet evening planned at home with Megan and instead you had to put up with—"

"The chuckle brothers," she laughs.

"The chuckle brothers?" I question.

"Yes, they're funny. Your family are fun to be around. They make me laugh," she smiles.

"They're a pain in the arse."

"No, they're not," she says as she playfully slaps me on the chest.

"Oh, they are. I love my sons very much, but they know how to play me." I pull her further into me but it's not enough. I know she's uncomfortable having Lucas and Joseph sat across in the living room even if they are consumed by the TV. "Come." I put my hand out to her and she takes it.

"Where are we going?" she questions.

"Lucas," I call out.

"Yeah," he answers, without taking his eyes from the TV.

"Listen out for the girls, I'm just going to show Holly the office," I say, desperate to have a few minutes with my angel in my arms.

"OK," he says.

I lead Holly out of the kitchen and down the narrow corridor that leads to the office, gym and the spare room where Sebastian and Izzy sleep when they stop over. I quickly point out each room and practically shove her through my office door. I round my desk, keeping hold of her hand. "In a hurry?" she asks.

"Yes," I answer firmly, sitting down in my chair and lifting Holly into my lap.

She chuckles at me, but I quickly turn it into a moan when I latch onto her lips with mine showing her how much of a hurry I was in to get her alone.

Our kiss is passionate and wild, and I find my hands feeling their way around her curves. I want to rip off her clothes, lay her out on my desk and run my lips, tongue and hands around every part of her gorgeous body. Listen to her moan and shout 'yes' while I keep her on the edge. Then fuck her into next week as she screams out my name. After we have our breath back I would carry her up to my bedroom and do it all again. Only I know we can't. Hesitantly, I break our kiss. Holly looks at me; her hair is wild, I must have had my hands tangled in her locks. Her lustful eyes hold mine and she is breathless. I love kissing the hell out of her. She always looks shocked as if she can't believe that she could get so high from just a kiss. But if she feels half of what I'm feeling then she must be floating in outer space.

Her head leans on my chest and we sit there in complete silence just listening to the peacefulness. Holly's hand is on my chest and one of mine strokes over her hip bone. I wanted to discuss her reservations about working with Izzy but right now I'm happy just holding my woman in my arms.

Chapter 22

Vlad

"How many cups of coffee have you had?" Sebastian asks, chuckling at me.

"Fuck off!" I spit out at him. He knows I don't mean it but I'm out of my mind this morning.

"Too fucking many by the looks of him," Nicholas interferes.

"He's very jittery," Daniel says, as I stand, pick up my phone, sit down again only to get back up and stride towards the window.

"He's on his fourth cup," Frank tells them. "In the last two hours."

"I am here," I say, trying to calm my racing heart down. "You don't need to talk as if I'm not," I tell them, sitting back down and rubbing my chest.

I'm not good with too much caffeine, it gives me indigestion and makes me anxious. Although I know this, I've drank my body weight in the stuff this morning.

When I telephoned Holly last night after she had left my home and got Megan to bed, I promised her I would not interfere between her and Izzy. It's their call if they want to work together, they don't need me, they have Sebastian if there's anything that needs checking over. Saying that, my little minx strolled in here at nine thirty, looking like the business woman of the year. She sported a two-piece dark grey suit. The skirt only reaching mid-thigh. A lemon fitted shirt, cut low. Her customary high heels and if I'm not mistaken a pair of stockings. And the worst thing is she has not bothered calling into the office to see me. No, not even to say hello or give me a good morning kiss.

"What's his problem?" I hear Daniel ask, as I rest my head on the desk and moan.

"Holly's in the building with Izzy, has been for the last three hours and he needs his fix of her," Sebastian tells him, chuckling at my expense.

After my number three son has stopped giggling like a little girl he says, "Shall I go ask them both to join us for lunch? That way you don't look needy." He stands there, hands in his pockets, waiting for me to answer.

I lift my head off the desk and look at him with pride because it's probably the best suggestion any of them have had all morning. But, I don't want to share her time with my sons today. I'm greedy when it comes to her, I need some time alone with her.

"Thank you, Daniel, but that won't be necessary." Standing, I crack my neck and stretch my back out. "Does anyone need the bathroom?" I ask, pointing towards the bathroom that has a shower and some items of clothing of mine. They all shake their heads. "Good. I'm going to go shower and change." I look down at my shirt that looks as if it's been through the ringer. "Then, I will go see if the girls want to grab a late lunch. You lot are not invited," I tell them, pointing between the four of them. I know Izzy will take the hint and leave us on our own. These bastards wouldn't. They would stay to wind me up.

Just as I'm stalking off towards the bathroom door, Frank calls out, "She's a good lass, Vlad old boy. You might want to keep her close…"

"Don't, Frank," I warn. I'm in no mood to listen to him or my sons take the piss today. They're all quiet for a few seconds but as soon as I close the door behind me, the laughing starts. Wait until it's their turn to fall in lo… And that's when I realise what this is. This feeling that has me going fucking crazy.

I watch Holly from one of the back tables. I've been sitting here with a glass of water in front of me for the last ten minutes.

After I had showered, I changed from the shirt and trousers I was wearing into a pair of black jeans and a polo shirt. As much as I wanted to stroll over, take her in my arms and kiss the hell out of her, I didn't. Her laughter caught me unawares, like it did the first night we met. So, I've sat here studying my woman from afar.

I watch as she throws her head back, laughing at something Izzy is telling her. Her eyes twinkle with amusement and her mouth turns up to show an impish grin. They are both animated when they speak, Holly throwing her arms around, causing her shirt to rise and show off her lightly tanned, soft skin. She takes my breath away. She reaches over the large round table to collect some paperwork, her left leg coming up behind her as she does. The short skirt she is wearing has a small slit at the back and I get a good view of her inner thighs. I'm so fucking glad my sons are not around. My heart rate ups at the beauty of her and I can't stand it any longer. I need to get to her.

I reach her just as she's zipping up a plastic wallet containing the paperwork they had been doodling on. My arm snakes around her waist and I pull her into me. She lets out a little squeal then turns her face to mine; her eyes gleam with humour. Without hesitation, my lips attach to hers, taking what they have wanted for over three hours. I don't care that we are not alone, if Izzy is uncomfortable she can avert her eyes.

The hunger for each other is poured out in this one kiss. It's so intense, we both moan at the same time. We are in the wrong place for what this kiss should lead to. But I can't stop it yet. I'm like a starved animal. Needing to feed. And Holly is my meal.

She places her hand on my shoulder and squeezes, pulling from me. I reluctantly let her and place my forehead on hers. There's just us. Breathless and ravenous for more.

We stare into each other's eyes while we catch our breath. I need to keep Holly close to me because my manhood has made a very large appearance and I really don't want to scare Izzy off. I'm hoping she has had the good sense to piss off and give us this moment alone.

I pull her into me and she lets out a giggle. There's a glint in her eyes. She's laughing at me. She can feel I'm in pain and she is highly fucking amused.

"Hi," she grins, biting on her lip to stop her laughter spilling out.

"Hi," I groan.

"Are you OK?" she asks, her lips twitching over my discomfort.

Am I OK? No. I would be if I could throw her over my shoulder and carry her off to my office, clear my desk and feast on her. And that is what I would do if my fucking sons were not in there.

I nod my head at her, unable to speak. I'm not sure I can form any words.

"Are you sure, because you look a little flushed there, Vlad?" She continues to goad me.

Oh, my little minx has found her naughty side which I enjoy extremely. I groan again, pushing my groin into her, letting her know what kind of pain she is inflicting on me.

"Hmmm," is her response. "It feels very painful," she chuckles again and kisses my cheek as she tries to pull out of my hold. I don't think so. She wants to poke the bear then she better be ready for its bite. I lower my mouth to her ear.

"Don't push me, sweetheart," I whisper, hoping she'll take up the challenge.

She swallows hard before she looks me straight in the eye, her lip curling up into a mischievous grin. "Why?" she goads.

Oh, she did not just say that. Her flirtatious banter tells me Izzy has long left us. Turning around to check, I don't see her and that's all I need.

I pick Holly up, throwing her over my shoulder. "Vlad, put me down," she squeals playfully.

She wiggles on my shoulder and kicks her legs. "I don't think so, angel, and keep still." My hand comes down on her arse and she lets out a squeal again.

"Stop!" she shouts while holding the back of my T-shirt.

"No." My voice is low.

"Where are we going?"

"You will see," I say, kicking open the door to one of the dancers' changing rooms. None of them are here and I know there's a lock on them. I close the door behind us and turn to drop the latch. There's just Holly and me.

I sit her on one of the dressing tables, manoeuvring myself between her legs. Her skirt hitches up and I can see the tops of her stockings. My hands run up her thighs. Her breath quickens, and she wets her bottom lip with the tip of her tongue when I stroke my thumb over the dampness of her lacey knickers. She's so ready for me. I lean in to take her mouth. We both moan on contact as we drink each other in. "Vlad," she mumbles against my lips.

"I need you, Holly," my voice husky and low.

"We can't," she utters, but still wraps her legs around me. Oh, I think we can. She's had me on edge since I watched her on the cameras saunter into the club. Keeping me waiting, then teasing me until any restrain I had left snapped. Yes, this is happening. Here and now.

"You can't walk in here wearing these," I run my hands over the lace at the top of her stockings, "or a skirt, this short." I brush the skirt further up until it's bunched up to her hips.

One of my hands travels up her shirt; my fingers make quick work of snapping the top button open. "Putting these on show." She gasps when I lean down and kiss the swell of her breasts that I've just uncovered. Her eyes are closed when I lift my head back up to face her.

"Open your eyes, Holly," I command. She obeys, showing her need for me. "Strolling in here and not coming to see me." I shake my head in disappointment, tutting. "Not nice, Holly," I whisper into her ear, giving it a little nip with my teeth. She gasps and grips the tops of my arms.

"I thought you would be busy," she says softly. Placing my fingers on her chin, I lift it and move my mouth to hers, so our lips are just touching.

"I'm never too busy for you, angel," I tell her, then steal her mouth again. This time our kiss is heated to the point of being combustible. She pulls my T-shirt out of my jeans and rakes her fingers across my bare back. My cock twitches on high alert, pressing up against her core. I need to be inside her, feeling her wrapped around me. "Put your arms around my neck, Holly." She tries to lift my T-shirt off but is struggling. I help her out then she wraps her arms around me, placing her face into my neck. Quickly, I place my hand under her and lift. My other hand goes straight for the lacey material that is barely covering her. In one swift movement I rip it off, tossing it on the floor. There's a sharp intake of breath from Holly and I chuckle as her eyes widen in shock.

My heart beats faster as Holly's hand trails over the bulge in my jeans. She reaches for the button, but her hands are shaking which causes her to fumble.

I step back slightly, to help with my restriction, then faster than the speed of light, my jeans and boxers have set me free.

There's no need for foreplay, we both need this now. I thrust deep inside her. "This is going to be quick, angel," I growl as I feel how she clamps around me. She moans into my shoulder then lifts her flushed face. I hold us there for a moment while we stare into each other's eyes. Everything about this woman, leaves me astounded. From her shy smile to her impish grin. How she embarrasses easily then says something that would make a builder blush.

She's such a contradiction.

A contradiction that has me spellbound. One that I crave for every minute of the day. One I want to cherish and never let go.

She's mine.

I pull out and slam into her again, causing us both to moan out loud. Holly's hands grip my neck as I continue to thrust in and out as my lips latch onto her neck. Her hips push towards mine, wanting me to quicken the pace. I know I'm not going to last long. I need her to be with me when it comes. My lips nip at her neck while my left hand seeks out her breast. She lets out a little whimper as I twirl the hard bud between my fingers.

She moans again and strokes the nape of my neck when I lift her off the dresser with one arm under her. Bringing her closer has a desirable effect because I can feel her tighten around me. The shock at the bottom of my spine lets me know I'm almost there. "Holly, you need to come, sweetheart," I whisper. She shudders in my arms.

"Oh my god, please don't stop," she pants. Not a cat in hell's chance that is happening.

Holding her with one arm I lean her over slightly and place my fingers on her clit as I keep on burying myself deeper. She screams and bites into my shoulder. My balls tingle and tighten when I feel her erupt in my arms, the pulsating of her dragging my orgasm out of me. "Fuck!" I roar, unable to hold back the intensity that she stirs inside me. I collapse on to my knees, keeping tight hold of the angel in my arms.

We shudder together and let out another moan.

Her face is buried into my neck when I roll onto my back, laying Holly on top of me. We're both breathless and sweaty when she lifts her head, to look at me.

The smile on her beautiful face fills me with elation and has me wondering how I have existed without her. She runs her soft hands up my stomach then lowers her head and kisses my chest.

Her feathery light kisses are tender. With every one that she places on my chest I feel light headed. Her lips are tracing over the broken pieces of my heart, fixing it back together.

And she has.

Every time I have looked into her gem-like eyes, held her tight within my arms, she has taken a piece and started to rebuild it until there's no more pieces left. It's whole again and it's all hers.

"Better?"

Her sweet voice brings me out of my thoughts. "Huh?" My revelation has me flummoxed.

"Do you feel better?" she chuckles as she sits up. I feel the disconnection straight away and reach for her, bringing her back into my arms.

"Much," I say as I nuzzle into her hair. We lay there for a few minutes, content with silence.

"Maybe we should get cleaned up," Holly breaks into the quietness.

"Do we have to?" I groan. I'm happy to just lay here with Holly in my arms. I know the floor's clean. This place is thoroughly cleaned every day after it's been used.

My little minx pulls away again and lets out a little chuckle. "I can't believe I've had sex in a club." She blushes as she gets up.

Instantly, I'm up off the floor, intrigued. "First time?" I query. Holly nods her head at me. She's pulled her skirt into place and adjusted her shirt. Placing my hands on her hips, I lower my head, nipping at her bottom lip. I love the fact that she hasn't been too sexually active and that I'm the one to break her club virginity. If I have anything to do with it I will be breaking many more. "Let's get cleaned up," I say, pointing her in the direction of the bathroom.

I follow her in and we clean up together.

"Vlad," she says, standing in front of me with one hand on her hip and the other one holding out her shredded knickers. We are out of the bathroom now, back into the dressing area of the room. I close the space between us, taking the scrap of silk from her and tuck it in my jeans pocket.

"Thanks," I say, smirking then adding a cheeky wink.

"Vlad," she stomps her foot, "I cannot go out without any underwear on," she scowls.

"Of course you can, sweetheart, people go commando all the time." I step back to put my T-shirt on. Holly tilts her head at me and then she scowls, giving me an evil eye. This is one I haven't seen from her before and I let out a chuckle.

"Oh, you think it's funny?" she grumbles. "Well let's see how funny you would think it is if I did this outside."

"Jesus, Mary and Joseph," I groan. My little minx has turned, giving me her back then she bends over, showing me her bare arse. "Why would you wear a skirt that fucking short?" I ask, adjusting my groin that's enjoyed the show very fucking much.

"Because I didn't expect to be knickerless," she argues but has a gleam in her eye. She knows I'm not happy about the belt she is wearing.

"But you would wear it knowing if you had to bend over anyone could get a flash of your underwear?" Before she has time to respond I'm in front of her, holding her by her hips. "Are you trying to kill me?" My hands move around to her bare bottom where I take a firm hold.

"Vlad, you are overreacting. I would not be bending down for anything." She places her hands on my chest. My caveman brain has kicked in and is crying out for me to throw her over my shoulder and hide her away in my cave. I don't want any man looking at her beautiful body and thinking any lewd thoughts of her. She's mine.

My thumbs smooth over the silky bare skin of her arse then both hands travel up her body. "This," I say as my fingers caress her skin, roaming up past her breast then to her face, "is mine," my voice is low and hoarse. Holly swallows but does not say anything. "No one sees or touches... I don't want men ogling what is mine," I state.

Holly stares into my eyes, not saying a word. For a moment we just stand there silent and when I think I fucked things up, she blinks then nods her head at me. "Holly," I whisper, tucking a loose piece of her hair behind her ear, "I need you to understand, I don't share, and I won't allow any man to try and take what's mine. Do you understand me, sweetheart?" I know my words will make her think twice about being with me but that's something I will have to deal with if she refuses to give me what I need. Knowing how I feel about this woman, that she drives me fucking crazy, to the point I become anxious if I can't get my fill of her, it will be one of the hardest things to give up.

Holly still has her eyes glued to mine when she nods her head at me. The breath I had been holding comes out in a rush and I close the distance between us. Not that there was much space between us anyway. "Holly, I need to hear you say it." I sound desperate, I know.

"Yes," she whispers.

"Yes, what, Holly?"

"I'm yours," she whispers. I pull her into my arms, burying my face into her hair. Inhaling her sweet smell.

"Thank you," I breathe into her hair.

"Vlad."

"Hmmm?" I'm content just holding her here in my arms.

"It has to be the same for you too," she says.

"What do you mean?" I question, pulling myself from her hair and holding her hands while I stand in front of her.

"You have to tell me you are mine." My lips move straight to hers, until they are just about touching.

"I've been yours since the first night we met, sweetheart," I utter. Then I show her in a kiss just what she does to me and how much I'm hers.

We break away from our kiss, breathless, and in the knowledge that we both need each other.

My stomach rumbles, reminding me that I haven't eaten and that I came down into the club to invite Holly to lunch. There's also the fact that she is still knickerless. "Come, let's find you some underwear then we can grab a late lunch," I say.

"I'm not wearing someone's cast-offs," Holly argues.

"We have brand new ones in the lockers," I tell her, chuckling as I open one and start rummaging through. Holly stands at the side of me, making faces every time I pull out a pair of frilly knickers. "Holly, they're all new. Look, they still have the tags on," I show her. She takes a few pairs from me, scrutinising them, screwing up her face then tosses them to one side.

"Them," she points, "they'll do."

"They're shorts, Holly," I say, passing them to her.

"Yeah, but they will cover better than the dental floss you keep choosing. I thought you didn't want any one seeing my arse?"

"I don't." My voice is almost a growl. Holly holds up a black pair of knickers I had picked out. They look fine to me until she turns them around and there's a piece of string. They're sexy as fuck and Holly would look fucking fantastic in them. But now is not the time. "I get your point," I say and toss the shorts back to her. She giggles as I shake my head at her then pulls the tags off them before she shimmies into them. Once she's ready, I take her hand and lead her out of the club and towards my restaurant.

We've only been in the restaurant twenty minutes. Our lunch has just arrived, and we were in the middle of discussing plans for the weekend. "There you are." The voice of my son Sebastian travels across the restaurant, causing some of the patrons to look around. "We've been looking all over for you two." He appears at the top of the steps and I have picked up on the we which tells me he is not alone. I've no sooner thought it when the rest of the brood join him at the top of the stairs.

"Oooh, lunch," Nicholas greets as he rounds the table and steals one of Holly's chips.

"You're not eating with us. Go grab yourselves a table," I tell them.

"This is our table," they all say together. Izzy has just appeared and is smirking at me.

"Vlad," Holly says, slapping my thigh. "Don't be mean," she chastises.

Looking at Holly, how she doesn't mind sharing her chips with Nicholas, how she laughs at his witty humour and daft jokes. At my sons who want to spend time with this woman, who has become everything to me. I count myself lucky.

Nodding my head to my boys and Izzy, "Sit, please," I smile.

"Great, I'm starving." Sebastian cosies up to the side of me, picks up my knife and cuts my steak sandwich in half. "Hmmm." He devours it. "I'll order the same and give you your half back." He continues to chew on my lunch. "I've been craving one of these all day," Sebastian grins and winks at Izzy who just shakes her head at him.

Holly sits there laughing at my boys while they steal chunky chips from her plate.

Daniel beckons over the waitress to take their order. Once it arrives my sons are happy and eat with passion while they laugh, joke, and chat about anything and everything.

Holly's hand is on my thigh with mine placed on top of it. She notices me watching them all interact together and rubs my leg a little. It's her way of telling me she's happy to be here. I can't help but lean into her and kiss her cheek.

Sebastian leans over to speak to Holly, finishing his meal and throwing the napkin on his plate. "I hear you had a very productive morning, Holly," he says.

"Yes, we did. Well, I hope we did anyway," she relays, smiling at him.

"Good, I'll look at your suggestions tonight," he tells her as he stands.

"Thanks," both Izzy and Holly say together.

"Well, are you ready?" he says to Izzy, picking up her zip wallets and folders. She nods at him and Daniel and Nicholas get ready to leave as well. "Oh." Sebastian turns to me. "I've invited Lucas to stay with us tomorrow night," he tells me with a gleam in his eye.

"Thank you," I say, giving him a fatherly smile. I fucking love him, he's always forward thinking and I'm happy he's thought about my love life.

"You are welcome, Romeo," he smirks, slapping me on the shoulder.

"Yeah, you really don't want cock blocking by a twelve-year-old," Nicholas verbalises, shaking his head with a straight face. Holly starts to choke on her water, while Izzy laughs so hard she needs to excuse herself, so she can get to the ladies' before she has an accident. My other two sons nod their heads in agreement with him. And I just sit there, open mouthed rubbing Holly's back.

I'm about to chastise my twenty-six-year-old son when Holly swipes him playfully round the back of the neck. "What was that for?" he asks, rubbing the stinging area while frowning at her.

"Mind your manners, Nicholas," she scolds him and it's my turn to laugh now because his expression is one of a mischievous child who's just been told off by his mother in front of his friends. It's priceless.

"Sorry Mum," he jests and scoots out from his seat just as Holly is about to prod him in his side.

I'm still chuckling at their playful banter as they all say their goodbyes, telling us to enjoy our date night. I think my mischievous son has met his match with my woman.

"Up for a date tomorrow then, Holly?" I ask, grinning while I place my arm around her shoulders.

"Well I don't see why not. It would be rude not to use our free pass." She smirks and winks at me. God, I love this woman.

Chapter 23

Holly

Vlad has brought me to a charming little Chinese restaurant. It has the usual décor of red and gold lanterns hanging from the ceiling. Brass dragons are sat along the partitions that separate the snug little booths and there's a rather large bronze Buddha stood in the middle of the floor. The staff are friendly, and the food is mouth-wateringly delicious.

I would have easily stayed at home, snuggled up with Vlad on the couch, watching TV, but Vlad wanted us to go out for something to eat then snuggle and watch TV.

After our bunk-up in the dressing room yesterday and Vlad getting his knickers in a twist over my lack of knickers as well as the too-short skirt I had been wearing, I concluded my man is indeed the something in my life that's been missing.

The fire and passion in his eyes, draw me in with such a magnetic pull, I feel light headed and dizzy with just one of his sexy winks. His touch ignites a desire in me that I've never known. How he strokes my skin with feather-light fingertips, bringing it to life from a long dormant sleep. Sparking electricity when his teeth graze and nip my flesh, the surge travelling to my core with such force and power, I feel as if I could light up the whole city.

His strong masculine arms hold me close and tight while his words tickle my senses. Nothing and no one has ever made me feel so needed and wanted. And I know his needing to hear me say, "*I'm his,*" should make me pull back a bit. The intensity in his dark eyes, should be a warning that I should keep him at arm's length. But it doesn't. I feel the same.

My birth mother showed no real love or affection towards me, discarding me like an old dish cloth so she could live her life. Men and drugs were her thing and there was no room for a small child.

My adopted parents cared for and loved me, giving me a safe and calm environment to flourish in. Only to be ripped from my life before I had even finished school.

My friends and their parents, Ivy and Jay, took me in and created a whole new family life for me but there was still something missing. Even with good friends I still never felt I belonged. The pub I worked in from eighteen years of age until it was sold without warning, seven years later, had kept me busy. Working long hours there and carrying on with my education dragged me out of the two-year loathing of the world I had been in after losing my parents.

Meeting Rob my ex-husband, and the offer of a new job had me believing that my life might be on the up. Only my loyalty to him was thrown back in my face when he deceived me, leaving me feeling lost and hurt all over again.

Ivy once told me that things happen for a reason and maybe I had to go through so many losses before I could find true happiness, and maybe she was right. Because right at this moment that's how I feel.

Happy, for once in my life. I feel I belong.

After Vlad's sons and Izzy had left us at the restaurant yesterday afternoon, we discussed our plans for the weekend. I hadn't planned anything special so when he asked me to join him tonight and stay at his for the weekend I jumped at the chance. Tonight, is our night until lunchtime tomorrow when Sebastian will drop Lucas off home. We will spend the rest of the day and the evening together with Vlad's youngest son. Then on Sunday, Vlad needs to work. He told me he always goes into the office early Sunday, staying until about two o'clock to attend to paperwork. That's fine with me, he will drop me off home and I can get on with looking over the notes and ideas that I had suggested to Izzy. Mrs White will be coming over to Vlad's on Sunday so that Lucas isn't alone, and Daniel or Nicholas will drop in to spend some time with their youngest brother.

I've yet to ask him if he and Lucas would like to come to a barbecue on Sunday afternoon. Olivia phoned this afternoon when I was getting ready for tonight and packing my bag. When I told her I was spending the weekend at Vlad's, she was more excited than me. So much so she put me on loud speaker. Jack, her husband, was very happy with himself, that I had listened to his lecture four weeks ago and started to enjoy myself. He was also very intrigued about Vlad and couldn't understand why I had not yet took him to meet him. Hence, the barbecue. Because it is May Day on Monday no one has work so Sunday afternoon is ideal for a get-together. I told them I would ask him tonight when we met up only I haven't had the chance, yet I wanted to talk to him about taking Lucas somewhere he will enjoy.

I don't know much about him other than he likes playing video games and he plays football for the local club twice a week. We've sat here for over an hour, eating our meal and trying to come up with something that is acceptable for a twelve-year-old. Vlad suggested a football match or just stay at home playing video games all day. Screwing my face up, with his recommendation, I don't fancy staying in all day or standing in a football stadium listening to the supporters curse at the players. My ideas were: bowling, go-kart racing or a drive to the coast. Vlad just shrugged his shoulders at me, telling me that he wasn't sure what Lucas would want to do. Best thing would be to leave it until he arrives home tomorrow and let him decide.

"Are you having a dessert?" Vlad asks over the noise of a very loud man that I think has had far too much to drink. It's only eight o'clock, a little early to be drunk. The man is with a group of men and women that look like work colleagues. A few of the women in the party have been giving him funny looks while one of the men has told him to shut the fuck up. Vlad's eyes shift to the drunk who is now trying to drag one of his female co-workers up to dance. She bats him away and he falls onto his seat, slapping the table with such force the glasses shake.

This isn't the type of establishment to behave in such a way and a few of the customers who have come out for a romantic evening or to enjoy a fine meal have started to complain.

Vlad, turns back to me. "Have you decided what you are having for dessert?" He takes my hand in his.

"No." I shake my head at him. "I'm stuffed. I don't think I could eat another thing," I say, rubbing my stomach. We've both had hot and sour soup for starter followed by duck in plum sauce. Then, various dishes for main course which we shared. I think salt and pepper king prawn, sweet and sour chicken Cantonese style, shredded beef in sweet chilli, noodles, rice and chop suey rolls is enough to feed me for the rest of the weekend.

"OK, sweetheart. I'll get the bill."

"You might have to get a crane to lift me," I puff out, leaning back in my chair. Vlad chuckles at my over-exaggeration and leans in to steal a kiss. "Can I use your gym in the morning? I'll need to get rid of these few pounds I've just accumulated," I ask as I pull away from his addictive lips.

"Hmmm." He gives me that hooded look. "You are perfect the way you are, angel, but I wouldn't mind watching you getting hot and sweaty." His husky voice seduces me. Making me quiver with need for him.

"You're such a flirt, Vladimir Petrov," I tease, slapping him on the chest and running my nails down to his abdomen.

"I know," he whispers, "but you love my kind of flirting," then nips the lobe of my ear. We need to leave this place and quick before he starts with his dirty talk because I might just create a whole new version of 'When Harry Met Sally' here at this table.

"Get the bill, I need to run to the ladies'. Then we're out of here, big guy." I jump up quickly, leaving him chuckling at my urgency.

Urgent to get back to the table so we can get out of here, my expectation running high of another mind-blowing night of Vlad's hot, muscular body entwined with mine, I'm out of the ladies' in two minutes flat. I swing past the bar, eyeing my man stood up at our table chatting leisurely with the manager. Not watching where I am going, my foot becomes entangled with something laying on the floor at the side of one of the tables. I can see myself stumbling and I know my hands and knees are going to take the brunt of the fall. *Oh, shit.*

Before I have time to connect with the polished wooden floor an arm snakes around my waist, pulling me up and spinning me around so I'm faced the opposite way in which I was going. "Wooh, there, gorgeous. You didn't have to fall at my feet to get my attention," slurs the voice of the arms that saved me from an embarrassing situation.

"What?" My shocked brain is dizzy, I've been spun around that fast. Focusing, I realise this man is too close, I can smell strong whiskey on his breath and there's a bit of what looks like seaweed stuck between his teeth. I try to pull out of his grasp, but he just pulls me closer to him, placing one of his hands on my arse. "Get off me!" I yell, my hand coming up to try and push him away only my hand lands on fresh air.

"Take your fucking hands off her!" I hear roar as I see the man who was just stood in front of me lifted into the air and thrown on to the bar.

Vlad has one hand around the man's throat. The whole restaurant has now become silent as they watch the drunken man that had been pissing everyone off, going purple in the face. Both his hands try to prise Vlad's fingers from around his neck. It's in vain. Vlad's grip is deathly. The muscles in his arm have expanded and show strength of a very powerful man. Dark blue eyes have now turned black. His expression is fierce. Like an angry bull ready to charge, his nostrils flare and the snarl that appears looks as if he's enjoying seeing the man struggle for breath. I need to stop him before he ends up choking the man.

"Vlad!" I screech, but he doesn't hear me. "Vlad!" I shout again; even the manager and a couple of the man's friends are shouting for him to let go. Our words don't penetrate through, it's as if he's so transfixed on hurting this man he's gone deaf.

My body has started to shake at the violent act that is happening right in front of me and I feel light headed but I know I need to pull myself together and stop this.

I walk over to Vlad, my hand quivering as I place it on his bulging bicep. "Vlad, let him go." My voice is soft but firm. I feel him twitch which tells me he has heard me. "Vlad," I say again. "Please let him go," my hand running up and down his arm. Slowly, his fingers unwrap from their hold and the man falls to the floor, coughing and gasping for air.

I bend down, checking that the man is OK and we're not going to have to deal with the police. I know he saved me from falling but that doesn't give him the right to grope me. And that is what has got my man looking murderous. The man has got his breath back and looks as if there's no lasting damage. I turn to look up at Vlad but see that he is now storming out of the restaurant.

Once I'm outside, I look up the street to where Vlad parked the car. His hands are braced on the roof and his head is bent down. He doesn't hear me when I call his name, so I pick up my speed to get to him. As I approach him, heels clicking the pavement, his head turns towards me. I'm shocked to see he has not calmed down yet; even though his eyes are not fixed and deathly black any more, there's still a steely look to them.

"Vlad," I whisper, placing my hand on his arm. I'm not sure what kind of reaction I will get from him. I don't think he would physically hurt me, in fact I know he wouldn't, but the look of him is telling me to be cautious. "Vlad," I whisper again. This time his eyes close and he breathes in deeply through his nose. His eyes open and I can see he's almost back with me.

Gently, I rub his arm again. "What was all that?" My voice is calm and soothing as I point back to the restaurant where he has nearly throttled a man one handed without batting an eyelid.

I should be scared at what my man turned into. I should be shocked at what he nearly did. I should be shouting at him and making him explain why he had to resort to such a violent act.

I know he has a past. I don't need a clairvoyant to tell me that the man I have fallen for has a history. I see it. Scrawled across his body in full colour. In his dark blue loving eyes, how they change to stony cold, intense and dark. But, I also see the caring, loving father, adoring grandad and the affection he holds for them. I also see the tender side of him when we're together. The desire in his eyes speaks in volumes and how he worships my body when we are together, we become one. His love for the people around him is in abundance. The richness all consuming.

"What?" The sternness of his voice tells me he is anything but calm.

"You need to calm down, Vlad. You could have killed that man."

"Calm down?" His body tenses as he takes my arms and manoeuvres me so my back is pressed up against the driver's door and he's stood in front of me. "Calm down?" he says again. "That man had his fucking dirty hands all over you and you expect me to be calm!" he bellows, causing a passing couple to flinch at the loudness. Placing my hand on his chest, I push him a little to try and get a little space between us. But he doesn't budge.

"You don't need to shout, Vlad, I was there." His breathing is heavy as he puts his hands on my hips. Bringing his mouth close to mine, he shuts his eyes and inhales deeply again. I know he's trying to rein in his anger.

"Have I not made myself clear, Holly, that you are mine? I do not share, and I will not..." He takes a deep breath again. "I will not stand by while another man tries to grope you. Do you understand me, Holly?" His eyes search mine for reassurance that I do understand, and I do. I would not be happy if some drunken floozy was mauling him, but I wouldn't try to strangle her.

"I understand, Vlad," I say, nodding my head. "But, you need to calm yourself. You could have hurt him and ended up locked up—" I don't get to finish.

"Don't defend him, Holly," he warns. "He is very lucky I didn't snap his scrawny neck." His jaw tightens, and his face is flush.

"I'm not defending him. If you had not grabbed hold of him when you did he would have been wearing my hand print across his face and probably had my heel jammed in his foot," I tell him. Vlad's hands come up to my face and I see a glimmer of the man I have fallen for as he glides his thumbs over my cheekbones.

His lips skim mine, causing a sensation to travel through my body. This is the man I want. The one who is tender and loving, not the one I saw back there in the restaurant. I don't ever want to see his handsome face take on such a hard, cruel look again.

"Vlad," I whisper against his soft lips.

"Hmmm," he mumbles.

"I don't want to ever see that side of you again," I tell him, shaking my head.

He nods at me then takes my mouth again and I can feel him growing hard as he deepens the kiss. I don't stop him. I let him have his fix.

When he breaks away his mouth travels across my cheek and to my ear. "What I need is you." His voice is low and layered with sexual desire.

I swallow, seeing the animalistic look in his eyes, making my legs turn to jelly and my heart rate skyrocket. "Get in the car, Holly," he demands.

For some reason the dominant sound of his husky voice strokes over my skin, sending a sensation to every nerve ending, exciting and arousing me, and I have no other choice than to follow his order.

He takes my hand and leads me to the other side of the car. Once I'm sat comfortably in my seat he leans in to fasten my seatbelt; he can't help himself from taking my mouth again.

He does not mess about getting us back to his home. We pull up outside and Vlad exits the car and is round to my side practically dragging me out. He races us both to the front door, where I pause. "What's the rush?" I smirk.

"Holly." He tugs gently on my arm as he opens the door. I don't move.

"Holly." He tugs again, and I can't help but let out a chuckle at his desperation. I don't know why I'm not hurrying through the door with him, ripping at his clothes, because I'm as desperate as him.

Vlad is in no mood for games as I am lifted off my feet and thrown over his shoulder. I let out a little squeal as he slaps my arse. "You deserved that," he moans.

"What for?" I chuckle.

"For wasting precious time, woman." Then slaps my arse again.

We make it through into the enormous entrance where I don't even get time to kick off my shoes.

I'm pinned up against the wall with Vlad's big body covering mine. His mouth attacks mine, his tongue wanting, seeking out its playmate. I don't hesitate in letting him in. Our tongues thrash and tangle together while my hands roam up his back to his neck. My fingers lightly run over the nape of his neck and I swallow the growl that erupts from his throat.

Vlad thrusts his hips, his erection rubbing against me. It's my turn to let out a little moan as it massages the sensitive part of me that's crying out for him.

Vlad breaks our kiss and we're both panting. "I fucking need you now," he states as he buries his face into my neck, nipping away while his hands are around my back pulling down the zip of my dress.

"Yes!" I cry out as he pulls my dress down to my waist, lifts the cup of my bra and ravishes my nipple. He sucks, bites and licks and I'm climbing him like a tree, the intensity too much.

He holds me under my bottom, my legs wrapped around him when I feel his other hand fumbling with his trousers.

He lowers me to the floor and pushes up my dress, with one swift movement my knickers are torn from me and flung across the room. Then he places his fingers against my heat as he latches on to my neck. My hand seeks out his hardness where I palm it, running my thumb over the tip. I hear a sharp intake of breath then his hand is holding mine as I'm lifted one handed again. He directs both our hands that are wrapped around him straight to my entrance. This time it's not slow or gentle. It's hard and it's fast and it's what he swore it would be the first week we met.

I rip at his shirt and one of his arms come up to help me remove it as he thrusts in and out frantically, still supporting me with his other hand. My fingernails score his sweat-soaked back as the sensation builds and builds. I'm not sure I can last much longer as I feel the quivering deep in the bottom of my stomach. His kiss is frenzied and when he swivels his hips I can't help but let out a loud moan. My arms are wrapped around his shoulders tightly and my hands delve into his hair. I tug at it and push my hips towards his, meeting with a swivel of my own. He growls and moans and moves his lips to my ear. "You nearly there, sweetheart?" he pants, still thrusting in and out like well-oiled machine.

"Fuck. Yes!" I scream. Vlad chuckles at my profanity and to be honest I find myself laugh because I've never felt this good. Sex has never been this intense or raw.

Vlad continues with his drive to take us both over the edge and within seconds we're both toppling from the highest of summits. Vlad's body stiffens and shakes in my arms as he roars out his climax. I'm wrapped around him afraid to let go as my pleasure tears through me with such power it leaves me week and dizzy.

Thank God for the wall behind me, as I think Vlad's having trouble keeping up straight. He has us both pressed against the wall, our foreheads resting together. Both of us panting like we've just ran a marathon. My arms and legs are tired and so am I. I know it can't be any later than ten but I'm ready just to fall into Vlad's bed and stay there until the morning.

*

I think Vlad had realised how tired I was because I'm just waking up in his bed. His side of the bed feels empty and when I reach out for him there's no sign that he's been there. Looking at the clock, I can see it says two fifteen. I lay there for a few moments, relaying in my head what happened after we had come down from our high. I remember him carrying me up the stairs, his face nuzzled into my hair. Then him undressing me, taking off my crumpled dress that had been scrunched up around my waist. My knickers were already gone, ripped off in the throes of passion, and my bra had been tossed somewhere as we continued with our pursuit to become one. I remember him tucking me into bed and him climbing in, cuddling into my back, his arm and leg spread over me while he whispered that he was sorry for his behaviour earlier in the restaurant.

I must have drifted off then because I don't remember anything else.

There's a rattle of something across the room that gets my attention and when I sit up I can see the door to the rooftop patio is slightly open. I climb out of bed and slip on my dressing gown that Vlad must have unpacked from my bag. The bag I had packed for the weekend was left in the boot of his car when we arrived here, too eager for other things. As I near the door there's a light on outside; it's dim but you can still see what's out there.

Soundlessly, I open the door and step out onto the cool floor. There's a small table and one solitary chair. A sun lounger lies next to it. Potted plants and shrubs line up around the edges. Fixed to the wall is a heater and I can hear the swishing of the tall trees in the garden. The railing that runs across the length of the patio is painted satin black, gleaming in the moonlight. And there stands Vlad.

He is leaning on the railing, elbows resting on the metal while he holds a small glass in his hand. His back is bare, and I can see his tattoos clearly as well as the scratch marks I made earlier. The muscles in his back flex as he moves slightly. I watch him roll his neck then take a drink of the clear liquid in his glass. He's stood there in nothing but a pair of black shorts and his body would be the envy of men half his age. From his broad shoulders, muscular arms, thick solid thighs, you can see he works out and takes care of himself. "Are you coming out? Or are you just going to ogle the goods, angel?" He smiles as he turns to see me.

I pad across and into his open arms. "I thought I had been quiet and you didn't know I was there."

"I didn't hear you," he says, passing me a drink from his glass. I take a sip and grimace. Neat vodka is not my thing. "I felt you," he whispers. I know what he means. There's a charge in the air whenever he is near. He feels it too.

"What are you doing out here?" I ask, nuzzling my face into his chest.

"Thinking," he answers, rubbing his hands up and down my back.

"What about?"

"You. Me. Us." He kisses my head and then lifts my chin so we're looking at each other. "When I first saw you three weeks ago, when we danced, and I held you in my arms, I knew you were special." He strokes my hair and kisses my head. "I knew I would never be able to let you go and I don't ever want to." He breathes in deeply.

I nod in agreement because the feeling was the same for me, still is.

"But," he pauses. "But, I have a past... A past that has fucked with this." He points to his head. "And, fucked with what's in here." He taps his chest where his heart is.

His eyes look sad and lost. This larger-than-life man, intimidating, tattooed and scarred, looks scared. I could cry for him.

My fingers swirl around his bare chest, circling the tattoos. "These," I tap his chest, "are part of your past." It's not a question, I know they are.

"Yes," he agrees.

"When you're ready you will tell me about it?"

"Holly," he pleads. "My past is dark, full of hurt, greed and deception. You. Your..." He shakes his head. "You don't need to hear or see what I have seen."

"You think I'm weak," I cut in.

"No. I don't want to tarnish you with my past. I don't want you to look at me differently and if I told you, you would," he murmurs, stroking my cheek.

I shake my head at him because we all have a past, things we are ashamed of, and whatever it is that has him scared we will deal with it together. "Vlad, we can't always control what life throws at us. Our pasts, whether they are good or bad don't have to interfere with the present or the future. Let them go," I say, reaching up and kissing the side of his mouth.

He nods at me, letting me know he will try.

"You will have to be patient with me, Holly. I'm going to fuck this up." He points between us both.

"I won't let you," I tell him, and he smirks at me.

"Good, because I don't want to lose you."

"You're not going to lose me. I'm not going anywhere. Why do you think this?" I ask.

"Tonight. That idiot in the restaurant. When he touched you and when I saw your face, you looked frightened. A red mist came over me and I had no control. If I hadn't had heard your voice, felt your touch, I could have—"

"Stop," I tell him, putting my finger to his lips. I know what he was about to say, and I don't want to hear it. "Do you know why you felt that way?" I ask him.

"Yes. Like my family, you are in here." He taps his chest again. "I have fallen hard for you, Holly, and I will protect you fiercely." He doesn't say the three little words but it's as good as. My heart skips a beat and my stomach flips with excitement. "And, like any hot-blooded male, I don't want any man touching my woman and you are mine," he states. He pulls me into him and ravishes my mouth and I let him. Comfortable with the knowledge that I am his and he is mine.

He breaks our kiss and cups my face. "But," his eyes blink and his head drops, "it scares me that one day I will lose you. Someone will try to take you away from me and I won't be able to control myself, my emotions; the anger and hurt will consume me. Eat away at me like a piranha devouring raw flesh and that comes from my past." He shakes his head.

I'm just about to speak when he puts his finger on my lips. "Please, don't ask me to explain it, Holly. Maybe one day I will but not now," he begs.

"OK." I nod. "Just so you know, though, I'm not going anywhere. You're stuck with me," I joke, trying to lighten the intensity of this conversation.

"Good," he smiles. "Now let's get you inside. You must be freezing." He looks down at my feet then his deep blue eyes roam up my body. "And I plan to warm you up," he says as he sweeps me up in to his arms, stalking towards the door that leads us back into the bedroom. And just like that, all the anguish of the night is forgotten.

Chapter 24

Vlad

"Morning, beautiful," I whisper, placing my lips on Holly's.

"Hmmm," she mumbles, stirring from her sleep.

I've been awake for the last hour, happy to just watch the woman in my bed sleep peacefully.

Grateful, that she is still here. After last night, I wouldn't have blamed her if she walked away.

My over-the-top performance in the restaurant should have sent her running, but it didn't. Although, some people may think the guy deserved it, me included, some may think a quick punch to the nose would suffice. But, there's nothing like watching a man's face drain from colour when he realises he could be snuffed out any moment and believe me, I would not have been letting go if I had not heard Holly's soft voice or felt her gentle touch. Not that I'm proud of myself. I'm not. Last night just verified for me what I already knew. That I love this woman who is currently sprawled out like a starfish, and that I become crazy when I see any man touch her.

Most men would. No man wants to see their woman mauled by another man. I wish someone would have told my wife back then, then maybe I wouldn't be as fucked up as I am over this woman.

It's not Holly's fault. She doesn't flaunt her beauty, her body, for every man to look or take. She doesn't have to. Her beauty starts within and oozes out through her sparkling sapphire eyes. Her radiating smile, beams brightly. In the warmth of her touch and how she forgives so easily. When she speaks, her ability to calm the most savage of beasts and how she laughs, filling the air with her presence. My angel.

I should let her go, push her away, but I can't. I need her like I need to breathe. I know, I will fuck up and she'll walk. And I will have to deal with the onslaught of my own wrath. Or, maybe I won't. Maybe this woman was sent to me to give me peace, love and forgiveness.

"What are you sat there thinking about?" Holly's soft voice asks.

"I'm thinking your breakfast is getting cold and so is your bath," I tell her as I snuggle in to claim her mouth. Once I've had my fill, I let her up.

"You know you could wait until I've brushed my teeth before you shove your tongue in my mouth," she moans, dashing down the bed sheets as she sits up straight.

"Nah, not happing, sweetheart. I've been awake an hour waiting for that," I say, going in again and nipping her bottom lip. She groans then giggles and slaps my arm. "Do you want your breakfast? Or have I slaved over this for nothing?" I exaggerate, putting the tray on her knees. There's chopped-up melon and strawberries which I know she likes. A bowl of her favourite cereal, hot buttered wholemeal toast and a large coffee.

"Wow, I hope this is for two because I can't eat all of that." She points at the food on the tray her eyes large. Maybe I've gone a bit over the top. There's two large bowls, both the size that Daniel uses. One with the cereal, the other with the fruit, and four slices of toast cut into halves.

"I could help you out," I grin, pulling out a spoon from the pocket in my shorts.

We share the breakfast. It's intimate and something I've never experienced before; sharing breakfast in bed is a first but with the woman I love, it feels right. We even share the oversized pot of coffee.

"Oh, I forgot to ask you," Holly says after she has swallowed a mouthful of toast, breaking the comfortable silence. She takes a drink of our coffee and then wipes her fingers on one of the serviettes. "What time do you finish work tomorrow?"

"Why? Do you want to take me on a date?" I joke, wiggling my eyebrows. She grins.

"What if I do?

"Well, angel, I would say I normally finish around two but could be persuaded to finish earlier if you have better plans." I take the tray from her and place it on the floor. Then I scoot over to the side of her and lift her into my lap. She doesn't struggle, she just gets herself comfy. "What do you have in mind?" I ask, stroking her thigh. Before she has time to answer, I add, "But if you're after getting into my boxers, angel, it's going to cost you, I'm not a cheap date." I can feel her shoulders jigging up and down and when she lifts her head from my chest to look at me, I can't help but pout at her. Her giggling increases, causing her eyes to water. She tries to rein in her giggles, but it just gets worse when she tries to speak. A mumble of jumbled words spills from her. "Pardon me?" I say, joining her with her bout of giggles. She takes a couple of deep breaths and contains herself.

"Wow. And here's me thinking you'd give it up for a trip to the local chippie and a bottle of beer." It's my turn to laugh now.

"Throw in a battered sausage and I could be persuaded." I throw her a cheeky wink.

"Stop," she says, slapping my arm and still laughing. "Otherwise, you'll end up distracting me and I'll forget to ask you again."

"OK. What was you going to ask?"

"Would you like to come to a barbecue tomorrow afternoon?" Her eyes hold a pleading look for me to say yes. She must know I will go anywhere she wants. "Lucas, Sebastian, Izzy and the kids are invited. And the chuckle brothers too," she says, smiling. I love that she has given two of my sons a nickname and that they are all invited to this barbecue.

"Whose is it?" I ask.

"Olivia and Jack. They want to meet you and your family. I've told them a lot about you."

"All good, I hope."

"Of course," she says as she kisses my chest.

"OK. Lucas will come but I will have to ring the others to check. I'm not sure what their plans are for tomorrow afternoon. Go have your bath. You will need to top it up with hot water, and I will go ring my sons," I tell her as I stand us both up, dropping my lips to hers, before I let her go.

She sashays off towards my dressing room, wearing one of my T-shirts. As she reaches the doorway, she turns. "Did you fetch my bag from your car last night?"

"Yes. Your clothes are hung up in there." I point to the room where she is stood. "And your toiletries are in the bathroom."

"Oh, OK." She stares into the over-large, walk-in-wardrobe. "Did you do this while I was sleeping?" Her hand waves around.

"Yes. Last night. When I couldn't sleep." I get up and join her in the doorway, observing the outfits she had brought with her that are now hanging up alongside mine.

"It's rather large." Her eyes sparkle as she views the room. Her eyes then fall on me and I can't help but lower the tone.

"So, I've been told," I chuckle as I lower my gaze to my crotch.

She slaps my chest playfully. "Go make your calls and get your mind out of the gutter." Her expression is full of amusement. I pull her into my arms, breathing her in.

"I will go and call my sons, but you better be out of the bath when I return," I warn her as I place her hand on my crotch. "Otherwise, me and my rather large friend will be joining you." Her eyes lower. That lovely blush creeps up her neck and onto her face as I turn and stalk out the room, happy with myself that I can still bring her shyness to the forefront.

When I return half an hour later, she's out of the bath and is just finishing getting dressed. My calls took longer than I thought they would do, then Mrs White rang to let me know she would be around tomorrow about eleven. I told her that Holly might still be here. I was hoping she could hang around here then when I return from work we could go to her friends' together. Mrs White was ecstatic that she would get to meet Holly. She's heard a lot about her from my sons and me but has not had the opportunity to meet her yet.

She grins at me, when she notices me leaning against the wooden door frame, watching her. "If I had waited any longer for you to wash my back, I'd have shrivelled up like an old prune," she says as she fastens up her jeans. Her smell engulfs the room. The scent of strawberries and peach mingle together as the sight of her in my room fills me with the need to always have her here. I can't believe I have missed the chance to sink into a hot bath with her. If I have my way, we will be sharing many baths and showers.

"Sorry, I couldn't get Lucas off the phone. He likes your idea of go-karting and will be home within the hour," I tell her as I sit on the bed, patting my knee for her to sit on. I can't help myself, I need to have her touch when she's close and crave it when she is not around.

Holly doesn't keep me waiting as she settles herself on my knee and puts her arm around my neck.

"Good. It will be fun," she says. "I haven't been go-karting since Jackson was a young teenager," she gushes.

"Jackson?" I query.

"Jackson is Lucy's twin brother. Olivia and Jack's eldest." She looks at me as if I should know this. I don't. Lucy is Megan's mum that I know, didn't know there was a twin.

"OK," I say.

"We used to go at least once a month before I got married then our little thing got less and less until we stopped going altogether," she sighs, putting her head into my chest. I can feel the tension in her body. I know something about her last statement has made her sad. I want to cheer her up, but I also want to know why they stopped going. I lift her chin, so our eyes meet.

"Why did you stop going?" I ask. She's quiet for a moment before she answers.

"Rob, my ex, didn't like taking Olivia and Jack's kids out and would moan at me for spending so much time with them." She lets out a little snort. "He said my friends were taking the piss and were just after a free babysitting service. What a dick. And what an idiot I was for giving him over ten years of my life." I can't help but hold her a little tighter and try to comfort her. I get the impression she gave up a lot for him and got nothing in return. I'm not going to judge, and I don't want to hear his name mentioned again. She's angry with herself, I can tell that, and it's my job to put that beautiful smile back on her face.

"Hey." I kiss her head and smooth her hair back off her face. Her eyes lift to mine and hold so much emotion. "Forget about him and the past, Holly, it's not worth beating yourself up about."

"Yeah, I know. My friends have told me many times. I just wished I had listened to them a long time ago."

"Well, for the record I can't wait to go go-karting with you and Lucas or anything else you want us to do together. I also think I'm going to get along well with your friends." I chuckle at myself because when did I start giving a shit about what people think of me?

She chuckles too. "You're right, you will get along. Olivia and Sarah already think you're fantastic and they've only seen you once. As for their husbands, yeah, you'll get along just fine." She rolls her eyes.

"What's that supposed to mean?" I ask. My fingers delve into her waistline then run up the side of her ribs. She lets out a squeal and jumps from my knee. She doesn't get far. I have her thrown on the bed, pinned under me before she has time to call my name.

"Vlad, stop," she giggles and now I have my Holly back. I nuzzle my face into her neck and keep my fingers on her waist. "Tell me?"

"Caveman," she chuckles out. "You're all cavemen," she says when she's contained herself. That, I can live with. I don't mind throwing her over my shoulder and I don't give a shit who's watching. If I need to stake my possession by growling at other men, then count me in because this woman is mine and I will do anything to keep it that way. I will also do anything to keep that beautiful smile on her face.

My lips take on hers fiercely and we're lost in each other for a few moments. When I pull away, there's that happy, content look back. I know the one very well, it's the one I've been wearing since we met.

"I need a quick shower and to get dressed, before Lucas arrives home," I say as I lean over Holly and steal another kiss.

"OK. I'll go make a coffee. Would you like one?" she asks, scooting out from under my arm.

"I'll have tea please," I answer. "If Sebastian turns up with Lucas, will you ask him to hang around? I need a word with him." She nods her answer and heads for the door.

"What did he say about the barbecue?" she asks, turning back to me.

"Sebastian, Izzy and the kids will be there, Nicholas too. They just need the address."

"What about Daniel?"

"Not sure. He said he has plans for tomorrow afternoon but if he gets time he'll call in."

"OK. I hope he makes it, even if it's just for an hour. It will be nice for us all to be together," she states on her way out of the door. I know what she means. Holly's friends are the closest things she has to family. I can imagine she will be a little nervous and will want to make a good impression. So, yeah, it would be nice if all my sons could make it too.

*

Today, could not have gone any better. Both Lucas and Holly got along remarkably well and had lots of fun at the go-kart track. We spent a couple of hours there after Holly had telephoned them this morning to get us booked in. Their interaction was sweet, funny and made my heart swell with love for them both.

Holly would ruffle his hair on purpose once she realised he applied more hair products than a teenage girl. He got past brushing her off and just let her continue. I think he enjoyed Holly making a fuss of him. She enquired as to what he liked at school. I was shocked, when he told her that he preferred art to most subjects; his eyes lit up when he spoke to her about sketching. Although Holly told him she didn't know much about art, she remained engrossed in his enthusiasm of the subject, his young face scrunching up with delight, as he buzzed with excitement, his wide grin making me wonder why I am just hearing about this.

We then decided to go and grab a burger and Lucas asked if we could go bowling. Again, both delighted to spend time together. As we walked from the carpark into the bowling alley, Holly put herself in the middle, linking both Lucas and myself. I couldn't be more surprised how Lucas has acted towards Holly. With never knowing his mother and not having the love and care a mother would give to her son, sometimes he struggles with women. Even though Mrs White has been around since he was six months old and Izzy since he was six years old, he can still be timid around them. Holly has not let his shyness get in the way, in fact she's brought out a different side to him. More confident and carefree.

Arriving home at seven, all of us hungry, my youngest and the woman I fall for a little more with each passing day, whipped up a chicken salad then prepared lots of snacks when we went to settle in the living room.

Straight away Lucas got out his PS4 and before I had time to think he was kicking both our arses on one of his games. A pillow fight was inevitable when I thought it would be OK to cheat. My little minx caught on and grassed me up to Lucas, which set him off launching cushions at me. I ducked, and one hit Holly that brought on a whole new game of Beat Vlad when I chuckled at the stunned look on her face.

Between them I was bombarded by small and large scatter cushions which they thought was hilarious until I picked them both up, threw them on the settee and set about tickling them both. Holly let out high-pitched squeals as I tickled her ribs and Lucas had tears rolling down his cheeks when I dug my fingers into the area just above his knee. Good to know their weak spots.

Once we had calmed down and tidied up, we put on a film, letting Lucas choose. But, now I'm sat here, my feet up on the coffee table, watching the credits run while I gently rub my thumb over Lucas' foot which is resting on my left knee. His head rests on the arm of the settee, and that's where it's stayed since he fell asleep halfway through the movie. I'm also stroking Holly's soft hair with my other hand as her head rests on my right thigh, her feet up on the other arm of the settee. She fell asleep before Lucas. I know I need to put them to bed but it's been enjoyable just to watch them sleep.

Lucas stirs, so I prop Holly's head under a cushion before I pick him up to carry up the stairs. He's not heavy. His size is a lot smaller than his brothers were when they were his age. Being two months premature and addicted to hard drugs will do that to a child. I thank God every day for keeping my baby alive and thank the hospital with substantial funds yearly for their medical intervention.

Lucas wakes in my arms just as I get to the top of the stairs and moans for me to put him down. "Thanks Dad but I'm a big boy now," he jokes, rubbing his tired eyes. I pull him into me and kiss the top of his head.

"You'll always be my baby boy," I chuckle as he screws up his face at me.

"I had fun today. Will you thank Holly for me?" his sleepy voice mumbles.

"Of course, but you can thank her yourself in the morning," he nods, realising Holly will be staying over. We haven't spoken about her staying here tonight, I just assumed he wouldn't mind. "Lucas…"

"It's fine, Dad," he smiles and stalks off towards his bedroom, leaving me with the thought that my youngest is now growing up.

As I make my way back to where I left Holly asleep on the settee, I see she is now awake, stretching as she turns off the TV. "Hey sleepy head," I whisper in her ear as I pull her back into my front.

"I thought you had gone to bed without me." She turns in my arms, her drowsy gaze flickering to focus.

Hell will freeze over first before that happens. "No, sweetheart, I've just got Lucas to bed." Her head falls into my chest.

"Hmmm, that's where I need to go," she mumbles.

"Come on then, angel," I say, sweeping her up into my arms and giving her a chaste brush of my lips. "Let's get you to bed."

Chapter 25

Holly

Making my way into Vlad's kitchen, I spot Lucas preparing breakfast. "Morning," I greet, with a smile on my face as he carefully chops fruit, arranging it neatly on a plate.

"Oh, hi," he greets back, shifting nervously on his feet. I know he is a little timid but yesterday he really enjoyed himself and didn't show any uneasiness around me.

"Need any help?" I ask, hoping we can pick up where we left off yesterday with him abandoning his shyness and enjoying spending time with me. If my relationship with his father lasts, and I can't see it not, then we will be spending a lot more time with each other. Saying that, I don't want to push him, he's not used to sharing his father with a woman, so I will tread carefully.

"Yes, please," he answers politely. "I thought I would make us breakfast." His eyes flick to the strawberries and melon he has chopped into chunks. "Dad's gone to work. He was running late; he overslept, and he never sleeps in," he chuckles. "So, I told him I would make our breakfast."

"Right, thank you," I say, nodding my head. I wondered how he knew I liked fruit for breakfast, and my favourite as well.

"We must have tired him out yesterday, huh?" I say, smiling, joining Lucas at the breakfast counter. "He is getting on a bit." He chuckles at my comment.

"Don't tell him that, you'll never live it down." He looks up at me, squinting when the morning sun appears through the blinds.

"Do you like fruit for breakfast?" I nod towards the plate that is now getting quite stacked up.

"Sometimes. I didn't know how much you liked." He shrugs, a little colour appearing on his face.

"What do you like with your fruit?" I ask. "Because you're going to have to share that with me."

"Sorry, I'm used to helping my dad prepare food for my brothers." He lets out a little chuckle, rising on his tiptoes and stretching his hands up, imitating the size of them.

I chuckle at him. He's such a cute, caring lad with a sense of humour when he's not being shy. "Well, as you've chopped enough melon and strawberries to feed an army of Petrov men, you're going to have to share it with me." I point at him.

"Dad, normally makes us pancakes with fruit," he says, biting his lip.

"OK, we can do that." I nod at him, knowing he's playing me and that's what he was after all along.

"And chocolate sauce," he beams.

"Wouldn't dream of putting anything else on my pancakes," I say as I turn towards the cupboards to look for the ingredients. God, I'm going to have to do some serious working out at the gym tomorrow to work off all the crap I've consumed this the weekend.

"Yesss," I hear the little mite hiss out. And just like that, Lucas is back to the boy I met yesterday.

Vlad arrived home from work just after two, taking me straight into his arms. "Where's Lucas?"

"He went to his room to get changed." I had only just got the last word out when the answer I gave him was swallowed up with such urgency it took my breath away. His lips were soft, warm and full of determination to get his fill. My back hits the island in the kitchen and I'm lifted onto the cold marble with Vlad nestled between my thighs.

"Hmmm, missed you," he utters into my lips.

"Missed you too," I whisper back, placing my hands on his firm chest.

Stroking my thighs, Vlad pulls away from my mouth. He looks tired and worried. I think he's a little upset with Daniel, due to him not coming to the barbecue this afternoon. Although, I would have liked to have had him join us, it's no big deal, he's only twenty-one and I'm sure he wants to spend his time with his friends. "Have you eaten?" I ask, knowing it's going to be after five before we eat at Olivia's.

"No. I was extremely busy this morning, so I missed out on lunch," he answers, taking a little nibble on my lower lip. I pat his chest to get him to move so I can get down from where he perched me, and he lets out a growl when we disconnect.

"Let me whip you something up before you waste away," I say, opening the fridge door to retrieve the pasta that Lucas and I had made earlier. Vlad's big body cuddles into my back as he lowers his lips to my shoulder and places his hands on my hips. "I'd rather eat you." His suggestive tone makes me shiver.

"Not going to happen, big guy," I chuckle, rubbing my bottom into him. I know I'm teasing him, but he needs to learn to restrain himself. "Young son upstairs that could walk in any minute so go sit down and let me feed you." His eyes widen, and that naughty grin appears on his face.

"Set to it then, woman, don't keep your man waiting," he says, swiping my arse before he saunters over to the dining table, taking a seat.

"Did you enjoy your morning, sweetheart?" he asks as I place the heated pasta on the table. It doesn't take long for Vlad to tuck in and devour the rather large plate of spicy chicken pasta.

"Yes. I spent some quality time getting to know Lucas. We made breakfast together then prepared lunch." Vlad raises one eyebrow when I chuckle, remembering how much fruit the poor kid had chopped up. "He's a good kid. He prepped enough fruit to feed the whole Petrov clan."

"Yeah, he's used to cooking for his brothers."

"That's what he told me. Mr and Mrs White called around. What a lovely couple," I gush. "They filled your freezer with lasagne, apple pies, chicken supreme and lots of other dishes." He nods his head and smiles.

"She spoils us," he mumbles around a mouthful of food. "Mary likes to make sure the freezer is stocked well and the cupboards too. She normally shops on a Wednesday, so expect lots of goodies to be stocked in them. That is until the vultures raid them and strip them bare," he chuckles. I know he means his four sons. Boy, they can eat.

"Hi, Paps," Lucas greets as he strolls into the kitchen. His hair has been gelled within an inch of its life and the smell of men's deodorant wafts through the air.

"Are you meeting a girl?" Vlad jokes, eyeing his twelve-year-old son while standing to get rid of his empty plate. He can't help but lean in, taking a sniff of his son as well as bouncing his hand off his hair.

"No," Lucas snaps. "I'm not going to meet Holly's friend looking like a scruff," he states as he takes a seat at the table. He might be the youngest, but he's got an old head on his shoulders. He turns in his chair and squints his dark blue eyes at his dad. "Are you showering and getting changed?" I can't help but let out a giggle at him, he's so cute. Vlad puts his hands on his hips and gives himself a once over.

"No. What's wrong with me? I was going to go in these," he exaggerates, his hand over his jeans and a creased shirt, throwing me a wink when Lucas lowers his head into his hands.

"Daaad," he drawls, shaking his head.

"What? It's not like I've been on a building site. I've only been sweating in an office for five hours," he says, trying hard not to crack a smile. Then he lifts his arm, sniffing under his armpit. It's so unlike the Vlad I know. I can't help but let out a snort of laughter. He walks towards Lucas with his arm raised. "I don't smell, do I?" he asks his son who is now moving away quickly. For the record he doesn't smell of anything but pure man, all woody with a touch of spice to add to his masculinity. The inky blue bottles of 'Sauvage' by Dior, sit in his bathroom and bedroom and give off the manly scent that suits my man immensely.

"Don't worry, Son, your old man won't embarrass you," he says, still chuckling at Lucas.

"It's not me I'm worried about, it's Holly. She doesn't need you humiliating her," he states, moving out of the way of his father when Vlad takes off his shirt and throws it at him. This is the fun side of him that no one sees but his family; the loving, playful father. Anywhere else he's professional with a superior quality about him. His deep, authoritative voice grips your attention and holds it for ransom without realisation. His long strides show determination and his strong features let you know he's not to be messed with. Vlad's presence oozes confidence with a slight mystery and arrogance about him which adds to his sex appeal. His employees respect and admire him even though he keeps many of them at arm's length, only ever greeting them with a nod of his head. The work colleagues that are privileged to know him better, love him like family. He's a smart, handsome man who prides himself on cleanliness and style. Could he ever humiliate me? No. Could he ever humiliate his family? No, and Lucas is aware of this.

An hour and a half later we're pulling into Olivia and Jack's drive, Vlad showered, changed and smelling so good I could eat him.

He hasn't even got the engine switched off when the front door opens, and Olivia comes barrelling out closely followed by Jack, who rugby tackles her and has her slung over his shoulder while she kicks her legs and screams at him to put her down. He slaps her arse and I can see his mouth saying, "No," then slaps her arse again.

"I like him already," Vlad chuckles as he gets out of the car.

"And so, it begins," I say as I stride towards my friends.

Vlad's by my side twining our hands together, his other hand on the back of Lucas' neck.

"Hi, you must Vlad," Jack greets, putting his hand out. "It's good to meet you at last, I'm Jack, her husband." He points to Olivia's arse. "And you must be Lucas?" Lucas shakes Jack's hand with a little grin on his face. "I'm sorry about my wife, she gets a little too excited when we have guests. You wouldn't have got out of the car before she imposed herself on you."

"I am here, you know," Olivia screeches while beating her husband on his back. "Put me down, caveman."

Jack brings her up then slides her down his front and smacks a kiss on her lips. "Love you," he says, not giving a shit that he has visitors stood in front of him.

"Yeah." Olivia rolls her eyes at him, then kisses his cheek. "Love you too," she whispers.

Then pounces on me.

"Holly, come here and give me a hug." She throws her arms around me, squeezing me in her embrace. Once she lets go, she surprises Vlad by jumping into his arms and planting a kiss on his cheek. Lucas' eyes bug out of his head while Vlad stands there frozen to the spot, his face pleading for me to save him. Not going to happen. Let Olivia have her moment. She's been dying to meet him properly; she's only seen him in the club when we first met. The man who has captured her friend's heart in such a short time.

She lets go of him and slaps him on his muscular shoulder. "Chill out, big guy, we're practically family." She smiles at him then turns to Lucas, who is probably wondering who this crazy woman is. He doesn't give her the chance to embarrass him.

"Hi, I'm Lucas," he says, holding out his hand. Olivia is polite and shakes his hand.

"Will you let them get in the bloody house?" Jack states as he gives me a hug. "Hi sis," he greets. "Just thought I'd get that in, don't want your man getting jealous," he whispers, chuckling.

"Behave," I chastise him, slapping his arm. Vlad knows these people are the closest I have to family.

We all make our way through to the back into the garden. The patio furniture is all out: tables, chairs, sun loungers and parasols. There's a bouncy castle blown up at the bottom of the garden and a music system is set at the top. The barbecue is off to the side and a small gazebo has been erected. Jay and Ivy are arranging plates of food and dropping bottles of wine and beer into ice buckets.

"Mum, Dad, Holly's here!" Jack shouts which has them both stopping what they are doing.

Ivy's wide smile greets us first. "Holly, look at you. You look so happy." Her hands take mine and she pulls me into a hug.

"Thank you," I say, because I am happy. I can't think of a time in my life where I was as happy, and I don't care who knows that it's because of this man at the side of me. "This is Vlad, and this is Lucas." I point to both at the same time, not wanting to put one before the other. "This is Ivy and Jay, Jack's parents," I relay back to my boys. And yes, I've took on Lucas as mine because what woman wouldn't? He's such a smart, funny, respectful boy any mother would be proud to have him as a son. If this weekend has taught me anything it's that he enjoys spending time with his father and me and doesn't mind me fussing over him like an old mother hen. The relationship between his father and me, although short is very serious and I would be privileged to take on this boy as my own.

Lucy steps through the patio doors, with Megan close on her heels. I introduce her to Vlad and Lucas while Megan is happy to brush her doll's hair.

Sarah, Nick and their children Jayden and Emilia are the next to arrive. As I look behind them, Sebastian, Izzy and their children are following. They must have met in the drive and come in with Jack's brother. Nicholas then appears, looking like his ever-mischievous self, and is soon being eyed up by my goddaughter, Lucy. I will have to keep an eye on her.

Megan and Rebecca screech the high-pitched noise they love so much and skip off together towards the bouncy castle. Emilia follows in pursuit, playing babysitter.

Turns out, Lucas and Jayden also know one another from school. They're not in the same class but are in the same year. Jayden asks Lucas if he wants to go meet his cousins, Nathan and James, who had taken residency in their games room since two o'clock according to Olivia. Joseph is asked to join them too, leaving Izzy and Sebastian child free for a little while. "We may have to come here again," Sebastian says, grinning. "We're not used to our children leaving our sides without having to prise them from us."

"I know," Izzy agrees, rubbing her belly. "We'll have another one soon too, with its little vice grip," she states, smiling.

"Oh, I love babies," Olivia announces. "All cuddly and snuggly," she gushes, screwing up her face and wrapping her arms around her middle.

"Don't get any funny ideas, woman," Jack warns. She slaps his leg playfully and gazes into his emerald green eyes.

"What, you don't fancy trying for another one?" her eyes flickering up at him.

"I don't mind trying at all," he flirts back with her. "But I'll be making sure there will be no little surprises, honey," he tells her as he pulls her in and kisses her cheek.

"I'm here as a guest, not to cook the bloody food." Jay's rumble breaks into their playful banter.

We've all got drinks and are just sat lounging around, chatting. Jay slaps Jack around the back of the neck. "Come on, you, I've put the steaks on, you can watch them."

"I'll do it." Nick jumps up. "If we leave it to him, we'll end up eating cremated offerings."

Everyone is getting along famously. The children have been fed, the boys have gone back to playing on the Nintendo and Rebecca and Megan are having a tea party with Emilia, Lucy and Nicholas. The women are talking babies and the men are discussing golf.

"That's where I know your face from." Jay points at Vlad. "I've been racking my brain over where I'd seen you before." Vlad shakes his head at him and looks a little surprised at Jay.

"Willow Bridge golf club, that's where you play? Right?" Jay's beaming at himself for figuring the answer to something that's been obviously bugging him for the last few hours.

"Yes, occasionally," Vlad enlightens him. Then he turns quickly to me. "Remind me I have something to ask you before we get home." He then swiftly spins back to Jay who is eager to ask more questions.

"Don't you and a few others organise fund-raising events, auctions and raffles for the children's ward at the hospital?"

Vlad nods his head and takes a drink from his bottle of lager, his face looking a little embarrassed. Wow, my man has a big heart, he has no need to feel embarrassed. I think it's the fact that all eyes are on him.

"I've seen your photo up on the wall in the entrance to the club and the bar, handing a cheque over to someone from the hospital," Jay states, then gets up out of his seat and puts his hand out to shake Vlad's. "It's very charitable of you." They shake hands and Jay sits back down.

"Thank you." Vlad says. "It's a worthy cause—" He doesn't finish because Sebastian steps in.

"Did you get our ticket, Paps?"

"Yes. I got one for you too." He turns to me. "I just forgot to ask if you would like to accompany me." He looks quite nervous as he rubs his thumb over my knuckles. As if I'd turn him down. Not bloody likely. "Will you come?"

"When is it?" I ask. I'm going, that's for sure. I just like to tease him a little.

"Hmmm." He reaches into his pocket and retrieves his wallet.

"June 2nd," Jay answers. "I bought two tickets a couple of weeks ago." He flashes two tickets around. Olivia jumps out of her seat and takes them from him.

"Are these for me and Jack?" She cuddles into him, trying to butter him up.

"I don't think so, lady, get Tight Arse to buy yours if you want to go. These cost me hundred pounds for them both." He takes them from her and shoves them back in his wallet.

"I'm not tight." Jack has just picked up on what his dad had said. "Please enlighten us to what this event is," curiosity getting the better of him.

Vlad places his bottle on the table and sits back in his chair. "It's a fund raiser, an auction. The proceeds from the sale of the tickets go straight into the fund for the children's ward. The items for the auction are collected throughout the year which could range from some obscure painting, an evening for two at a restaurant, a spa break, a weekend away at some lavish hotel, it varies. There's usually around twenty top items that've been donated from different companies. We raise a lot of money. There's quite a few stuck-up suits that like to bid high when they've had a few," he chuckles, mimicking a drink in his hand and bringing it to his mouth. "There's also a band and food which the golf club pays for. And it's a black-tie event," he finishes.

"It's a good night," Izzy adds. "The bands are good. Caterers are brought in. The auction is a lot of fun and there's raffles too." Her enthusiasm for the event captures everyone.

"You haven't answered me yet," Vlad leans in and whispers in my ear. I think I've left him hanging long enough.

"Yes, I would love to go with you," I tell him. Then without a thought to who is around us I grab his shirt and pull him in, placing my lips on his. He has one of the kindest hearts going. The biggest. He works hard. He loves fiercely and gives unconditionally. I'm so lucky he's mine.

When we pull away from each other, I don't blush, and I don't say a word to the friends and family around us who are speechless at my blatant love for this man.

"Count me in," Jack says, breaking the silence.

"And me," Nick follows.

"What about me?" Lucy looks around at everyone as if to say, 'You're not leaving me out.'

"I better have three then," Jack says. There's a big smile on Nicholas' face when he turns. I'm the only one to pick up on it as Olivia is gushing about going shopping for dresses.

"It's OK for you lot." Izzy waves her hand at the women in the garden. "I have to buy something to fit this in." She puts her hands on her cute belly and jiggles it about.

"Right, ladies, shopping day. Get your phones out, we need to fix a date. You too, Ivy," Sarah orders. "There's a cute little shop in the high street that's very classy, they stock a variety for pregnant women," she says to Izzy. "We went in by mistake. They have some beautiful one-offs. We could go there first." Her face is full of excitement.

"Oh, what about that all-in-one?" Olivia reminds us.

"God, yes. If I was pregnant I'd definitely wear it," Sarah states.

We all set a date and time in our phones to meet next week. Then decide to higher Sarah's sister's friend to come and do our hair and nails on the day of the event. Olivia plans that all the women should get ready at her house and meet the men there; we all agree but get a grumble from the men. Especially Jack, who will be getting ready at his dad's whether he likes it or not.

Vlad excuses himself to go out to the car. When he comes back he has a bottle of brandy in his hand and a couple of bottles of wine. We were told not to bring any alcohol because Jack and Nick had been to the wholesalers and bought in bulk. Vlad wouldn't listen and said they were a gift. Only, we forgot to bring them from the car when we arrived.

He hands the wine to Olivia, who thanks him with a sweet kiss on his cheek. Jack takes the brandy from him and shakes his hand. When he sits back down he puts his arm around my shoulders and pulls me in, giving my hair a nuzzle. I know he's addicted to the smell of my hair products, so I just let him inhale away. "I've just texted Dave and ordered five more tickets. I'm going to pick them up from him tomorrow," he tells me when he's finished breathing me in.

"Who's Dave?" I ask, snuggling in to his warm chest, his arm moving around my waist, holding me tight.

"He's a consultant at the hospital and a member of the golf club who helps to organise the fund-raising events."

"Oh. Is that how you met him and got involved with raising money for the hospital?"

"Yes and no," he says, stroking my waistline. "It's a long story. I'll tell you when we're not in company."

"OK," I say, knowing that's there's quite a lot I don't know about Vlad, but I am willing to wait till he is ready to tell me.

We sit a while. Our heads resting together. His arm around me and my hand placed on his chest. Just happy listening to the chatter around us. The boys have been out of the games room, attacked the bouncy castle, nearly collapsing it. They filled their boots with more food then charged through the house back to the games room. They were all brought back out and given a warning to calm down with the threat of Olivia coming in to put them all to bed. That soon sorted out the little darlings because they tiptoed like little mice when they went back in.

Something tugs at my leg and has me sitting up. The same thing must have happened to Vlad because he sits up quickly too. When we both look down at the offending entity, two pairs of curious saucer-size eyes stair back at us. Two little chubby mitts attach to my legs and work their way up until I have a four-year-old bundle of curls sat on my lap. When I turn to look at Vlad, he too has a bundle of curls sat on his lap. Well, more like hung around his neck. Rebecca has her arm tightly around her granddad's neck and her head resting on his shoulder with her thumb stuck in her mouth. She looks so bloody cute. Megan wraps herself around me and opens her mouth.

"Ask him." She directs her words towards her little friend who is scrambling to kneel up on Vlad's lap. Settling herself, she takes his chin in the palms of her hands and taps her little fingers on his cheeks. Vlad, bites his lip, trying to hide his amusement but you can see a glint of humour in his blue eyes. Rebecca narrows her eyes and scrunches up her freckled face, concentrating hard. A little chuckle escapes from Vlad, causing Rebecca to press two of her fingers on his lips squashing them together so they pucker. This gets a few giggles from the ones who are watching.

"Are you Holly's boyfriend?" Rebecca questions, tilting her head to the side and placing her hand on Vlad's chest to balance herself. He helps to steady the little inquisitive pixie by grabbing her waist, so she doesn't topple. She narrows her eyes again as if to say, 'Answer me,' and this time a giggle slips from my lips. It's adorable to see. Vlad looks out of his depth with all eyes glued on him to answer the question.

"Hmmm," he considers, sitting up a little straighter. "Well, I am a boy." Rebecca and Megan both cover their mouths and giggle at him. "And, I am Holly's friend. So, that would make me Holly's boyfriend," he tells them.

Megan shuffles on my knee so she is sat facing Vlad. "But we saw you kiss her," she says, pointing her finger to me and swinging her legs. I can see Nicholas. And I can hear him sniggering at her comment. I know it's him that's got them asking questions. He's such a mixing shit.

"No, I didn't," Vlad says, biting his lip trying hard not to laugh.

"Aw, you lied," the two of them say in unison as they cover their open mouths with their hands, eyes wide.

"I did not lie," Vlad says, chuckling. "She kissed me," his voice higher than normal as he answers them truthfully.

They both giggle again and jump down from our knees, joining hands. Chocolate curls mix with fiery red as their heads come together, whispering not so quietly. Every word is heard before they even ask the question they've just conjured up.

Quiet sniggers come from Ivy and Jay. Howls and hoots from the rest of the crew who have heard what the girls were mumbling.

"Can we be bridesmaids at your wedding?" they ask us both, one placing their elbows on my knee, the other on Vlad's. This time I cover my mouth because I can't contain my laughter any longer.

"Answer them, will you?" Nicholas buts in.

"Yeah, they'd look adorable in little frilly dresses," Olivia announces, linking Nicholas' arm.

I'm all but crying. In fact, tears form in my eyes as I watch Vlad stare at the two little mischief makers with nothing but shock on his handsome face. Doesn't he realise, it's every little girl's dream to be a bridesmaid? Frilly frocks, glittery shoes and a sparkling tiara. Of course he doesn't, he's brought up four boys.

His eyes shift from the girls to family and friends that are now all waiting for one of us to answer. I'm not even going there. Then he gets that cheeky smirk on his face, one corner of his lip lifting as his eyes connect with mine and a cheeky wink is thrown at me. "When," he pronounces, his gaze now shifting back to the girls, "we get married." He takes my hand in his and all the women sigh. I'm just a pool on the floor. He doesn't say 'if'. It's 'when'. And I know we have only been together a short while but we're not kids. We both know this relationship isn't just a fling. It's so much more.

"You two," he breaks my thoughts and I watch him tap both girls on their noses, "will be the first to know." Both beam at him, milky white teeth show as they let out a squeal. "And, yes, you can be bridesmaids," he finishes, sitting back in his chair as he blows out a breath and kisses my knuckles.

That's all the little whirlwinds needed as they skip off towards the bouncy castle, giggling.

"Wow!" I hear Sebastian blow out. "How many months did I put on that bet?" he asks Nicholas, turning in his seat to look at his brother.

"Just a minute, I've got the list in my pocket." He fumbles in his back pocket, bringing out a black leather wallet.

"What bet?" Olivia asks, looking confused at the two brothers, only because she hasn't got a clue what's they're talking about. Which is a first for her, not to be in the know.

"Oh my god!" she screams. "Look at this!" She passes the piece of paper that Nicholas has given her around the table, and I curl into a ball against Vlad, who is highly amused at my embarrassment.

"Oh, I'll have some of that." Sarah's wide eager smile meets her eyes as she rummages in her bag, to get a pen so she can have in on the bet.

"Please, tell them to stop," I plead at my man who is bent over wiping his eyes, his face red with elation. The note has gone around the table and everyone has bet on when they think Vlad and I will get married.

"No," Vlad answers me as he pulls me into him. "I told you not to encourage him," he chuckles, as he throws his hand up pointing to Nicholas. Jack examines the piece of paper that he's just took from his dad.

"Holly love, your name's down on this list." His arm snakes around Olivia's shoulders and they both explode into a fit of laughter. Then Jack scribbles on the paper and passes it back to Nicholas. He glances at it then looks at Jack. "What?" he says shrugging his shoulders. "I'm not going to bet against the bride to be. If anyone should know when the wedding will be, it's her."

"Nicholas Petrov, I'm going to beat you with a blunt instrument," I call out to him, amusement in my voice. He's soon by my side being the drama queen his father says he is.

"Aw, Mum," he drawls, placing his hand on his heart. He could be an award-winning actor. "You know you love me." He then bends and kisses my cheek. "Sorry," he whispers with that cheeky Petrov smirk on his face. He's not sorry at all.

Izzy explains to everyone about Nicholas predicting on how long it would be before she and Sebastian would get married when they first met. She then went on to tell them that he also predicted that Vlad and I would be married in six months. That's how the bet started. They all find it highly amusing as they watch us both cuddled together shaking our heads at them, and agree with Nicholas. I think they've had too much alcohol.

I never thought I would marry again. Never thought I would trust anyone enough again. Being held safely and lovingly in Vlad's arms, knowing this man is everything I ever wanted, I can see what they see. But, we still have a lot to learn about each other, so marriage might not be on the cards. Well, not as quick as they are presuming.

The girls are tired and getting cranky. Lucy decides it's time to get Megan ready for bed. Sebastian and Izzy collect their children, give their rounds of goodbyes and head for the door, Nicholas joining them. Sarah and Nick follow, leaving just shortly after.

Ivy and Jay say their goodbyes and we get ready to leave too. Everyone has helped tidy up and the men have indulged in a couple of glasses of the brandy that Vlad had brought round for Jack. We leave the car in the drive and order a taxi to get back to Vlad's.

The alcohol, fresh air and laughter has tired us all out and we head straight to bed when we arrive back at Vlad's home.

Startled, I sit up and struggle with my surroundings. The blackout blinds are drawn, and I can't tell what time of day it is. Scrubbing my hands up and down my face, I focus on what it was that woke me from my deep sleep.

The sound of an angry voice, Vlad's voice, has me climbing out of bed and looking at the clock. It's seven thirty and I'm curious to what he's shouting about and where in the house he is. I hear raised voices again just as I'm heading for the bathroom. Quickly, I finish up in there and slip on a pair of jeans and a T-shirt. As I make my way down the stairs, I stop when I hear a cracking of wood splintering. "I've fucking warned you before, Daniel. I do not want those people in my house!" Vlad's voice bellows when I look over the banister, past the kitchen into the front room I see two men, one of them scowling at the other.

"OMG," slips from my lips and I put my hand over my mouth to silence myself.

The table is layered with beer cans and wine bottles. The cushions that were all sat in their place on the settees are scattered on the floor and if I'm not mistaken there's plates with died out butts of cigarettes. In fact, there's a strong smell of an illegal tobacco.

The wood I heard cracking is an acoustic guitar, broken into pieces, strings snapped, laying at the side of the table.

Vlad glares at his son. Hurt and anguish in his eyes. Body stiff. He places his hands on to Daniel shoulders. "Why won't you listen to me?" he asks, shaking his head. "These people you think are your friends, are not. All they see is a young man with more money than sense. Someone they can leech off." He takes a deep breath, trying to calm his emotions. Daniel doesn't move, I don't think he dare. Obviously, after we got in last night and went to bed, Daniel must have turned up with a few of his friends. Looks like they had quite the party.

I hear a noise coming from the kitchen area, so I tiptoe down the rest of the steps to see who's there. Nicholas is leaning on the counter, drinking from a cup. He spots me and beckons me with his head to join him.

"What's going on?" I whisper. He puts his finger to his lip and shakes his head, telling me not to ask.

"And this!" I hear Vlad shout, as he points down to one of the plates which is full of the left overs of rolled up joints. "I see this again," he snarls, "in my house, and I will not just throw the lowlifes you call friends out, I…" He stops, trying to rein his anger in. I don't think he has to say anything else. I think Daniel gets the message because his face has just stripped of all colour. He looks petrified. Vlad steps back from him, realising his son is scared. "Get this cleaned up before Lucas gets up." His voice is firm and not to be challenged. With that, he turns, not even seeing me, and strides towards the stairs. Taking two at a time when he reaches them. The sound of the house rattling when the bedroom door closes, tells me he is very angry.

"What the hell, Daniel?" Nicholas says as he steps up to his brother.

"I know," he says, putting his hand up. "I fucked up. I fell asleep. We'd only had a few cans when we got back here. I didn't know they were going to smoke this shit. Look at my fucking guitar," he moans, picking it up and holding it out.

"You're lucky he didn't wrap it round your neck, you stupid bastard. Stop being so naïve. You know exactly what Toby and his girlfriends are like, I've told you before." Daniel looks at his brother, knowing he's let not only them down but himself.

228

"Clean it all up and I'll take Holly home," he says.

"What?" I ask, looking at them both, not knowing why the hell I'm going home. All I want to do is go to Vlad and hold him. Help take away all the stress that this in front of me has caused.

"Believe me, Holly, you don't want to be around him now. He'll calm down and come to you," he says as he lifts my bag off the kitchen worktop, where I left it last night. I stand there torn between flying up the stairs to see Vlad, who is very upset, or listening to Nicholas, whose eyes plead with me to take his advice. It's probably the first time I've seen him looking serious, so I take his warning.

I take my bag from him and open it to get my apartment keys, then slip on the shoes I'd kicked off in the doorway last night and follow him out of the door.

Chapter 26

Vlad

My legs take the stairs two at a time to get to Holly's apartment, too impatient to wait for the lift. I haven't seen her since Monday morning; well, technically it was Sunday night because I didn't see her in the kitchen watching my frustration with Daniel get the better of me.

Waking early on Monday and in need of water, I quietly slipped out of bed. I hadn't noticed Daniel and his friends when I stepped into the kitchen to get a bottle of water from the fridge, it wasn't until I turned around to face the living room that my eyes met with four semi-naked bodies sprawled out on the floor. One of them being Daniel, two females and the other one, Toby the pot-smoking idiot that I have warned my son to stay away from.

This was the third time I had come across this guy lounging around my house with the smell of illegal tobacco filling the air. I know Daniel doesn't smoke it, but having any addictive substance under my roof, near his younger brother, is enough to have me raging.

Throwing his friends out before they had chance to dress properly did not satisfy my rage nor did yelling at my son for being so stupid. Smashing his beloved guitar over the coffee table grounded me slightly when I saw the look of hurt on his face. The upset in his eyes wasn't just because he had let me down. It was that he had angered me that much that he had pushed me to breaking something I had bought him for his sixteenth birthday, that I knew he treasured. I don't get angry with my boys, never had the need to punish them as they were growing up, but Daniel knew he had overstepped the mark, bringing any friends of his who deal with drugs to my house.

Only afterwards, I was the one feeling guilty and upset.

Entering my bedroom, I realised Holly was not there. I could only assume she had seen me yet again raging like a wild animal. Soon after, I heard that Nicholas had driven her home. I knew I would have to phone her to explain myself.

Dinner time came around, then I was ready to talk rationally with Daniel. We sat and ate dinner together discussing what had happened that morning. I knew my son wouldn't have smoked any of the shit his friends brought into my home. He was sorry, and he had had words with Toby for smoking it while he was asleep.

I apologised for getting angry with him and breaking his guitar. He promised me that he would not bring Toby here again and I promised to replace his guitar the following day.

I haven't taken much interest in Daniel's musical pursuit, I always thought it was just a hobby that he would lose interest in. But, when we spoke Monday afternoon I could see the passion in his eyes as he told me about the band he had been practicing with. Apparently, they had been together for a while and that's where he had been Sunday afternoon. I was a little shocked that he had kept his passion for music from all of us.

I also phoned Holly to explain myself to her. She was very understanding, which let me off the hook. Missing her already, I suggested to her to come and stay at my house on Tuesday, only she knocked me back. She had work to do.

Since her meeting with Izzy last Thursday, she's on Project Revamp Aphrodite but with spending so much time with me she hasn't made much progress.

Missing her was an understatement so when she suggested for me and Lucas to stay at hers tonight, I jumped at the offer. Lucas did not want to come, not because he doesn't like Holly, no. It was due to his brothers offering to have a games night with him which he was overjoyed with.

I think they just wanted the grumpy bastard out of the house. Holly would normally have her goddaughter staying over on Wednesdays but tonight the little cherub is with her mother. Lucy, Megan's mum, has a week off university before she goes back to sit her exams. Which I am so grateful for. The scowl that I have had for the last couple of days has now become an award-winning grin.

As I approach her door which is slightly ajar – she must have opened it when she buzzed me in – I know tonight I won't be able to hold back on telling her how in love with her I am.

It's all new to me, this overwhelming feeling to want to spend every waking moment with her. I miss her so much when we are not together, I find I need to phone her to hear her soft voice. I text her constantly; the fact she is always happy to hear from me keeps me going until I can hold her, touch her, smell her sweet smell and get my fix of her addictive smile. She deserves to have a man who would want to give her the world and I thank my lucky stars every day that it's me who gets to be that man.

Slipping my jacket and shoes off as I enter her hallway, I place my bag that holds my clothes for tomorrow on the floor.

I study Holly from where I am, leaning against the wall with my arms folded across my chest. She's chopping salad, swaying her hips in time to the music she's playing. The seductive tone of her voice sings along to the lyrics and as much as I want to go to her and wrap myself around her, kiss her neck, breathe her in while my hands roam over her body, I don't. I stand frozen watching my woman be herself in her own home. This is what she does, where she's relaxed and content.

She puts the knife down, still singing along to some song about Havana, her hips taking on a very sexy sway. She's a mastery of movement, which holds me captivated. The way she sings overwhelms me causing the hairs on my skin to stand on end.

The music ends, and she turns to see me watching her. Her bright eyes and the way she bites at her lower lip to stifle her laugh has me off the wall and going to her. My hands grip her hips as I look down into her gem-like eyes. "Enjoy the show?" she asks as her hands travel up my chest and on to my shoulders.

"Very much," I say, pulling her into me and stealing her lips.

She moans into me as our kiss deepens. Almost three days without my angel has left me pining and from the way her tongue is dancing in my mouth, the way her hands have found their way under my shirt and are stroking my heated skin, lets me know she feels the same.

We break away from the passionate kiss that could have quite easily led me to lift Holly onto her worktop, step between her thighs and bury myself in her until we were both sated.

"Missed you," Holly mumbles as she snuggles in to my chest.

"So fucking much," I mumble into her hair. She chuckles at my words as we both stand in the middle of her kitchen, content in just holding each other.

"How was your day, honey?" Holly asks, as she steps back, keeping hold of my hand.

"It was good, but it's just got a whole lot better," I answer, pulling her back into me and nuzzling into her neck. We keep that way for a short while, silent. Filling our starvation with the desire and love we hold for each other. A couple of days apart has left us both hungry for each other, but I'm sure that will be rectified tonight.

Holly is the first to break the silence.

"Where's Lucas?"

"Oh, I forgot to mention, he's stopping at home. Nicholas and Daniel are staying with him, they're having a games night."

"Are you staying the night?"

"Of course," I say, wrapping my arms around her and kissing her again. It's never felt strange to want to spend time with Holly, whether we are at mine, hers or out. Introducing her to my family and me meeting her friends just came naturally. This what we have, what we share is something I never thought I wanted. Now, it's all I want.

"Good. Let me pop this in the oven, it shouldn't take long," she tells me, picking up the tray that's lined with chicken wrapped in bacon. "How did Izzy's scan go this afternoon? Do they know the sex?" she asks, her beaming smile filling the room.

"Izzy and the baby are both fine, but they couldn't tell whether it's a boy or a girl, I think it had its legs crossed."

"Yeah, that happens a lot," she says, crouched down by the oven door. I nod my head at her, knowing the same thing happened when they were expecting Rebecca.

"Do you like feta cheese?" Holly asks, once she shuts the oven door, rinsing her hands before she tosses the salad into a bowl.

"I do," I answer, as I wrap my arms around her waist and press my front to her back. Bringing my mouth to her ear, "Even if I didn't the fact that my woman wants to cook for me would have me eating it anyway," I say, pressing my lips onto the bare skin between her shoulder and neck.

"Hmmm, you're so easy to please," she says, chuckling at my comment. "It's inside the chicken, but if you don't like it, I could whip something else up."

"Well, I do like it and where you're concerned I am always pleased." I rock my hips into her, getting a slap with the tea towel for my teasing.

"I thought we could eat out on the balcony, it's such a lovely evening and there's a beautiful view of the park."

"Sounds good to me."

"Good, 'cause the alternative would be to sit at the breakfast bar." She points at the small area that probably would be a very tight fit to seat two for dinner. "Or, we could sit on the floor and eat around the coffee table in the living room. It's not very big…"

"Aw, sweetheart," I say, placing my hand on my chest and averting my eyes to my crotch. "That's not what you said the other night when I had you bent over the settee," I say, wiggling my eyebrows and sending her a flirty wink.

"Oh my god," she squeals, covering her blushing face with her hand. "I can't believe you." She throws the tea towel at me, chuckling at my comment.

"Sorry, couldn't help myself. Plus, you did set yourself up for it." She's still laughing at me when I wrap my arms around her and lower my lips to hers.

"Well, I need to go set the table," she says, pulling out of my arms. "Because the chicken and jacket potatoes will be ready in about twenty minutes," she says, retrieving a tablecloth from the drawer and two wine glasses from the cabinet.

I'm still in the shirt and trousers I had worn for work, didn't want to waste any more time away from Holly.

"I need to change. Can I jump in your shower? I was running late so I haven't had time to freshen up yet."

"Of course. You don't need to ask. You're better off using the shower in the bedroom, it's bigger than the one in the bathroom." She places the glasses on the worktop. "I'll show you where the towels are." Holly strolls off towards her bedroom and I go to fetch my bag from the hallway then follow her into her room.

She passes me two soft bath towels, then opens one of the built-in cupboard doors. As I'm stripping off my shirt and trousers, Holly turns to me. Her sapphire eyes rake over my naked chest then lower to my bottom half that is just clad in black boxers. My angel's lips moisten, and that naughty look appears on her face as her lust-full eyes roam back up my body and reach mine. My little minx wants to play. "Something you want, sweetheart?" I ask, lowering my voice while I lean against the wall.

"What? No." She shakes her head, flustered, realising she's just been caught ogling. I don't mind, she can watch all she likes; if she wanted me to put on a show to music, I'd gladly get my kit off. I close the distance between us, knowing if we get into this now we won't be eating until midnight. "Stop." She puts her hand out, placing it on my chest. There's a smirk on her face and her breath catches when I remove it and run my lips over her wrist then pull her in to me.

"Are you teasing me?" I whisper into her ear.

"No. You need to stop flaunting this..." Her hand waves up and down my body; the smile on her face and glint in her eye, tells me she was enjoying watching me strip.

"Aw sweetheart, you know you can't resist me," I tease, pressing up against her so she can feel my very hard length. Her eyes fill with lust and her chest rises and falls as she breathes in and out deeply. Holly's hand reaches out and grips hold of me. I swallow hard. Didn't expect this before dinner. Her mouth moves to the middle of my chest where she places a soft kiss. With my dick still gripped by her hand she drops tender kisses along my chest and throat then continues until she is stood on her tiptoes and her mouth is next to my ear.

"Hmmm," she breathes. "As much as I would love to finish what we have started," she looks up at me and pats my chest with her other hand, "we will have to continue later because dinner will burn, you need a shower and I need to find the parasol in that cupboard, so I can set the table." She smirks at me then throws me a cheeky wink. What the hell? I can't believe the little minx is going to leave me hanging. Her hand drops me, and she sashays off towards the cupboard she had opened when I first started to strip.

I chuckle at her boldness, happy that it is me who brings out her naughty side that she didn't even know she had. I think we both bring out a different side in each other, but I can't leave my little angel without giving her a taste of her own medicine.

She turns to me as she stretches to reach something from out of the cupboard. Her T-shirt rises, showing her slim waist and that little naughty smirk is still fixed in place. Oh, let's see if it's still there when the shoe is on the other foot.

My finger runs up her exposed skin and she lets out a little shudder. "Holly, sweetheart," I whisper into her ear, making sure our bodies are touching. "If you're going to rouse the beast..." I move my hands to the firm cheeks of her arse and take her bottom lip in my teeth, giving it a little nip, then stroke my tongue over soft flesh. Holly moans against my lips, her eyes closed, loving the feeling of me stroking and squeezing her bottom. My lips run up her neck as her breath quickens; once I reach her ear I finish what I wanted to say. "Tease the beast, Holly, and this..." I slap her arse hard and she lets out a squeal, "will suffer later."

I wink, turn and saunter off towards the bathroom, chuckling when she shouts out, "Bastard."

I'm not long in the shower. Once I'm dry, I slip into a pair of faded jeans, and saunter back into the bedroom. Expecting to find Holly either in the kitchen or out on the balcony, I'm surprised to see her sat on the floor propped up against the wall. Around her are lots of old nick knacks and a tatty carboard box that is tipped upside down. Hugging her knees with her head bent down touching them, her right hand holds an old rag doll. She lets out a sniffle which has me moving faster than lightening, I'm by her side. My hands go straight to the sides of her face that I gently lift and that's when my heart lurches out of my chest. Tears spill down her cheeks. Using my thumbs to wipe them away, I look at the woman I love, broken. Her face is red and blotchy and her lip trembles as more tears fall from her bloodshot eyes.

"Holly, sweetheart, what's wrong?" My concerned voice cracks because if there's one thing I have come to realise is that seeing this woman so upset breaks my heart.

Moving a loose piece of hair behind her ear, I place my cheek on hers. "What's happened?" I whisper, placing soft kisses on her damp cheek. She shudders in my arms and moves back out of my hold. Her palms press into her eyes wiping away the tears.

"Sorry," she sobs while reaching for the tatty old box that's been held together with tape. She drops the doll in it then picks up one of the crumpled photographs. Putting my hand on hers, I stop her and lift her chin so she has to look at me.

"Holly, tell me what's happened."

"Nothing, I'm being silly," she sniffles, wiping at the tears that have dampened her face, the face that was full of fun and happiness when I went to shower not more than fifteen minutes ago. Looking at the picture that's still in her hand, I can see it's one of a small child and a young woman. There's a few more of them on the floor and a letter addressed to Holly.

I'm not stupid, I can see this small shabby box holds some of her past and it's remembering that, that has her sobbing like a little girl.

"Holly, stop. You're not being silly." This time I lift her into my arms and carry her to the bed where I sit down and position her so she is sat across my knee. She wraps her arms around my neck and buries her face into my chest. We sit there silent for a little while. Me, waiting for her to divulge something that is painful for her but will help her so much if she can let it out.

Her sobs have stopped when she lifts her head, looking at her sad childhood laid out on the floor. "I didn't know it was in there," her voice shaky as her foot lifts and points at the worn-out box. "It fell out when the parasol got stuck on it," she sobs. I take the photo from her trembling hand, looking at the scrawny, ill-treated girl. It's easy to see the child is Holly and the woman with dark-rimmed sunken eyes is her mother. Although they both look like they could do with a good meal and a hot bath, there's a look of happiness on their face. "Olivia and Sarah must have put it up on the shelf when they helped me move in here. I haven't looked in that box in years." Her eyes stay fixed on the box as a heartfelt sigh makes her shudder and my arms automatically hold her tighter. My lips kiss her hair and I rub her back gently.

"Is this your mother?" I ask. Holly nods her head and takes the photograph from me. Her eyes cast downwards, and her body lets out a shiver as she continues.

"I don't remember much from living with my real mum, just certain things that're hard to forget. In this photo she was off the drugs and we were spending quality time together, we were happy for a little while.

"I was four years old and had seen my mum drugged up to the eyes too many times. Listened to too many men come to see her while I hid in the wardrobe in the bedroom, too scared to sleep in my own bed. The parties, the arguing would have me taking my pillow and blanket and hiding in the bottom of the single wardrobe."

I don't say anything as Holly moves out of my arms to pick up the little rag doll. She holds it for a while then returns to me. My arms hold her tight as I look at the tatty doll that probably kept her company on those lonely, daunting nights.

"She was my only friend. I'd cuddle her all night long. I had a habit of rubbing her hair between my fingers for some reason it would relax me, and I'd fall off to sleep, curled into the tiniest ball until the morning. Then I would creep downstairs, listening to make sure there was no one there, and eat whatever I could find for breakfast."

My heart rips apart for the little girl who had no one to turn to but an old doll. Holly's never once mentioned anything about her mother or why she was adopted, and I've never asked. We both have a past, Holly's being one of continuous loss and hurt of people she loved, mine being one of deception, immoral activities and greed from the people I loved.

"Sometimes…" Holly's voice trails off as she holds tightly onto the doll, sitting up a bit on my knee. My arms stay around her, holding her. One of my hands reach out to hold hers, the one that is holding the doll. My other hand lifts her chin, so she can see my eyes. I want her to know I will always be here for her. If she wants to fall apart while remembering her childhood, I will pick her up afterwards. If she just needs an ear to listen to her then I have two that will hang on to every word while she gets it off her chest. If she needs me to take her high amongst the stars in the throes of passion, so she can forget just for a while some of the hurt from her upbringing, then I'm on it. Every day, I will make it my life's work that she never has to remember any hurt from her past. She sees the warmth and love I hold for her in my eyes and her mouth moves to mine; she places her lips to the side of mine and tenderly kisses me, before sitting back up.

"Sometimes, I would find her slouched across the settee, her discarded drug paraphernalia on the table and beer bottles scattered about the room. I'd quietly put them in the bin, cover her with the blanket that had slipped off her then I would rummage in the kitchen for something to eat. Once she woke she would find me back in my room looking at the books she had bought me or playing with my doll. She'd tell me what a loving daughter I was and either drop me at nursery or take me to the park for an hour." She looks at the photo and rubs her thumb over it. I don't speak. I just pull her into my embrace, my head resting on hers, so she can't see the tears that threaten my eyes. While her mother slept off the effects of her partying, my angel was left to fend for herself. To hide in the darkness of the night without her mother to comfort her if she had a bad dream or if she was unwell. To clear the mess that had been left from her so-called mother and her friends and to search for scraps for her breakfast. My heart bleeds. Swallowing the lump in my throat, I sit up. Holly doesn't need to see the anger and hurt building in me. She needs me to be strong just like her.

"In this photo, I think she was trying to come off the drugs. I remember people coming to the house, I think they must have been from child services because they would ask lots of questions. I had started reception class and she couldn't get away with keeping me at home anymore, too stoned to get me there half the time. However, it didn't last because not long after that photo was taken, she left me alone while she nipped out. It wasn't the first time but usually she would be back within a couple of hours. She always left me a watch, it's that one on the floor." Holly points down towards some of the photos. I hadn't noticed the old watch with a large clock face, the photographs partly covering it. Holly leans down and picks it up then gets herself comfy again. "She would tell me to watch the big hand go around the full clock twice and she would be back and often she got back before. Only, this time she didn't. I watched the darkness descend twice and listened to the birds sing their morning song twice before someone came knocking at the door."

I can't keep quiet anymore. "Holly," I whisper, running my hands over her face and brushing her wavy hair back behind her ears. "I'm so sorry you had to go through such…" She puts a finger on my lips to stop me. I kiss it then move in and kiss her cheek. "You must have been petrified," I utter into her hair. She nods her head at me, pulling back a little, then she continues with her story.

"When I didn't answer the door, it was kicked open. I remember hiding behind the settee, holding that box." She nods her head towards the box that's on the floor. "I'd made a bed inside it for my doll, and when someone knocked at the door, I was scared. I'd always been told not to answer the door so the first thing I did was pick up the box with the doll in it and hide behind the settee. The police were the first to enter, I could see their uniforms, then a man and woman followed them. I'd seen them both before when they came to speak to my mum. They were from child services and they explained to me that my mum had been arrested and that I was going to stay with a nice couple by the name of Mr and Mrs Spencer. I took the box with me."

She stops, and a lone tear slips from her eye and runs onto her cheek. My thumb wipes it away and I pull her into my arms, my lips gently kissing her hair. I'm not sure if the tear was for her mum or for Mr and Mrs Spencer, who ended up adopting her then were taken from her in her teens when they were killed in a car crash.

A high-pitched beeping noise pulls us apart and scrambling off the bed. We race into the kitchen to find smoke billowing out of the cooker. Quickly, I cut the electric supply and open the oven door, wafting the tea towel at the smoke. Holly opens the windows before coming to my side, bending down to look at the burnt offerings that I'm lifting out of the oven. I drop it in the sink and turn on the cold water. It sizzles dramatically. As the smoke disperses we can see our dinner is thoroughly fucked. "Looks like we're eating takeout," Holly chuckles. Although, there's a hint of a smile on her beautiful face, there's still sadness in her eyes. I want to see my Holly back and I know exactly what will do it.

"No, sweetheart, we're going out." I kiss Holly hard on the lips then go retrieve my mobile phone from my jacket pocket. I send a quick text; within minutes I have the reply I need.

"I can't go out. Look at me – my face, it's blotchy, I'm a wreck," she says, her hands covering her face. I take her hands away and put mine there, so I'm holding her face in my hands. "You have every right to be upset and every right to cry but it's my right as the man who loves you." I stare into her glazed eyes, hoping she sees that I mean what I am saying. I watch her swallow and the acknowledgement of my declaration to her registers. Her lip trembles and her eyes fill up again. "I love you so much, Holly, and I will do anything and everything to make sure that you see it every day." I kiss her fiercely, swallowing her moans, taking away the pain that had her distraught and giving her me. Me to depend on. Me to show her that she is wanted, desired, even when she thinks she is not looking her best. Me to always be there for her. I break away from our kiss. "Come," I say, holding out my hand. I lead us back into the bedroom and towards the en-suite bathroom. "Go shower and I will get this cleaned away," I say, pointing to the box and photos on the floor.

"Thank you," she says, lifting her hand to stroke my face. I turn my head and kiss her hand then send her off into the bathroom with a slap on her arse. I don't need a thank you from Holly, I need to see that playful smile back on her face.

I text Nicholas, to ask him if he will bring me a clean shirt and suit over to Holly's. I had only put jeans and T-shirt in my bag, which I was going to wear tomorrow for work, not that I planned to go in for long. I was hoping to spend most of the day in Holly's bed with us both wrapped together like vines.

Within half an hour, I have put everything back in the box, cleared away the burnt offerings in the kitchen, picked out a very sexy lingerie set for Holly and an elegant wraparound dress with matching shoes for her to wear to the restaurant. I'd texted my manageress to have my table set for two and to have a bottle of champagne on ice ready for when we arrive. Nicholas has dropped off my suit and I'm just slipping on my trousers when Holly comes out of the bathroom with just a towel covering her. She looks refreshed and as beautiful as always. Her hair is pinned up and she's put a light touch of make-up on. I saunter over to her as I'm fastening up my pants. "I chose a dress and underwear for you, I hope you don't mind." My lips turn up a smile when she picks up the underwear, raising her eyebrows at me.

"Sexy, I forgot I had these," she smirks, holding up the silky transparent bits of material. "Bought by my two interfering friends from some underwear party." She screws her nose up at them, chuckling, then looks at the dress I picked out for her. "Good choice." She nods her head then drops her towel, baring her beautiful body to me. Her body screams for me to claim her, throw her on the bed and bury myself deep inside her. Pushing her to the limit, eradicating all the hurt she felt this evening and replacing it with ecstasy. But, I don't, I have plans for us tonight. Making love to her is on the agenda but so is showing that I know what she enjoys.

We dress quickly and make our way out to the lift. "Where are we going?" Holly asks.

I tap my nose in response. "Wait and see," I tell her, taking her hand as the lift door opens for us to step in. The lift door closes; Holly turns to me, taking my jacket lapels in her hands. She has something to say. Her tongue strokes her bottom lip before she bites it nervously. "I forgot to tell you," she whispers. I tilt my head at her questionably. Her eyes flicker. I know she's nervous about whatever she's forgot to tell me.

"What is it?" I ask, stroking her cheek with my thumb. She rises on her tip toes, so our lips are just about touching, then her sapphire eyes gaze into mine.

"Hmmm. I forgot to tell you. I love you too," she whispers then shares her lip gloss with me. Our kiss lingers until the lift lands and the doors open. My heart beat is racing, and the temperature has just gone up a few degrees. It's the first time that a woman has ever told me she loves me and meant it. Placing my head on hers, I catch my breath that she has just taken away. Then I lower to her ear. "Good, because if you hadn't had told me before we got home tonight I would have had to fuck it out of you."

She gasps at my comment and slaps my chest while I chuckle at her. I knew she was in as deep as me but hearing it warms me and makes me ecstatic. We walk to the car hand in hand, me getting a telling off for my inappropriate comment. Holly knows I like our banter. My dirty inuendoes make her blush and have her covering her mouth to stifle a giggle. I'm normally subjected to a jab of her elbow or a playful slap and a prod from her finger. Love taps. Occasionally, she'll play along with me, letting all her inhibitions go and giving in to the little minx inside her.

*

Falling through the door of the office that I have in Eruption, Holly has my shirt untucked and is tugging at the zip of my trousers. I love how eager she is to get me naked.

Leaving the restaurant where we had eaten our weight in seafood and drank a bottle of champagne, we made our way to Eruption. It was eighties night and I knew Holly would love the music. If there was anything that would help rid her of the hurt she was feeling earlier, music would be one. Seafood, champagne and me being amorous would seal the deal.

After having our hands all over each other on the dance floor for the last two hours, I could see the lust in her eyes. When we dance, the passion intensifies between us. It happened within minutes of meeting in this very place only five weeks ago. Our bodies join, and our hands feel their way around, arousing and igniting a fire so hot we should come with a warning label.

It was no surprise when Holly dragged me off the dance floor. Well, I didn't need much dragging because if she hadn't have moved when she did, I would have probably thrown her over my shoulder and marched us both up to the office, too urgent to wait until we got home. Knowing what she wanted, I was only too happy to help her out.

Stripped down to my boxers, my little minx beckons me to join her. She's perched on my desk, wearing just her silky knickers and heels. Her hair is still pinned up.

Settling between her legs, I pull the clips out that holds it in place. Shaking her golden locks, so they fall in ripples down her back, she's a vision of perfection. I drop my boxers and take her in, running my fingers down her face to her kissable lips. Tracing down her flawless skin until I reach the swell of her breast. Perfect. My hands feel their way over her soft curves.

Holly's eyes smile at my erection; she places both her hands on my desk and lifts her bottom. Her mouth smirks at me, anticipating my next move. She's come to know her underwear will be soon ripped from her. I don't keep her waiting. I know she's eager to ignite the flame that's been burning for hours. With one swift movement the garment is removed and lying on the floor as we join our bodies together.

Our bodies entwine as we clear the desk of its contents which clatter onto the floor. My mouth moves manically down her neck, across her collarbone then latch onto her hard nipple. Nipping and twirling my tongue, Holly moaning and grinding her hips into me. I pick up the pace, knowing this will be the first of many orgasms tonight.

The dull music that echoes around the club helps to drown out the moans and growls that escapes from me when Holly's hand strokes over my skin and her teeth score at my neck and shoulder. Her mouth moves to mine as she sucks on my tongue. I can't help but drive myself deeper into her while my fingers grip her hips so tight I'm sure I will bruise her.

The feeling of Holly tightening around me, carries me away into another world. Where the smell of summer meadows, rich with colour, the soft sound of the rippling stream that sparkles like diamonds in the summer sun and the sweet sound of the blackbird enhances my senses has me growling out my release as tears pool in my eyes. This is what she does to me. Takes me away from a world of pain and replaces it with her overwhelming love.

I fall onto Holly breathless, nuzzling my face into the crook of her neck, hoping she doesn't feel the wetness from my eyes. With my heart beating as if it's going to break out of my chest, I try to think of any other time that I was with a woman when my emotions came to the fore. I can't think of any. Only with my angel.

We lay contented with Holly stroking her nimble fingers over my back. "Are you OK?" she murmurs, moving her hand so she's now running her fingers through the back of my hair.

"Hmmm. Yeah." I lift, holding Holly to me, then carry us both over to the two-seater settee.

Settling comfortably, Holly straddles my hips as she kisses up my neck onto my chin then takes my lips. Her hips rotate, causing me to harden again. Within minutes we're making good use of the settee, the walls and the floor.

Exhausted, I flop down onto the softness of the sofa, relishing the feeling on my back. Holly has taken off into the bathroom to freshen up, leaving me to get my breath back. Looking at my watch, it's three o'clock in the morning and I know I will have to move soon before Frank and the manager do their check, so they can lock up.

My little minx appears in the doorway. "Are you moving any time soon?" She smirks at me, walking over to where I am sat she gives me her hand.

"I can't move, I think you've broke my back and my dick," I groan, shifting from my seat, so I'm stood in front of her.

"How are you still walking?" I chuckle while tapping her nose gently.

"Oh, believe me, I doubt I'll be getting up from my bed tomorrow or the next day." She stretches her back out and covers her mouth when she yawns. "Look, I'm ready to fall asleep where I'm stood. You go get dressed and I will tidy up in here. I don't want your sons walking in here thinking they've had burglars." Her laugh is contagious, and I can't help but laugh with her as I collect my shirt and trousers that are crumpled on the floor. Just picturing their faces if they were to see the state of this place, almost has me leaving it as it is.

Once I'm dressed and we have put things back in place, I order a taxi to take us back to Holly's. I don't think we will be moving out of bed tomorrow, so a quick text to my sons asking them to drop Lucas at school then pick him up and drop him at Holly's afterwards. We'll get a takeout when he arrives and hopefully I will able to persuade Holly to come and stay at mine at night. I don't want to leave her alone. I was supposed to be calling into work tomorrow for a few hours, but I've just decided I'll take a few days off, so I can spoil her. Hopefully, I can keep her mind off the hurt she endured when she was only the age of my granddaughter.

Chapter 27

Holly

"Don't walk so bloody fast," Ivy says as we make our way down the narrow-cobbled street towards Kitted Out, the small boutique where we hope to be able to buy something suitable for a black-tie event. Our appointment there is for ten thirty; Sarah had telephoned them two weeks ago after we had arranged to go with Vlad to the golf club's annual fund-raising night.

Ivy links Olivia's arm as we pass by the variety of chic shops that fill the busy street. The whiff of coffee coming from the pavement café mixed with the fragrance from the scented candle shop and the aroma of smoke coming from the jacket potato stall, floats through the air. I inhale the smells and take in my friends old and new, more than happy to be here with them.

"I hope the shop we want isn't as small as some of these," Ivy waves her hand around, getting our attention, "because you'll be lucky to get your chest in, never mind the six of us." She looks down at Olivia's boobs, shaking her head with a smirk on her face.

"Cheeky mare," Olivia says, unlinking her arm from Ivy's and stopping in her tracks. "There's nothing wrong with having ample boobs and I'll have you know your son loves my chest." Her hands are on her hips now as she turns up a smile at her mother-in-law. They have a fantastic relationship. All the years I have known them they have got along like two best friends. Always taking their little digs in a bit of fun. Olivia's chest size and Ivy's choice in hair colour get a mention often.

"Oh, I know. I've watched him drool many times when you've had them on display." She lowers her glasses from the bridge of her nose, so her eyes look over them and thins her lips as if she is some type of old school mistress.

"Mum, Nanna, will you stop? You're showing us up," Lucy chastises them like children.

Chuckling at them, I look at Izzy who is giggling away at their interaction.

"It's not that small and if we don't get a move on, we'll be late," Sarah says.

"Oh, don't get me started on you with your arse hanging out of everything you wear."

"What?" Sarah snorts, out covering her mouth to stifle her laughter.

"Oh my god," both Lucy and Izzy say in unison, giggling as Izzy leans on Lucy, putting one hand on her shoulder and crossing her legs as if she will wet herself.

"Listen you two," Ivy points at Sarah and Olivia. "When you both choose something to wear can you please choose something that covers your assets?" she tells them, biting on her lip to stifle her laugh.

"Nanna!" Lucy shouts. "Come on, let's get moving before that man over there, who has heard every word that you have said, dies of a heart attack." She links her nanna and sets off walking towards the shop.

"Hang on," Olivia says, catching them up. "What about Holly?"

"What about Holly?" Ivy asks.

"Doesn't she get told what she can and can't wear?"

"No. Holly always dresses accordingly." She looks across to me and winks with that conniving smirk of hers. She's a mischievous old bugger.

"Oh, Holly always dresses accordingly, does she?" Olivia and Sarah say together. "Well ask her what she was wearing the night she met Vlad because believe us, she gave him easy access to all her assets." They both link arms, passing by us smirking at me and nodding their heads at Ivy.

Ivy looks at me and winks. "Don't worry, Holly, I'm sure you looked the picture of elegance," then picks up her feet again and sets off.

Chuckling at them, Izzy complains she is going to wet herself and Lucy tells them it's like shopping with teenage girls. I can't help but join in with them. "Oh, you never know, I might buy something that sends my man into a frenzy for the night out." My hand rakes through my hair as I give them a sideways glance.

"Just remember it's not a night club. It will be full of sophistication, style and elegance, so choose suitably, ladies," she tells us.

"Have you forgotten I was married to a wanker?" Shaking my head, I amend my statement with a chuckle. "Oh, sorry, I meant banker."

"Nice," Sarah gleams. "I think you was right the first time."

"You know? That's the first time I have heard you slag him off, without you looking upset," Olivia says, placing her arm around me to give me a hug. "Well done you and well done Vladimir Petrov for showing you how a woman is supposed to be treated."

"Yes, I shall have to thank that man for putting that new smile on your face, it's one I've not seen on you before, Holly," Ivy says.

"It's a beam from bonking constantly," Sarah says. "You see it on us two all the time." She points between Olivia and herself. Olivia nods in agreement, flashing all of us a wide excited grin. Ivy shakes her head at them and Lucy gives out a little shiver, not wanting to think about her mum and dad getting it on.

We walk quietly towards the shop that is just ahead of us; Olivia moves in close to me.

"It wouldn't matter to that man of yours what you wear, Holly, I think when he looks at you he sees a beautiful, caring lovable woman." She nods at her own words. "I also think," her eyebrows lift, "when he looks at you, he sees you naked because I swear the times I have seen you together he always looks as if he wants to feast on you."

"Yeah, that man has it bad for you," Sarah declares, walking alongside us.

They're not wrong; I never know when he's going to pounce on me. The last week has gone by so fast, it's been a whirlwind of sightseeing, eating and mind-blowing orgasms. I've lived here all my life and never realised how beautiful the Yorkshire countryside is. Eating extravagant meals in romantic settings, my man knows how to charm me. He can have me wanting him with just one look.

Having sex outside the bedroom has become an everyday occurrence. Up against trees, me straddled across him while we're hidden in the long grass. Him sneaking into the ladies' of his own restaurant, his hand covering my mouth to stifle my moans and him biting down on my shoulder to drown out his growl. Over desks, back seat of the car, shower and most walls in his home. Acting like two young twenty-year-olds, we couldn't get enough of each other.

We would fall into bed exhausted from our shenanigans throughout the day and the evening. Then in the early hours his tender kisses would rouse me, and we would make love with a passion so strong, emotions so high, I'm sure if anyone was passing outside they would see bloody fireworks coming out of the roof.

Since my meltdown last week he has not left my side, but he's never once mentioned it either. Our night out was one to remember and there's been many more since. Spoiling me and keeping a smile permanently on my face has become his mission. Lavishing in each other has kept me from remembering the past and given me hope for a better future, and I think that was his intention.

"We're here," Sarah lets us know. Opening the door, an old-fashioned bell rings above it. The shop is bigger than it looks from the outside and a bubbly middle-aged woman gushes towards us.

"Come in," she smiles. "I'll be with you in a few minutes, I'm just finishing serving this lady then I'm all yours. Please look around." Her hand twirls in the air then she returns to a tall brunette woman who looks down her nose at us all pouring into this classy shop.

We mooch round, taking in the fine garments hung on

mannequins and lining the walls, feeling the silk and lace as we go. "It's like the bloody Tardis in here," Izzy jokes.

"Yes, it is. It's bigger than it looks," Lucy agrees, running her hand over a black embroidered gown. "And there isn't a price tag on any of these dresses," she whispers, looking at the gown again. I can see she has fallen for that one already, but she is right about them not having any price tags on.

"That's because they don't want to scare you off," Olivia says to Lucy. "Do you like that one?" Olivia asks her, looking up at the gown.

"Hmmm, it has caught my eye," she answers, tilting her head to the side as she scrunches her lips up.

"You know the saying, don't you?" Ivy asks Lucy.

"What saying?"

"If you need to ask the price you can't afford it," she tells her. "And you, my dear, don't need to worry because your grandad is treating you."

"No. You both spoil us enough," she argues, knowing her grandparents spoil all their grandchildren and if I know Ivy, Lucy will be walking out of this shop with that dress belonging to her.

"Well who else are we going to spend our hard-earned money on, if not our grandchildren?"

Olivia stands in front of Ivy pointing into her chest, mouthing, 'Me.' Ivy slaps her hands away. "Oh, stop, you. Your husband gives you anything you want."

"Yeah, he does, but he gets this in return," she smirks, running her hands down her body.

"Mum! Stop!" Lucy snaps, shaking her head at her floozy of a mother. You would think the poor girl would be used to her mother and father's explicit suggestions and harmless flirtatious behaviour.

Jack adores Olivia and would do anything for her. He's worked hard over the years to provide for his family, but Olivia has worked equally hard by his side.

"Oh, baby, I'm only having a laugh." She gives Lucy a cuddle and kisses the top of her head. "Wait till you meet the love of your life, we'll see what your behaviour's like then." She kisses her head again and tells her to pick whatever dress she wants – Nanna and Grandad are paying – and that she and Jack will buy her shoes and bag and anything else she needs.

Lucy doesn't argue; she knows she isn't going to win this battle.

We continue to admire the gowns on display when two more women make an appearance from what looks like the changing room. They greet us all with a smile and introduce themselves as Barbara the seamstress and Michelle, one of the sales assistants.

The doorbell dings again as the snooty cow leaves and the lady who welcomed us in drops the latch on the door. "I'll close while we're attending to you ladies," she says.

She introduces herself as Leana, the owner, and doesn't mind closing when she has a few ladies in all at once. Izzy raises her eyebrows at me and I know exactly what she is thinking.

That this only happens in very expensive ladies and gents' shops.

Leana informs us that any gown we choose can be altered by Barbara, free of charge, and will be delivered to our home addresses if we wish.

Michelle pops a bottle of champagne and pours a glass for everyone then we set about looking for the perfect gown.

Crickey, anyone would think we were looking for a wedding dress with the over-the-top treatment from these ladies. I'm sure the prices will reflect on the style and service of this boutique. Maybe I should have took Vlad's offer to pay for my outfit for the evening.

A chuckle escapes my lips when I remember the look on his handsome face as I threw his bank card back at him while ripping up the pin number he had sneaked into my bag this morning.

He growled and grunted while mumbling to himself. Then when I informed him I would be staying at home tonight, he pinned me to the mattress, trying to seduce me into staying with him. And it might have worked if I hadn't already arranged to have a girls' night in with Olivia and Sarah.

We have a lot of catching up to do, mainly them wanting to get all the dirty gossip on my relationship with Vlad. Plus, the new project that Izzy and I have going for Aphrodite.

*

If I thought it felt strange last night not having Vlad to snuggle up with, this morning was even worse. Waking without him wrapped around me or me sprawled across his broad chest, with the light sprinkling of hair tickling my face, feels wrong.

Shopping with the girls yesterday, couldn't have gone better. We spent an obscene amount of money on the most exquisite dresses I have ever seen, and I've seen quite a few. Not one had to be altered and we opted for them all to be delivered to Olivia's as that's where we will be getting ready the night of the fundraiser.

We then went on to buy some real pricey sexy underwear that if my man tries to rip off, I will put him on rations in the bedroom. Not really, I bought them with him in mind and can't wait to see that animal look in his eyes when he does.

We had bought shoes, bags and accessories, which I was told not to buy. Apparently, Vlad had texted Izzy and put her on 'stop Holly from accessorising' duty because he would like to treat me. I couldn't say no; Izzy was too bloody cute when she pleaded with me to give him a break and let him spoil me.

After we had eaten, Izzy and Ivy made their way home and the rest of us took a taxi to Sarah's and that's where we stayed until nine thirty. I had spoken to Vlad over the phone when we finished shopping. Nicholas and Daniel were staying with him and Lucas tonight, having a lads' night in. I texted him when I arrived home and he telephoned me telling me he wouldn't be able to sleep if he didn't hear my voice. He's so mushy but I knew what he meant.

We stayed on the phone for nearly an hour, him only letting me go when I complained I had a headache. I thought it was because of the champagne we had while shopping, and the couple of glasses of wine I had had at Sarah's, but waking this morning tells me otherwise.

A wave of nausea hits me as I push the palm of my hand into the left side of my head to try and combat what feels like a streak of lightning traveling from my temple into the back of my eye. Curling into a ball and laying back on to my bed, I cover my head with the quilt.

My bedroom curtains are not very thick and let in the morning sun which doesn't help with the migraine attack that started with a mild throb last night but has become a full-blown one now.

I haven't had one for a very long time but when I do it hits me like a sledgehammer to the side of my face, leaving me unable to leave the house for a couple of days.

Breathing through the sickness and pain, I get out of bed. My medication is in the bathroom cabinet and the cool pack for my eyes is in the fridge. Collecting my meds, I pick up a pillow and make my way into the living room. The curtains in there darken the room better than the bedroom, so I think curling up on the settee would be beneficial to my condition.

After taking the two oval tablets, I place the glass of water and the other tablet I can take if these don't kick in, on the table, then get cuddled up with my quilt. Quickly, I send a text to Vlad, explaining that I can't meet him for lunch. He won't be happy, but it can't be helped. Then I place the cool pack over my eyes, sinking into the soft cushions. Hopefully, I can get a few hours' sleep which might help with the pain.

Sleep overtook me swiftly and when I wake a few hours later, the nausea has subsided a little. Knowing this is the best time for me to try and eat something I stagger into the kitchen to make some toast.

Finishing my toast and a cup of tea I pop the plate and cup in the sink, ready to climb back onto my makeshift bed when there's a rather loud knock at my door. I wasn't expecting anyone, and I don't really want anyone visiting me today. Maybe if I ignore it whoever it is will go away. Knowing my friends are all busy this morning and Vlad is in a meeting with his accountant till mid-day, I decide not to bother answering it. As I turn to walk towards the settee, dizziness overcomes me, and I find myself having to grip the back of it.

There's another knock at the door and I wince at the thunderous sound. Lowering to the floor and crouching on all fours, I crawl the short distance towards the hallway. Standing on shaky legs, I open the door where I'm met with one very upset-looking man.

With hands braced on the door frame and a face that looks like thunder, I move to let my distressed man in. Just then I'm hit with another dizzy spell and I find myself being lifted off the floor with a pair of thick muscular arms supporting me. "Fucking hell, Holly, let's get you sat down," comes the concerned voice of a man who now looks worried. He sits us both down, me on his knee, wrapping his arms around me with my face snuggled into his chest. Best place in the world. "Do I need to take you to a doctor?" He lifts my chin, looking into my eyes. I must look like shit, but Vlad looks at me as if I'm the most beautiful woman in the world. I shake my head.

"No. It's a migraine, I have medication for it."

"I knew I should have come over last night when you said you wasn't feeling well," he moans into my hair while rubbing my back. Funny, I feel a little better already just snuggled into Vlad's warm chest, listening to the steady rhythm of his heartbeat while his strong hands lovingly rub up and down my body.

"It felt just like a normal headache last night," I mumble, still happy been pressed against him. "I thought you were in a meeting till lunch."

"I was. I should be, but I cancelled it when I saw your text." He kisses my head and shuffles a bit to get comfortable.

"You didn't need to do that." I lift my aching head to look at him.

"Holly," his hands come up to my face and his thumbs stroke over my cheekbones, "please don't tell me what I don't need to do when it concerns you. I'm not going to leave you alone when you're not well," he affirms.

Even if I wanted to argue, that I'm used to been left on my own when I'm not well, I haven't got the energy to, and in truth I like the fact that he wants to take care of me. I would do the same for him.

"Wow," he says. "You must be ill, you're not being your normal pain in the arse when you disagree with me," he chuckles, rubbing his nose against mine.

Nuzzling into his neck and inhaling his masculine smell, I murmur, "That's only because I don't have the energy to give you a hard time." My finger gently prods him in his ribs and I'm suddenly being carried towards the bedroom.

"Good, because you're coming home with me."

There's no discussion.

He just carefully places me on the bed, rummages around in my wardrobe and drawers, filling a bag, then stalks off to the bathroom, returning with my medication. I don't stop him. Nor do I stop him when he gently takes off my shorts and vest and replaces them with jogging bottoms and a sports T-shirt.

My make-up bag, handbag and contraceptive pills are put inside the hold-all while he collects the spare set of keys from the kitchen drawer. Sitting there, I just watch mesmerised at this larger-than-life man who looks to any outsider, unapproachable and menacing, but is anything but.

In no time at all, the items of clothing that Vlad had packed for me are hanging alongside his with the clothes I had left here yesterday morning. My toiletries have joined Vlad's. There's a DO NOT DISTURB notice on the bedroom door and I am nestled into the middle of his oversized bed with his blackout blinds closed.

My head hurts, my eyes ache, but my heart is full of love for the man who makes me feel wanted like no one before. There's nowhere I would rather be.

I must have drifted off into a peaceful sleep and when I wake, it's four o'clock in the afternoon. On the edge of the bed, sits my handsome man rubbing my back. Sitting up, the nausea, dizziness and the feeling that my head might explode has lessened to just a dull ache behind my eyes. "How are you feeling, sweetheart?" Vlad asks, his voice soft and warm. He climbs onto the bed and lays on his stomach at the side of me. I lay back down again, turning on my side so I'm facing him.

"Much better, thank you." I snuggle into him as his arm comes over me and his hand comes up, lightly stroking my hair.

"You look better than you did this morning."

"Yeah, I bet I looked a sight for sore eyes."

"You always look beautiful to me," he whispers, the words drifting across my cheek like a soft feather as he tenderly places a kiss.

"Hmmm. You're such a charmer." I close my eyes, relishing the feeling of his hand massaging my head and his soft lips touching my eyelids.

"Only with you," he murmurs.

Vlad sits up and looks towards the bedside table. "I've made you a light snack, if you're up to eating."

I could eat something. I haven't had anything since eating two slices of toast this morning.

"Thank you." I sit up as he passes me a tray with a chicken salad sandwich and some berries in a dish.

"Wasn't sure what you would want, so I opt for a small sandwich." His smile is comforting and warm.

"This is fine. I'm lucky the nausea has eased off or I wouldn't be able to get this down."

I finish the sandwich in no time at all and eat just a couple of the berries. Vlad opens me a bottle of water and finishes off the berries.

"I've telephoned Olivia to let her know where you are just in case; she was worried if she couldn't get hold of you."

"Thanks, I'll ring her tomorrow."

"I told her you would be staying here for a while, so just to call over whenever…" He trails off as his dark eyes gaze into mine and he tucks my hair behind my ear.

"Vlad." I take his hand in mine and he strokes his thumb over my knuckles. I love being here with him and had a wonderful time when I stayed for a week. But, I have only just gone back home yesterday, and he needs to be at work after taking a full week off to be with me. He also has his family to take care of. Well, Lucas anyway.

"I should be able to go home tomorrow. I'm feeling a lot better than I did early this morning. The migraine hasn't lasted as long as it normally does, so there's no need for you to take time off work to be with me," I say, shuffling closer to him.

He sighs gently then plants a soft kiss on my lips. "Holly, I love you," he breathes in deeply through his nose and out again, "and I love having you here," he smiles.

"I love you too and love being here…" He puts a finger on my lips to stop what I was going to say.

"Your clothes are in my wardrobe and hang very well at the side of mine. My suits would get lonely without them." He smirks then kisses my cheek. "Your toiletries sit in my bathroom as if that's where they belong, it would be a shame to move them." He kisses my other cheek. I might be feeling off colour, but my heart rate has just picked up speed with the thought of where he is going with this.

He inhales deeply. "Can you smell that?"

I sniff a little and shake my head. "Close your eyes, breathe in and tell me the first thing you smell?" I lay down and do as he asks.

With my eyes closed and the silence in the room, my senses are on high alert. I feel the soft touch of his fingertips lazily drawing circles around my stomach. The sound of him breathing on my skin sends tingles down my spine. Gently, he puts his lips to mine and straight away my tongue comes out to taste him. Licking my lips, the sweetness of the berries he had eaten and a faint hint of peppermint from his mouth wash linger.

Inhaling again, I'm overcome with the smell of his masculine scent mixed with his aftershave and shower gel. I also smell me. Me and him mixed together, creating a unique scent of its own.

My eyes flicker open and focus on the man who is loving and caring but is as deep as the ocean. His finger runs over my bottom lip. "What was it, Holly?" his low tone sending another shiver down my spine.

"You and me," I whisper as I sit up, headache now gone and the overwhelming want of this man who has given me something I've never experienced before – true love. I want him to lay me down and take me amongst the stars.

"Us," he says with his devilish grin. "Best fucking smell in the world," he chuckles. "I might bottle it."

"Wow," is all I can say to him because I know what he means.

He leans over me, so I lay my head back down on the pillow. Strong arms stretch out at either side of my head. His warm lips meet mine then they travel towards my ear. "Why would you not want that all the time?" He lifts his body from mine and throws me a cheeky wink. Then he's up off the bed retrieving the tray he had brought the sandwich and fruit on, disappearing out of the door.

And why wouldn't I want this all the time?

Chapter 28

Vlad

"Is my tie straight, Dad?" Lucas asks, looking up at me with a nervous smile on his face. He's a little anxious that he will stand on Holly's toes. She's told him he can have the first dance tonight. Although he was a little excited, the poor boy doesn't know how to lead a lady round the dance floor. We have a swing band playing later, so it has been left up to me to give him a few lessons. He did quite well, but nerves have the better of him and I can see Holly will be limping home, if he doesn't settle down. I adjust the knot on his grey striped tie and pat his chest; his dark eyes screw up as he looks at me.

"It is now," I tell him. He's a handsome-looking boy, all suited and booted in his charcoal trousers, white shirt, shiny black shoes and tie. It's a warm night so he didn't want to wear a jacket, not like the rest of us who are all dressed in suits, waist coats and fucking dickie bows. I pull at mine to try and stop the thing from choking me.

"Everything looks in order," Dave says as he walks towards us, pointing out at the stage all set up, with the band at one side and the podium at the other. "Old Sam looks like he might hit someone over the head with that auctioneer's hammer," he chuckles. Looking over I can see that he looks a little flustered, there's a lot of donations for the auction plus a generous amount of raffle prizes.

"He'll be fine, he always gets himself in a tizzy beforehand, but comes up trumps when the auction starts." The old guy took on the responsibility of the auction when we first started fund raising and enjoys the excitement during the bids; he drags quite a bit of money out of the crowd that attend.

I take in the room which is usually gloomy with dark wood and old brass fittings but is now bright and updated. The tables have been layered with white banqueting covers and the wooden chairs have been replaced with black and chrome seats. The curtains have been removed and replaced with white blinds and the bar area has had a makeover, about time too. All the money this club makes with members' fees and it hasn't had a lick of paint in years.

"You're looking very dapper," Dave tells Lucas, ruffling his hair, but quickly removes his hand when he gets spiked by what can only feel like a hedgehog. My son likes to put lots of products on his hair; even though it's short he still gets it to spike and it sets hard.

"Thanks, Doctor Young," Lucas says, his cheeks heating up a little. He does embarrass easily.

"You know, Lucas? I'm not your doctor anymore so you can call me Dave."

He nods his head at Dave, telling him OK, but he won't. He's known Dave since he was a baby and always refers to him as Doctor.

"Where's the lovely Holly?" he smirks, wiggling his eyebrows at me.

"She'll be here in about fifteen minutes, along with Izzy and a few friends." My heartrate kicks up at the mention of Holly's name and I've become far too hot.

She left my home this morning to meet her friends at dinnertime and I miss her already.

In the last month we have spent three weeks of them together. After, having Holly with me and my family for one full week, I wanted more. When she became unwell the following day, I knew there was only one thing for me to do. Take her home with me and show her why she should stay.

In the last two weeks, Holly has stayed every night. She let me take care of her when she was ill and once she felt better, we both slipped into a routine.

We woke together. Ate breakfast together, along with Lucas and the rest of the brood if they turned up. My sons love Holly and I can tell she adores them, especially Lucas. We drove Lucas to school, picking up my grandchildren on the way who have also taken to Holly very well. Holly would then meet up with Izzy, so they could continue with their plans for the club, and I would meet Sebastian and Nicholas. The plans for buying an old building in the hopes of building apartments are going well and we've had meetings with the council for planning permission. Jack and Nick are in the building trade so after speaking with them last week, I decided to offer them the contract for the building work.

Most days Holly and I would have lunch together, either at my restaurant or in my office. Holly thinks I don't eat enough through the day or that I eat lunch too late. So, she would surprise me, turning up with lunch at mid-day where we would sit and eat together on the settee in my office. Most times lunch would last a lot longer than it should due to our dessert, which was each other.

Once we had both finished work for the day, we would pick the children up from school and take them out for tea or if Izzy and Sebastian were picking them up they would meet us at home. The night she was due to have Megan, the poor kid had toothache which led Olivia and Jack wanting to keep her at home.

Evenings would consist of family time either with mine or Holly's friends, sometimes both. We had many romantic evenings just for the two of us and learnt a lot more about each other's likes and dislikes. I learnt my woman hates people who raise their voice unnecessarily but loves to massage my back. Which I also love because when Holly massaged my back it led to other things being massaged. Win-win situation, really.

"It's the real deal then?" Dave asks, bringing me out of my thoughts as I remove my jacket, placing it on the back of one of the chairs. I don't need to ask what he's talking about, he's known me a long time. Besides my sons, except for Lucas, he's the only person in England that knows that Lucas was born with a drug addiction due to his mother and that I don't normally get into relationships.

"Yes," I answer firmly. I want everyone to know that Holly is mine and hopefully that's how it will stay. He nods his head at me with a genuine smile on his face.

"Good for you," he says, glancing out towards the terrace where the bellowing of laughter comes from Jack as he listens to Nicholas who is being very animated while he speaks.

"With you?" He nods towards where Sebastian, Nicholas, Jack, Nick and Jay are in fine flow, swilling pints of beer down their necks like water. Nodding my answer, I ask Dave to come and meet the rowdy bunch that are getting a few looks from some of the members. It's still early but people like to arrive well before the auction starts.

There's a few handshakes from some of the regular golfers that I haven't seen in a while and I'm given the once over by a couple of women as we pass the bar. I smile politely and pay them no more attention. I only have eyes for one and she will be here shortly.

Outside I introduce Dave to everyone then Mark, his daughter and his new wife arrive so there's more introductions.

As I'm chatting to Jack, Lucas tugs on my sleeve to get my attention. "Holly will be here any minute, are we going to meet her in the car park?" His dark eyes squint at me as the evening sun catches them and his hand shoots up to cover them. "Looks like you're not the only one who's smitten," Jack states, smiling at my youngest as he tries to ruffle his hair.

Lucas adores Holly. With no mother in his life, he's never had that unconditional love that a mother would give. None of my sons have and it's never seemed to bother them. Mrs White has been around for years cooking, cleaning and giving sound advice to them. But there was still something missing.

Holly catapulted into our lives, stealing my heart in an instant. Sebastian took to her straight away because of her friendship with Izzy. Nicholas, well what can I say? His humour bowled her over and the fact that she can take a joke won her a place in his heart. Daniel and Holly have yet to find their connection, but they get along fine, whereas Lucas finds that unconditional love with Holly.

She dotes on him.

Over the last month she's given him endless hours of her time. Preparing breakfast together, packing up his lunch for school. If we're not eating out she's in the kitchen making his favourite food for after school. I thought it was because she loved my kitchen so much. Only I see her fuss over him at meal times and the gleam in her eye as we eat together and chat about the day's events, taking an interest in everything he does, makes my heart expand even more for her. He revels in having Holly's attention. A bit like his father, really.

Any problems with his homework she's there, giving him advice and support.

His art work that he enjoys so much, sketching, now hangs in frames around the house. Courtesy of Holly, enjoying them. We've even had a trip to the art gallery. "Dad." I look down at my son knowing in the short time he has known Holly, he has now come to regard her like a mother.

Let's hope I don't fuck up.

"Come on then," I smile at him as I place my hand on the back of his neck, letting him lead the way to the car park.

"Wait for me," Jack says, taking another drink of his pint. "If I'm not there to meet Olivia, she'll have my balls…" He stops, looks down at Lucas then at me and mouths the word 'sorry'. He needn't have bothered; he's probably heard a lot worse than what he was going to say from his brothers and me. I chuckle at Jack, shaking my head.

We make our way to the main door that leads out to the car park, closely followed by the rest of the men who are waiting for their lovely ladies to arrive.

The limousine I had arranged to pick them up has already pulled in and the driver is helping Ivy get out. Lucy holds one of the doors for Izzy as Sarah steps out closely followed by Olivia. They're all beautiful in their long flowing gowns. Their husbands go to greet them, and I'm left captivated by the slender, lightly tanned legs that have just made their appearance.

Silver sequins cling to her body as she rises from the gleaming black vehicle, looking like the goddess she is. Holly's gown runs the full length of her gorgeous figure, with a split that travels from the top of right thigh to floor where it pools at her feet. God help any man that looks at her tonight.

Her hair has been pinned up, with ringlets falling at either side, showing her delectable neck. My heart rate kicks up speed and has just broken the speed barrier.

Her mouth is turned up into a perfect smile, highlighting her cheekbones. Beyond beautiful.

Hypnotised, I can't move. Her pose is award winning and as I try to prise my feet from the floor they have stuck to, she turns to me. The sparkle of the diamond drop earrings and necklace I bought her as a gift catch the sunlight, glimmering like the stars.

My angel.

"Dad." That word circles around the air but it doesn't register; only this magnificent woman that is mine exists. "Dad." I hear the word again and this time feel a slight jab in my side.

Bringing me out of my frozen state, I glance down at Lucas who has his head tilted to one side giving me a questioning stare. Realising I have left Holly waiting far too long, I'm off like a greyhound, stumbling over my own feet as I do. Rectifying my step before I make a fool of myself, I'm in front of her taking her hands in mine.

"Fucking hell, I have no words," I breathe in her hair. She chuckles into my chest and I pull her closer into me. If that is even possible. We stay like that for a little while, holding hands, chests pressed firmly together, my nose in her hair breathing her in and hers pressed against my chest. When we pull away our eyes meet and I'm a mess. Lost for words, she speaks first.

"Are you OK?" she smirks with that little mischievous smile of hers.

"No." And I'm not. She looks fucking edible, which means I'm going to go fucking crazy if one man dares to roam his eyes over her bare legs or up her fucking irresistible body. Taking a few deep breaths, I try to combat the paranoia spinning around my head when Holly rises on her toes and places her lips on mine. That has the desired effect because in my heart I know she would never pay any attention to another man but try telling my fucked-up head that.

She pulls away, wiping her subtle pink lipstick from my lips.

"You look…" Shaking my head, I can't put into words how I see her, so I just throw a few that are an understatement if there is such a thing. "Stunning… Beautiful… Exquisite."

"Thank you, I get the picture," she laughs. "And look at you." Her hand touches my bowtie as her other hand opens my jacket. She pats my chest with wide eyes and nods her approval of my choice of attire for this evening's event. A low whistle escapes her lips. "Wow, looks like I'm going to be fighting the ladies off tonight," she chuckles, patting my chest again. I take her hand in mine and bring it to my lips, kissing it softly.

"There's only one lady for me and she is stood right in front of me," I say, placing my lips on her cheek. "And I will be glued to her all evening, so that every man knows you are mine and every woman knows I am yours," I whisper in her ear.

"Come on, you two. Leave it alone till you get home," I hear Nicholas laugh. Turning with my hand now holding Holly's, I see everyone has gone into the building leaving just Holly and me.

Our pace is quick as we enter, and Holly makes a beeline for Lucas who is stood with Sebastian and Izzy. I feel bad for taking up her time outside. I knew my boy was eager to see her. It doesn't seem to faze him because as soon as Holly grabs hold of him to give him a hug, his face beams and he gives those puppy-dog eyes. "Look at you," she gushes, fiddling with his tie. "How handsome do you look?" She ruffles his hair and chuckles when she gets spiked. My son just stands there proudly lapping up the attention from Holly then the rest of the women who give a little tug on his tie as they pass.

I join my son and Holly, leading them to the bar before the mad rush. We grab a glass of champagne then make our way to our table. An hour later the room is full, and the auction has begun.

*

All the items have been auctioned off, Nicholas paying well over the odds for a weekend in Edinburgh and Jack ending up with a spa break due to his lovely wife Olivia interfering with him during the bidding. Most of the raffle prizes have been won, Nick coming away with one year paid-up membership to the golf club and Holly got all excited when her numbers were called out; she wasn't bothered what it was, just that she had never won anything in her life. Turns out, she had won a magnum of champagne.

With the auction and raffle over, the music starts up and we all sit back and listen to the guy who is doing a fine rendition of a Frank Sinatra song. The women all swoon at him, Olivia saying he sounds like Michael Bublé and Jay moving first to lead his lovely wife onto the dance floor.

An hour later champagne, wine and beer are flowing well, everyone has been up dancing and I've just sat down after handing over Holly to my son Lucas who has finally built up the courage to get Holly on the dance floor.

It's so fucking cute watching him lead Holly round the floor as we all sit back and watch Holly chat with Lucas, putting him at ease. I hear Olivia speaking to Daniel.

"Wow, I'm sure Holly would love to come and see your band play," she says. "In fact, we could all come and make a night of it." She excitedly turns to Jack, Sarah and Nick. They all nod in agreement then she turns back to Daniel. "Your dad hasn't mentioned it…"

"That's because I didn't know," I cut in.

"Oh well, then you know now." She stands from her seat and walks round to the back of my chair. "Holly would love to go," she leans in to say.

"Well we will go then." I don't know what the big deal is, if Daniel had told me and invited us I would have said yes.

Sebastian and Izzy won't be left out and Seb gives Daniel a playful slap around the back of the head for not telling his family about his first gig. Nicholas follows Sebastian with the telling off then everyone agrees to making it a night out. Jay and Ivy offer to watch Lucas, Joseph and Rebecca if Mr and Mrs White are unable to have them which is very kind of them.

"You know, Daniel? You could get Holly up to sing, she has a fantastic voice." My ears prick up at this little bit of information.

"She does?" questions Izzy.

"Yeah. While she worked in the pub when she was younger, she was always asked by the bands to belt out a few tunes. We all went to watch her." Olivia points around the table at the friends of Holly's that know so much more about her than I do. Not that I haven't heard her sing, I have. Along to the radio and when we dance, she sings sweetly into my ear; she has a lovely voice.

"She can't half belt out a tune," Nick adds. "She sung at our wedding, voice like an angel," he beams. Daniel listens attentively to everyone giving their opinion of Holly's singing voice. With his head nodding he takes in all they are saying.

"Do you think she'll get up and give us a few songs next week if I just invite her up on the stage?"

"Get a couple of drinks down her, she will," Olivia suggests. "Don't tell her beforehand though, she'll be nervous all week. Wait till the night."

"You can't do that," I butt in. I'm not letting them just put her on the spot, what if she doesn't want to and feels obligated to just because she doesn't want to let Daniel down?

"Vlad," Jack says.

"I don't think it's right not telling her and I will not have her looking embarrassed if she doesn't want to," I say a little harshly.

"But she will want to, she always did. It was only due to that prick she married that she stopped singing, well, that and that the pub being sold from under her nose," he argues.

"After she lost her job we always went out. Open-mic bars, karaoke, bands, that sort of thing and Holly always got up to sing but once she married that fucking waste of space, who was never good enough for her, it all stopped." Jack's red face tells me he wasn't happy with her ex and the brotherly instinct in him is coming to the fore, telling me I should trust him on this one. They do know what she likes, and I don't want to be the one to spoil the evening. I nod my head at him, letting him know that I'll go with their plan, but God help them if it backfires and my angel is left feeling uncomfortable.

My eyes drift to the dance floor where Holly and Lucas have just finished their dance and are headed back to the table. Suddenly, my blood runs cold and my hands grip the table when I see a ghost from the past approaching them. He greets my son. I'm not sure whether Lucas will remember him, it's been five years. I watch with a chill running through my veins as Lucas, the ever so polite boy, smiles nicely then introduces Holly. Again, another genuine smile is presented to him and what I can only surmise is him asking Holly to dance. Lucas heads back to the table while Holly is left with a sly, devious, coward of a man. I can see her shaking her head and putting her hand up to say no but he ignores her. She smiles uncomfortably as he takes her hand and spins her so they're on the dance floor.

Something erupts in my chest and I hear myself growl like a rabid dog. Slowly his head lifts and that sly smirk appears when our eyes meet; the back of my knees hit the chair so fast it sends it skidding, crashing into the table at the back of me. My hands shake the table hard, spilling the drinks as I launch myself towards the man who hates me with a passion and will do anything to make me pay for the games he and his ex-wife get off on.

I don't get far when two of my strapping sons block my path, one of them holding the door to the terrace open with one of his arms. Sebastian and Daniel hold my stare, letting me know they will not be allowing me to step one foot near the man who is spinning Holly around the dance floor.

I know they're concerned, they have every right to be, my past showing that I won't think twice about annihilating this man.

Following them both out into the darkness of the night, the solar lights giving off a soft blue glow around the edges, Sebastian puts his hand on my shoulder. "Father," he soothes. My sons, all of them, have a way to calm the beast that lives within me whenever it rears its ugly head. I walk to the railings, placing my forearms on it and untying the bowtie around my neck.

"Ignore Andrew, he's just trying to rile you up. He knows if you kick off in here tonight that your membership will be revoked," Sebastian says, leaning against the railing with Daniel stood next to him.

"It's been five years since your argument," Daniel informs me. Since our argument, if only it was that simple.

"Yeah, and he's not letting it go." I turn to face them, Sebastian knows it's not just about the bust-up five years ago, it's much more.

The door opens and Nicholas steps out, holding a large brandy in his hand. "Thought you could do with this," he chuckles, passing me the tumbler. Only he could find any of this amusing. "Hmmm, I'd get yourself calmed down pronto, big man, your lady doesn't look very happy." Fucking hell, how am I going to explain this one to her, my angel who can't bare arguing, never mind me about to rip some bastard's head off.

"Where is she?"

"She went to the ladies', but I think she wants answers. She saw your little outburst and came off the dance floor straight away. I told her and Jack, who was wondering what had got you looking like you could kill someone, that you and Andrew had issues a few years ago and him dragging Holly onto the dance floor was just to get to you."

I nod my head at him and tell him and his brothers to go in, I will follow shortly. Daniel and Nicholas go ahead leaving Sebastian and me outside. Taking a large mouthful of the brandy, I try to calm the war I have inside me. "Holly is nothing like her," Sebastian quietly says. I know who her he is referring to and he's right, my angel is nothing like his mother. But it still doesn't help the torment I feel when a man puts his hands on her.

The door creaks open and Sebastian retreats from my side. The whisper of two voices, announces that Holly has joined us. The door closes, and I hear the clicking of her heels on the floor.

"Hey," she says, placing her hand on the middle of my back. Straight away her touch soothes my soul. "What's got you all worked up?" she asks, rubbing my back while standing at the side of me. What do I tell her? That I'm a jealous bastard and my demons make me paranoid? Do I tell her about Andrew and his wife? I'm not sure she would understand any of it.

Turning to her, I take her hand in mine and offer her a drink from my glass. She takes a sip and passes it back all the while not taking her sparkling eyes from mine. I choose not to go into to detail and shake my head at her.

"Nothing," I say as calmly as I can, then pull her into me. But she is not taking this answer and I get the wrath of my angel.

"Don't you dare lie to me!" She all but stamps her foot. I'm a little taken back by how angry she has just become. She drops my hand and prods me in the chest. "I saw you. I saw the anger on your face, just before Sebastian and Daniel stopped you from charging like a bull onto the dance floor," she rages at me, her normal tranquil manner gone. She prods at me again, rising on her tiptoes, getting right in my face. "So, don't you dare try and fob me off with 'nothing'." She's angry with me and this is a first. Tears threaten her eyes. I just want to pull her in and hold her. I have done this to her.

I try to take her hand, but she bats me away. She wants the truth.

Turning to the railing I breathe in the night air and hope I am not about to fuck up the best thing that has ever happened to me. "I fucked his wife." I hear Holly's breath catch and she recoils from me. I turn my head to her; I could have phrased that better. The tears that threatened are now trickling down her cheeks, her hand covers her mouth and I feel like shit.

"Sorry." I put my hand out to her. "What I should have said was I slept with his wife."

She doesn't take my hand but wipes the tears from her eyes. She sniffles then speaks.

"It doesn't matter how you sugar coat it, Vlad, you still slept with another man's wife." She glares at me, shaking her head.

She turns to look out onto the golf course, the darkness blocking out the view. I move so I'm closer to her. "I didn't know," I whisper.

"What?" She turns to face me, her head tilted to one side and her eyes now narrowing.

"I didn't know she was married when I slept with her."

"Vlad." She shakes her head at me. "I don't understand. Well, I understand that you slept with a woman who was married to the man who dragged me up to dance. What I don't understand is why you looked as if you wanted to kill him when it should be the other way around," she says. I let out a sarcastic chuckle and get a glare from my angel. "It's not bloody funny." She prods me. Again. This time I take her hand and keep it firmly in mine. I'm not letting it go, I need her touch if she wants me to explain how I was played by a vindictive wife who wanted to get back at her cheating husband.

Holly looks at our joined hands then looks up at my face; seeing that I need to be touching her, she doesn't pull away. "Explain."

And I do.

I explain to Holly how five years ago I was in a club with Mark and Dave when I met this attractive woman. One thing led to another and we booked into a hotel room. A few hours later after pleasuring each other, I was back home tucked up in my own bed not giving it a second thought.

She tells me to continue and I do.

"Two weeks later, I'm in the bar," I nod my head towards the door indicating to the bar here, "when Andrew walks in with this woman draped all over him. I wouldn't have recognised her if it wasn't for the tattoo in the middle of her back." I don't go into how I had admired it while I was sinking into her from behind. "Anyway, as she passes me she runs her red painted nails down my arm and that's when I see the tattoo on her back. The dress she was wearing had no back and I knew then that this was the same woman I had slept with a couple of weeks before."

"Had you not seen her before in here?" Holly asks.

"No. Never. I knew Andrew, I'd played golf with him, but I don't do small talk. So, I'd never asked about his wife or if he had children, it's not my thing. And I'd certainly not noticed her in here before."

Holly chews on the inside of her cheek and I move in a little bit closer to her.

"As soon as I saw their wedding rings, I knew I'd fucked up. She wasn't wearing one the night I met her so I'm assuming she was out to cheat on him."

"Sounds that way," Holly agrees. She looks a little calmer, but I don't want to chance my look. Continuing with what happened next, I watch Holly's face turn from shocked, amused, anger then calm and playful.

"I thought about leaving but Dave and Mark persuaded me to stay, telling me that Andrew is always playing away from home and if they had seen the woman that night they would have told me to stay away."

"They didn't see her that night?"

"No." I shake my head. "They had just left, and I wanted one for the road. I met her at the bar and within half an hour we were on our way to the hotel." I shrug my shoulders. Holly knows I've been no angel for the past twelve years. She breathes deeply through her nose and shakes her head as if she's disgusted with me. I'm a little vexed at my angel because we met in a club and it didn't take long for me to get into her knickers.

Raising my eyebrow at her, I challenge her to make a comment.

She realises, apologises and I continue.

"Not long after, she must have been knocking back the wine because she was drunk and all over me. I told her to go away, that she was making a show of herself and that it was just one night, it shouldn't have happened. Only, it was too late, her husband caught her with her hands on me and overheard me telling her to go away. It was then when he told her to leave me alone and that she spurted out that she had already had me." Holly's mouth falls open then she closes it and she giggles, covering her mouth when I frown at her.

"It's not funny, Holly." My firm voice stops her sniggering. "I was used." I know I sound like an old fucking woman but it's true. Holly sniggers again.

This time I pull her into me, putting my nose in her hair and breathing her in then. "I would never sleep with another man's wife knowingly."

"I believe you," she says, unfastening my waistcoat, putting her arms around me and snuggling in. My arms wrap round her tightly and I thank God that I have met this woman.

"So, what happened next?"

"Next. Holy hell broke loose. Andrew took a swing at me, I moved out of the way and he hit Mark. Mark went for him but was stopped by Dave and me. Andrew's wife, Alison, flipped her lid and laid into her husband. Apparently, she wanted to get back at him for his cheating ways and I was her pawn. When she saw me in the club she knew who I was even if I didn't know her. That's when she set her sights on me, knowing which evening I went into the golf club; she set it all up to unveil her infidelity. She was planning on leaving him anyway, but she wanted to let him know that two could play his game."

"Bloody hell, what a pair of bastards." She looks up at me, tears now dried away and the hurt gone.

"It didn't end there," I tell her.

"No?" her eyes wide, and her head shaking.

"No. He had me suspended from the golf club and the committee of the fund-raising team, pending an investigation. He told them I couldn't be trusted, that I knew Alison was his wife and that I was the one who had instigated the fight in the club. He also called the police, accusing me of blackening his eye when it was his wife." My words turn harsh when I think how he could have ruined me. At the time, I had two licenced premises and getting into brawls could have had my licence taken from me.

"Did you get arrested?" Holly's concerned voice calms me.

I shake my head, remembering how scared I was that my sons would be without me if he got his way. "No, too many witnesses." She blows out a breath and runs her finger across my cheek then standing on her tiptoes, gently puts her lips to mine. I lean down to give her better access. Our kiss is soft but meaningful. It's her letting me know that whatever it is that has me worked up, she will be there for me. But there's a lot more she needs to know about me. She knows it and so do I. But, my past must stay there for now, until we're are both strong enough to cope with the hurt it will bring to our relationship.

"Let's go back inside." Holly breaks our kiss, while she fastens the buttons of my waistcoat.

"Hmmm, I was happy with you attached to me," I pout. She giggles at me and takes my hand.

"You know? I know it's more than just this Andrew dragging me on to dance that had you all worked up, Vlad," she says, raising her eyebrows at me. "But," she pats my chest, "I'm willing to let it go for now, but you will have to tell me soon. Whatever it is we will deal with it." She wipes her lip gloss from my lips and doesn't say anything else on the matter. I just nod at her knowing eventually I will have to divulge my past.

"Come." She puts her hand out for me. "I let you spin me around the dance floor, then you can take me home. And I might just let you rip these very sexy knickers off me," she teases, showing me her sexy underwear by just lifting where the split starts in her dress.

She's lucky I don't throw her over my shoulder and storm off with her into the woods that surround the golf club. But I don't. I whisper into her ear, "There's no 'might' about it, my little minx. They'll be off before we get home." I kiss her neck and drag her back inside and onto the dance floor.

Chapter 29

Vlad

Tonight, is Daniel's big night. It's the first night that his family and friends will hear his band play. He's nervous and I'm at the stage where I might fake a headache or something where I can stay at home. I know I should be over the moon he has got himself a gig and I am, I'm more than proud of him. But I'm terrified I will spoil the whole evening.

I've snapped at everyone who dare to speak to me this week; my staff won't even look at me and my sons are giving me a wide berth. I know I should be happy that I have a loyal, loving family and a woman who cares and loves me fiercely, but it's Holly that has my demons on the rampage.

All week she has been in the club with Izzy, meeting with men and women from different bands, eager to get the live bands and themed nights up and running. Over the weeks, I've left them to it, but when I called into the club on Monday wanting to take her to lunch, I had no over choice than to walk back out.

With my blood boiling due to my head reverting to when I was married, I stormed into my office, slamming my fist into the door as it shut. This had my eldest Sebastian up out of his chair faster than a leaping leopard attacking its next meal and me cursing as my watch that was bought for me by my sons, smashed into pieces.

Explaining to Sebastian what had put me into a foul mood, he shook his head and reminded me that Holly is nothing like his mother. And I know that, but seeing other men fawn over her, flirting with her and putting their grubby fucking hands on her, had me green with envy. I know Holly didn't think anything of it when one of them put his arm around her waist, giving her a cuddle and when another placed a soft kiss on her cheek; she knows some of these people from years ago. I shouldn't be jealous because I know she only has eyes for me, but I can't help but want to rip the head off any man who isn't family that goes anywhere near her. When Andrew from the golf club dragged her up to dance last Saturday night, it wasn't the history we had between us that had me feeling murderous. It was the fact that he had put his hands on my woman, but I didn't mention that to Holly. I didn't need to. She listened to what I told her about Andrew and his wife even though she knew there was more to my reaction than him just trying to aggravate me over an incident that happened five years ago. She also knows I've been like a bear with a sore head all week and I'm sure there's times within the week she has wanted to strangle me as I tell her I'm fine.

Every day she has asked what it is that's bothering me, and every day I have lied to her with an excuse that I am stressed with work. I feel like I'm fighting a losing battle because if I tell her the truth then she will leave me and me knowing it's only a matter of time before I explode, not able to keep my monsters at bay, she will be out of here like a bat out of hell. I'm fucked if I do and fucked if I don't.

Stripping down to my boxers, I sit on my bed and place my head in my hands when the bedroom door opens. Lifting my head to see who it is because let's face it, in my house it could be several people, Daniel stands there leaning against the door frame with his hands stuffed in the front pockets of his jeans. "You OK, Paps?" He asks, as he stands up straight and joins me sat on the bed.

"Yeah," I tell him, not wanting to go into details about my insecurities and spoil his night.

"Are you sure because you look like you have the worlds troubles on your shoulders?" He smirks, knocking his shoulder into mine. I can't tell him what is bothering me, I don't think he would understand my turmoil, so I lie to my son, telling him everything is good, and I've just been a bit stressed with work. He lifts one of his eyebrows at me, seeing straight through my lie but doesn't question it.

"OK, I'm setting off in ten minutes," he says, getting up and walking towards the door. "I'll see you there then?" He turns to look at me.

"Yeah, I'll be there." And I will be. I have never let my sons down and I'm not about to start now. Standing up, I meet him at the door. "Good luck tonight," I say, placing my hand on his shoulder. "We'll be there about eight." Meaning me and Holly, who I know is on her way here and should be here any time.

"Thank you," he says. I know he's nervous and where some people would be more nervous knowing there will be family and friends there, he wants our support and will thrive with it.

"You don't need to thank me for supporting you, it's what I do. Now get out of here, so I can get dressed." I push him out of my bedroom door and vow to myself that I will not let my demons spoil his night.

Just as I'm closing my bedroom door, I hear the sweet voice of my angel as she makes her way up the bedroom steps, telling Daniel she will see him there. She laughs at something he says, and my spirits lift. With all the hours she's been working this week we haven't had much time to ourselves and maybe it's that that I am missing quality time together. Just Holly and me. I might have to share her tonight but now and the rest of the weekend I will make sure it's just the two of us.

She strolls into my room with a bag in her hand, still laughing at whatever Daniel had said. Straight away she walks into my arms and I wrap them around her, needing this moment with her. When we're alone or with family and friends, my thoughts are calm, but when we are out in public they are anything but. They circle like sharks waiting to strike at the bait. The bait being any man that happens to drop his eyes on my angel. She doesn't notice the way they look at her, wanting what they can't have, nor does she see the beauty that radiates from her. Her vivacious and positive attitude to life has people wanting to be around her when we are out because let's face it, she's the life and soul of the place. Her friends love her, my family adore her, and I worship the ground she walks on.

She's too good for me, I know, but I'll be damned to hell before I let her go. Even then I would challenge the dark one himself to get back to her. I pull her closer in, relishing the warmth that surrounds her and inhale that sweet smell of her that I can never get enough of. She does the same.

"Hmmm, you smell bloody delicious," she mumbles into my shoulder. I chuckle at her when she nibbles at my skin and a stirring starts in my boxers. She feels it and pulls out of my embrace.

"Oh no, we don't have time for that." She stands back, giggling while taking in my growing erection. I've hardly seen her all week. Her eyes roam up my body until they meet with mine and that's when she sees the determination in me.

I stalk towards her, smirking as she tries to backtrack her steps but it's in vain as she backs into the closed door. My hands take her hips as my lips claim hers. Kissing her hard and rubbing my erection against her has her moaning. My mouth travels across her jawline and down her neck then across to her shoulder where I take a little nibble of my own. She moans into me and I know I've got her. She is mine and right now I will take what's mine.

*

"You look happy," Holly says as I button up my shirt while she dries her hair. We decided to take a shower together after I had my way with her up against the door. She might have been complaining that we didn't have time but that didn't last long. In five minutes, I had her climbing the door and screaming my name; the only complaining I got was to get her there quick.

I send her a wink and stride over to the dressing table where she is stood. "I am, but then I always am when we're together."

"Yeah, not this week. You've looked a little sad, distant and annoyed a lot," she says, putting down the hairdryer as she puts her hand on my chest.

"That's because I have missed you," I tell her, running my hands through her soft hair, knowing it's only half the truth.

"We've seen each other every day."

"I know, but we haven't had any time alone." I place a quick kiss on her soft lips then make my way over to the bed and pick up my trousers, not wanting to get into what has really been bothering me.

She takes her dress off the hanger and turns to me.

"I agree," she says as she shimmies into the too-short, off-the-shoulder, white floral dress. It's not really that short but anything above the knee when we're going out has me going crazy.

She turns her back to me and lifts her hair, so I can zip her up. Once I have zipped up her dress and adjusted the material, exposing the smooth bare skin of her shoulders, my lips kiss one then the other and she shivers as I place my hands on her hips.

"When we arrive home tonight, I'm locking the door, and nobody is coming through it until Monday."

"Hmmm," she mumbles as I place a kiss on the side of her neck. "Sounds good to me, but what about Lucas?" she asks, turning in my arms.

"He's spending all day tomorrow at Sebastian's. Tom is going to drop him off and then Olivia's sons have invited him over for the day on Sunday and she said he can stop at hers. Which means it's just you and me, sweetheart, all weekend. In our oversized bed." She tilts her head at me, giving me a questioning look.

"Our bed?"

"Yes, our bed, where we will eat, drink watch too many bad movies and I might let you take advantage of me." I wink at her, turn her around and slap her bottom. She chuckles at me as she continues to get ready for our night out.

"Are you not going into work on Sunday?" she asks while she puts her earrings in.

"No and I'm not going in next Sunday either because I'm booking us a weekend away just for you and me," I tell her as I zip up my trousers.

"Oh, did you ask me if I wanted a weekend away? I might be busy." I can see that mischievous grin appear on her face as she disappears into the walk-in wardrobe. I might just lock the little minx in there and not let her out until next week. I follow her in, pinning her against the shelving. My hands hold onto the shelves, so she is trapped between my arms as she gazes up at me, trying hard not to laugh at the expression on my face.

"You don't want a weekend away with me?" I try to sound offended at her last comment and look at her like she has just upset my feelings. She studies me with her beautiful blue eyes then pulls me into her, wrapping her arms around me and laying her head on my chest.

"I'm sorry, Vlad. I was joking. I would love it," she says as she reaches up to kiss me. I lower my head and let her take my mouth. "Thank you," she says when she pulls away.

"Good, I'm glad you're happy about it. I just think we need some time alone. We spend a lot of time with my sons and your friends, it will be nice just you and me."

She nods her head at me. "You're right, we do spend a lot of time with family and friends so yes, it would be nice to get away for a few days. Just you and me."

"That's settled then, I'll book it tomorrow."

"Where are you taking me?" she asks, picking up her shoes from one of the racks. I'm behind her in a flash; you can almost see her fucking knickers when she bends over. I'm going to have a hard time tonight keeping my hands off any bastard that looks at her.

"Please, don't dare bend over like that while we're out otherwise I won't be responsible for my actions." She stands up, knocking my hands off her arse then holds on to me while she puts on her shoes.

"Oh, stop overreacting," she says with an amused expression. "If I went out wrapped up like an Egyptian mummy you would still go all caveman on me." Yeah, she's right, I would because she would still look like a goddess and still have men ogling her.

I try to calm my anxieties down and pull her into me. "That's because you're mine," I tap her arse, "and I don't want any man looking at what's mine." I kiss her passionately, causing her to moan, then I pull away leaving her wanting more.

We arrive at the pub half an hour late; the music is blaring as my son and his band blast out a favourite of mine, 'Something Just Like This' by Chainsmokers and Coldplay. Coldplay being one of the bands I can listen to daily. The pub isn't quite full, but the bar area is busy as we make our way across to the far end of the room towards our friends and family.

Sebastian sees us and gestures to the table where he has a bottle for me and a glass of wine waiting for Holly. Nobody mentions that we are late, they're all too enthralled in the band. Holly snuggles her back into my front and I wrap my arm around her waist, resting my chin on her shoulder as we stand there listening to the song end.

"Wow, they're really good," Jack says as he lifts his bottle to his lips, his other hand rubbing his wife's back.

"Yes, they are," I reply as I nod my head at Daniel. He's just noticed that we have arrived and that smile on his face lights up the stage as he breaks into another song. I have the same smile on mine, knowing that it is my son and his friends that have the whole pub gripped with their performance.

Nicholas and Sebastian bring a couple of chairs from another table and everyone moves round so we can sit down. Contented just listening to Daniel's gravelly voice, nobody speaks. He's on to his third song before Nicholas breaks the silence around the table.

"I knew he could sing, but boy he knows how to work that stage." His eyes are wide as he tilts his head towards the other side of the small stage where a group of young women watch with love-struck eyes. They sway in time with the music before making their way on to the dance floor.

Daniel and the other band members are dressed in faded jeans, Timberland boots, and they're all wearing a ripped white T-shirt. My son owns the stage, baring his lightly tanned muscles through the tears on his shirt. Strumming his guitar as the band take on a very popular song, 'Give Me Everything Tonight' by Pitbull. Between the other guitarist, Daniel and the female drummer, the song starts off well. The women on the dance floor screech and the women around our table do too, jumping up from their chairs and on to the dance floor.

Mesmerised by my son's talent and how he flirts with the women, I chuckle as he gives them the Petrov smile and throws in a cheeky wink while bending down to kiss a dark-haired woman on the cheek. "What a fucking flirt he is," Jack bellows over the loud music as we watch him, and the other guitarist work the women into a frenzy; even our women are screaming at them.

My older two sons decide they don't want to be left out and join the ladies on the dance floor. Nicholas manoeuvres himself so he his dancing with Lucy and Sebastian snuggles into his wife.

Jack studies them for a moment before he turns to me with a 'what the fuck?' look on his face. Nick sniggers at Jack and I can't help but let out a chuckle as well. He doesn't comment on how close Nicholas and Lucy are dancing, he just shakes his head and joins his wife, running his hands up and down her curves. Nick joins Sarah and I grab hold of my little minx who is wiggling her fine arse at me.

Daniel's first spot has ended, and the juke box is playing in the background as he introduces his band members to all of us. Sophia the female drummer isn't their usual drummer, Daniel informs me. She's the lead singer from another band who is helping him out tonight due to their drummer being ill. Apparently, he has invited her band to the club next week for a formal chat with Izzy and Holly in the hopes they can get a gig there.

Half an hour later Daniel and his band are back on the stage for their second spot. When he finishes his first song, he addresses the audience once they have finished applauding them.

"Thanks," he says, covering his eyes from the light so he can see out into the crowd.

"We don't normally do this but there's a special little lady in the audience tonight that I have heard sings like an angel and we're hoping she'll do us the honour of joining us on stage tonight." He turns to our table with his beaming smile that no woman could say no to. "Holly, get your arse up here." He strides to the end of the stage and leans, putting his hand out for her to join him.

"Holly, Holly, Holly!" is chanted by her friends and when I turn to look at her, she is looking at me for support. Her smile lights up the room when I wink at her and stand, taking her hand. She stands with me and the room applauds her. My woman makes her way to the stage where Daniel helps her up, passing her a microphone that fits across her head, so her hands are free. They whisper to each other, then Daniel speaks to his band. Once Holly is settled the band cue her in. She looks a little nervous and misses her cue. Daniel strums his guitar again waiting for Holly; this time she's on time and fucking hell, my heart bursts with love for this woman.

Chapter 30

Holly

My hands shake as Daniel helps me onto the stage. I can't believe my friends have set me up for this. It must have been them that told him that I loved singing back in the day before I was married. I still enjoy singing but haven't sung in front of anyone for years. I look out to my friends, shaking my head at them, and I can see them grinning at me. They know me well and know I was at my happiest singing to the crowds.

Daniel asks me what I want to sing, and I try to think quickly of a up-to-date song that I know all the way through. Knowing I'm a little nervous and out of practice, I opt out of singing a slow one which would show any uneasiness in my voice.

"Better When I'm Dancing, by Meghan Trainor. Do you know it?" I whisper to Daniel who nods his head at me, giving me a reassuring smile.

"Good choice," he says, then informs the rest of the band.

My nerves get the better of me and I miss my cue. Glancing over to Vlad, he's sat there, long muscular legs parted. His arms crossed over his broad chest. Our eyes meet; the warmth from his smile engulfs me and that cheeky wink he throws at me combats my anxiety. The strum of Daniel's guitar prompts me in again and this time I close my eyes and follow his lead.

Hmmm, hey

Hmmm

Hey!

Don't think about it

Just move your body

Listen to the music

Sing, "Oh-hey-oh."

Just move those left feet

Go ahead, get crazy

Anyone can do it

Sing, "Oh-hey-oh."

Show the world you got that fire

Feel the rhythm getting louder...

When I open my eyes the dance floor is full. Shifting my gaze to our table, I'm able to make out with the restriction of the lights that apart from my man they are all on their feet dancing. Vlad sits there, still watching. I can't make out his eyes, but his smile tells me everything. It's good to see that the burden he's been carrying all week has lifted and he's enjoying the evening.

I continue with the song, Daniel by my side. His hip hits mine and I knock back into him. He leans into me while his fingers pick at the strings and when I finish the song, there's a round of applause; mainly from friends and family. Daniel kisses the side of my cheek. "Well done," he whispers. "Come on, everybody, let's hear it for Holly." He claps with everyone else. "It takes a lot of guts to come here," he directs to the audience. "But, I'm sure if you clap a little louder Holly will give us another song." He gives them the Petrov smile and I watch as young women go crazy over him. I'm shocked that he would want me to sing again after cocking up the start of the first one and I'm sure my nerves were apparent all the way through.

To my surprise, I must have sung better than I thought because just about everyone in the pub is on their feet cheering for me to sing another.

I'm back in my comfort zone, standing here in front of a pub full of people I don't know and a crowd I do. Seeing the smiles on their faces and the cheering sounds gives me the confidence to sing again. There's a song I would love to sing and if I have the nerve should have my man grinning from ear to ear. I lean into Daniel and whisper, "Ain't Nobody, by Chaka Khan." He lets out a chuckle, knowing where I'm going with this song because let's face it, he was there that night when I threw caution to the wind to pursue what Vlad was offering. I also have it as my ringtone for him only.

Daniel speaks to the other band members; one of them places his guitar in its stand and takes his place behind the electronic keyboard. Once everyone's in position, Daniel approaches his mic. "This one's for you, Paps."

The electronic keyboard starts, and I wait for my cue.

Captured effortlessly

That's the way it was

It happened so naturally

I did not know it was love

The next thing I felt was you

Holdin' me close

What was I gonna do?

I let myself go

Now we're flying through the stars

I hope this night will last forever.

I've been waiting for you

It's been so long...

My stare does not leave Vlad as I step off the stage and slowly make my way towards him. With a sway in my hips, I weave my way through the crowd and past my friends who are dancing. I get a cheer from them and continue with my pursuit.

"You knew I could not resist, I needed someone..." I carry on with the chorus and into the next verse, curling my finger to beckon Vlad to join me on the dance floor. If he's nervous he doesn't show it. Sebastian, Nicholas and the rest of our friends cheer as he joins me.

Taking my hand in his, he places his addictive lips on the side of my neck and slips one arm around my waist.

My arms raise into the air giving him full range of my body, letting his fingers roam where ever they please. I'm lost within the song, the feel of his touch and his breath on my skin. Just as I'm about to start the next verse, he spins me round so my back hits his chest and this is where I want to be.

"And first you put your arms around me." His arms swiftly grab my hips, gyrating his hips into me. Mine mimic his as my whole body sets alight with the way he commands it.

"Then you put your charms around me." His lips trail down the side of my neck.

"I can't resist this sweet surrender Oh! My nights are warm and tender." He spins me back around again and our eyes lock. Filled with love, lust and so much more.

We stare into each other's eyes

And what we see is no surprise

Got a feeling most would treasure...

And just because I'm feeling all kinds of sexy. My arms around his neck, I take a chance and stroke that little area that I know gets him going; the nape of his neck. A low sexy growl escapes from him as he raises his eyebrow at me and I chuckle at his predicament. Knowing I'm pushing his buttons and that he might just throw me over his shoulder and charge outside to get his fill, I remove my hand from his neck as I continue to sing.

And a love so deep we cannot measure

Ain't nobody

Loves me better...

His fingers spread across my waist as he nuzzles into my neck and I'm overheating with the connection of our bodies. Oh boy. I didn't quiet think this through when I invited him to join me, as another growl erupts from his chest when I grind my bottom into him, I carry on singing regardless. Vlad's fingers run up and down my sides the heat between us becomes like an inferno.

Throughout the last chorus, Vlad and I play a slow, seductive tune with our bodies on the dance floor.

Ain't nobody

Loves me better than you.

I'm glad to see we're not the only ones on the dance floor as I finish the song.

Vlad steals my lips, lingering languidly until he's had his fill.

"Wow," I hear Daniel's voice. "Looks like someone's gonna be getting laid tonight," he chuckles. Vlad flips him the middle finger, that cheeky smirk plastered across his handsome face as he winks at me.

I return the mic to Daniel who gets the audience on their feet giving a round of applause.

*

The night has gone superbly, and Daniel is on his final spot when I leave Vlad sat chatting with Jack and Nick. The women are all on the dance floor and Sebastian and Nicholas are at the bar. As I make my way down the short passage to the ladies', my arm is grabbed, and I'm yanked to one side, my back hitting the wall with a thud. "What the hell!" I yell. It's then I hear the slurred voice of the man that I was married to.

"That's some show you put on earlier, Holly." His finger strokes down my cheek. "How come I didn't get to see this sexy side of you?" His fingers trail down my neck as he turns up a smile. I bat his hand out of the way and try to move from his hold, but his hips are pressed up against me.

"Let go of me," I spit at him. He's drunk and a little less put together than his usual neat self. His hair is a little longer than normal and where he was always clean shaven, he looks like he hasn't shaved for a couple of days.

He breathes in deeply and closes his eyes. "I always loved your smell, so fruity and inviting." His eyes open and when I look closely their filled with lust. I feel sick.

"Get off me, you idiot." I push at him and he lets go of me. Never one to cause a scene, he stares at me as if he's shocked himself. "Don't touch me again. You lost that right over a year ago when you cheated on me. My smell wasn't good enough then..." I rage at him. He takes a step back from me, but his eyes rake over my body. I don't want him looking at me in that way. "Stop that," I say, not understanding why he is here. He doesn't live anywhere near this pub and it's not the sort of place he would frequent anyway. He's into wine bars and restaurants and hanging out with his snotty-nose bankers.

"Stop what, Holly?" he asks as he trails a finger down my arm. "You never minded my touch before." He steps closer this time and his overpowering aftershave leaves me nauseated. "How about you wiggle those hips for me, baby, or is it just the gangster that gets that treatment?" He laughs at me. "Your taste in men has fell to an all-time low, Holly. From a banker to a jumped-up gangster." He shakes his head, tutting. Arrogant bastard. Who the hell does he think he is?

"How dare you?" I push him out of my way and he staggers a little, he's that unsteady and he's bloody crazy. "You," I point at him, "do not have the right to question me on who I am with. He is twice the man you are and will ever be. And while we're on the subject where is Rachel, the mother of your child? Huh?" I prod him in his chest, but he doesn't answer me. "You cheated on me and left me for another woman and you have the audacity to question my life. You try and come on to me knowing I'm with someone." I need to calm down and get him to leave before someone sees him. Although Vlad doesn't know what he looks like, my friends do and if they see him they'll be trouble. I don't want to think about what Vlad would do if he finds out. "I think you better leave," I say as calmly as possible.

"I'm with friends, Holly. I'm not going anywhere yet," he states with that cocky attitude. Always full of his own self-importance; well, this time he might just rue the day he didn't listen to me. If he can't take the hint, then be it on his own head if something happens.

"OK," I say. "Just don't come near me again or touch me." I try to brush past him, but he grabs my arm again, pulling me into him.

"Come on, Holly, you don't want a quick bunk-up for old time's sake?" he says as his lips brush across my cheek. Bloody hell, he must be pissed because in the years I'd known him we had never had a quick bunk-up. Our sex life was confined to our home and mainly in the bedroom.

"Holly, what's going on?" I hear two shocked voices ask and that's all I need, Olivia and Sarah seeing him. They're bad enough sober; with a few wines down them, they're likely to tear him limb from limb and won't think twice about informing Jack that he is here. Nick is the more rational one of the two and wouldn't interfere; Jack will take it as his big brother duty to knock his head off for cheating on me. I know Nick has seen and spoken with Rob since our divorce, Jack has been biding his time but that's not my only worry. Vlad will sense there's a problem and will have a coronary if he knows Rob has been anywhere near me, never mind touched and propositioned me. I need to get the arrogant twat out of here because as much as I can't stand him, I don't want to witness him getting a good hiding.

"He's just leaving," I tell them, pushing out of his hold.

"Am I? I think I told you I was with friends and I'm not going anywhere." He stands up straight and pushes out his chest. I rub the top of my arm that he had hold of. Sarah notices it and sees the red mark that's been left there.

"What's he done to you, Holly?" she asks, taking hold of my arm. Olivia's eyes follow what Sarah's looking at.

"It's nothing," I tell them, taking back my arm. "We need to get him to leave before Jack sees him," I say. He sniggers at my comment and gets the wrath of Olivia.

"I don't know what you think you're doing here and why you think it's OK to corner Holly. But if you don't leave now it won't be Jack you need to worry about," she says, getting right in his face. Which is calm for my overprotective friend because she's always hated him. I know she's always wanted to smack his smug face.

He doesn't back down from her and continues with this delusion of me and him.

"Oh, I think I'll stay where I am and finish the conversion I was having with my wife." He grabs my hand tightly.

"Ex-wife," the three of us say together. Now I know he's lost it. I try to take my hand from his, but he keeps hold of it.

"Let go of me, Rob." I'm getting more and more annoyed at him. He ignores me, so I bring my other hand up and slap his face. Shocking myself. That has the desired effect; he drops my hand to rub his cheek. As I turn to give Olivia and Sarah a look to say he's lost it that's when I see my man striding towards us and he doesn't look happy.

Nostrils flaring and the curl of his lip, a snarl that would be enough to scare off a pack of wolves, I can almost see the pulse in his neck breaking out as it beats like a time bomb. His eyes are ablaze with anger and glare at the man in front of me. I do the only thing I can and place myself in his path, grabbing him around the waist to stop him in his tracks.

"Holly, let go of me." His voice is firm but not angry with me as his strong hands lay on my shoulders and try to gently move me out of the way. I stand firm.

"No," I say, gazing up at him, but his eyes are fixated on Rob. I know he won't try and move me, he would never hurt me, and he would never stop me from wrapping my arms around him.

"Why?" He's still glaring at Rob and I can hear Olivia and Sarah pleading for him to go. They know as much as I do what Vlad would do to him.

"Why what?" I ask.

"Why won't you let go of me?" His voice is low enough for just me and him to hear.

"Because you'll hurt him," I answer.

"And what does he mean to you, Holly?" He gazes down at me now. His arms by his side while his broad chest heaves heavily under his fitted shirt. Our eyes connect, and I can see hurt in his dark eyes. As much as he is angry and that is what other people around us will see in his eyes, I see a man who has endured a world of pain in his life and now I am adding to that.

Reaching up with one hand, I stroke over the scar that lives above his eye. My finger follows the scar down the side of his face until I reach the end of it. I let it trail over his cheekbone and onto his soft lips where I trace round them. "He means nothing to me," I tell him, still gazing into his eyes. "But you do." Standing on tiptoes, I gently touch his lips with mine. I whisper. "He's not worth…" I don't manage to get the rest out when I hear an almighty ruckus behind us.

I turn my head, careful not to let go of the man who would rip up my ex like a tornado whipping up anything in its path, and I'm not about to let that happen. Violence isn't my thing. The first sign of blood has me shaking like a leaf.

I must have missed Jack pass us while I was trying to calm Vlad down because him and Rob are just been pulled apart. Jack flexes his fist, I assume after hitting Rob in the nose. Blood trickles down from it as two of his friends from the bank help him to his feet. "Get him out of here before I break his fucking neck!" Jack shouts at them. Olivia drags her husband away from the men, one of them mouthing, *'Sorry Holly.'* I know him from the bank and I now know why Rob ended up drunk and tried coming on to me.

With such high regard for himself and not wanting to show what he had, he let go. Rob will have got it into his head that he could show his friends that if he wanted me back then he could get me. Of course, they will have seen my performance on the dance floor with Vlad and ripped into him for cheating on me. I never thought I was good enough for him, but my friends told me he was lucky to have me. Now after being with Vlad for the last few months, who constantly reminds me how beautiful I am, I believe they were right. I was too good for him and he never deserved a woman who stood by his side through his career and gave up pursuing hers for him.

Since meeting Vlad and his family, I've become involved with recruiting bands and acts for one of their clubs and have been able to stand on a stage and sing again. They have also become my family who I adore and the man who currently has his arms wrapped around me, is my world.

I didn't notice that my nerves had got the better of me, but Vlad did. He manoeuvres me out of the way of the arguing that is still going on, keeping his arms tightly around me but not taking his dark eyes off Rob who still wants to have a go with Jack. A couple of bouncers turn up and are ready to throw the lot of us out when one of them smiles at Vlad and shakes his hand. He loosens his hold on me and speaks to the man who nods at what he is saying then turns to the two men that are with Rob. "Get him out of here before we do." He's a beefy man who shouldn't be argued with and even though Rob's friends have taken the hint, Rob's drunken state has given him some Dutch courage to argue back.

He steps forward, getting a little too close to his intended target –

me. I'm spun around so fast my head spins. I'm now standing, sandwiched between Vlad's back and the other bouncer's front. Vlad still has a hold of me by my hand as he looms over Rob who is at least four inches shorter than the man he is trying to antagonise.

I don't need to see Vlad's face to know he will be snarling and glaring at this lunatic who thinks he can take on such a force. I've seen Vlad when he's worked up. When it involves me, he could drop a man with just his glare. His back is rigid and the muscles in his forearms tense and expand as Rob tries to outstare him. Not sure if this could be called a pissing competition, one man trying to stake his claim, but it needn't be.

There's only one winner out of this and that's Vlad. Rob had his time with me, over ten years and not once did he make me feel as wanted as this man does. Glancing around everyone stands waiting, anticipating their next move. I'm not sure if they are as shocked as I am that Rob would try and take on this beast of a man. In fact, I'm shocked he had stuck around after his bust-up with Jack.

After what seemed like long minutes but I'm sure wasn't, Rob takes a step back and looks around at everyone. He puts his hands up in front of himself, admitting defeat, shakes his head and throws a smug smirk as if to say, 'Fuck the lot of you,' then storms out closely followed by his two mates.

"What an arsehole," Olivia comments while examining Jack's hand. He delights in the attention from his wife, wrapping his arm around her and pulling her into him as the bouncers warn him to behave for the rest of the night or he'll be thrown out. He takes their warning then turns to Vlad and me.

"He's had that coming for a long time." Vlad nods his head, his lips tight and the muscles of his jaw still pulsating. "Not sure what his problem was with Holly though, but if I was to hazard a guess, I'd say he was jealous."

"Hmmm," Sarah muses. "I think you're right but, let's not him ruin our evening. We need to get back to everyone else before they think we've deserted them and Daniel."

We make our way back to the table where Sebastian raises his eyebrow at his father. Vlad mumbles something in Russian; Sebastian closes his eyes and shakes his head. I'm not sure what has been said, and I don't ask. It's not often they slip into their native language when talking but I suspect it has something to do with what has just happened.

For the next hour we listen to Daniel sing; I make conversation with our friends while Vlad sits there with my hand in his, resting on his lap. He hardly speaks unless spoken to, everyone around our table knowing he is stewing over Rob.

With the band finished and most of the evening having been one of lots of dancing, singing and drinking, we say our goodnights and head out for our taxis. The ride home we share with Izzy and Sebastian, dropping them off first. Izzy should be the only sober one amongst us, but the incident with Rob in the latter part of the night has sobered both Vlad and I up. Izzy yawns, showing her tiredness, and to be truthful I'm hoping Vlad doesn't want to discuss what happened earlier because I'm beat. He hasn't asked why I was slapping my ex around the face or why he had hold of my hand, but I know it's eating away at him. This could be just another thing to add to his darkened mood that he's been wearing like a lead weight all week. Which is a shame because through most of the evening since arriving at Vlad's home then arriving at the pub, some of that weight had lifted and he was enjoying himself.

We travel the rest of the way in silence, Vlad's jaw still ticking away, so I snuggle my head into his chest hoping he will reciprocate my cuddle. He doesn't let me down. His arms wrap around me and his lips gently touch the back of my head.

"If your ex comes near you again, Holly, you walk away from him and let me know. It should be me dealing with him, not you or Jack," are the first words he speaks when we get home.

He kicked off his shoes, marched into the kitchen and retrieved a bottle of water from the fridge. His eyes watched me over the bottle as he drank it then without a word he strode off to the toilet. It was then he brought up what had happened, when he returned.

I stare at him for a moment, trying to gauge why he thinks Rob would come near me again and why he thinks I cannot deal with him myself. "He was pissed, Vlad. I haven't heard from him in over a year and I don't expect to hear from him again. I know he can be an arsehole but I'm sure when he wakes up tomorrow he will regret what he said and did," I tell him.

"Whether he was drunk or sober, he knew you was with someone, but he still tried it on." He's not shouting but his voice rises as he stands at the kitchen island. "And you should have walked away from him or at least sent Olivia or Sarah to come and get me…"

"I tried to walk away but he grabbed—"

"He grabbed you and stopped you from leaving, Holly!" he rages, standing up, and I wish I had kept my mouth shut. "Tell me what he did and said to you," he says as he stands in front of me. He doesn't touch me, but his eyes lock on to the tiny red mark that has appeared on my arm. He knows it wasn't there before we went out and I'm trying to come up with something where I don't lie to him, but I don't give him the full details.

"He grabbed me as I was making my way to the toilet. He wanted to talk, and I refused. When I tried to pull away from him, he grabbed me again. That's when Olivia and Sarah turned up. They argued for a while and when I tried to leave again he grabbed my hand. I slapped him. You know the rest." I shrug my shoulders. I'm not going into details and enraging him over it. I witnessed his state of mind when he saw Rob had hold of my hand, I'm not about to tell him he wanted a quickie for old time's sake. God, no. I wouldn't put it past him to go out looking for him if he knew the truth. I'm sure Jack and Olivia would be only too keen to give up his address to Vlad.

He nods his head, his eyes searching mine for something else. He knows I'm not telling him everything and I'm not going to. I'm tired and need my bed. It's been a long night and I need sleep. Putting my hand on his chest, I reach up and brush my lips over his. "I'm going to bed," I whisper. He doesn't follow me which shocks me because he always follows me. Usually throwing me over his shoulder and racing up the stairs with me or carrying me in his arms.

I'm so exhausted that once I wash my make-up off, slip on one of Vlad's T-shirts and snuggle under the sheets, I fall asleep. I don't hear Vlad come to bed. Not sure whether he did.

Chapter 31

Holly

This night out is turning into one of those nights where you wish you had stayed in. Vlad tried to get me to stay at home with him and now I wish I had taken up his offer to snuggle on the sofa and watch a film.

I declined his offer just to piss him off. His over-the-top caveman attitude the last few times we had been out as well as that he still is refusing to tell me the truth as to what is bothering him, is pissing me off. I love him with all my heart, but his constant brooding has got to me. Even after our talk the day after my ex had showed up in the pub where Daniel was playing, there's still no change in him.

He tells me work has been stressful, but I know all is well in all the Petrov establishments. The restaurant practically runs itself. They have a manageress in place who runs the show with Vlad just turning up to make sure any paperwork and wages are all in order. Eruption runs like clockwork; it might be owned by Vlad, but it happens to be run by Nicholas with help from Sebastian and Daniel. Izzy oversees Aphrodite along with Sebastian and I know that even though they have had work done and are changing the entertainment, everything's running smoothly. That leaves the buildings that Vlad has purchased with hopes to turn them into apartments. This project is in its early stages, so yes, this might be causing him a bit of stress, but not to the extent that I have seen him in.

I catch him staring off into space with a worried expression on his face. Sometimes I feel his eyes boring into me and when I turn to see him he looks anxious. He's stewing over something and until he tells me what it is, I can't help him.

So, when I was asked to join Olivia and Sarah on a night out – they were tagging along with Lucy and some friends of hers from university – I jumped at the chance to spend some time with my friends without the men being there. Lucy had finished her exams and was having an evening out. Nicholas had given them free passes into the club, so they could celebrate. They have become good friends over the last month and spend a lot of time texting each other.

We've been here a couple of hours and I still feel off. I'm not sure why, but the feeling I should have stayed at home washes over me. Lucy and her friends have been in full-on party mode since arriving here while Sarah struggled with a headache. She's telephoned Nick to pick her up twenty minutes ago. I would have gone with her, but Olivia asked me to stay. She's enjoying spending some time with her daughter, and I didn't want to take that away from her. If I'd left to go home, she would have felt that she had to come with me.

The dance floor is full to bursting with hot, sweaty bodies and I'm sick of getting my feet trod on. I'm extremely sick of the man at the back of me and his two friends thinking it's OK to get a little close and personal. I've tried to be diplomatic about it, laughing it off when one of them put his hands on my hips and tried shimmying up to me. Turning to him, I put my hand on his chest, smiled nicely and pushed him away. Only he didn't take the hint. He's been grabbing my arm and spinning me around then pulling me into him. I've told him to leave me alone, he just isn't listening. Vlad would be like a raving lunatic if he was to witness this man putting his hands on me. Imagining his face, I move away from the man and his two friends again.

We moved to the far side of the dance floor and fifteen minutes later his hands were on me again. This time I didn't say anything, I just stepped back into him making sure the heel of my shoe hit hard onto the instep of his foot. This got him cursing, then I turned to him, telling him next time it would be his balls that my foot would be connecting with if he didn't leave me alone. Who am I kidding? I wouldn't have had the guts to kick him in the balls. He snarled arrogantly at me, but his two friends took the hint and dragged him away. Olivia raised an amused eyebrow at me, telling me I should have done that earlier.

And maybe I should have, or at least gone to see Frank or one of his bouncers, then maybe I wouldn't have had to put up with him being prick all evening.

As I try to enjoy the evening, I'm still wishing I had stayed at home. This intensifies when Olivia grabs my attention, pointing to the set of steps that lead down onto the dance floor. Seeing who she is pointing at sends a cold shiver down my spine. The man who wouldn't leave me alone, now watches me and doesn't look happy. He also looks like he's on something. Deciding it's time, I informed one of the bouncers about him because he is now creeping me out. I leave Olivia, Lucy and her friends on the dance floor, telling them I'm going to the ladies', and then to find Frank. Olivia offers to come with me, but I tell her to stay with Lucy, I will be fine. It's not like I don't know anybody in here; all the staff and bouncers know who I am – they see me often enough either in here or next door in Aphrodite. If I'm not with Vlad, on a night out, then I'm with him in his office when we have lunch together. I'm also with Izzy a few times a week. Every member of staff knows me by my name and I've come to know them.

I see Frank leaning over the bar speaking to one of the staff. He isn't hard to miss; he makes Vlad look small. The music is thumping and it's hard to hear what you are saying without getting close.

Just as I'm within three feet of him his back to me, my elbow is yanked back. "Where do you think you're going? You little tease." My skin crawls in disgust at his words and touch because I know when I turn I'm going to see the man from the dance floor.

Before I have time to react, the bellowing of another voice thunders over the music. "Take your fucking hands off her!" Hearing the thick Russian accent, has me concerned. I have come to know that two things bring out the thickness of Vlad's accent. One: when passion is running high and our bodies are wrapped together, he can't help but speak words in his native tongue which gets stronger as his sexual desire intensifies. Two: when he gets annoyed. And that is one angry man.

"Fuck you," comes a choked-out yell.

My body turns in slow motion and what I'm witness to, I never want to witness again.

The man from the dance floor is suspended in the air, dangling from Vlad's arm. His hand wrapped tightly round his neck. With one swift movement Vlad's head connects with the man's nose which explodes with the sound of a crack. Blood oozes out, spraying over Vlad's shirt. I'm not sure who screams the loudest, the people stood around or me.

My legs turn to jelly and I stagger backwards into the bar. I'm caught by two large hands and pushed to the side of the bar. "Fuck," Frank growls out then speaks into his mic that is attached to his earpiece as he strides towards the two men that are now covered in blood.

I can't move, I'm stuck, supported by the bar which I'm grateful for because my legs feel like they might give way.

I watch as two men who I know were on the dance floor jump Vlad from behind, who is still holding the other man by his neck. His doesn't give. His shoulders and back are solid and as they swing from him, trying to connect a punch, he jabs one of them in the side of the head with his elbow, throwing the other one over his shoulder onto the floor. He drops the man who has now turned purple and with one swift powerful kick to his chest he sends him flying into the crowd, who Frank and a couple of bouncers are trying to move out of the way. The two men lunge themselves at him again and are quickly dispersed. As he strikes out at them, showing strength and power of ten men, one of them connects a punch to Vlad's lip. He doesn't feel it; he looks like a man who could kill. He walks at speed towards the man he had by the throat as the other two are trying to scramble up from the floor.

Again, he picks him up and this time punches him in the face, not letting go of his neck. The other two men come barrelling towards Vlad again but are intercepted by four bouncers who make light work of leading them out of the club. Two more approach Vlad along with Frank, looking wary of their boss. Frank doesn't. I think they are right to be wary because this man looks anything but approachable.

His dark blue eyes are now black and fierce. His jaw is tight and his nostrils flare as his stare fixates on the man who had his hands on me on the dance floor. Blood drips from his lip and his charcoal shirt is ripped, showing the tattoos that span his thick muscles.

Frank steps in, catching the next punch in his hand, stopping it from hitting its intended target. He speaks, saying something to Vlad, and his focus disconnects from the man who now looks anything but arrogant like he did on the dance floor.

Vlad snarls at the man then drops him like a sack of potatoes. The man is quickly picked up and escorted away by the two bouncers.

Frank places both his hands onto Vlad's shoulders and whispers something to him. There's a curse from him and when Frank steps to one side I see a man I hardly know. His eyes are wild, chest heaving, and his overall look is menacing.

I try to steady my shaky legs but it's in vain as my whole body has joined in. I'm in shock, I'm sure of it. Watching this violent behaviour unfold in front of me, involving the man I love, has me shocked beyond belief. This family man who has so much love and care for his family, who has held me tight while I sobbed like a baby, took care of me when I was ill and loved me like no one before, the man that stands before me is no longer that man.

With a snap of his head his eyes are on me, penetrating my soul. Instantly he's in front of me, grabbing my hand as he trails me behind him around the bar and through the door that leads down the corridor towards his office. He doesn't speak. His strides are quick, and I struggle to keep up with him, losing my shoes in the process. "Vlad, stop!" I call out, but he's suddenly gone deaf or he's just ignoring me. Probably the latter.

Once we're through the office door he slams it shut, causing me to flinch.

I don't have time to speak when he turns, wiping the blood from his mouth. "Why?" He questions, getting in my face. I step back, hitting the door. I don't understand his question or why he's angry with me, I'm not the one who has just beaten the shit out of three men.

"Why what?" I reply.

"Why the fuck did you let him put his hands on you?" he spits out, causing the blood to spray into my hair and on my cheek. I can't believe what he is insinuating, he thinks I led him on. "I didn't…"

"Don't fucking lie to me!" he roars, stopping me from finishing what I was going to say. He wipes his mouth again with the back of his hand then pulls his shirt over his head to wipe the blood from his hands. His chest is still heaving, and his anger is outlining and expanding his muscles. The shirt is tossed onto the floor as he looks to the ceiling then closes his eyes, muttering something I don't understand.

His breathing calms a little and he turns to look at me. "You let him touch you." His eyes meet mine and this time they hold so much hurt and sadness. I want to move and go to him wipe the blood from his lip that I think needs gluing. Hold him, explain to him that I didn't lead the man on. That I told him to leave me alone and was just on my way to speak to Frank about him, but I stop myself. Because something just came to me. How did he know?

My question is answered when I look over to the far wall and see the CCTV all lit up. All monitors are showing different areas of the club. He's been watching me. Why didn't he just come and see me on the dance floor or send Frank? Looking towards the desk I see a bottle of vodka, over half of it gone.

Suddenly, I'm brought back to the man in the room when my wrists are pinned above my head and Vlad's body is pressed against mine. He holds both my wrists in one of his hands and rests his forehead on mine. His other hand strokes down my ribcage, fingers traveling to my thigh. "Is my touch not enough for you?" he whispers. "Do I not turn you on any more, Holly?" I close my eyes at his words that are thick and laced with sarcasm. I'm at a loss for words and a little scared of the man in front of me.

"Stop," I say shakily. It's all I can manage to get out without bursting into tears.

"Stop what, Holly?" he asks as he trails kisses across my cheek until his lips are barely touching mine. "Am I not what you want? Have I not always…" He takes a couple of deep breaths and moves his hand so he's holding my waist. "I would do anything for you. Give you anything you wanted." He closes his eyes again and places his cheek on mine.

My arms are aching and the grip he has on them is making them sore. I rub my cheek against his, hoping that my touch will calm him. The sadness I saw in his eyes as he spoke just before he closed them, breaks my heart, but I need him to let go of me.

"Vlad, let go of me, you're hurting me," I utter as calmly as possible.

"Hurting you?" he sneers, his accent thick as he curses in his own language, while shaking his head. His chest starts to heave again as his breathing becomes erratic. I thought I would be able to calm him but he's getting worked up again. And so am I.

How dare he treat me like this? Who does he think he is? If he'd have come to me in the club instead of drinking and watching the cameras we wouldn't be in this state now.

"Did you do it to get my attention?" His dark eyes burn into mine.

"You're crazy and drunk," I spit out at him. I might be nervous because of his behaviour and comments. But I'm also angry with him.

"Vlad, let go of me," I say sternly.

He drops my hands and moves away from me, picking up his shirt off the floor and wiping his face on it. I wait there, not knowing what to do. Do I leave? Or do I hash it out with him?

His head is bent down, buried in the shirt that's covered in blood. I think he must have bit the inside of his cheek when he was punched in the mouth because there seems to be a lot of blood. He turns his head to look at me and the look I get is one of disgust, like I'm something he just stepped in. "Get out!" he shouts then turns, stalking over to his desk and picking up the half empty bottle of vodka.

"No. You're not doing this to us," I argue, stepping forward, rubbing my wrists that have purple welts on them. He picks up the bottle, wincing when it hits his lips. He downs it in one and when he finishes his facial expression has not changed.

"Hurting you," he continues with what he was going to say before he let go of my wrists. "And what have you just done to me?" He prods his chest as he sways a little, grabbing hold of the desk to steady himself. He sways again and falls back into his chair then pins me with his dark stare. "I am crazy," he slurs, nodding his head. "To think I could trust a woman again."

Trust. I know he hasn't let me in fully. Tonight, and the last couple of weeks have proved that. Whatever has been bothering him, if he had trusted me, he would have told me. I know this has something to do with his wife and I would put money on it that his issues run a little deeper than just her. I can't challenge him tonight about it, there's no reasoning with him.

Why didn't he just talk to me? I've told him things about my ex-husband, when I was a small child living with my mother and her drug addiction. I've cried in his arms about it.

He took me into his home, introducing me to his family, and I know that was a first for him but his love for me didn't run as strong as I thought it did. If it had he would have trusted me enough to tell me what was going on in his head. I can't be with him anymore and I don't think he cares anyway. I'm not going to stay with a man who can't give me his all, I had enough with Rob. Looking at the CCTV, it angers me that he sat here watching me, getting drunk and thinking the worst.

Standing between the door and his desk, I can't leave without saying what I need to say. "Whatever you think you saw on them fucking screens..." My head flicks towards them and I kick myself for swearing. My language needs taking in hand; I sound like him. He lifts his head to look at me. He has no remorse in his eyes, just blackness. "You're wrong," I say slowly. "But I don't care anymore." Shaking my head at him. "You're not the man I thought I knew and loved." I'm just about to walk out of the door when I hear him move from his chair. I take another look at him; he's leaning over his desk, palms flat on the hard surface where we have made love numerous times. His dark gaze runs up and down my body before he staggers back into his chair.

"Get out, Holly. I don't need you," he spits out. "You're just like her," he says, picking up the empty bottle of vodka and dropping it back on his desk.

Those were the last words I heard as I turned and ran out of the door. I can't take his hurtful words.

My head is spinning with what has taken place here tonight and all

I can think of are the last words that came out of his mouth.

I spot my shoes as I hurry down the corridor. Picking them up, I hear breaking glass coming from Vlad's office which I'm sure is the vodka bottle hitting the wall. The sound of furniture being thrown has me moving quicker and when I reach the door, I'm met with one worried-looking man. Nicholas moves forward, placing his hands on my shoulders. "Holly, what the hell just happened out there?" He points out into the club. I can't speak. I just want to scream, cry for the hurt that has just taken place here tonight. An animalistic roar and another crash of furniture echoes up the corridor. My heart breaks at the wounded noise and Nicholas' face turns pale. "My father?" he utters.

"Yes."

"Please Holly, don't leave," he pleads, his concerned eyes searching mine. "Wait here. Let me speak with him then I will come back." I nod my head and he takes off down the corridor towards the man I love but can no longer be with.

Tears stream down my face as I make my way through the bar. "What the fuck's happened, Holly?" Through my clouded vision, Olivia comes into view. "You have blood in your hair, Holly, what's happened?" She takes me into her arms, running her hand down my back, soothing me.

"It isn't mine," I say through my sniffles, shaking my head.

"Whose is it?" Her hands are on my cheeks and she gives me that 'I don't want any bull shit' look. I can't go into what just happened, not yet.

"Just take me home," I sob, leaning into my best friend who has always been there for me. Well, she might just get a little more than she signed up for because getting over a man like him, might just take the rest of my life.

Chapter 32

Holly

"Are you sure going away on your own is the right thing to do, Holly?" Sarah asks as she passes me a sweet cup of tea. Shrugging my shoulders, I blow my nose and wipe the millionth tear from my eye.

"I don't know what's right or wrong anymore." I croak out my answer once I've taken a sip of the overly sweetened tea. According to Sarah, sweet tea is the answer to everything but it's doing nothing to lessen the pain I am feeling.

If I thought that my heart had broken before then I was wrong. The feeling of abandonment, loneliness and loss because of my mother's wild ways was a walk in the park. The hurt, uncontrollable crying and the unanswered questions as to why my adopted parents were ripped from my life was nothing but child's play. The unfaithfulness of my husband was a light breeze compared to the way I feel now.

"Let me enlighten you to a few things, Holly," Jack says as he takes a seat round the dinner table. Olivia rolls her eyes at him and shakes her head.

"Holly does not want to hear any of your cavemen opinions, thank you very much." She pats his knee as if to say, 'No offence,' but it's not the right time for one of his rambles.

"I know she doesn't but…" He rubs his hands up and down his face, focusing on his beard. "Men are simple creatures, Holly."

"That we are." Nick agrees with him, holding out a cup of coffee for his brother. He takes the spare seat next to Jack and places his cup on the table. All four of my friends have taken turns being with me over the last three days. I know we've been here before but this time I've decided I need to get away. I'm a mess and don't want to put on them anymore, it's unfair. They have their own families and lives to look out for and I'm sick of being the one that they need to rally around after. I know they don't see it that way, they tell me all the time that I have done a lot for them over the years. I'm not just a friend to them, I'm their family and they are mine but this; what I am going through, this whole new feeling of pain, I need to be on my own to get my head round what I am feeling.

"Two things, Holly." He holds two fingers up, bringing me out of my thoughts. "One, our home is our castle, never a truer word spoken. The other is the woman in our life." He takes hold of Olivia's hand and kisses her knuckles. "Men can and will do the stupidest of things if we think another man is trying to get into her knickers." Olivia slaps him on the shoulder for being so straight forward but to be honest I wouldn't expect anything else from Jack.

"Jack, you can say some idiotic things sometimes," Olivia chastises him.

"He's right. We can." Nick defends his brother. Getting out of his seat he walks over to Sarah, shifting her until she is snuggled up on his knee. My heart hurts and I swallow the lump in my throat; just seeing this most natural thing upsets me as I remember that every time Vlad and I were together he would do the same thing.

"If we think a man his chasing our woman, we don't think rationally, and if we've had a drink we're even worse," Nick states.

"You need to let him explain himself, Holly," Jack says with a look of concern on his face.

"It's not that simple," I tell him, my throat still croaky with all the crying I have done in the last three days.

"It never is but if you don't give him the chance you might kick yourself later. Everyone deserves a chance, Holly."

"You didn't say that about Rob."

"No, because he didn't deserve one. He was and still is an arsehole, he proved that last week. Vlad is a good man who dotes on you, anyone can see that."

My phone lights up with a message. I don't need to look at who's texting me, the tune it plays tells me it's Vlad. It hasn't stopped ringing nor have the text messages stopped piling up from the man I loved and treasured so deeply. Every voicemail begs for forgiveness and to hear him out. Every text message reading the same. The buzzer to my apartment I switched to privacy because I couldn't bear the sound of it anymore; knowing he was just outside the building was too tempting. That's when I knew I had to get away.

Arranging to pick up the keys to Jay and Ivy's cottage this morning from Olivia and Jack had me here early, eager to get away.

I know if I answer his call or let him into my home, I would end up giving in to him. I'm not strong enough to say no to him and that would lead us back to where we were before. Me not knowing what brings out such intense rage that he becomes a different person.

Violence scares the shit out of me; I'd heard enough of the screams, slaps, things being smashed and maddened voices when I was a young child. Hiding in my bedroom, shaking in the bottom of the dark wardrobe, praying it would stop and hoping I would not see another bruise on my mum's face.

Living with my adopted parents in a calm, loving environment, slowly those cold scary nights faded into the past until they were buried so deep they were almost forgotten. Even married to Rob they stayed at bay. We never argued. I was a pushover and gave in to him all the time, but it wasn't in his nature to raise his voice or get angry. The way he was in the pub the other week was out of character for him; maybe all is not rosy in his new life.

Meeting Vlad, taking on someone so intimidating, shocked the hell out of me but from day one he made me feel feelings I never thought existed except in books or in other people's lives. The way he looked at me, held me and spoke to me was always with so much passion he stole my heart straight away.

"When are you going to return his calls, Holly?" So many questions. *Are you sure you're doing the right thing? When are you going to return his calls and give him a chance to explain?* I can't cope with this; my head feels like it's been trapped in a vice and could explode any minute. I need to get away.

"I'm not."

"You're not?" Sarah questions, her mouth open and eyes wide. I know I've shocked her, but I can't speak to him and I won't let him think he can fob me off with his smooth smile and sexy wink. I know he would never physically hurt me but when he's in that place, the one only he is privy, to that's when he becomes a different person. The one I don't know.

"No." I turn my phone off, throwing it into the bottom of my hand bag. As I stand, Olivia gets up from her seat and takes me in her arms.

"We're here for you, Holly, don't stay away too long," she says as she lets me go. Jack is the next one to embrace me and a sob breaks out from my throat.

"Text him. Let him know you're going away for a few days," he whispers into my hair. I break away from him and Nick passes me a tissue. Wiping the tears from my eyes and blowing my nose, I pick up my car keys and the keys for the cottage. If I don't leave now, I might just give in and stay.

"His sons know, they will tell him. When they called last night, I'd already decided I was going away, so I let them know."

"Good. How were they?" Sarah asks.

"Concerned," I choke out, remembering the look of worry and despair on their faces. How they pleaded for me to speak with him. I wouldn't expect anything else from them. They love their father and he them. But, it wasn't just their father they were concerned for, it was me as well. The whole family make me feel part of them and I have come to look at them as part of mine. I will miss them deeply.

I wipe at my face again. "They were concerned for both of us."

"When will you be back?" Sarah asks as she takes her turn to hug me. I shrug my shoulders, not sure how I answer that I might not come back.

"I don't know," I say.

"I thought you were just going for a few days, Holly." Jack looks at me then to his wife, shock on his face.

"I can't say how long I'll be gone for, but I'm only a few hours' drive away. My mobile will be off, but you can get me on the landline if you need me at all," I tell them, not knowing whether I might be back in a few days, a week, or it could be a couple of weeks or months. I just don't know. All I do know is that I met a man who turned my world upside down and all I could see was him. Now all I see is the damage that man can do. He's like a force of nature that you're told will be a light storm blowing in, but when it's over you're left with the aftermath of a force-ten gale, destroying what's in its path, and in this case my heart.

To be continued...

About the Author

I am fifty years old and work full-time as a learning support assistant. I live in Leeds, West Yorkshire, England, which is where I was born. I come from an extremely large family which has two sets of twins, me being the eldest of one of the sets. I am kept exceptionally busy with my job and family commitments where I take care of my elderly mother. I enjoy spending quality time with my partner of thirty years, stepdaughter, two grandchildren, my twin sister and her family. Any spare time I have, I can be found reading a good romance novel, contemporary, erotic or thriller. If not reading I will be using my newly found creative side, writing. When I have the chance to take a holiday, you will find me in the breathtaking province of Alberta, Canada, where I get to take in the scenery, sample all they have to offer and spend time with my older brother and beautiful nieces.

Printed in Great Britain
by Amazon